A Gate at the Stairs

A Gate at the Stairs

A NOVEL

LORRIE MOORE

BOND
STREET
BOOKS
DOUBLEDAY
CANADA

The Bond Street Books colophon is a trademark of Random House
of Canada Limited

Grateful acknowledgment is made to Hal Leonard Corporation for
permission to reprint excerpts from "Ain't No Mountain High Enough,"
words and music by Nickolas Ashford and Valerie Simpson,
copyright © 1967, 1970 (renewed 1995, 1998) by Jobete Music Co., Inc.
All rights controlled and administered by EMI April Music Inc.
All rights reserved. International copyright secured.
Reprinted by permission of Hal Leonard Corporation.

Library and Archives of Canada Cataloguing in Publication has been
applied for

ISBN: 978-0-385-66824-8

This book is a work of fiction. Names, characters, places and incidents are
products of the author's imagination or are used fictitiously. Any resemblance
to actual events or locales or persons, living or dead, is entirely coincidental.

Printed and bound in the USA

Published in Canada by Bond Street Books, an imprint of Doubleday
Canada, a division of Random House of Canada Limited

Visit Random House of Canada Limited's website: www.randomhouse.ca

10 9 8 7 6 5 4 3 2

This book is for
Victoria Wilson and Melanie Jackson

"As for living, we shall have our servants do that for us."
—VILLIERS DE L'ISLE-ADAM, *Axel*

"Suzuki!"
—*Madama Butterfly*

"All seats provide equal viewing of the universe."
—MUSEUM GUIDE, HAYDEN PLANETARIUM

Acknowledgments

For their myriad insights, my deepest appreciation goes to Max Garland and Charles Baxter. Also for their help, many thanks to Ashley Allen, David McLimans, Elizabeth Rea, the Emily Mead Baldwin family, the University of Wisconsin Arts Institute, the UW Graduate Research Committee, and the WISELI/Vilas program. My boundless gratitude, too, to the Lannan Foundation.

A Gate at the Stairs

I

The cold came late that fall and the songbirds were caught off guard. By the time the snow and wind began in earnest, too many had been suckered into staying, and instead of flying south, instead of already having flown south, they were huddled in people's yards, their feathers puffed for some modicum of warmth. I was looking for a job. I was a student and needed babysitting work, and so I would walk from interview to interview in these attractive but wintry neighborhoods, the eerie multitudes of robins pecking at the frozen ground, dun-gray and stricken—though what bird in the best of circumstances does not look a little stricken—until at last, late in my search, at the end of a week, startlingly, the birds had disappeared. I did not want to think about what had happened to them. Or rather, that is an expression of politeness, a false promise of delicacy—for in fact I wondered about them all the time: imagining them dead, in stunning heaps in some killing cornfield outside of town, or dropped from the sky in twos and threes for miles down along the Illinois state line.

I was looking in December for work that would begin at the start of the January term. I'd finished my exams and was answering ads from the student job board, ones for "childcare provider." I liked children—I did!—or rather, I liked them OK. They were sometimes interesting. I admired their stamina and candor. And I was good with them in that I could make funny faces at the babies and with the older children teach them card tricks and speak in the theatrically sarcastic tones that disarmed and enthralled them. But I was not especially skilled at minding children for long spells; I grew bored, perhaps like my own mother. After I spent too much time playing their games, my mind grew peckish and longed to lose itself in some book I had in my backpack. I was ever hopeful of early bedtimes and long naps.

I had come from Dellacrosse Central High, from a small farm on the old Perryville Road, to this university town of Troy, "the Athens of the Midwest," as if from a cave, like the priest-child of a Colombian tribe I'd read about in Cultural Anthropology, a boy made mystical by being kept in the dark for the bulk of his childhood and allowed only stories—no experience—of the outside world. Once brought out into light, he would be in a perpetual, holy condition of bedazzlement and wonder; no story would ever have been equal to the thing itself. And so it was with me. Nothing had really prepared me. Not the college piggy bank in the dining room, the savings bonds from my grandparents, or the used set of World Book encyclopedias with their beautiful color charts of international wheat production and photographs of presidential birthplaces. The flat green world of my parents' hogless, horseless farm—its dullness, its flies, its quiet ripped open daily by the fumes and whining of machinery—twisted away and left me with a brilliant city life of books and films and witty friends. Someone had turned on the lights. Someone had led me out of the cave—of Perryville Road. My brain was on fire with Chaucer, Sylvia Plath, Simone de Beauvoir. Twice a week a young professor named Thad, dressed in jeans *and* a tie, stood before a lecture hall of stunned farm kids like me and spoke thrillingly of Henry James's masturbation of the comma. I was riveted. I had never before seen a man wear jeans with a tie.

The ancient cave, of course, had produced a mystic; my childhood had produced only me.

In the corridors students argued over Bach, Beck, Balkanization, bacterial warfare. Out-of-state kids said things to me like

"You're from the country. Is it true that if you eat a bear's liver you'll die?" They asked, "Ever know someone who did you-know-what with a cow?" Or "Is it an actual fact that pigs won't eat bananas?" What I did know was that a goat will not really consume a tin can: a goat just liked to lick the paste on the label. But no one ever asked me that.

From our perspective that semester, the events of September—we did not yet call them 9/11—seemed both near and far. Marching poli-sci majors chanted on the quads and the pedestrian malls, "The chickens have come home to roost! The chickens have come home to roost!" When I could contemplate them at all—the chickens, the roosting—it was as if in a craning crowd, through glass, the way I knew (from Art History) people stared at the *Mona Lisa* in the Louvre: *La Gioconda!* its very name like a snake, its sly, tight smile encased at a distance but studied for portentous flickers. It was, like September itself, a cat's mouth full of canaries. My roommate, Murph—a nose-pierced, hinky-toothed blonde from Dubuque, who used black soap and black dental floss and whose quick opinions were impressively harsh (she pronounced Dubuque "Du-ba-cue") and who once terrified her English teachers by saying the character she admired most in all of literature was Dick Hickock in *In Cold Blood*—had met her boyfriend on September tenth, and when she woke up at his place, she'd phoned me, in horror and happiness, the television blaring. "I know, I know," she said, her voice shrugging into the phone. "It was a terrible price to pay for love, but it had to be done."

I raised my voice to a mock shout. "You sick slut! People were killed. All you think about is your own pleasure." Then we fell into a kind of hysteria—frightened, guilty, hopeless laughter I have never actually witnessed in women over thirty.

"Well," I sighed, realizing I might not be seeing her all that much from then on in, "I hope there's just hanky—no panky."

"Nah," she said. "With panky there's always tears, and it ruins the hanky." I would miss her.

Though the movie theaters closed for two nights, and for a week even our yoga teacher put up an American flag and sat in front of it, in a lotus position, eyes closed, saying, "Let us now breathe deeply in honor of our great country" (I looked around frantically, never getting the breathing right), mostly our conversations slid back shockingly, resiliently, to other topics: backup singers for Aretha Franklin, or which Korean-owned restaurant had the best Chinese food. Before I'd come to Troy, I had never had Chinese food. But now, two blocks from my apartment, next to a shoe-repair shop, was a place called the Peking Café where I went as often as I could for the Buddha's Delight. At the cash register small boxes of broken fortune cookies were sold at discount. "Only cookie broken," promised the sign, "not fortune." I vowed to buy a box one day to see what guidance—obscure or mystical or mercenary, but Confucian!—might be had in bulk. Meanwhile, I collected them singly, one per every cookie that came at the end atop my check, briskly, efficiently, before I'd even finished eating. Perhaps I ate too slowly. I'd grown up on Friday fish fries and green beans in butter (for years, my mother had told me, margarine, considered a foreign food, could be purchased only across state lines, at "oleo" stands hastily erected along the highway—PARK HERE FOR PARKAY read the signs—just past the Illinois governor's welcome billboard, farmers muttering that only Jews bought there). And so now these odd Chinese vegetables—fungal and gnomic in their brown sauce—had the power for me of an adventure or a rite, a statement to be savored. Back in Dellacrosse the dining was divided into "Casual," which meant you ate it standing up or took it away, and the high end, which was called "Sit-Down Dining." At the Wie Haus Family Restaurant, where we went for sit-down, the seats were red leatherette and the walls were covered with the local *gemütlichkeit:* dark paneling and framed deep kitsch, wide-eyed shepherdesses and jesters. The breakfast menus read "Guten Morgen." Sauces were called "gravy." And the dinner menu featured cheese curd meatloaf and steak "cooked to your likeness." On Fridays there were fish fries or boils at which they served "lawyers" (burbot or eelpout), so-called because *their hearts were in their butts.* (They were fished from the local lake, where all the picnic spots had trash cans that read NO FISH GUTS.) On Sundays there was not only marsh-mallow and maraschino cherry salad and something called "Grandma Jell-O," but "prime rib with au jus," a precise knowl-edge of French—or English or even food coloring—not being the restaurant's strong point. *A la carte* meant soup *or* salad; *dinner* meant soup *and* salad. Roquefort dressing was called "Rockford dressing." The house wine—red, white, and pink—all bore the requisite bouquet of rose, soap, and graphite, a whiff of hay, a hint of hooterville, though the menu remained mute about all this, sticking to straightforward declarations of hue. Light ale and dunkel were served. For dessert there was usually a *glückschmerz* pie, with the fluffy look and heft of a small snowbank. After any meal, sleepiness ensued.

Now, however, away and on my own, seduced and salted by brown sauce, I felt myself thinning and alive. The Asian owners let me linger over my books and stay as long as I wanted to: "Take your tie! No lush!" they said kindly as they sprayed the neighbor-ing tables with disinfectant. I ate mango and papaya and nudged the stringy parts out of my teeth with a cinnamon toothpick. I had one elegantly folded cookie—a short paper nerve baked in an ear. I had a handleless cup of hot, stale tea, poured and reheated from a pail stored in the restaurant's walk-in refrigerator.

I would tug the paper slip from the stiff clutches of the cookie and save it for a bookmark. All my books had fortunes protrud-ing like tiny tails from their pages. *You are the crispy noodle in the salad of life. You are the master of your own destiny.* Murph had always added the phrase "in bed" to any fortune cookie fortune, so in my mind I read them that way, too: *You are the master of your own destiny. In bed.* Well, that was true. *Debt is a seductive liar. In bed.* Or the less-well-translated *Your fate will blossom like a bloom.*

Or the sly, wise guy: *A refreshing change is in your future.* Sometimes, as a better joke, I added *though NOT in bed. You will soon make money.* Or: *Wealth is a wise woman's man. Though NOT in bed.*

And so I needed a job. I had donated my plasma several times for cash, but the last time I had tried, the clinic had turned me away, saying my plasma was cloudy from my having eaten cheese the night before. Cloudy Plasma! I would be the bass guitarist! It was so hard not to eat cheese. Even the whipped and spreadable kind we derisively called "cram cheese" (because it could be used for sealing windows and caulking tile) had a certain soothing allure. I looked daily at the employment listings. Childcare was in demand: I turned in my final papers and answered the ads.

One forty-ish pregnant woman after another hung up my coat, sat me in her living room, then waddled out to the kitchen, got my tea, and waddled back in, clutching her back, slopping tea onto the saucer, and asking me questions. "What would you do if our little baby started crying and wouldn't stop?" "Are you available evenings?" "What do you think of as a useful educational activity for a small child?" I had no idea. I had never seen so many pregnant women in such a short period of time—five in all. It alarmed me. They did not look radiant. They looked reddened with high blood pressure and frightened. "I would put him in a stroller and take him for a walk," I said. I knew my own mother had never asked such questions of anyone. "Dolly," she said to me once, "as long as the place was moderately fire resistant, I'd deposit you anywhere."

"Moderately?" I queried. She rarely called me by my name, Tassie. She called me Doll, Dolly, Dollylah, or Tassalah.

"I wasn't going to worry and interfere with you." She was the only Jewish woman I'd ever known who felt like that. But she was a Jewish woman married to a Lutheran farmer named Bo and perhaps because of that had the same indifferent reserve the mothers of my friends had. Halfway through my childhood I came to guess that she was practically blind as well. It was the only explanation for the thick glasses she failed often even to find. Or for the kaleidoscope of blood vessels burst, petunia-like, in her eyes, scarlet blasting into the white from mere eyestrain, or a careless swipe with her hand. It explained the strange way she never quite looked at me when we were speaking, staring at a table or down at a tile of a floor, as if halfheartedly plotting its disinfection while my scarcely controlled rage flew from my mouth in sentences I hoped would be, perhaps not then but perhaps later, like knives to her brain.

"Will you be in town for Christmas break?" the mothers asked.

I sipped at the tea. "No, I'm going home. But I will be back in January."

"When in January?"

I gave them my references and a written summary of my experience. My experience was not all that much—just the Pitskys and the Schultzes back home. But as experience, too, I had once, as part of a class project on human reproduction, carried around for an entire week a sack of flour the exact weight and feel of an infant. I'd swaddled it and cuddled it and placed it in safe, cushioned places for naps, but once, when no one was looking, I stuffed it in my backpack with a lot of sharp pens, and it got stabbed. My books, powdery white the rest of the term, became a joke in the class. I left this off my résumé, however.

But the rest I'd typed up. To gild the lily-livered, as my dad sometimes said, I was wearing what the department stores called "a career jacket," and perhaps the women liked the professionalism of that. They were professionals themselves. Two were lawyers, one was a journalist, one was a doctor, one a high school teacher. Where were the husbands? "Oh, at work," the women all said vaguely. All except the journalist, who said, "Good question!"

The last house was a gray stucco prairie house with a chimney cloaked in dead ivy. I had passed the house earlier in the week—it was on a corner lot and I'd seen so many birds there. Now there was just a flat expanse of white. Around the whiteness was a low wood Qual Line fence, and when I pushed open its gate it slipped a little; one of its hinges was loose and missing a nail. I had to lift the gate to relatch it. This maneuver, one I'd performed any number of times in my life, gave me a certain satisfaction—of tidiness, of restoration, of magic me!—when in fact it should have communicated itself as something else: someone's ill-disguised decrepitude, items not cared for properly but fixed repeatedly in a make-do fashion, needful things having gotten away from their caregiver. Soon the entire gate would have to be held together with a bungee cord, the way my father once fixed a door in our barn.

Two slate steps led, in an odd mismatch of rock, downward to a flagstone walk, all of which, as well as the grass, wore a light dusting of snow—I laid the first footprints of the day; perhaps the front door was seldom used. Some desiccated mums were still in pots on the porch. Ice frosted the crisp heads of the flowers. Leaning against the house were a shovel and a rake, and shoved into the corner two phone books still in shrink-wrap.

The woman of the house opened the door. She was pale and compact, no sags or pouches, linen skin tight across the bone. The hollows of her cheeks were powdered darkly, as if with the pollen of a tiger lily. Her hair was cropped short and dyed the fashionable bright auburn of a ladybug. Her earrings were buttons of deepest orange, her leggings mahogany, her sweater rust-colored, and her lips maroonish brown. She looked like a highly controlled oxidation experiment. "Come in," she said, and I entered, mutely at first and then, as always, apologetically, as if I were late, though I wasn't. At that time in my life I was never late. Only a year later would I suddenly have difficulty hanging on to any sense of time, leaving friends sitting, invariably, for a half hour here or there. Time would waft past me undetectably or absurdly—laughably when I could laugh—in quantities I was incapable of measuring or obeying.

But that year, when I was twenty, I was as punctual as a priest. Were priests punctual? Cave-raised, divinely dazed, I believed them to be.

The woman closed the heavy oak door behind me, and I stamped my feet on the braided rug I was standing on, to shake off the snow. I started then to take off my shoes. "Oh, you don't have to take off your shoes," she said. "There's too much of that prissy Japanese stuff going on in this town. Bring in the mud." She smiled—big, theatrical, a little crazy. I had forgotten her name and was hoping she'd say it soon; if she didn't, she might not say it at all.

"I'm Tassie Keltjin," I said, thrusting out my hand.

She took it and then studied my face. "Yes," she said slowly, absently, unnervingly scrutinizing each of my eyes. Her gaze made a slow, observing circle around my nose and mouth. "I'm Sarah Brink," she said finally. I was not used to being looked at close up, not used to the thing I was looking at looking back. Certainly my own mother had never done such looking, and in general my face had the kind of smooth, round stupidity that did not prompt the world's study. I had always felt as hidden as the hull in a berry, as secret and fetal as the curled fortune in a cookie, and such hiddenness was not without its advantages, its egotisms, its grief-fed grandiosities.

"Here, let me take your coat," Sarah Brink said finally, and only then, as she lifted it off me and headed across the foyer to hang it on a hat rack, did I see that she was as thin as a pin, not pregnant at all.

She led me into the living room, stopping at the large back window first. I followed her, tried to do what she did. In the yard most of a large oak tree split by lightning had been hacked and stacked by the garage for winter firewood. Near its old stump another tree—tenuous, young, with the look of a swizzle stick—had been planted, trussed, and braced. But Sarah was not studying the trees. "Oh, for the love of God, look at these poor dogs," she said. We stood there, watching. The dogs next door were being kept in the yard by an invisible electric fence. One of them, a German shepherd, understood the fence, but the other one, a little terrier, did not. The German shepherd would get a game of chase going around the yard and lead the terrier right to the electrified border and then stop short, leaving the terrier to barrel on ahead into the electricity. The stunned terrier would then come racing back, shrieking with pain. This amused the German shepherd, who continued to do this, and the shocked terrier, desperate for play, would forget, and get started again, and barrel on into the electricity again, yowling. "This has been going on for weeks," said Sarah.

"Reminds me of dating," I said, and Sarah spun her head, to size me up again. I could see now that she was at least two inches taller than I was; I could peer up her nostrils, the weave of tiny hairs like the crisscross of branches seen from the base of a tree. She smiled, which pushed her cheeks out and made the blush beneath them look shadowy and wrong. Heat flew to my face. Dating? What did I know of it? My roommate, Murph, had done all the dating and had essentially abandoned me so that she could now sleep every night with this new guy she'd met. She had bequeathed me her vibrator, a strange swirling, buzzing thing that when switched to high gyrated in the air like someone's bored thick finger going *whoop-dee-doo*. Whose penis could this possibly resemble? Someone who had worked in a circus, perhaps! Maybe Burt Lancaster's in *Trapeze*. I kept the thing on the kitchen counter where Murph had left it for me and occasionally I used it to stir my chocolate milk. I *had* once actually gone out on a date—last year—and I had prepared for it by falling into a trance in a lingerie store and buying a forty-five-dollar black Taiwanese bra padded with oil and water pouches, articulated with wire, lifelike to the touch, a complete bosom entirely on its own, independent of any wearer, and which when fastened to my particular chest looked like a dark animal strapped there to nurse. I was filled with a pleasing floating feeling while wearing it; I felt heated and sacrificial, and so I imagined it improved my chances in the world, my own actual bust having been left (I once joked) on a plinth in the basement of the Dellacrosse library, the better to free my spine for erect walking.

All that preparation was the futile preening of a fly: my poor date cleared his throat and told me he was gay. We lay there together on my bed, only partially disrobed, our black underwear misadvertising our experience. His back was full of rosy pimples: "bacne," he'd called it. I rubbed my fingertips across it, a kind of Braille, its message one of creaturely energy and worry. "Queer as Dick's hatband," he announced into the room, candor—or a pretense to candor—being the cheapest and most efficient assault on hope (a hope, I had to admit, that had, to use my dad's expression, gilded its own lily-liver and become an expectation). "Dick's hatband?" I'd repeated, staring at the ceiling. I had no idea what that meant. I thought mutely and appallingly of the band on a hat that Dick Hickock might wear. We'd stayed up for an hour after his confession, both of us trembling and teary, and then got up and for some reason decided to make a cake. We had wanted to have sex but ended up baking a cake? "I really, really like you so much," I said when the cake was done, and when he said nothing in reply, a hard, stubborn silence entered the room and reverberated as if it were a sound. I said awkwardly, "Is there an echo in here?"

And he looked at me pitifully and said, "Well, I wish there were, but there's not." Then he went into the bathroom and came out wearing all my makeup, which for some reason made me believe he had lied about being gay. "You know," I said, testing him, but mostly pleading, "if you concentrated you could be straight. I'm sure of it. Just relax, close your eyes once in a while, and just do it. Heterosexuality—well, it takes a lot of concentration!" I said, a begging sound in my voice. "It takes a lot for everybody!"

"It may take more than I have," he said. I made him coffee— he asked for cream, and then cold cream and then paper towels— and then he left, taking a slice of warm cake with him. I never saw him again, except once, briefly, from across the street when I was walking to class. He had shaved his head and was wearing thick violet boots and no raincoat in the rain. He walked in a bouncy zigzag movement, as if avoiding sniper fire. He was with a woman who was more than six feet tall and had an Adam's apple the size of a small swallowed fist. A long scarf—whose was it? I couldn't tell; at points it seemed to belong to them both—flew exuberantly behind them like the tail of a kite.

Now Sarah turned back to the window. "The neighbors just put in that invisible fence," she said. "In November. I'm sure it causes MS or something."

"Who are they?" I asked. "The neighbors, I mean." I would show some anthropological interest in the neighborhood. No one I'd interviewed with had yet called me back. Perhaps they'd desired a lively take-charge type and I'd seemed dull, slow to get involved. It had started to worry me that if I wasn't careful my meekness could become a habit, a tic, something hardwired that my mannerisms would continue to express throughout my life regardless of my efforts—the way a drunk who, though on the wagon, still staggers and slurs like a drunk.

"The neighbors?" Sarah Brink's face brightened artificially, her eyes wide. Her voice went flat and stagey. "Well, in that there dog house there's Catherine Welbourne and her husband, Stuart, *and* Stuart's lover, Michael Batt. The Welbournes and the Batts. Who could make up these names?"

"So—Michael's gay?" I said, perhaps now showing too much interest.

"Well, yes," said Sarah. "Much is made of Michael's being gay. 'Michael's gay,' the neighbors whisper, 'Michael's gay. Michael's gay.' Well, yes, Michael's gay. But of course the thing is, *Stuart's* gay." Sarah's eyes looked merry and bright—the frantic but pleased cheap sparkle of Christmas dreck.

I cleared my throat. "And what does Catherine think of all this?" I ventured. I tried to smile.

"Catherine." Sarah sighed and moved away from the window. "Catherine, Catherine. Well, Catherine spends a lot of time in her room, listening to Erik Satie. The beard, poor thing, is always the last to know. But look." She wanted to change the subject now, get down to business. "Have a seat. Here's the deal." She motioned with an arm tossed suddenly out in a spasm. "Childcare," she seemed to begin, but then stopped, as if that were sufficient.

I sat down on a small sofa that was upholstered in a kind of pillow ticking. *Childcare,* like *healthcare,* had become one word. I would become a dispenser of it. I opened my backpack and began fumbling through it, looking for a copy of my résumé. Sarah sat across from me on another pillow-ticking sofa, the very brightness of her looking as if it might stain the cushions. She twisted her legs up and around each other in such a way that the lower half of one gave the illusion of jutting out of the upper half of the other, as if she had the backwards knees of a crane. She began clearing her throat, so I stopped fumbling and set the backpack aside.

"Already the winter air is getting to me," she said. She turned and coughed again loudly, in that parched fashion that doctors call "unproductive." She patted her flat stomach. "Here's the deal," she said again. "We are adopting."

"Adopting?"

"A baby. We are adopting a baby in two weeks. That's why we're advertising for a sitter. We'd like to line someone up ahead of time for some regular hours."

I didn't know anything about adoption. I'd known only one adopted girl when I was growing up, Becky Sussluch, spoiled and beautiful and at sixteen having an affair with a mussed and handsome student teacher that I myself had a crush on. In general I thought of adoption much as I thought of most things in life: uneasily. Adoption seemed both a cruel joke and a lovely daydream—a nice way of avoiding the blood and pain of giving birth, or, from a child's perspective, a realized fantasy of your parents not really being your parents. Your genes could thrust one arm in the air and pump up and down. *Yes!* You were not actually related to *Them!* Strangely, at the stamp machine at the post office, I had recently bought the newly issued adoption postage stamps—*Adopt a Child, Build a Family, Create a World*—and gleefully adhered them to my letters home to my mother. It was a form of malice I felt entitled to. It was quiet and deniable.

"Congratulations," I murmured now to Sarah. Was that what one said?

Sarah's face lit up gratefully, as if no one had yet said an encouraging word to her on the matter. "Why, thank you! I have so much work at the restaurant that everyone I mention this to acts peculiar and quiet, so meanly worried for me. They say, 'Really!' and then all this tension springs to their mouth. They think I'm too old."

I accidentally nodded. I had no idea, conversationally, where we were. I searched, as I too often found myself having to do, to find a language, or even an octave, in which to speak. I wondered how old she was.

"I own Le Petit Moulin," Sarah Brink added.

Le Petit Moulin. I knew of it a little. It was one of those expensive restaurants downtown, every entree freshly hairy with dill, every soup and dessert dripped upon as preciously as a Pollock, filets and cutlets sprinkled with lavender dust once owned by pixies, restaurants to which students never went, except if newly pinned to a fraternity boy or dating an assistant dean or hosting a visit from their concerned suburban parents. I knew Le Petit Moulin served things that sounded like instruments—timbales, quenelles—God only knew what they were. I had once tried to study the menu in the lit window near the entrance, and as I stared at the words, the sting of my own exile had moistened my eyes. It was a restaurant that probably served my father's potatoes, though my father would not have been able to go in. The lowest price for dinner was twenty-two dollars, the highest, forty-five. Forty-five! You could get an oil-and-water bra for that price!

I fumbled in my bag again for my résumé, and found it folded and bent but handed it to Sarah anyway. I spoke. "My father supplied a few of the restaurants around here. A few years back it was, I think."

Sarah Brink looked at my résumé. "Are you related to Bo Keltjin—Keltjin potatoes?"

It startled me to hear my father's potatoes—Kennebecs, Norlands, Pontiacs, Yukon golds, some the size of marbles, some grapefruits, depending on drought and digging times and what the beetles were up to—all summed up and uttered that way right here in her living room. "That's my dad," I said.

"Why, I remember your father very well. His Klamath pearls were famous. Also the yellow fingerlings. And his purple Peruvians and Rose Finns were the first to be sold in those little netted berry pints, like jewels. And those new potatoes he called 'Keltjin duck eggs.' I had a theory about those."

I nodded. Returning from his English honeymoon with my

mom, my father had actually smuggled a many-eyed jersey royal straight through Chicago customs, and upon returning to Dellacrosse, he'd grown them in pots and troughs in the barn in winter and in the ground in spring and sold them to restaurants as "duck eggs."

"I'd rush out to the farmers' market at six a.m. to get them. Come April, I should put those back on the menu." She was getting dreamy. Still, it was nice to hear my father spoken well of. He was not really respected as a farmer back home: he was a hobbyist, a truck farmer, with no real acreage, just some ducks (who every fall raped one another in a brutal fashion we never got used to), a dog, a tractor, a website (a website, for Christ's sake!), and two decorative, brockle-headed cows of dubious dairiness. (They were named Bess and Guess, or Milk and Manure, according to my dad, and he would not let them trample the stream banks the way most of the farmers around us did with their cows. I had once milked Bess, carefully cutting my fingernails beforehand, so as not to hurt her; the intimate feel of her lavender-veined and hairy breasts had almost made me puke. "All right, you don't have to do that again," my dad had said. What kind of farmer's daughter was I? I'd leaned my forehead against Bess's side to steady myself, and the sudden warmth, along with my own queasiness, made me feel I loved her.) We had also once had an ebullient pig named Helen, who would come when you called her name and smiled like a dolphin when you spoke to her. And then we didn't see her for a few days, and one morning over bacon and eggs, my brother said, "Is this Helen?" I dropped my fork and cried, "This is Helen? Is this Helen?!" and my mother, too, stopped eating and looked hard at my father: "Bo, is this Helen?" The next pig we got we never met and its name was #WK3746. Later we got a sweet but skittish goat named Lucy, who, sometimes along with our dog, Blot, traipsed around the yard, free as a bird.

My dad was chastened down at the Farm & Fleet for having only a few of the props. His farm was a mere kitchen garden that had gotten slightly out of hand—and only slightly. And he had painted his barn not the cheap, blood-camouflaging red of the country (which against the green fields and shrubs reminded my mother too much of Christmas) but blue and white like the sky, the silliness of which was spoken of often in the county feed shops. (Though these colors pleased my mother, I supposed, with their reminders of Hanukkah and Israel, though she professed to despise both. My mother's capacity for happiness was a small soup bone salting a large pot.) Plus, our farmhouse was too fancy by local standards—cream city brick mixed in with chicago to form a pattern of gold and dusky rose, with the mansard roof of an affluent farmer, though my father wasn't one. The dentals on the soffits my father sometimes painted brown or orange or sometimes a lurid violet—he altered their color every other summer. What was he, "some pillow biter from the Minnesota Ballet"? He sometimes pretended to be deaf and carried on with his own sense of humor and purpose. He had added a family room by hand, in the green way, the first in the county, and he mixed his own earthen plaster and hand-troweled it onto some wired bales of hay stuffed between the beams. The neighbors were not impressed: "I'll be damned. Bo's gone and built a mud and straw hut and he's attached it to his damn house." The sills were limestone, but reconstituted, and so they were just poured in. He was seldom deterred. He loved his old blue dairy barn with its rusty pails never thrown away and its adjacent stream that could still cool milk and which ran down to a small fish hatchery. He had a woodlot and few tillable fields. It was simple hill farming, really, but to the locals he seemed a vaguely contemptuous character, very out-of-town. His idiosyncracies appeared to others to go beyond issues of social authenticity and got into questions of God and man and existence. My father tried not to use hybrid seeds—wouldn't even plant burpless cukes—and so his lettuce bolted early. Perhaps this seemed hilarious—along with the low acreage, even lower attendance at church suppers and county fairs, plus an eccentric spouse of indeterminate ethnicity who slept too late for a farmer's wife and did not keep herself busy enough with chores. (My mother laid full-length mirrors on their sides in the back of the flowerbeds to double the look if not the actual volume of her gardening.) Worse than farming out of a book, my father seemed to be farming out of a magazine article: the ginseng farmers were held in higher esteem. Still, he would try to ingratiate himself—plant a small field of decoy soy to enliven the soil and lure the pests over from the neighbors' alfalfa, help them out a little. He rotated crops, not just for soil but in a fun game to confuse the enemy: if one year one put wheat in where the potatoes were and put the potatoes where the soy was, one seldom got borers. Or, one got bored borers—incapable of the excitement required to track down a snack. Our soil looked chocolatey and had structure, like wine, whereas the Atrazined dirt of our neighbors was often a sad heap of dry gray clods. My dad was local and green and organic and correctly slow but had years ago refused to be bought up by any of the organic cooperatives who were buying up the old truck farms. This just isolated him further. He was known as a Tofu Tom, or Bo the Tofu Prince, or sometimes just "Bofu," even though he grew potatoes.

"Yeah, his potatoes have a rep—at least in certain places," I hastened to add. "Even my mother admires them, and she is hard to please. She once said they were 'heaven-sent' and used to call them *pommes de terres de l'air*." Now I was just plain talking too much.

"That's funny," said Sarah.

"Yeah. She felt no name existed that accurately described them."

"She was probably right. That's interesting."

I feared Sarah was one of those women who instead of laughing said, "That's funny," or instead of smiling said, "That's interesting," or instead of saying, "You are a stupid blithering idiot," said, "Well, I think it's a little more complicated than that." I never knew what to do around such people, especially the ones who after you spoke liked to say, enigmatically, "I see." Usually I just went mute.

"You know, Joan of Arc's father grew potatoes," Sarah now said. "It was in her father's potato fields that she first heard voices. There're some legendary potatoes for you."

"I can understand that. I've heard voices myself in my father's fields," I said. "But it's usually just my brother's boom box clamped on the back of his tractor."

Sarah nodded. I could not make her laugh. Probably I was just not funny. "Does your father ever grow yams?" she asked.

Yams! With their little rat tails and their scandalous place in contemporary art, about which I'd read just last year. "No," I said. I feared, as interviews went, I was in freefall. I wasn't sure why either of us was saying what we were saying. "Potatoes are grown from the eyes of other potatoes," I said, apropos of God knows what.

"Yes." Sarah looked at me searchingly.

"In winter my brother and I actually used to shoot them out of pipes, with firecrackers," I added, now in total free association. "Potato guns. It was a big pastime for us when we were young. With cold-storage potatoes from the root cellar and some PVC pipe. We would arrange little armies and have battles."

Now it was Sarah's turn for randomness. "When I was your age I did a semester abroad in France and I stayed with a family there. I said to the daughter Marie-Jeanne, who was in my grade, 'It's interesting that in French-Canadian French one says *"patate"* but in France one says *"pommes de terres,"*' and she said, 'Oh, we say *"patate."'* But when I mentioned this later to her father? He grew very stern and said, 'Marie-Jeanne said *"patate"*? She must never say *"patate"*!' "

I laughed, not knowing quite why but feeling I was close to knowing. A distant memory flew to my head: a note passed to me from a mean boy in seventh grade. *Laugh less,* it commanded.

Sarah smiled. "Your father seemed like a nice man. I don't remember your mom."

"She hardly ever came into Troy."

"Really?"

"Well, sometimes she came to the market with her snapdragons. And gladioluses. People here called them 'gladioli,' which annoyed her."

"Yes," said Sarah, smiling. "I don't like that either." We were in polite, gratuitous agreement mode.

I continued. "She grew flowers, bunched them together with rubber bands. They were like a dollar a bunch." Actually, my mother took some pride in these flowers and fertilized them with mulched lakeweed. My father, however, took even greater pride in his potatoes and would never have used the lakeweed. Too many heavy metals, he said. "A rock band once crashed their plane into that lake," he joked, and though a plane had indeed crashed, the band was technically R&B. Still, it was true about the water: murky at best from gypsum mining up north.

It was strange to think of this woman Sarah knowing my father.

"Did you ever travel into town with them?" she asked.

I fidgeted a bit. Having to draw on my past like this was not what I had expected, and summoning it, making it come to me, was like coaxing a reluctant thing. "Not very often. I think once or twice my brother and I went with them and we just ran around the place annoying people. Another time I remember sitting under my parents' rickety sales table reading a book. There might have been a another time when I just stayed in the truck." Or maybe that was Milwaukee. I couldn't recall.

"Are they still farming? I just don't see him at the morning market anymore."

"Oh, not too much," I said. "They sold off a lot of the farm to some Amish people and now they're quasi retired." I loved to say *quasi.* I was saying it now a lot, instead of *sort of,* or *kind of,* and it had become a tic. "I am quasi ready to go," I would announce. Or, "I'm feeling a bit quasi today." Murph called me Quasimodo. Or Kami-quasi. Or wild and quasi girl.

"Or quasi something," I added. What my father really was was not quasi retired but quasi drunk. He was not old, but he acted old—nutty old. To amuse himself he often took to driving his combine down the county roads to deliberately slow up traffic. "I had them backed up seventeen deep," he once boasted to my mom.

"Seventeen's a mob," said my mother. "You'd better be careful."

"How old's your dad now?" asked Sarah Brink.

"Forty-five."

"Forty-five! Why, *I'm* forty-five. That means I'm old enough to be your . . ." She took a breath, still processing her own amazement.

"To be my dad?" I said.

A joke. I did not mean for this to imply some lack of femininity on her part. If it wasn't a successful joke, then it was instead a compliment, for I didn't want, even in my imagination, even for a second, to conflate this sophisticated woman with my mother, a woman so frugal and clueless that she had once given me—to have! to know! to wear!—her stretch black lace underwear that had shrunk in the dryer, though I was only ten.

Sarah Brink laughed, a quasi laugh, a socially constructed laugh—a collection of predetermined notes, like the chimes of a doorbell.

"So here's the job description," she said when the laugh was through.

Walking home, I passed a squirrel that had been hit by a car. Its soft, scarlet guts spilled out of its mouth, as if in a dialogue balloon, and the wind gently blew the fur of its tail, as if it were still alive. I tried to remember everything Sarah Brink had said to me. It was a mile home to my apartment, so I replayed long snippets of her voice, though the cold air was the sort that bullied a walker into mental muteness. *This is an incredibly important position for us, even if we are hiring at the last minute. If we hire you, we would like you to be there with us for everything, from the very first day. We would like you to feel like part of our family, since of course you will be part of it.* I tried to think of who Sarah Brink reminded me of, though I was sure it wasn't anyone I'd actually met. Probably she reminded me of a character from a television show I'd watched years before. But not the star. Definitely not the star. More like the star's neatnik roommate or the star's kooky cousin from Cleveland. I knew, even once she had a baby, she would never be able to shake the Auntie Mame quality from her mothering. There were worse things, I supposed.

In the sky the light was thin and draining. Dusk was beginning already, although it was only three in the afternoon. The sun set earliest in these days before Christmas—"the shortest days of the year," which only meant the darkest—and it made for a lonely walk home. My apartment was in one of those old frame houses close to campus, in the student ghetto that abutted the university stadium. It was a corner house, and the first-floor apartment I shared with Murph was to the south, on the left as one walked up the stairs to the porch. Murph's real name, Elizabeth Murphy Krueger, adorned our mailbox along with mine on an index card in sparkly green glue. Across the street the gray concrete stadium wall rose three times higher than any building around, and it overshadowed the neighborhood in a bleak and brutal way. In spring and fall convening marching bands, with their vibrating tubas and snares, routinely rattled our window-panes. Sun reached our rooms only when directly overhead—in May at noon—or on a winter morning when reflected from some fluke drifts of a snowstorm, or in the afternoon when the angle of its setting caused it to flare briefly through the back windows of the kitchen. When a generous patch of sun appeared on the floor, it was a pleasure just to stand in it. (Was I too old or too young to be getting my pleasure there? I was not the right age, surely.) After a rainstorm, or during a winter thaw, one could walk by the stadium and hear the rush of water running inside from the top seats, dropping down row by row to the bottom, a perfectly graduated waterfall, although, captured and magnified within the concrete construction of the stadium, the sound sometimes rose to a roaring *whoosh*. Often people stopped along the sidewalks to point at the exterior stadium wall and say, "Isn't the stadium empty? What is that sound?"

"It's the revolution," Murph liked to say. To her, stadiums were where insurgents were shot, and this caused her to have mixed feelings about living so close, to say nothing of her feelings about the home football games, when curb space was scarce and the parked cars of out-of-towners jammed our streets, their cheers from the stands like a screaming wind through town, the red of their thousands of sweatshirts like an invasion of bright bugs. On Sunday mornings, the day after the games, the sidewalk would be littered with cardboard signs that read I NEED TICKETS.

Murph was now only technically my roommate, since she mostly lived a mile away in a subletted condo with her new boyfriend, a sixth-year senior. I had a tendency to forget about this—looking forward to telling her something, wondering what we might cook up for supper, expecting to see her there, brooding, with her sweater thrown over her shoulders and her sleeves wound round her neck, a look that was elegant on her but on me would have made me appear insane. And then I would come home to realize, once more, that it was just me there. She would leave the telltale jetsam and flotsam, hastily changed clothes, carelessly written notes. *Hey, Tass, I drank the last of the milk— sorry.* So I was left with the ambivalence of having to pay with aloneness for an apartment I could not alone afford. It was not miserable—often I did not miss her at all. But there was sometimes a quick, sinking ache when I walked in the door and saw she was not there. Twice, however, I'd felt the same sinking feeling when she was.

The porous dry rot of our front steps still held weight—six slim tenants, single file—but every time I climbed them I worried it could be my last: surely the next time my foot would go through and I would have to be pried from the splintery wreckage by a rescue squad phoned by the watchful Kay upstairs. Our landlord, Mr. Wettersten, was classically absentee, though he believed in good boilers and, when school was in session, did not stint with heat, perhaps fearing the lawsuits of parents. You could shower several times a day, or at the last minute: your hair would dry in a snap over the radiators. Sometimes my apartment would so overheat that my fingernails would dry up and crack and break off in my gloves, chips of them stuck in the woolen fingertips. Now, as I unlocked the door and pushed in, the pipes were clanking and letting loose with their small internal explosions; no pipe had ever yet burst, though if the boiler kicked on at night, the quaking could pull you alarmedly from sleep. It was, at times, like living in a factory. Kay, who lived in the largest flat, was middle-aged and the only tenant not a student; she was always in some skirmish with the landlord about the building. "He has no idea what he's up against, letting this building go the way he has," Kay said to me once. "When something's off here I have nothing else to think about. I mean, I have no other life. I can make this my life. He doesn't appreciate what he's up against. He's up against someone with no life." So we all let Kay manage the troubles of the house. She had been there for more than a decade. Murph sometimes referred to the tenants of the house as the Clutter Family, by which I assumed—I hoped, I prayed—she meant all their clutter.

When I walked across the front room to throw my stuff on the couch, the floorboards, paradoxically worn and tentative, creaked loudly—more so now that all humidity had fled the place. Despite the busy, complaining crackle of pipe and floor, the rooms had a wintry loneliness. Our fireplace, cold and unused, a safety hazard—what hope for comfort without the risk of fiery death? should we risk? yes, I once begged, yes!—we used as a storage nook for CDs. In the corner leaned my electric bass and amp, yearning for a workout, but I ignored them. I had a see-through Dan Armstrong lucite, like Jack Bruce of Cream, and I had contrived to know stray licks not usually played on bass: I knew some Modest Mouse, some Violent Femmes, and some Sleater-Kinney ("Isn't that the cancer hospital in New York?" my brother once asked me), plus, from the olden days, Jimi Hendrix, "Milestones," "Barbara Ann," "Barbara Allen," "My Favorite Things," and "Happy Birthday" (as if played by Hendrix but on a bass!). Once, in Dellacrosse, I had agreed to give an actual concert—I played "Blue Bells of Scotland" and wore a kilt. A kilt with a see-through electric guitar! which managed to sound very much like a bagpipe, and because the concert was part of a county fair, they gave me a green ribbon that said *Lyric Lass.* Everyone at that stupid fair had their head up their hinder as far as I was concerned, including me, and I never played there again.

In the hallway of my apartment the phone machine light was blinking and I pressed Play, turned up the volume, then went on into my bedroom, where I flopped down on my bed, in the icelandic afternoon dusk, door open, to listen to the voices of women, one after another, and their various desires and requests.

First there was Murph's sister. "Hi, it's Lynn. You are not there, I know, but call me later when you are." Then there was my mother. "Hello, Tassie? It's your mother." Followed by a bumping, banging hang-up. Had she dropped the phone, or was this just one more example of her strange personal style? Then there was my advisor, who was also Dean of Women. "Yes, this is Dean Andersen looking for Tassie Jane Keltjin." I kept forgetting our outgoing message contained no indication as to whose phone it was. It simply had Murph screaming (we thought hilariously), "Leave your message after the tone, if you have to! We are *so not here!*" Dean Andersen's voice was gentle but forceful, a combination I would spend many hours of my young life attempting to learn, though they would have been better spent on Farsi. "Tassie, could you leave a copy of your spring registration forms in my mailbox in Ellis Hall? Thanks much. I need to officially sign off on them, which I don't believe I did, though I'm not sure why. Have a great break." There was a long, uncertain silence preceding the final message. "Yes, hello, this is Sarah Brink phoning for Tassie Keltjin." There was another long, uncertain silence. I sat straight up to hear if there was anything else. "Could she phone me back sometime this evening? Thank you very much. 357-7649."

First I phoned my mother. She had no voice mail of any sort, so I let it ring ten times, then hung up. Then I rewound our machine and played the message from Sarah Brink again. What was I frightened of? I wasn't sure. But I decided to wait until the morning to phone her back. I got into my nightgown, made a grilled cheese sandwich and some mint tea, then took them back into my room, where I consumed them in bed. Ringed by crumbs and grease, newspapers and a book, I eventually fell asleep.

I woke up in a blaze of white sun. I had neglected to pull the shades and it had snowed in the night; the morning rays reflected off the snow on the sills and on the low adjacent roof, setting the room on fire with daylight. I tried not to think about my life. I did not have any good solid plans for it long-term—no bad plans either, no plans at all—and the lostness of that, compared with the clear ambitions of my friends (marriage, children, law school), sometimes shamed me. Other times in my mind I defended such a condition as morally and intellectually superior—my life was open and ready and free—but that did not make it any less lonely. I got up, trudged barefoot across the cold floor, and made a cup of coffee, with a brown plastic Melitta filter and a paper towel, dripping it into a single ceramic mug that said *Moose Timber Lodge.* Murph had gone there once, for a weekend, with her new BF.

The phone rang again before I'd had time to let the coffee kick in and give me words to say; nonetheless, I picked up the receiver.

"Hi, is this Tassie?" said the newly familiar voice.

"Yes, it is." I frantically gulped at my coffee. What time was it? Too soon for calls.

"This is Sarah Brink. Did I wake you up? I'm sorry. I'm calling too early, aren't I?"

"Oh, no," I said, lest she think I was a shiftless bum. Better a lying sack of shit.

"I didn't know whether I'd left a message on the correct machine or not. And I wanted to get back to you as soon as possible before you accepted an offer from someone else." Little did she know. "I've talked it over with my husband and we'd like to offer you the job."

Could she even have called the references I'd listed? Had there been enough time to?

"Oh, thank you," I said.

"We'll start you at ten dollars an hour, with the possibility of raises down the line."

"OK." I sipped at the coffee, trying to wake my brain. Let the coffee speak!

"The problem is this. The job starts today."

"Today?" I sipped again.

"Yes, I'm sorry. We are going to Kronenkee to meet the birth mother and we'd like you to come with us."

"Yes, well, I think that would be OK."

"So you accept the position?"

"Yes, I guess I do."

"You do? You can't know how happy you've made me."

"Really?" I asked, all the while wondering, *Where's the new employee's first-day orientation meeting? Where is the "You've Picked a Great Place to Work" PowerPoint presentation?* The coffee was kicking in, but not helpfully.

"Oh, yes, really," she said. "Can you be here by noon?"

The appointment with the birth mother was for two p.m. at the Perkins restaurant in Kronenkee, a town an hour away with a part-German, part-Indian name that I'd always assumed meant "wampum." The social worker who ran the adoption agency was supposed to meet us there with the birth mother, and everyone would cheerfully assess one another. I had walked the half hour to Sarah Brink's house and then waited twenty minutes while she scrambled around doing things, making quick phone calls to the restaurant—"Meeska, the Concord coulis has got to be more than grape jam!"—or searching madly for her sunglasses ("I hate that snow glare on those two-lane roads"), all the while apologizing to me from the next room. In the car, on our way up, I sat next to her in the front seat, since her husband, Edward, whom, strangely, I still hadn't met, couldn't get out of some meeting or other and had apparently told Sarah to go ahead without him.

"Marriage," Sarah sighed. As if I had any idea what that meant. Yet it did seem odd that he wasn't with her, and odder still that I seemed to be going in his stead.

But I nodded. "He must be busy," I said, giving Edward the benefit of the doubt, though I was beginning to think Edward might be, well, an asshole. I looked sideways at Sarah, who was hatless, with a long cranberry scarf coiled twice about her neck. The sun caught the shiny artifice of her hair as well as the stray tufts of white lint on her peacoat. Still, especially with the sunglasses in winter—something I had seldom seen before—she looked glamorous. I was not especially used to speaking to adults, so I felt comfortable just being quiet with her, and soon she turned on the classical music station and we listened to Mussorgsky's *Pictures at an Exhibition* and *Night on Bald Mountain* for the entire ride. "They've told me the birth mother is very beautiful," said Sarah, at one point. And I said nothing, not knowing what to say.

We waited in the second booth in at Perkins, Sarah and I sitting on the same side, to leave the seat opposite fully open for the two people we were waiting for. Sarah ordered coffee for us both and I sat looking over the plasticized Perkins menu, with its little pictures of golden french fries laid out on frilly, verdant lettuce next to tomato slices the size of small clocks. What would I order? There was the Bread Bowl Salad, the Heartland Omelette, and various "bottomless" beverages, for the greedy and thirsty— I feared I was both. Sarah ordered Perkins's Bottomless Pot of Coffee, for the entire table, and the waitress went away to bring it.

"Oh, look, here they are," murmured Sarah, and I looked up to see a heavily made-up middle-aged woman in a deep pink parka holding the arm of a girl probably my age, maybe younger, who was very pregnant, very pretty, and when she smiled at us, even from that distance, I could see she had scarcely a tooth in her head. We stood and moved toward them. The girl wore an electronic bracelet on her wrist, but was clearly unembarrassed by this because she energetically thrust her hand out from her sleeve in greeting. I shook it. "Hi," she said to me. I wondered what she had done, and why the bracelet was not around her ankle instead. Perhaps she had been very, very bad and had both.

"Hi," I replied, trying to smile companionably and not stare at her stomach.

"*This* is the mother, *here*," the woman in the pink parka told the pregnant girl, indicating Sarah. "Sarah Brink? Amber Bowers."

"Hi—it's so wonderful to meet you." Sarah grasped Amber's hand warmly and shook it for too long. Amber kept turning back hopefully toward me, as if she were as baffled as I was to be in the company of these mysterious middle-aged women.

"I'm Tassie Keltjin," I said quickly, shaking Amber's penalized hand yet again. The delicate knobs of her wrists and her elegant fingers were in strange contrast to her toothlessness and the hard plastic parole band. "I'm going to work for Sarah, as a childcare provider."

"And I'm Letitia Gherlich," said the adoption agency woman, shaking my hand though not letting go of Amber's coat sleeve, as if she might escape. Amber did have the face, if not currently the body, of someone who perhaps more than once had suddenly made a run for it.

"Hey, Letitia," said Sarah, who threw her arms around her as if they were old friends, though Letitia stiffened a little. "Here, come sit down," she added. "The waitress is bringing coffee."

After that, things moved with swiftness and awkwardness both, like something simultaneously strong and broken. We hung up coats; we ordered; we ate; we made chitchat about the food and the snow. "Oh, there's my probation officer," Amber said, giggling; her face brightened, as if she had a little crush on him. "I think he sees us. He's sitting right over there by the window." We looked up to see the probation officer, his blue jacket still on, his bottomless Diet Coke stacked with ice. A going-to-seed hunk in a windbreaker: the world seemed full of them. We all just stared to buy ourselves time, I suppose, and to avoid the actual question of Amber's crimes.

Letitia began to speak to Sarah, on Amber's behalf. "Amber is happy to meet Tassie as well as you, Sarah." Here Amber looked across at me and rolled her eyes, as if we were two girls out with our embarrassing mothers. I had been noticing Amber's face, which was as lovely as advertised but sassy, with a strange electricity animating it, and with the missing teeth she seemed like a slightly educated hillbilly or an infant freak. Her hair was a gingery blond, shoulder length, as straight and coarse as a horse's tail. "Amber is wondering, of course, about your religious plans for the baby. She is very interested in having the baby baptized Catholic, aren't you, Amber?"

"Oh, yeah," said Amber. "That's the whole point of this." She pulled out the front of her bulging stretchy sweater and let it snap back.

"And of course, she would hope you would have the child confirmed as well, when the time came."

"We could do that. We could definitely do that," Sarah said agreeably.

"Were you raised Catholic?" asked Amber.

"Uh, well, no, but my cousins were," said Sarah, as if this solved everything.

Letitia, nervous about the sticky parts of a deal, said cheerily, "The birth father is white. I did mention that to you, didn't I?"

Sarah said nothing, her face momentarily inscrutable. She picked up a lone cold french fry the waitress had yet to clear and began to chew.

Letitia continued. "Tall and good-looking, like Amber."

Amber smiled happily. "We broke up," she said, shrugging.

"Do you have a picture of him, though? To show Sarah?" Letitia was selling the idea of the handsome white boy-dad.

"I don't think I ever had a damn picture of him," said Amber, shaking her head. Now she looked at me, grinning. "Except in my mind. My mind's a regular exhibition." The phrase was oddly reminiscent of the Mussorgsky we'd listened to in the car.

And her mouth, with its few and crooked teeth, bits of shell awash on a reef of gum, seemed a curious home for her voice, which was slowly surprising, with its intelligence and humor. There was a lull now. Amber suddenly leaned back, physically uncomfortable. "So, where's your husband?" she asked Sarah.

I examined Sarah's face for the stiffened look of the accused. "He's, oh, he's at a meeting his lab is having with the university. I run my own restaurant in town, so I can make up my own schedule as far as meetings go. But, well, he's at the beck and call of others—at least today he is."

"Do you think you really have time for a baby, owning a restaurant and all?" Amber was not shy. If she had been shy, not one of us would be at Perkins right now.

Sarah refused to be flustered. She'd heard remarks of this sort a dozen times. But before she could speak, Letitia spoke for her. "That's why Tassie is here. Tassie's the backup. But Sarah will always be around. She'll be the mom. And she can do a lot of her work right out of the house—isn't that right, Sarah?"

What work could Sarah do from the house? Yell at Meeska about the coulis?

"Absolutely," Sarah said. "Oh, I forgot. I brought you a present, Amber." She took a CD from her purse. "It's a mixed CD of my favorite classical music."

Amber took it and stashed it in her bag with the most fleeting of glances. Perhaps she'd had a slew of these lunches as a means of collecting goodies, which she would later sell on eBay. "And I have a present for you, too," she said, and handed Sarah a foil-wrapped pat of butter she plucked from the bowl on the table. "It's wrapped!" Amber said, smiling wickedly. The CD hadn't been. A scalding boldness gripped Amber's face, then a kind of guilt, then drifty blankness, like songs off a jukebox list, flipped through unchosen.

"Thanks!" said Sarah gamely. You had to hand it to her. She

opened up the butter and applied it to her mouth like lip gloss. "Prevents chapped lips."

"You're welcome," said Amber.

When we all walked out to the parking lot, the probation officer followed. The American flag was flapping noisily next to the Perkins sign; the air was picking up wind and snow. The probation officer walked to his car and got in but did not start it. Amber's face was completely lit up. I saw that she was fantastically in love with him. She was not concentrating on any of us, and something about this provoked Sarah.

"Well," she said, studying Amber with an artificial smile.

"Yes, well," said Amber.

"All right then," said Letitia.

"Can I give you some advice, Amber?" Sarah asked, standing there, as Letitia clutched Amber even tighter. Letitia was ecstatic to have a white birth mother in tow, one with a little white bun in the oven, and did not want a rival agency to get ahold of her. Or so Sarah would say later. The windbreakered parole officer gave a wave and drove off.

"What?" Amber said to Sarah, but to me she smiled and said, "He was definitely following me."

"When I was your age, I had some rebellious ideas," Sarah continued her unsolicited advice to Amber. "I got in trouble now and again, here and there, but I realized it was because I was doing things I wasn't any good at. Look at this." She tapped Amber's electronic bracelet with a gloved index finger. "You're eighteen. Don't sell drugs. You're no good at it. Do something you're good at."

Sarah meant this tough-love speech compassionately, I could see, but Amber's face flushed with insult, then hardened. "That's what I'm trying to do," she said indignantly, and tore herself from Letitia's grip, walked over to what was apparently Letitia's car, and got in on the passenger's side.

Baby, it's scold outside, Murph would have said if she were there.

"We'll talk later," Letitia called to Sarah, waving good-bye and hurrying off to Amber. Perkins's flag was whipping loudly in the snowy wind.

"Well," said Sarah as we both got into her car. "That was, for all intents and purposes, a complete disaster."

She started up the engine. "You know?" she continued. "I always do the wrong thing. I do the wrong thing so much that the times I actually do the right thing stand out so brightly in my memory that I forget I always do the wrong thing."

We rode home mostly in silence, Sarah offering me gum, then cough drops, both of which I took, thanking her. When I glanced over at her, driving without her sunglasses, her scarf wrapped now around her head like a babushka, she seemed watery, far away, lost in thought, and I wondered how a nice, attractive girl—for I'd thought I had glimpsed on the way up the girl I imagined she once was, her face still and thoughtful, her hair in the sun ablaze with light—how a girl like that became a lonely woman with a yarny shmatte on her head, became this, whatever it was. After a childhood of hungering to be an adult, my hunger had passed. Unexpected fates had begun to catch my notice. These middle-aged women seemed very tired to me, as if hope had been wrung out of them and replaced with a deathly, walking sort of sleep.

Sarah's cell phone played the beginning to "Eine kleine Nacht-musik," its vigorous twang not unlike a harpsichord at all, and so not completely offensive to the spirit of Mozart, who perhaps did not, like so many of his colleagues, have to roll about as much in his grave since the advent of electronic things.

Sarah pulled the phone from her bag and slowed the car slightly while she did. "Excuse me," she said to me. "Yeah?" she said into the phone. All this despite the bumper sticker on her car that read PERHAPS YOU WOULD DRIVE BETTER WITH THAT

CELL PHONE SHOVED UP YOUR ASS. She also had one that said, IF GOD SPEAKS THROUGH BURNING BUSHES, LET'S BURN BUSH AND LISTEN TO WHAT GOD SAYS. It was interesting to me that such a woman, one with such rhetorical violence adhered to her car, had gotten past the adoption agency's screening processes, whatever they were. She also had a third bumper sticker that said BORN FINE THE FIRST TIME—though cell phones and Christianity were going to be the very things to bring her a child. Her fourth was no more promising: BEHIND EVERY SUCCESS-FUL WOMAN IS HERSELF.

I don't know why I could hear so clearly—perhaps Sarah was a little deaf and had the volume on everything turned up high.

"Sarah, hi, it's Letitia," I heard.

"Hi, Letitia." I believed I wasn't supposed to listen, so I looked out the window at the bleak snowy landscape; the sun was low and feeble, dissolving whitely like a lemon drop. Each town we passed through had a Dairy Queen, with customers lined up, even in winter. When I looked back at Sarah I saw her powdered, thinning skin like a crepe, with the same light freckles as a crepe, her gnarly-knuckled hand, arthritic from chopping herbs, going through her spiky russet hair, knocking back her scarf. How did her stand-up hair defy not just gravity but even the additional weight of a scarf? Why did my own hair always lie flat, defeated by atmospheric physics of all sorts, unimproved even by the most widely advertised of sticky gels? Education had not entirely elevated my concerns in life. It had probably not even assisted my analyses of these concerns, though that was the most I could hope for. I was too fresh from childhood. Subconsciously, my deepest brain still a cupboard of fairy tales, I suppose I believed that if a pretty woman was no longer pretty she had done something bad to deserve it. I had a young girl's belief that this kind of negative aging would never come to me. Death would come to me— I knew this from reading British poetry. But the drying, hunch-ing, blanching, hobbling, fading, fattening, thinning, slowing? I would just not let that happen to *moi*.

Sarah switched ears, making it harder for me to hear, but then switched back and slowed to let a convoy of trucks pass. I could hear Letitia. "If this doesn't work out with Amber, there are babies on the international market. We've had a lot of luck with South America. Paraguay has opened up again, and other countries, too. And they're not all brown there, either. There's been a lot of German influence, and some of these kids are beautiful, very blond, or blue-eyed, or both."

"Well, thanks for the info," said Sarah brusquely. "Get back to me on Amber." Letitia then said something I couldn't make out, and Sarah said quickly, "Gotta run—there's an ice patch ahead," and snapped the phone shut.

"The babies of Nazis," Sarah said, shaking her head. "They're hawking Nazi babies. Racially superior. Unbelievable." She raked her fingers yet again through the bright desert grass of her hair. I didn't ask her how a tiny baby could be a Nazi. What did I know? Maybe it could. "Blue eyes!" she cried. "The human race has really come a long way!" She shook her head again, this time with a horsey, nasal exhalation of disgust. "I knew someone in cooking school who was a blue-eyed Jew. He said his sperm was in great demand at the local sperm bank and he was making a lot of spare cash. He was at first a funny story and then a kind of expression we all used: 'Gettin' over like a blue-eyed Jew in a sperm bank.'"

"Yeah," I said dopily.

"You may be too young to know this yet, but eventually you will look around and notice: *Nazis always have the last laugh.*"

Then we were wordless through the towns of Terre Noire and Fond du Marais, places named both whimsically and fearfully by French fur traders, before the subsequent flattened pronunciations by Scandinavian farmers made the names even more absurd: "Turn Ore" and "Fondue Morass." "You'll find I say about eighty-nine percent of what's on my mind," Sarah said. "For the other eleven percent? I use a sauna." She put a CD in the car player. "Bach's first French suite. Do you know it?"

After some clicking and static, it began, stately and sad. "I think so," I said, not sure at all. My friends had already begun to lie, to bluff a sophistication they felt that at the end of the ten-second bluff they would authentically possess. But I was not only less inclined this way but less skilled. "Maybe not, though," I added. Then, "Wait, it's ringing a bell."

"Oh, it's the most beautiful thing," she said. "Especially with this pianist." It was someone humming along with the light dirge of the Bach. Later I would own every loopy Glenn Gould recording available, but there in the car with Sarah was the first time I'd ever heard him play. The piece was like an elegant interrogation made of tangled yarn, a query from a well-dressed man in a casket, not yet dead. It proceeded slowly, like a careful equation, and then not: if $x = y$, if major $=$ minor, if death equals part of life and life part of death, then what is the sum of the infinite notes of this one phrase? It asked, answered, reasked, its moody asking a refinement of reluctance or dislike. I had never heard a melody quite like it.

"You live near the stadium, right?" asked Sarah. We were already back in Troy. She swung the car down Campus Avenue toward the tiny street, Brickhurst, where I lived. The neighborhoods near the university were already mostly empty for the Christmas holidays, but in houses that were not student housing, frequently there were lights strung along the soffits and the brightened gutters seemed to shout cheerily, "WE are here! WE ARE HERE!"

"I'm at 201 Brickhurst," I said.

"Brickhurst?" I suspected she was one of these out-of-staters who'd moved here a while back but had only a pieced-together knowledge of the town, a mind map assembled on a strictly need-to-know basis. But she was there in less than a minute.

She put the car in park. She patted me on the shoulder, then let her hand run down my coat sleeve. "Thanks," she said. "Phone me when you get back into town after Christmas." Her face looked fantastically sad.

"OK," I said, not knowing what else to say. "Sounds good." It was the midwestern girl's reply to everything.

II

Christmas morning I slept in late. So did my younger brother, who had picked me up at the Dellacrosse bus station the night before, driving my father's truck, the one with EAT POTATOES AND LOVE LONGER emblazoned on the back. He'd stood waiting in the parking lot for me to get off the bus, sporting his cheap brown parka and no hat, seeming glad to see me, as if he had something to share, though I didn't really expect anything: my brother rarely shared. He helped with my suitcase and with my electric bass (which I'd brought with me), sticking both in the back of the truck, and he refrained from his usual remark about only boys playing bass. The electric guitar had been invented fifty miles from here! I was always ready to counter, to no particular person at all, as Robert himself was as steeped in the local myths about Les Paul as I was. I also had an acoustic upright bass at home in my bedroom, with a satchel full of bows attached to its belly. It looked like a fat abandoned archer in the corner, a quiver full of arrows gathering dust. "Ole Bob," Robert called it, lumping it in with him and my dad. "At least you're not lugging Ole Bob."

Robert, it had often seemed to me, failed to apply himself—musically or academically. Perhaps having an older sister had stymied him a little. He knew I was quietly nuts about my guitar. The Jewish part of us both sort of understood that to worship God was to siphon off the worship of doodads—and we loved doodads (my instruments were insured up the wazoo)—but it didn't always work that way: sometimes God adhered to something material and physical and earthly, and then all was a little misty for the holder and beholder of the doodad. But my brother was nice to me about it all; in fact, when I thought back to our many years together, he was, essentially, always nice to me, though he did gun the engine a little wildly as we pulled out of the parking lot. To his friends he was known as Gunny, a name my parents hated.

On the ride back to the house he told me how he was doing, though I had to ask two times. Sometimes a stammer came over him, which made him hesitant to speak at all—I'm sure he felt that the slightly choked and garbled voice did not accurately reflect his mind, though who knows, maybe it did. Sometimes you could see him trying to pick up speed when he spoke, velocity smoothing things over and getting him to the end sooner. Gunny, indeed.

On the bus I'd eaten nothing but some supermarket sushi, half a plastic tray of which was still in my purse, and hunger made me a more eager listener. Every word seemed a morsel. He was in his last year in high school and hated it. He had gotten four Fs and a D this past semester. His face showed no dismay in the relating of this. Apparently my father, not always one for helpfully stern parenting, had stared at the report card and said, "Well, Robert, what can I say. Four Fs and a D: it looks like you're spending too much time on one course!" My brother chuckled drily, telling the story. Then we both fell silent, driving slowly toward home, the dark trees going by us with their branches set in the soft mush of the night sky like wrens' feet or a spiky brooch in a cotton-bedded box. We passed the First Methodist Church and its spotlit plywood crèche, where the expressions of the dozing sheep were the least imbecilic in the scene. A sign out front advertised the title of the Christmas sermon: LOVE YOUR ENEMIES; YOU MADE THEM. We passed the Vanmares' old farmhouse, where they had decorated the front yard again in a completely random holiday fashion: silhouettes of penguins, palm trees, geese, and candy canes all lit up as if they were long-lost friends at a gathering. Still, I was not immune to other people's responses to Christmas, their whatnot compositions, whether it was art or just exuberance. Whimsy and fuss could still rivet me.

I got out my sushi and began to snack. "Want some?" I asked Robert.

"No way," he said.

We passed the Drift Inn, which had lost its *D* and become the Rift Inn. The parking lot at Buck Rub Bowling was jammed for some knockerheimer tournament. We drove right down the main street of Dellacrosse, which was lined with single-story storefronts and diagonal parking out front. Squeezed in side by side were Larry's Resale Shop, Terry's Taxidermy (formerly Dick's Deergutting), and Walt's Worms, all of which we sailed right past. Chewing, I concentrated my stare, as if I were in fact the stranger I felt myself to be, studying the metal rickrack of the bridge across Wahapa Creek. We passed the road to the township dump and at the turnoff the dump-tender's cabin, which the tender had outfitted proudly and spectacularly with items gleaned from the dump itself. A large glittery reindeer with broken-off antlers sat atop his roof.

Putting away my sushi, I said, "If you eat a bear's liver, will you die?"

Robert laughed. "I have no idea." Then he added, "I do know that if you're a squirrel you should stay away from hot electrical boxes or you will get so electrocuted that your teeth will fuse together." And he pointed this gruesome thing out to me, on the power line that edged our road, close to our own gravel driveway.

"How's Mom?" I asked before we entered the house. The truck lights in the driveway would have already signaled our arrival.

"Mom's a little emo. In other words, just the same," he said, grabbing my bag and bass again for me the way the college boys rarely did. My parents had raised a nice farm boy, though I wondered if they knew this. It had not been their conscious, active intent. I went to follow him, but he signaled that I should walk ahead. I climbed the porch stairs and rapped on the aluminum storm door, then opened it and shouted hello. My mother was never one for Christmas Eve, and so coming home for the holidays I was often greeted like a neighbor stopping by on Sunday after church, a neighbor she saw all the time but did not want to be unkind to.

"Oh," she said. "Hi there." This year there was the smell of baking ginger in the air. The house struck me once more with its warm neglect and elegant poverty—the Hitchcock chairs that were beat up, uncared for, never treated as special antiques but as serviceable items that had to earn their existence on this planet the hard way: at our house, a kind of hard-knocks house for furniture.

My mother had sprung for eggnog, and a little brandy, and although my father had already gone to bed she and Robert and I sat up for twenty minutes or so, with a coffee log burning low in the fireplace and a plate of gingersnaps on the mantel before we were all too tired to pretend. The coffee log was a favorite of my mother's, though to me it smelled less like coffee and more like a burning shoe. "I'd light the menorah," said my mother, "but remember what happened last year with the curtains catching on fire." The curtains had gone up in a blaze and we had thrown a punch bowl of eggnog on them to douse the flames, and the eggnog had sizzled and cooked into the fabric until the whole house smelled like a diner omelet.

"That's OK," I said. "I'll light the menorah tomorrow for you." Though I would forget to do it. Every year it was my job to clean it, scrape off the previous year's wax with pins and a fork, so perhaps my forgetting was convenient.

"Thanks, honey," said my mom, who never called me "honey." Almost never. The television was on, murmuring low and flashing its colors. My mother flicked it off with annoyance. "A grinch who stole Christmas?" she said. "With all that's going on in the world we should have to deal with *that*?"

In the morning my brother and I came downstairs within ten minutes of each other. The Christmas tree this year—or Hanukkah hemlock, as my mother still called it—was a pre-lit affair ordered online. The McLellans' Christmas tree farm had recently gone out of business and my parents had resorted to an environmentally sound plastic pine from Hammacher Schlemmer. Ornaments like blue fish and beribboned, clove-studded oranges were clustered in the middle. Old dangly earrings that had lost their mates were hung on the more delicate branches. My mother had placed at the top a large tinselly Star of David, angled rakishly, like a geometry problem. Possibly, in late-morning light, this was just how all irony presented itself.

My parents were at the kitchen table eating cold cereal but offering to make us latkes with applesauce or regular pancakes or both, both being a holiday tradition. "I chopped the potatoes and onions up yesterday," said my mom. Soon, I knew, she would get a skillet of oil going, or fire up the stove griddle, and the house would fill with slick oniony air, like the greasy spoon on Main Street, permeating our clothes and hair.

"Thanks, maybe later?" I said with the question mark our generation believed meant politeness but which baffled our parents. Outside the morning was bright. I liked the holy, rejoicing look of it: the many gray Christmases of my childhood had depressed me. And apparently not just me: one year the holiday card my mother sent out was an October photo of my brother and me, with a caption that read *The children. In some dead leaves.*

The light covering of snow on the fields out back and in the yard between the barn and the house was already melting in the morning sun. Ochre grass was poking through in patches. Beyond, the incline part of the acreage—which my father had sold off last year "for a pretty penny, or, maybe not pretty exactly, but a penny with a great personality"—had been resold by the Amish to others and was already being developed into something called Highland Estates. The weather was so warm that construction had continued into December. There were two yellow backhoes jutting into the sky. The houses were going to be huge, my mother said, with treeless lots and phony gazebos and turrets and patios to look back at us in mutual rebuke.

"They don't like trees because squirrels climb up them and get in their attic and chew on the exercise equipment no longer in use. Now, without trees? The squirrels'll head elsewhere and the attic will fill up with moths and moles." It made one secretly grateful for the Amish, who did not do this, but unfairly annoyed with them when they sold to people who did. Still, mostly the Amish were buying up farms as is, and holding services in their parlors, though it was bitterly said in Dellacrosse that their wagons and trotting horses chipped and dinged the roads, and that their houses were declared churches in order to stay off the tax rolls and that they bred like rabbits and dressed like bats.

"Watching the snow melt?" I asked my brother.

"Yeah, I mean, what the hell kind of weather is this?" asked Robert, continuing to look outside at the sky. Clouds were starting to balloon there, as if a party were getting ready to begin.

"Your language," said my mother.

"My language is English," said my brother.

"It's beginning to look nothing like Christmas," I sang. "Everywhere I go."

"Nice voice," said my brother, sounding sincere, which surprised me. But then he added, under his breath, "Blah, blah, fuckin' blah."

"Conversation inside needs brightening," I tried singing again, "because the climate change is frightening!"

"Global warming," said my father. "They've found prickly pear cactus as far north as the Hottomowac River. And even the Costco has taken to putting fake spray frost on their windows this year."

I tightened my bathrobe. It was nice to have my father here. Often during past holidays he had been too busy supplying the high-end restaurants in Chicago with their gourmet vegetables— not just cold-storage potatoes but little purple eggplants and shallots; supplying them over the holidays meant driving the truck all the way to Illinois in the snow, and he could never make it back in time for dinner. The local farming, like art, had always catered to the rich in one way or another. The dairy farm down the road, I knew, kept the county's doctors and lawyers and ministers as private customers, selling them their best premium butter. The rest of the butter—known as Dellacrosse grease—went wherever. And the local cheesemakers were in some strange condition of reversal. One of the old cheese factories had gone under and become a school. And one of the old schools had become a cheese factory. But an *artisan* cheese factory, done with syringes of mites and vegetarian rennet. This was the kind of cheese factory that had the best chance of making it—food for yuppies— like my father's dainty potatoes, arranged by hue in purple net bags. These cheesemakers gave their cheeses eccentric names like Unplugged and Washed Midget: wacked food for wacked people, my brother said disdainfully. The producers of conventional cheese were busy with the governor trying to find niche marketing in Japan.

In the morning sunshine my parents looked cleansed of their reinforcing farm dirt. They looked translucent and a little frailer than they had even in the fall, when the black potato muck beneath their nails and the mud on their shoes and clothing seemed to anchor them to the earth. Now they could—and might—ascend in a shaft of light, for all I knew. I scarcely recognized them, as if they were only slightly animate in their holographic shimmer. In the past their soil had warmed and defined them. Now they were like figurines made not even of glass but of translucent sugar. I felt hearty and fleshy and bloody by comparison, feeling the thick heated meat of myself even in my bathrobe. We were all in our bathrobes, which struck me as funny. Probably we would all get dressed before opening presents, bowls of Fiddle Faddle on the coffee table. The presents I was giving this year were merely three-by-five cards with drawings of the items I had intended to give but had had no time to get and so would get later. This was something of a traditional joke. This year I had drawn them all pictures of sports cars, a cruel spin on the tradition, since it meant I had given it very little thought and was probably getting them nothing. I even ran out of three-by-five cards and for my brother's used a four-by-six, with a larger drawing of a larger car—and so a larger jokey lie. Arguably, it was better than that unfortunate year when I was twelve and too old for such a thing but had nonetheless wrapped a candy box jammed full of puppy poop from our dog, Blot, and given it to Robert, with a little tag that said *MMMMMM . . . good. Merry Christmas from Blot.* "Look what the dog-do did," I said at the time, studying his reaction. Which remained one of quiet perplexity.

My mother was now smoking. "Should I make breakfast?" she asked again. My father, who'd been too tired to talk last night, said, "Yeah! Make breakfast! Robert and I want to sit Tassie down and make her tell us about college."

"Yeah, right," said Robert. He padded out of the kitchen. "I'm taking a shower," he called back, claiming our one bathroom.

"Sooo . . ." My dad smiled at me. "How's college?"

"Oh, OK," I said inarticulately, but I figured all my dad really needed to hear was positive things in a tempered tone he could trust. My mother was heating up oil and had taken the cold bowl of latke mixture out and peeled the Saran Wrap off the top. I started to help her, molding handfuls into plump mounds, the oil and egg white slimy in my hands.

"Any boyfriends?" My father's eyebrows went up and down, dismissively, mockingly, letting me know I need not answer. My mother gave him a look anyway. "Bo." She said his name like that to warn him of trespass. She claimed to call him Robert in private, never liking his family nickname but needing within the house to distinquish between Robert junior and senior.

I liked my dad. Nothing he did ever bothered me, not even his recent drinking, which didn't usually begin until late afternoon anyway. Still, my unblaming affection had not kept me from feeling the occasional shame of him. "Your father's a farmer? What does he farm?" acquaintances back in Troy would sometimes ask. In Dellacrosse he was barely considered a farmer at all. "Nothing," I would sometimes reply. "He farms nothing. Dadaist agriculture."

"Oh, I get it," an East Coast boy with a glass boot of beer might say, or a girl with narrow dark-framed glasses like the Nana Mouskouri of my mother's old LPs.

I'm not sure where this small, slightly thrashing, not quite deforming shame had come from. Somehow I had learned it, perhaps even at Dellacrosse Central, where having a father-farmer should have been no shame at all, and wasn't, despite my father's miniature operation. People knew his produce was coveted. And among the kids the more obscene jokes were saved for the ginseng farmers. But I remember once in seventh grade, our homeroom teacher had gone around the class and asked us what our fathers did. When she got to Eileen Reilly, Eileen turned red and said, "I would rather not say." This astounded me, for her father was a handsome, charming salesman at Home Savings Shoes on

Main Street—Stan the Shoe Man, my mother affectionately called him. But his daughter had absorbed some disappointment—his, or her mother's—and did not want to speak of how he earned his living.

Perhaps that was the moment I learned this as a source of personal shame, or observed the possibility of it.

"So your classes then," said my father. "Sit down on this lovely Christmas morning and tell your old dad about the ones you took and the ones you're going to take when you go back. How did that philosophy class go?"

"Did you know that Alexander the Great left all his money to Aristotle?" I asked brightly.

"That's how he got his name," said my father. "Aristotle gave it to him! Before that he was just Alexander the Fine."

"Bo! Sheesh." My mother shook her head.

A sizzling sound came from the griddle, where she was pouring oil. We had an old-style stove, with the griddle built in. You had to clean it with rags and paper towels, or pry it out with a barbecue fork and go at it with steel wool and water. The hot latke mix steaming into the air now smelled good to me and helped cover up the kitchen's perennially faint reek of mice. My mother was stirring regular pancake batter as well.

"It's OK to sit while you help," said my mother to me, "but remember these latkes aren't hamburgers. Don't cup them into thick shapes."

I ignored her and continued with my fat latkes and my dad.

"Next term?" he asked.

"I've registered for another literature survey—Brit Lit from 1830 to 1930—Intro to Sufism, Intro to Wine Tasting, a music appreciation course titled Soundtracks to War Movies, and a geology course called Dating Rocks." The Sufism did not throw him.

"Dating rocks?"

"I need to learn!" I said, laughing.

"Don't let them kiss you," he said, not smiling. The random assortment of my courses lacked the sound of serious direction. I'd left out my PE requirement, which I was filling with a double-listed humanities and Pilates course called The Perverse Body/ The Neutral Pelvis. I didn't want to provoke him.

Still, I murmured, as if in self-pity, "They don't kiss. That's why they're called rocks."

"Wine tasting?" He raised his eyebrows. It had the sound of a father not getting his money's worth.

"I need a gut course, to make the others go better," I said. "I didn't really have one this past semester, and things were too intense."

"But aren't you underage?"

"Technically, I guess. But it's for a course, so I guess they let you."

"Will you make dean's list again?" asked my mother.

"Possibly," I said.

"Well, you have to be careful which dean," said my father. "You don't want to get on the wrong list!"

"Besides, I'm going to be working next semester."

"You got a job?"

"You got a job?"

"Is there an echo in here?" I said.

"Well, tell us," said my mother. "Don't just sass us to death."

"It hasn't really begun. It's a babysitting job. But there isn't a baby yet."

"Oh, yes, one of those," said my father, amused.

"What do you mean, no baby yet?" asked my mother, who looked puzzled. My father was grinning ear to ear, as if to say, *Now here's a how-de-do.*

"There *will* be one. Or should be. In January," I explained.

"The mother's pregnant?"

"Well, the birth mother is pregnant, and the woman I'm working for is going to adopt the kid."

There was silence all around, even from my dad, as if this were a situation to be considered for all its various and deep sadnesses.

"It's a good thing," I added. "This girl—she could never be a good mother. And the lady who's hiring me? She's kind of neat. She's nice and pretty and she owns a fancy restaurant in town."

"That's why she needs you," said my mother, concerned. "She's too busy for a child."

I was about to try to defend Sarah when my father asked with unfeigned interest, "What restaurant?"

"Le Petit Moulin," I said.

My mother turned and made a knowing face. "A *fineschmecker* running a place for other *fineschmeckers*."

My father smiled broadly. "Oh, I remember her. Very nice woman." My mother turned her back to us, flipping the flapjacks and throwing the latkes into hot oil, refusing to let go of her skepticism regarding the whole matter. My father continued. "She would come and check out those potatoes as if they were diamonds. But she would sometimes take the ones with a bit of rot in them anyway, knowing that once the rot part was cut out the rest of the potato would be sweeter than most. Smart lady."

"Why can't she have her own children?" asked my mother, continuing in her doubt.

"Mom, I don't know. I can't ask. I hardly know her."

"What about her husband?"

"What *about* her husband?"

"Who is he?"

It was a little surprising even to me that I knew so little about him. "I think he's probably a professor of some sort, but I'm not sure."

"Hmph," said my mother. "Academics." Now she was muttering. "They all shoot from the hip. And the hip is always in the chair."

"What did you say?" asked my father.

"Nothing," said my mother. "Keeping a safe distance never keeps one from having an opinion, is all. Having no dog in the race doesn't keep people from having extremely large cats." Then she added, "Pull your seat up to the table. The food is ready."

My father had more of a sense of humor than my mother. "Just because I'm hard of hearing," he said to her now, smiling, "doesn't mean you're not mumbling!" Yet it was his sense of adventure she had had to sign on for long ago, good-naturedly, and in reluctant love, and he had taken her on something of a journey, out here to the country, to this farm. But she had been game. At least at first.

"Oh, well, someday maybe *I'll* open a restaurant," she said now, sighing brightly, which seemed about as happy as she got—a sigh with some light in it. She then added a remark that typified the sort that filled me with loathing for her. "You know, with the new year approaching, I've come to realize I've done nothing these past decades but devote my energies to the interests of others. So, soon? I'm going to start focusing on myself."

"Well, before you get started, darling," said my father, "could you please pass the syrup?"

Once when I was a kid my father planted ten acres of corn and rye and then midsummer plowed just the rye, making a graphic ribbon effect through the rolling fields. "This would be best seen by air," said my dad. The whole reason he had become a farmer is that he thought it would be fun. And so he hired a guy from Minneapolis to take an aerial photo of it, and we stuck it up on the fridge with little spud magnets. It looked beautiful—the gold of the mown rye striping the green corn and both undulating through like a performing pair of lovebird dolphins. This, I pretended, was a picture of my parents' marriage. My mother had thought she was marrying a college president's son but got a hobby farmer instead, yet she'd followed him. She stayed with him wherever the hell it was they were going. She was like a stick-

leback fish caught inland as the glacier retreated and the rivers—
the only access to the sea—disappeared. She would have to make
do, in this landlocked lake of love. I knew, as she had mentioned
it, that she'd thought there'd be money—he'd grown up in a
house with columns—but she hadn't realized there was none: the
house was owned by the college. Even when she and my father
came to Dellacrosse and bought our old brick house, with its
falling-apart shed and barn but its flowerbeds gorgeous with pan-
sies and impatiens, she didn't understand that those particular
flowers were annuals, and so she waited for them to return the
next year, feeling dashed and betrayed when they didn't. Another
mirage! But eventually she learned to plant her own. And for a
while she was a pro. Until she got too tired. That was when she
installed mirrors in the flowerbeds, slowly learning the art of
mirage herself.

After our late breakfast the winds picked up, and soon there was a
thunderstorm, the sky yellowish and the clouds filled with the
crunch and rip of lightning. The leafless trees looked frail and
surprised. The sudden downpour eliminated practically all the
snow on the ground, and because the drainage on the county
roads was so poor, they filled like canals with water, just sitting
there glistening, ready to turn to ice when the temperature
dipped later in the afternoon. Which it did.

Our actual Christmas ceremonies for the day, outside of breakfast, had been so painfully casual—no hamentashen, no pfeffer-
nüsse, no kringle from Racine—that I wondered why we had
bothered. Perhaps my mother, the keeper of ritual, had lost interest in this ostensibly Christian custom now that we had grown,
and my father didn't really know how to take over. Where was
the turkey, its yankable heart in a baggie jammed up its butt?
On the other hand, my mother had given me a carefully wrapped

present of a pearl necklace and watched, teary-eyed, as I opened it. "Every woman should have a pearl necklace," she said. "When I was your age I got one." From my father, I knew. And now, with no man in my life, even though I was only twenty, she would be the one to bestow this artifact of womanhood, this rite of passage, this gyno-noose, upon me. That I might in fact never have an occasion to wear such a thing or that I might look like the worst sort of Republican doing so probably never occurred to her. I think she saw it as a kind of ticket off the farm and out into the world, wherever *that* was.

"Thanks, Mom," I said, and kissed her cheek, which was simultaneously powdery and damp. I thrust the velveteen box of pearls high, as if making a toast. "Here's to Jesus," I said.

My mom looked at me from a great and concerned distance. Their present to Robert was a handheld instant star and constellation identifier.

Another flurry of thunderclouds passed by overhead and hail came pounding down on our roof, and down the chimney, crackling in the fireplace as if to mock the sound of fire and then bouncing out from the hearth onto the wood floor. It was as if I had unstrung my mother's pearls and just flung them around.

Afterward we sat around and watched TV. Only once do I remember our going to church on Christmas—the Norwegian Lutheran church in town. My father had cast his WASP eye around at the stained-glass windows and their bright, jellied scenes and designs, and then murmured, perhaps recalling his churchier past or struggling against some ancestral Puritan pride, "I think that's an original Koshkonong window. Or, wait a minute, let me see, maybe it's not—" and my mother had whispered in a fond hiss, "Let's face it, Bo: You know nothing about the goyim."

"There's lots of strange weather all around the country," my dad said now, sitting down to join us.

"What do you mean?" I asked, a little frightened. Like a child, I still trusted him to know all.

"Well, there are a lot of storms in odd places and high winds"—he slowed down to subdue his own dark report—"and eerie calms . . ."

"Eerie calms?" I asked.

"There's a pregnant pause outside Kenosha that's scaring the pants off 'em."

"Dad!" And I laughed, to please him.

At four o'clock, with the sun just about set, my brother and I went outside for a walk, and we slid around with our shoes on the new ice. It had been sunny enough before noon so that my mother had put laundry out, and now in the light wind it billowed from her clotheslines, snapping the ice from its threads like the sails of an arctic whale ship. How many Christmases had we ever been out without boots? Not many.

"How are Mom and Dad *doing*?" I asked my brother.

"Oh, OK, I guess," Robert said. "They still go at each other tooth and nail, but I've learned not to pay too much attention. It's really all nothing. And better than when they turn their attention to me. Yikes!"

"They after you about school?"

"Oh, yeah." He skittered a stone across the ice with his shoe. "I screwed up a question on a test and got sent to the principal's."

"What do you mean?"

"I said Gandhi was a deer."

"A deer?"

"I got Gandhi mixed up with Bambi."

"What?" He was bright, so he came to things quickly without patience. He tended to blurt. If he hit a blank spot he just said something fast. And it was sometimes absurd. He had once said *asteroids* instead of *hemorrhoids,* which made me bury my face in my arms.

"I don't know—words remind me of other words. Like the word *hostage* makes me think of *sausage*. I don't know why. I just hate all that shit, I'm telling you. But don't worry, I'm not going to go postal or anything." We were scooting along inefficiently, hardly lifting our feet so as not to slip. "My grades aren't good enough, and college applications have to be in first of the month. I may just join the military."

"Why?" Alarm struck a note in my throat.

"It's peacetime. I'm not going to get killed or nothing—"

"Anything."

"Anything. Two years and the government'll pay for some of college, and Mom and Dad'll be off my back."

"The government will only pay for some of it?"

"Well, apparently there are different packages, depending on how long you sign up for. A recruiter came to our high school."

"A recruiter came to your high school? Is that legal?"

Robert snorted. "It is at Dellacrosse Central."

"Sheesh," I said.

"Yeah, when I bring the whole thing up Mom gets upset. She's threatening to phone the recruiter at his house in Beaver Dam and give him a piece of her mind."

"It's amazing she has a piece left. But it's true—I believe she does."

"What does she want me to do? Go to DDD?"

"I hope not."

The Dellacrosse Diesel Driving School was the hellish Plan B—Plan D, it was jokingly referred to—for all the kids who'd bombed out in their courses. "I've been taking yoga for PE credit," he said.

"Really?" Things changed so fast, it whipped your head around. Yoga had entered the corridors of Dellacrosse Central High, but so had the army recruiters.

"Yeah. Deep breathing: a triumph of me over me."

"Oh-ho. You have your own personal and hygienic mat?"

"I do."

Here he looked up at me with great earnestness, his eyes asking me to hear him in the deepest way I knew how. "And I sit there in the dark gym," he said, "and just think. Signing up for the army seems the only thing. It's either that or diesel driving school."

"But it's not really peacetime. There's Afghanistan," I said. These faraway countries that had intruded on our consciousness seemed odd to me. It seemed one thing sixty years ago to go over and fight for France, a country we had heard of, but what did it mean now to fight in or at—there was no preposition . . . for?— a place like Afghanistan? To their credit, students in Troy were eager to find out, and the Intro to Islam course had filled up for spring semester, which was why I was stuck with the more narrow, and reputedly fluffier, Intro to Sufism. We would read Rumi and Doris Lessing.

"Afghanistan's over."

"It is?" I'd been studying for finals.

"I dunno." He skittered a stone again. "Yeah, I think so."

"What happened? Did we win?"

"I dunno." He laughed. "I guess so."

"Yeah, well, soldiers without a war get bored and sometimes they get stationed in hot, edgy places and start to want one. They don't know why they're there otherwise. And if one doesn't come they just start shooting the sky and then each other."

"How do you know so much?"

"Movies."

"Ha!" Then he added solemnly, too solemnly, "If I don't come back, you know, alive, don't let them bury me in some big-ass coffin. I don't want to take up space."

"Well," I said, "I guess that's why you're taking yoga: so we'll be able to squeeze you into a pretzel box! We'll all declare, 'Oh, he would have wanted it this way!' "

"Thanks." He smiled.

"I'm not sure I like the idea of *enduring* freedom."

"How about letting freedom ring?"

"Even that. Shouldn't freedom just be free? Why do you have to let it do anything? That suggests it's kind of locked up and then being sprung on people."

"You like college, don't you?"

Aloft in the trees, the squirrel nests, hidden all summer, sat exposed like tumors—composed of the flesh of the trees but still jealous and other. "Quasi sort of. Did you do any hunting this year?" He had never been an enthusiastic hunter. How would he manage in the military?

"Nah."

"No animal population control?" The ostensible reason for hunting always made me snort.

"No, actually this year I've been part of a program that does deer-condom distribution."

"Excellent!" I was working on a laugh that was more than my usual pleased grunt, but all I had right now was a kind of blast that culminated in a bleat.

We continued walking on the edge of the icy road, past a stand of birches that in the distance looked like my mother's cigarettes stubbed out in the dirt, barely smoked. My brother's boy's life seemed lonely and hard to me. He still had one snaggletooth that poked out of his smile. This was because there had been only enough orthodontia money for one of us, so it went to the daughter, whose looks would matter (wasted on me! a smileless girl I felt sure no man would ever desire—not deeply). I got the braces. He got the chores. The expectations that he help my dad around the farm were so much greater than any that had been laid upon me, and so I could see his life was a little harder than mine, though he was a good-looking boy, bright in a general way, and with many friends. As a young kid his plans were entrepreneurial. Once, years ago, he'd drawn up a design for a hotel chain, and believing his greatest competitor would be the Holiday Inn, he decided to name it in an opposing, competitive spirit: Normal Night Out. The Normal Night Out Hotel.

He had, however, the same loneliness in him that I did, though he had always been my mother's favorite. Where had that gotten him? My mother's love was useless.

We pushed past the gate at the far end of our property and walked down one of the old half-frozen cow paths terraced slightly with old roots and stones to form steps. A small fly buzzed past my ear, then vanished. I had never seen a fly before at Christmas, and I swatted at it, feeling, as we had been taught to feel in Art 102, the surrealism of two familiar things placed unexpectedly side by side. That would be the future.

We hiked down past the copse of sycamore and oak (as children, animating some dormant urban fear, we had witlessly shrieked, "The copse! The copse!" and raced through the underbrush, thrilled by our own concocted, dreadless terror). Now Robert and I weaved among the piss elms toward the old fish hatchery, which in winters of the past we would have skated on; it was a former nineteenth-century mill pond that had long ago lost its falls, though the old paddle wheel still leaned against a tree, coated with squirrel shucks. Sometimes we'd tobogganed down the snowy trail all the way to the hatchery, where now there was no snow at all, just the matted hard grass and dirt and the dried, icing stalks of angelica and milkweed and bee balm. My brother liked to fish at the hatchery sometimes, even in winter, sometimes even in the stream, even if the fish were really now just trash fish, and even though it was stupid to ice fish in a stream. But summers down this path I had always liked, and when the gnats weren't bad I had sometimes accompanied him, sat in the waist-high widgeon grass beside him, the place pink with coneflowers, telling him the plot of, say, a Sam Peckinpah movie I'd never seen but had read about once in a syndicated article in the *Dellacrosse Sunday Star.* Crickets the size of your thumb would sing their sweet monotony from the brush. Sometimes there was a butterfly so perfect and beautiful, it was like a party barrette you wanted to clip in your hair. Above and around us green leaves would flash wet with sunsetting light. In this verdant cove I recounted the entire plot of *Straw Dogs*.

But bugs were the thing that drove us back. *Flies as big as raping ducks!* we used to say. Mosquitoes with tiger-striped bodies and the feathery beards of an iris, their wings and legs the dun wisps of an unbarbered boy, their spindly legs the tendrils of an orchid, the blades of a gnome's sleigh. Their awfulness and flight obsessed me, concentrated my revulsion: suspended like mobiles, or diving like jets, they were sinisterly contrapted; they craved color; they were caught in the saddest animal script there was. Once I whacked Robert's back, seeing a giant one there, and killed five, all bloody beneath his shirt.

Now we stood at the cold stream's edge, tossing a stone in and listening for its *plonk* and plummet. I wanted to say, "Remember the time . . ." But too often when we compared stories from our childhood, they didn't match. I would speak of a trip or a meal or a visit from a cousin and of something that had happened during it, and Robert would look at me as if I were speaking of the adventures of some Albanian rock band. So I stayed quiet with him. It is something that people who have been children together can effortlessly do. It is sometimes preferable to the talk, which is also effortless.

We found more stones and tossed them. "A stone can't drown," said my brother finally. "It's already drowned."

"You been reading poetry?" I smiled at him.

"I've just been thinking."

"A dangerous thing."

"A little goes a long way."

"A little's a dangerous thing. But so is a lot. And so is none." I paused. "It's all a minefield."

"Are you high?" asked my brother.

I almost skipped a stone. It wanted to. I could feel it, the desire of the stone. "If only," I sighed. I threw a stone way out left past the old fish hatchery, toward the tennis meadow. There was actually an old tennis court on our property, built by the original owners of the house. It had long been broken up with reedy weeds, had reverted almost completely to ad hoc prairie, though if one walked through there were still cracked pieces of concrete underfoot and on opposite sides two old chipped white posts for a net. In my lifetime no one had ever played tennis here. It seemed a ghostly glimpse of an old affluence that once protected the place, a counter to the signs of the old poverty—outhouses and stick pumps—that underlay most of the farms and houses nearby.

I threw another stone. And at that we headed back to the house. New snow fell silently through the sky until an updraft whistled in and caused the flakes to go up, as in a shaken-up snow dome. Robert had worked as a camp counselor for part of the previous summer and now began to sing. " 'I know a song that gets on everybody's nerves, everybody's nerves, everybody's nerves. I know a song that gets on everybody's nerves, and this is how it goes: I know a song that gets on everybody's nerves . . .' " We arrived back home damp and pink looking in the vestibule mirror, though the mirror was petaled with my mother's reminder Post-its, which made our faces look momentarily like flowers in a kids' play. My mother had baked a noodle kugel and instead of turkey had made a Christmas brisket, and we all sat down to eat. She brought the hot brisket in on a platter from the kitchen and, standing behind me, swooped it onto the table, barely missing my head. "Duck," she ordered me as she did this, and I let my head fall to one side.

"What is that?" asked my brother.

I stared at him hopelessly.

"You're the son of a Jewish mother," said my dad, "and you don't recognize brisket?"

"I do recognize brisket," he said. "But I thought she said it was duck."

It was our one big family laugh. The brisket itself, made with ketchup and one too many onion soup packets—perhaps my mother had not seen that she'd already put one in—was salty and not her best. We all piled condiments on top—cranberry sauce and a vegan relish we called "cornfield caviar"—then we drank a lot of water the rest of the night.

At home in Dellacrosse my place in the world of college and Troy and incipient adulthood dissolved and I became an unseemly collection of jostling former selves. Snarkiness streaked through my voice, or sullenness drove me behind a closed door for hours at a time. When afternoon came, I tried to go for little walks—one should always get out of the house by two p.m., my mother once advised—and I would sometimes take Blot, though once we ran into the garbage truck still trawling the roads. Blot hated the garbage truck, feeling, I think, that the men were taking away things that rightfully belonged to him, if not to all dogs in general. He barked wildly as if he were saying, *You bastards, we're going to find out where you live and come take all your garbage and see how you like that!* I was often back by two-thirty, returning to my room until dinner. I would come down, not helping my mother, and find a foaming stew pot, vesuvial and overflowing, because with her bad eyesight she had put baking soda in it instead of cornstarch, or once, I discovered, she had made little salads and put them in the ceramic dog dishes.

"Mom, these are the dog dishes," I said, pointing out the little dog heads printed on them.

Indignation tensed the muscles of her face, but she said nothing.

Once she shouted up to me and I had to come down and see what was the matter.

"You and your fancy food," she said. She had taken the sushi I'd brought home on the bus and left it on the counter, then accidentally knocked the wasabi onto the floor. Whereupon Blot had automatically lapped it up and, startled by the sensation, which he construed only as pain and heat, began to howl and tear up and run around the house. He attacked his water dish so urgently that it too fell over, and so I took him outside, where he ate snow—what little there was—and drank from a puddle. It took him an hour to settle down. The remark about fancy food, however, lingered longer. I had once gone out to dinner with my mother and ordered cabernet sauvignon, and instead of objecting that I was underage, she'd said, "Oh, fancy, fancy."

I read, flopped across my bed in my old room, its pink walls and white trim a comforting peppermint candy womb, as snow at last did begin to pile up outside. Occasionally lightning flashed again in the middle of a blizzard. What planet was this? The sky purpled, and roaring bursts of light seemed briefly to set fire to the snow as if it were the dusty landscape of a moon. Tree branches clawed into the soggy wool of the sky. I remained the nerdy college girl under siege of the weather, my days full of books that were rabbit holes of escape. Christmas music from the radio downstairs, playing through all twelve days of it, wafted up: "Rejoice, rejoice," sounded like "Read Joyce, read Joyce"— and so I did, getting a head start on my Brit Lit. "Emmanuel . . ." I made my way through *The Critique of Pure Reason.* Some days grew so bland and barren, I found myself perusing Horace, though between books I would open up my electric bass, put on the headphones, and make up little riffs for an hour or so, experimenting with the reverb. It always amazed me what a mere four strings could do. I had started with cello when very young, and then descended. Ole Bob sat in the corner, winking, I believed. Playing a guitar was so much less effort. Like a girl taking a pee. One didn't even have to stand. One could lie on the floor and just go at it with one finger like James Jamerson's magic claw. One could pretend to be Jaco Pastorius in Weather Report—especially in this weather. Here would be my report! Or Jaco on "Hejira." Here would be my Hejira! Or Meshell Ndegeocello, whose low voice I could imitate but not well.

The days ended, then started over again, like dull redos. The heat kicked on; the heat kicked off.

I made no attempt to see my few friends left from high school, who when I conjured them in my mind seemed dull and thickened strangers. In the fall I had written a note to one, my friend Krystal Bunberry, who for no real reason (but unwitting prophecy) we used to call Krystal Berry Bun; her father had worked his whole life in the toilet paper factory and on retirement received not only a free lifetime supply of toilet paper but a diagnosis of colon cancer. He then received a colostomy as well. "Rusty drainpipe removal" it was called by Krystal herself. She had written me to see if I needed any toilet paper—they now of course were giving it away. And so I had written her with my condolences, even though her father hadn't actually died. The previous year I had been in one of my friends' weddings, Marianne Sturch's; she had worn a sequined, strapless wedding gown, and left her bridesmaids to wear brightly flowered dresses fit for a kind of pornographic milkmaid: low-cut and laced up the midriff with a sort of shoelace. "What Scarlett O'Hara might have done with a shower curtain, if she were trying to snag a plumber," said my mother, who perceived the loud ugliness of the dress even through the fog of her bad eyesight. Our shoes were white patent leather, what Marianne called "pattin' leather," though I was never sure whether this was on purpose or not. Not just the outfits but the entire wedding in a rental hall at the Ramada felt tawdry and embarrassing; thirty minutes in, I found I never wanted to marry. The bride carried what looked to be a cord of pink and gold gladioluses but were really only three scepterlike stems in yellow and peach; reminded of my mother, I was woozy, seeing them. After that, I couldn't muster the energy to phone Marianne—she and her husband, Brendan Brezna, went to Orlando and Cancun for their honeymoon, a busy five-days, four-nights package with a cruise—and our paths, especially with my staying in the house like a shut-in when I came home, failed to cross.

Everyone here seemed a stranger, if not an outright alien. Before I was born, the town of Dellacrosse had been preposterously named Little Spread Eagle, after a local Indian warrior hunted down like a dog by government militiamen and turned first into the name of a golf course, then a motor lodge, then finally a town—everything about the place had been a kind of jokey curse from the start. When the village councilmen changed it to Dellacrosse, they also decided to try to remarket it as an extraterrestrial tourist site. Rumors of spaceships in the outlying cornfields and fiery brassy things floating through the night sky and even one or two probings of overweight Little Spread Eagle housewives (or the occasional passing-through truck driver) by strange creatures in black helped create the possibility of a mystique. It caused Dellacrosse to become the self-declared "Extraterrestrial Capital of the World." ("Not another anal probing," my mother took to saying, reading the *Dellacrosse Courier.* Or once, rather angrily to my father, "Why don't they just name this town what it is: Buttfuck, USA!" "Gail!" chided my father. "Get a grip!") Little paper alien heads were fastened to the streetlights on Main Street, and people sold Venusian vanilla sundaes with Mars Bar crumbles. At first it was hoped that people would come from all over the country and camp out and stay put to try to see the spaceships and aliens that might appear in the roadside parks and fields outside town. The burst of commerce and national publicity lasted less than a year and then it vanished, like the spaceships and aliens themselves. People said the council had packed everything up in a rocket and sent it back to its planet, leaving some strays behind.

The strays I felt were my own friends, who were now like martians to me. They guzzled brandy straight from the bottle, drank TheraFlu recreationally like toddies on weekends (though, truth be told, I still did that myself). They wore T-shirts that said DELLACROSSE: IT'S JUST THE TICKET, since the place had now acquired some notoriety as a speed trap. Prepositions mystified. Almost everyone said "on" accident instead of "by." They said "I'm bored of that" or "Wanna come with?" They pronounced "milk" to rhyme with "elk" and "milieu" as "miloo," as in skip to my loo—when they said it at all. And they used tenses like "I'd been gonna." As in, "I'd been gonna to do that but then I never got around toot." It was the hypothetical conditional past, time and intention carved so obliquely and fine that I could only almost comprehend it, until, like Einstein's theory of relativity, which also sometimes flashed cometlike into my view, it whooshed away again, beyond my grasp. "I'd been gonna to do that" seemed to live in some isolated corner of the grammatical time-space continuum where the language spoken was a kind of Navajo or old, old French. It was part of a language with tenses so countrified and bizarrely conceived, I'm sure there was one that meant "Hell yes, if I had a time machine!" People here would narrate an ordinary event entirely in the past perfect: "I'd been driving to the store, and I'd gotten out, and she'd come up to me and I had said . . ." It never reached any other tense. All was backstory. All was preamble. The past was severed prologue and was never uttered to be anything but. Who else on earth spoke like this? They would look at the tattoo on my ankle, a peace sign, and, withholding judgment but also intelligence, say, "Well, that's different." They'd say the same thing about my electric bass. Or even the acoustic one—*That's different!*—and in saying it made the same glottal stop that they made pronouncing "mitten" and "kitten."

And they'd grown fat, especially the boys, it was said, from air-conditioning. There were no more hot summer spaces to take away their appetites and sweat them thin—the diners, the houses, even the tractors, were newly air-conditioned inside. It was increasingly difficult to recognize people. I began to think of everyone I knew there in the derisive terms my mother some-times used—"schnooks and okey-dokes"—meaning hicks who pretended to mean well, or rubes with some plan up their sleeve. To me, they had taken on a repellent creatureliness, like ancient monsters that were thought to live in deep northern lakes, or like the dinosaurs rumored still to be roaming the vast interior of Africa, the world having rushed forward into the future without them. And so, I imagined, when the glacier had retreated it had trapped the resident driftless knuckleheads of Dellacrosse, whom time forgot. Or else they all were the dimmerwits from outer space who'd forgotten to get back on the spaceship and so the ship had left without them. Deliberately! Dellacrosse had the aspect of having been left behind by many ships. It seemed the outer space of outer space.

Added to this was my own tuned-in sense of the uncanny. When I was younger, odd strangers were said to be roaming the streets, perhaps space aliens looking for natural resources. Or were they tourists looking for space aliens or aliens looking for abandoned colonists and ancestors? Perhaps nothing had been a hoax after all. Perhaps body snatchers or the undead or creatures from another planet were really, truly attempting to walk among us here in town. My old friends from high school seemed proof enough: ominous androids who'd perhaps been hatched from young humans but who now were just inadequate and unattrac-tive impersonations hoping to pass as actual people. They would loiter for a while on this planet, until they were summoned home, where they would be decoded and tossed in a junk heap, their zombie-cookie faces eventually devoid even of their faultily assigned facial expressions, their boring experience all stored on subcutaneous data-processing chips.

We are not alone. But, hell, we sure wish we were.

I was capable of little homicides like this. My mind, when I came home to Dellacrosse, became full of them. Which in its own way enlivened the town for me, the way an obituary briefly brings back the dead. It was a hopping town, people exclaimed in what was a community joke, because everyone's toes had got cut off from frostbite! But that was the least of it for a town full of graduates of the Dellacrosse Diesel Driving School, for a town that was just one of a thousand forgotten poppy seeds scattered across the state map. Scorched grains of cornmeal on the bottom of a pizza. A thousand black holes. Pinpricks with little names. On New Year's Eve I stayed in the house rather than accompany my brother up the road to join the rowdy group of neighbors who had gathered at Perryville and County M. I didn't want to hear a single voice say, "Hi, Tassie, how's college?" Or "You've been reading? Whatcha been reading?"

"Why, I've been reading Horace!"

The fireworks every year grew more explosive and raucous, beginning days before New Year's Eve, and every year they were still legal. I could hear the whistle and pop of them, the metallic shower of pellets. They were no longer the fireworks of my childhood—simple ladyfinger firecrackers jammed like sausages into tangerines or dried goat bladders that had been hung on the Christmas trees, then yanked off and lobbed, loaded, across the field in a kind of snowball fight. (One did this with one's friends to destroy the enemy. Who was the enemy? One's friends. Who else would you want to see jump as a tangerine exploded at their feet?) As the winters grew less cold and white, the fireworks grew fancier. They now had evolved from homely grenades that could give you no more than a small blistery burn to cherry bombs and M-80s, weapons-grade devices used most often in military training. Last year the detritus of one had set a marsh on fire—in winter.

Outside, the lulls between explosions were accompanied by both children and grown men banging on tin pots and whooping. These were people who would be snowmobiling if only there were snow. If the lake were frozen they would drive their pickups out on it and go bar to bar, parked on the ice all night. They would be ice fishing from their shanties—"I got a hole out there dug!"—and they would be mumbling their taciturn joy over tip-ups and fish bites. But now there was just another round of heart-stuttering booms, the *rat-a-tat-tat* of war made jolly—but not for me. Oh, where was Ira Gershwin when you needed him for a real song, a country protest song, not just some whiny piano-bar lament? One year, I feared, someone would take the occasion to slyly shoot an actual gun, without notice, and I just hoped it wouldn't be me. That was a bleak, wintry joke I told myself. And my brother. But still.

Late on the afternoon of New Year's Day, Sarah Brink called my house. My mother answered, said, "Yes, she's here," then handed me the receiver.

"Hi, Tassie," Sarah said, sounding breathless. "Just calling to see if there's any chance you're coming back into town a little early."

I looked out the window at the purpling patina of the snow. My father and brother were in the next room, talking about snowblowers. "Like when?" I asked.

"Oh, say . . ." She stopped not for consideration but for nerve, it seemed, and dragging out the words like that made them sound like the beginning of the national anthem. "I hate to sound pushy. But like by the third?"

"Of *January?*"

And then she laughed, and I laughed, and we were both sort of laughing at each other and at ourselves in a confusing manner, having no facial expressions to assist.

III

I took the bus back the next day, on the second. Having been, as my brother used to say, "crowded as a beehive" on my way out of town, the bus during winter break was now empty and clean and morose. In Troy at dusk, the isolated patches of gray snow were like dryer lint. The heat in my building had not been turned off—that would freeze the pipes—but had been cranked down to a chill fifty-five. Generous when the students were there, the landlord knew they had gone home and did not warm the house as amply. Not just for Kay. In my absence the floorboards had readjusted and acquired new creaks. When I stepped into my own living room, it felt like someone else's house. There was some frost creeping up the panes of my windows, on the inside, and Murph's long-bequeathed vibrator/immersible blender still sat on the counter. (She had purchased it at a shop called A Woman's Touch, where I'd gone with her when she went to look for one. "Come on, come with," she'd implored. My mind had been trying to be open to such an object but kept slamming shut. "A woman's touch?" I'd asked her as we walked in. "Isn't what we want a *man's* touch?" The place had been a tiny chapel to the penis, phallic devices of all makes and creeds, on display like shoes in a shoe store though without the bannicks and special chairs needed to be properly fitted. Two large, cheerful women behind the counter who installed batteries and would wrap and deliver in plain brown wrapping, if desired, smiled and asked us to be sure to let them know if they could help. All this had at first amused then oppressed me. For days, however, I thought about going back alone and having one of the more welcoming, less motorized versions—pink and pliable—sent to me in the mail.)

Because the apartment was so unusually cold, I made my way to a coffee shop to warm up. During the school year, for study breaks, I alternated between Starbucks with its Orwellian sizing—"tall" means "small"!—and a place near the law school called On What Grounds, where "tall" meant "medium" and which had, in addition to coffee, a variety of teas in glass jars, multi-colored confetti as pretty as sachets, though once when I asked for a cup of one, the clerk shouted to someone in the back, "Hey, Sam. Is the lemongrass the one with the larvae?" After that I mostly ordered coffee—at first the espresso, in the tiny doll cups I'd never seen before moving to Troy, and then lattes in glass mugs to warm my hands. They sometimes had cookies, usually choco-late chip or oatmeal raisin, in the singular, it was said, because there was only one raisin or one chip in every cookie. Sometimes I went next door to Baby B Burritos—named after the owner's child, supposedly, though Baby B was also said to be a kind of acronym: Burritos As Big as Your Bum." Or so said Murph. There was the pizza and shake shop two blocks down, with its sign in the window: NEVER FEAR, NEVER QUIT, STOP IN. There was also an Indian buffet: ALL YOU CAN EAT FOR A DOLLAR. But if you ate too much and stayed too long, they started showing you slides of their home village, which made you feel pretty awful.

I had inadvertently left bananas to blacken on the counter over break, and even though I'd wrapped them in plastic, and even though the air was chill, when I came back from Starbucks, the apartment had by then warmed a little—the radiators steamed like trains; had the landlord spotted my return?— and I could see there were fruit flies beginning to flick around the sink. Flour moths fluttered like the tiniest angels from somewhere—who knew? The leftover boxes of cereal? Flour moths but no flour. I grabbed at them midair like a mad person. The Mexican straw-berries in the refrigerator had grown the wise and cheery beards of Santa Claus, and some Peruvian pears were cauled with mold. The cream cheese was a tub of dull green clay. In contrast to the few bucolic snowflakes of my visit home, this place seemed a sort of soiled, surreal, shaken-up snow dome of student life, so I turned off the lights. Murph had left hers on in her room, includ-ing the neon THINK OUTSIDE THE BOX, which she had saucily, instructionally, hung over her headboard. And so I unplugged it. Then I put on a sweatshirt and long underwear and went to bed, hoping that in the morning the new year would reveal its new-ness: so far it seemed painted too familiarly in my heart's old sludge.

The phone rang early. Sarah's voice was bright and on. "I'm going to have the taxicab swing by and pick you up at eleven o'clock. We're flying to Packer City," she announced.

"We are?" I was scarcely awake. I was going to have to become a new person biologically just to associate with her.

"Do you mind? Just pack a little overnight bag, and we'll be back tomorrow. We just got a phone call about a baby up there, and we're going to meet with the birth mother."

Another birth mother. How long could this go on? And did it matter, as long as Sarah paid me?

"Good, fine," I said. I had never been on a plane before. I had never been in a taxicab, but I didn't dare tell her this.

I didn't really have an overnight bag. I had a backpack, and in it I put a nightgown, underwear, and a different shirt. Otherwise, I would wear the same clothes I had on now. I threw in a book—*Zen Poems,* from a friend from last year who had transferred to a small Buddhist college in California. "So, now you're going to Zen State," Murph and I had said, and he gave us the book to reform and silence us. It had poems in it like "The world is a wake / vanishing behind a boat / that has rowed away at dawn."

Okay... Let the Buddhists depart the world and subdue their despair. Still, I did not think one necessarily had chosen wisely by leaving the party altogether and going home early to a kind of walking sleep. I preferred the mentally ill witch Sylvia Plath, whose words sought no enlightenment, no solace, whose words sought nothing but the carving of a cry. An artful one from the pitch black.

Oh, if only she had married *Langston* Hughes!

I had written on a Post-it, as if to mock my mother's own list making, my favorite line: "I'm no more your mother / Than the cloud that distills a mirror to reflect its own slow / Effacement at the wind's hand." Then I had stuck it—oh yes, oh well—on the frame of my mirror.

We stand around blankly as walls.

Motherhood like radar or radiation was radiantly in the air.

I saw the cab from my window, and when I came down the porch steps the cabbie jumped out and opened up the trunk for my backpack. "Hi," he said, smiling. How old was he? Thirty? What had he studied? French literature? The cabbies in this town seemed all to have law degrees or PhDs or unfinished dissertations on ancient Greek pottery design or the hegemonic hedges of Versailles. A slightly disputatious animation in his face caused me to take him for a law degree type—there were too many of them here, since law students didn't have to take the bar exam if they stayed in town, and so the town had long ago begun overflowing with lawyers, many of whom were now at the wheels of city buses, FedEx vans, and taxicabs. I got in the backseat and there was Sarah, beaming. She was wearing not a peacoat but a long shearling one. Perhaps she had gotten it for Christmas. "Another adventure in prospective motherhood!" she exclaimed.

"Yes," I said, thinking the phrase sounded like something Murph would say about a careless romantic fling. I found myself wondering again where Sarah's husband was.

As if reading my mind, she said, "Edward's going to try to meet us there. He's flying back from a conference in L.A., via O'Hare, and if the flight's on time we should see him at the Green Bay airport. We'll rent a car and all drive back together."

"I'll get to meet him," I said stupidly.

"Yes, of course," she said. "Or, you can do what a lot of people choose to do: just go through the motions." She expelled a quick, ambiguous bark of a laugh.

The cabbie, I believe, hated her already, but when the meter tab came to twenty even, which she gave him, and then when she couldn't find anything smaller for a tip and dug a quarter out of her pocket apologetically, he handed it back to her. "Ma'am, you need this more than I do."

She turned briskly away from him. He popped the trunk without getting out, and we lifted out our own bags and hurried into the airport. "I'm really a good tipper, ordinarily! I really am!" she said. "I'm known for my good tips!" I nodded. I believed her, though she had yet to pay me a dime. I remembered a remark my often frugal father used to make: *I only like to be gratuitous when it is absolutely necessary.*

"There are no manners in the Midwest anymore," Sarah said. "You have to go to the South. And even there it's getting patchy."

At the ticket counter they checked our IDs, Sarah keeping hers a little hidden from me, as if she disliked her picture. She stuck it quickly back into one of the many zippered pockets her burnt umber handbag contained. "This pocketbook has so many compartments, it's hard to remember where you've put things," she said. "It's like an intelligence test." I had only ever heard one other person use the word *pocketbook* instead of *purse:* my mother. "But it's magical. There's so much room. You can keep loading it up and discover so much you didn't know was there! It's like the stream of endless clowns that keeps coming out of the Volks-wagen! Still, if I were my own mother? I'd have every zipper labeled."

To me, Sarah herself was like a Volkswagen endlessly expelling clowns. "You have a mother?" I said. "I mean, your mother's alive?"

"Yes," she said.

"Awesome," I said, in that peculiar way, I knew, our generation had of finding that everything either "sucked" or was "awesome." We used *awesome* the way the British used *brilliant:* for anything at all. Perhaps, as with the British, it was a kind of antidepressant: inflated rhetoric to keep the sorry truth at bay.

"My mother and father had a real relationship," she said.

"Well, they were married."

"Anyone can get married. They had a relationship!"

"Do your parents like your restaurant?"

"My father died before he saw it. But he never liked to eat out. I once took him to a Benihana in New Jersey, but the sizzling hibachi table made him very jumpy. I think it conjured all these memories of the war and the firebombing of Tokyo. After that he refused to eat out with me. He would say, 'Come see us! Your mother has made a beautiful kugel!' He was a rich old man scared of the sizzle of a grill."

"He was rich?"

"Well, sort of. Is your dad rich?" Her eyebrows arced and her eyes bugged out. We were in a dialogue that was about something other than what we were saying. At least I hoped so.

"People thought we were, but we weren't," I said. Actually, I wasn't sure. I repeated the conventional wisdom. "Farmers aren't rich. They have land but no money." Actually, my father didn't even have that much land. He had once stood on the porch and flung his arms out and said, "Someday, kids, all this will be yours." But his knuckles had hit the porch supports. Even the porch wasn't that big.

"Farmers are rich when they die," I added.

"I suppose," said Sarah. "I never think of anyone as rich when they die. I think of dead as about as poor as you can get."

"Gate two, upstairs," said the woman at the counter, handing us our boarding passes, and since we only had carry-on bags, we went directly upstairs, except that Sarah, seeing that no people were on the down escalator, decided to try to go up it. "Watch this," she said to me. "This is how you get a little exercise before getting on a plane." And she ran quickly up the moving steps, using it like a treadmill, and waving goofily to me from the middle, as if she were Lucille Ball. "Ma'am, that's the wrong escalator," said someone on the other side, going up, and then because it was taking Sarah so long to get to the top, someone else came riding up and said, "Do you know you're going up the down side?" No one understood what she was doing, and so no one smiled.

"Exercise!" exclaimed Sarah. This burst of eccentricity in her I could see was familiar to herself, and unresisted. Such self-permission I don't believe I'd ever witnessed before in almost anyone of any age. I myself went up the up escalator and watched as, still holding her carry-on bag, her shearling coat lifting behind her, she took the flying gazellelike leap necessary to get off the descending stairs, and which if her timing had been even a moment different could easily have left her maimed. That all this failed to draw the notice of anyone in security was a relief.

"Not too bad for an old gal, eh?" said Sarah, breathlessly grinning and pink in the cheeks. I made a smile of some kind—I have no idea what kind—and we then moved quickly to the elaborately cordoned security line, where a beefy, bloat-faced man took our nail clippers and Sarah's tweezers. "A girl just can't groom anymore!" she said to me. I chuckled to please her. She had an anxious energy swimming around her, which laughter—hers, anyone's—seemed to dispel.

As for me, tension gripped my neck. I couldn't distinguish my own fears of flying from my general disorientation regarding this sudden trip. The plane was small, only a fifty-seater, hardly a hijacking target, and from my window seat the gray pieces of the wing seemed fitted together both randomly and intricately, like the plumage of a goose. The handles on the emergency exit doors were grizzled, crooked, and beat. Was this good luck? The January day was blue, sun sparkling off the evergreens, the air clear as a bell; it was state-of-the-art light, as noon in January sometimes could be: not rich but pale and cleansing as lemon wine. Watching from the plane window, I saw dozens of planes negotiating the small grid of runways: a bee dance of near collision and narrow escape. Oh, where, oh, where was the nectar? There was just the busy dance and commerce of a hive. Robert's word—and true.

Then suddenly we were taking off, racing down the runway and lifting into the air like a carnival ride, the plane with a seabird's wobble. It seemed to me like a ride you'd spend extra tickets on at the state fair. I felt the lift in my gut and the plane tipping side to side, finding itself. For a split second I darkly imagined all the workers at Boeing or wherever this puddle-jumper had been made (Brazil! I would later find out) as carnies, toothless and tattooed. Beneath us the ground shot away—if the world vanished like the wake behind a boat rowing away at dawn, would that really be such a bad thing? The twenty-five minutes of farmland between Troy and Green Bay became a snow-splotched checkerboard of drained olive, khaki, gold-gray, and nut brown—not unlike the roasted bean display, green to french roast, that Starbucks had set up near the register, and which I sometimes found myself staring at as if the displays were glass vats of pistachios or M&M's or gumballs one might get from a machine if one only had the right change.

The right change. I thought of this phrase now and its meaning for Sarah. Her desire for a baby. Her undertipping of the cabbie. I had yet to see her get ahold of the right change.

Contents may shift during the flight, we had been told. Would that be good or bad? And what about the discontents? Would they please shift, too? And what if oxygen deprivation in the cabin caused one to think in idle spirals and desperate verbal coils like this for the rest of one's life? Below us moved the continued squares of greens and browns that Rothko never got to. The ground mottled with mud and snow, broken occasionally by the shiny shoe print of a lake. Beneath us was a tone of ochre that when the sun hit looked like a vellum lamp.

"So, here's the story about this birth mom," Sarah said softly, for privacy, though the plane engine was loud and I had to ask her to repeat things. *Birth mom.* It was one of those faux-friendly terms invented by the adoption business itself. I studied the intricate construction of the plane wing as she spoke. One had to fix one's gaze somehow. Apparently this birth mother had been working with Catholic Social Services, who had been looking to place her baby daughter, but when too many months had gone by and the family they had found suddenly backed out (they had prayed and their God had told them no; "*their* God," emphasized Sarah, "no one else's. Everything's been privatized, even the Creator"), the birth mother switched agencies, and the one she hired had been in touch with Letitia Gherlich, with whom we'd had lunch at Perkins. They had a fee-splitting arrangement.

What about Amber?

Amber was no longer in the picture, apparently, having violated her parole, and not having liked any of the prospective parents well enough. She was considering keeping her baby.

"I kind of liked Amber," I said—a mistake.

Sarah's face became a polished stone. "Amber was a coke addict and a meth-head. Both," she said. Amber was past tense. We were covering her inanimate face in the white sheet of *was.* Only her bare feet were sticking out, an ankle monitor brightly in place, perhaps one tiny toe wiggling good-bye: I *had* kind of liked her.

The new birth mother in Green Bay was named Bonnie and was apparently in her late twenties. A grown-up! Her baby was well over a year old, possibly two, already languishing in foster homes. "And after we pay them both a visit, we may see why, though I think I already know."

I was quiet. The plane was now descending and my ears were closing from the pressure. Everything she said seemed to be coming to me from under water.

"The baby's black," she said. "Part black. And nobody wants her. People would rather go to China! All the way to China before they would take in a black kid from their own state."

When I was a child the only black kids I ever saw were indeed in Green Bay. I would see them when we went there to shop: children of the professional football players who lived in big suburban houses and were said to move every three years, when their dads got injured or traded. "I warn my kids not to bother getting to know them," clerks said openly in the stores. "They're just going to move." This was how bigotry got conducted among people who swore they weren't prejudiced at all.

"I'm sure that's what it is with this baby," said Sarah. "Race."

I wondered whether the birth father might be a Green Bay Packer. That would be cool. When I was a freshman there was a girl in my dorm named Rachel. Because her dad was black and her mom was white, her friends called her Inter-Rachel. She would always laugh.

The plane bumped down, and I swallowed hard to open my ears and settle my stomach. I dug some chewing gum out of my backpack. I hadn't eaten very much and that, combined with my slight queasiness, had surely given me bad breath.

Out in the airport we looked for Edward, but he wasn't there. Sarah asked about the flight from Chicago, but it had arrived fifteen minutes ago and all passengers had already deplaned. "Maybe he's at the baggage carousel," she said, and I traipsed after her. We circled the luggage belts and wandered over to the Hertz counter, where Sarah filled out the forms for renting a car, and then we waited near the men's room. He just wasn't there. I thought the men's room should also have a big yellow sign that said HERTZ.

Sarah sank against the wall, beneath the sign that did not say HERTZ but instead the restroom one that said MEN. Her eyes were starting to mist. She closed them, and when she opened them again she shook her head and sighed. "This," she said, "is why God invented the fetal position."

I was starting to admire her. Or at least I was fearing her less.

She reshouldered her bag and pulled her coat tighter. "Oh, let's just go," she said, car key and map in hand. Her features had fallen but I saw her lift them again, one by one, the way one rights light porch furniture after a wind. I wondered what her marriage could possibly be like. Made up as it went along, no doubt. Women now were told not to settle for second best, told that they deserved better, but at a time, it seemed, when there was so much less to go around. They were like the poor that way, perhaps. What sense did anything they were being told possibly make, given the scarcity of their world?

We found the car, a shale-colored Ford Escort, in the far end of the lot. I got in and felt how clean it was, cleaner and tidier perhaps than any car I'd ever been in. Sarah handed me the map. "Mind being the navigator?" she asked, or sort of asked.

"Not at all." I opened the map, knowing it would never again be folded back correctly, at least not by me. I had map skills, but not that kind.

Out the windshield the busy grid of a small mill city full of bridges stared back at me. The giant sports arena with its glistening white top on the horizon, or the big bowl of the stadium, all this took up a good portion of the sky. I navigated as well as I could. I remembered that once on a Miss America broadcast Miss Wisconsin, when asked by one of the judges, hadn't known what "the Bay of Pigs" referred to and had said anxiously, "Green Bay?"

The fire hydrants were painted lime—it was strange to see green in winter at all—and there were green trolley buses, as if this were all some hilarious tourist town where one came to visit the Jolly Green Giant himself. I'm sure some people came looking but found only Vince Lombardi, the pope of Green Bay, in statue form. Plus factory after factory slipping waste into the river. "I wonder if there's a high incidence of cancer here," Sarah ventured out loud. "Or birth defects . . ."

"I know there's a high incidence of football," I said. In the distance I could still see the light roof of the arena and the new high boxes of the stadium, in a ring of towers like castle lookouts. Sarah fiddled with the radio until she found the soul station and the snake-rattle opening of "Heard It Through the Grapevine." Her left foot tapped the car floor, and I thought I saw her shoulders shimmy through her coat. A car passed us with a BEARS STINK bumper sticker.

"Is that referring to football or actual bears?"

"Football," I said.

The lawyer's office was in a creepy old hotel downtown. We circled the parking lot, looking for spaces. "When trying to park I tend to go into fortune-teller mode," Sarah said. "As in I have a hunch there's a spot right around this corner. Or else into defense attorney mode, where I argue with the signs: Why *aren't* I an authorized vehicle? I'm as authorized as the next guy, also as handicapped as the next guy, and as for the hour limitations, well, on the East Coast, where *I'm* from, it's four o'clock right now. Crap like that. Sometimes I will vibe and seize the *intent* of a rule and go with that—rather than with the rule itself."

There was only a tight space next to a black sedan that had parked jauntily—much space on the right, none on the left. Nonetheless, we pulled up on the left to see the driver was still there, slumped down, waiting for someone, a Packers cap pulled down over his brow. He rolled down his window. "Lady, why don't you find some other place to park," he said.

Sarah muttered, "Why on earth should I?" then turned off the engine, opened the window on my side, and shouted, "If you could move over a few inches there would be room for everyone. This is the only spot left in the lot."

"I was here first," he shouted indignantly.

"What on earth difference does that make?"

"Lady, you've put me in a tight spot. I'd hate to see your car all banged up and scratched."

She got out and slammed her door. "Yes, sir, and I'd hate to see the air let out of all four of your tires." I got out carefully, and we walked quickly toward the building entrance. "The rental insurance covers everything, I do believe," she said to me with great confidence. "Or else the credit card. I once murdered someone and American Express covered everything!"

I smiled. The lobby was dark with faded scarlet and maroon. The elevator was brass and tarnished, and it wheezed and shuddered slowly to the third floor. When its doors crashed open, I stepped out quickly before the contraption changed its mind altogether and swiftly shot its way to the basement in a jangle of steel. "Suite Three D," said Sarah, reading from a business card that said *Roberta Marshall, Attorney-at-Law,* and soon we were in a large sunlit room, decorated in green and pink. The wallpaper was olive with great swirling blossoms of lilies and roses ballooning and bursting or mating and probing and flipping out, in repetition, across the walls.

"We're here to see Roberta Marshall," said Sarah to the receptionist, a large woman with hair dyed a tarnished gold hue and gelled into a stiff hood.

"Your name?" said the receptionist.

"Oh, sorry. Sarah Brink."

The receptionist dialed three numbers and waited with the receiver against her ear. She moved her head back and forth, rolled her eyes a little, looked at her watch, looked at me and gave me a quick tight smile, then looked at her manicure, which seemed in need of new paint. "Sarah Brink is here," she said. "Along with . . . I'm sorry, I didn't catch your name."

But as I was saying "Tassie Keltjin," she was simultaneously repeating Sarah's name into the phone so that the utterance of my name was wiped out by the utterance of hers. "Sarah Brink. Yes. Brink." Then she slammed the phone down and sighed. "She'll be with you in a minute."

We sat down and waited. It was hard to tell where we were or what year it was. It could have been anywhere, anything.

Roberta Marshall burst through the door but then shut it closely, secretly, behind her. She was a small, dark-haired woman with a wide smile that had long ago given her marionette lines and crow's-feet. Though it was daytime she wore a tailored black velveteen jacket with a notched lapel that cut in and out in a way that gave her angles and flattered her, and which she probably hoped made her look rich. I was already becoming a woman who sized up another one fast—I was becoming typical.

We all stood, we shook hands, and then we sat back down. Roberta looked at me and smiled her big cracked-open smile. "Sarah told me you'd be coming," she said approvingly. "No Edward?" she asked, looking around, knitting her brow.

"Next time," said Sarah. Still, she had a bit of happy hope in her face. Roberta Marshall opened a manila envelope. "So here's our little girl," she said, pulling out some Polaroids. "Just barely still a baby," she added. "She's been sitting in the foster care of Catholic Social Services awaiting an African-American couple." This was the same story I'd just heard. "They did find one, but then the couple changed their minds: said they had prayed to their God and their God had advised against it. So they turned the baby down. And then the birth mother, who is white, finally left Catholic Social Services and came to us."

"Well, then, just as well," said Sarah with her happy confidence still working her gaze, which cast itself eagerly toward the snapshots that Roberta was holding.

"I don't know who 'their God' was that it was so different from the rest of ours," said Roberta, rolling her eyes; you could see she had no truck with ditherers. "Once I did an international, and the couple spent two weeks in a Santiago hotel and flew back childless because they said they 'couldn't bond with the baby.' So, just as well; yes, just as well." She was still hanging on to the photos for some reason. "The birth father is African-American, or at least part African-American, though he seems to have skipped town. We have put in the ads we're supposed to before we sever his rights."

"What ads?"

"The ones telling him to show up or else. But this happens a lot. Even if we find these guys, we usually can meet with them at McDonald's, buy them a burger, and let them know that giving up their rights is the best thing. Even if they're in prison we go and talk to them, though that's a little harder. A guy in prison won't give up anything. He's given up a lot already." She paused, as if she thought that might sound brutal. "No one is coerced. They are convinced in completely compassionate and reasonable ways. Everything is legal. These are usually young guys who've come up from Milwaukee or Chicago for a job in the canning plant and one Friday night just had a couple beers, if you know what I mean." Then she added, "The birth mother is white— did I say that already? She didn't know the father for very long; Victor—we're on a first-name-only basis here all around. But the birth mother is not romantic about motherhood: she would like to pull her life together and go back to school. She doesn't have much." She thrust the photos toward me. Uncertainly, I went to take them but she quickly pulled them back. "I'm sorry," she said, touching her head as if she had a headache. "You," she said to Sarah. "I meant to give them to you. Sorry."

Sarah took it in stride. She didn't want to upset the applecart in any way. She gently took the photos as if they contained the baby herself. "Oh, look at her," she said with pleasure. "She's beautiful."

"She'll darken up, of course," Roberta Marshall said quickly.

"Of course. It's not as if that's a problem!" Sarah arranged a look of benign indignation.

"Well, I didn't mean to suggest it was a problem. I just think people should understand. I have a biracial son myself. And he has been raised with a sense of total racial blindness. It's a beautiful thing. He knows his adoption story by heart, how mommy's tummy didn't work, and he has completely embraced it." The adoption business seemed to be full of women's "broken tummies." "When he was ten years old he was watching Gregory Hines dance on TV, and he said, 'Look, Mom, that dancing man is adopted.' It was the cutest thing."

It didn't sound that cute. It sounded odd. It sounded like it had the sharp edge of a weird lie poking into it. Perhaps, as we said in Dellacrosse, the former home and hope of extraterrestrial visitation, she had her head up her hinder. I glanced over at Sarah, who was remaining tight-lipped and nodding. I always had the sense with her that she didn't suffer fools gladly but that life was taking great pains to show her how. Although later I would hear her say, repeatedly, "Racial blindness—now there's a very white idea," right then she merely asked, "When were these pictures taken?"

Roberta craned to look at them again. "They were taken by the birth mother the day before yesterday, I think."

"She's healthy? The baby?"

"Healthy. A little allergy to her formula, initially, but that all got worked out. She's eating regular food now, I do believe. We'll have to see what the foster family says. I have to warn you about the foster care from Catholic Social Services: it's not the Pfister Hotel."

"And what else do we know about the birth parents?"

"Well, the birth mother you'll meet today—everyone on a first-name basis only. She needs to interview you and see if you are the right parents—right mother—in her mind. The birth father, well, we don't know much. And there are privacy issues. She didn't know him well. It was, I think, only a fling, of sorts. Possibly it was a—no, I take it back. I don't think it was a date rape."

A dry quiet descended on the room like snow.

Finally someone stirred stiffly, as if shucking off ice. Sarah. "Can we meet the baby?" she asked.

Roberta grinned. "You've come all this way. Of course! But first you need to meet Bonnie. The birth mother." And here she lowered her voice. "She's just going to ask you a few questions. Her concern is religion. The baby's already baptized, but Bonnie wants a promise that she'll be confirmed." And here Roberta lowered her head and her esses made a hiss: *"Unenforceable, of course."* She then resumed a normal tone and what seemed to me an attorneylike posture. Broom up the back. "You wouldn't have any problem with that, would you?"

"I don't think so," said Sarah. "I have attended the Unitarian Church and often there they have ceremonies that—"

Roberta did not like the word *Unitarian*. She interrupted with an ominous richness of voice. "This is a birth mother who spends her Saturday nights ice-skating with nuns. You wouldn't have any problem with having the child confirmed *and* taking First Communion in a Catholic church."

"Uh, no, I wouldn't," said Sarah, on cue.

"Good." Roberta stood. "Now let's meet Bonnie." She opened

the door to her office and signaled to someone inside. "We're ready for you," she said quietly, and then opened the door wide.

Bonnie was not bonnie. She was dressed formally, in a beige knit suit, pantyhose, and brown flat shoes, to make her look professional, I supposed, which she wasn't but wanted someday to be. She was heavy, perhaps still from the pregnancy. Her hair was thick and pale, the color of a wax bean, with roots of darker doorknocker blond. She was older than I was. Maybe she was even thirty. She wore glasses, and behind them I could see her eyebrows were shaved into a thin line—the stubble showing both above and below. The thin line was lengthened at the end with an eyebrow pencil, which looked about as natural as if she had just taped the pencils themselves over her eyes. I had always been told never to pluck above the brow, only below but never above, and never, ever shave them, and seeing her standing there, in the muck of her mistake, I finally knew why people had said all that stuff about plucking. I stood to greet her. She looked puffy and medicated. I wondered how it would be for her going back to school, inconveniently carrying around this ironic name—like the birth father, Victor. I wondered if she thought it mocked her. When everything else in her life probably was a source of sorrow, on the other hand, why would she care about the rhetorical mockery of her name?

She walked toward us slowly, with the fibrous, brushing sound of pantyhose, and then she sat down on the sofa next to me, so I sat back down with her. Beneath her stiff composure and mask of a face she gave off a whiff of bacon grease and gum. The smell of spearmint grew, and I began to wonder whether she had a wad stashed in the back of her mouth to disguise a terrified breath. Close up the odd art of her eyebrows seemed more a mild madness than a mere miscalculation.

I smiled at her, thinking she could see me in her peripheral vision—and she could. She turned and nodded but then focused her attention back on Sarah, who sat across from us.

"Have you met my daughter yet?" she asked Sarah.

All the words in that question felt wrong. There was an awkward pause, and Roberta jumped up. "I'm going to have Suzanne bring us some coffee." She got up and went looking for Suzanne, who for some reason had left her receptionist's desk and gone into Roberta's office, as if they had traded places and it didn't really matter who was who. That of course was what this whole adoption agency was about: women switching places.

"No, I've only seen pictures," said Sarah. "She looks very beautiful."

"Yes," said Bonnie, her eyes suddenly welling. "She is."

"She looks like a little Irish Rose," said Roberta, overhearing as she returned to the room, carrying a tray with two bowls: one piled with creamers and one jammed with yellow packets of sweetener that I'd learned from friends had been invented accidentally by chemists during a reformulation of insecticide. Death and dessert, sweetness and doom, lay side by side: I was coming to see that this was not uncommon. Such sugar, of course, was corrupt. Death, on the other hand, was pretty straightforward. I knew several kids who for money had been lab rats in pharmaceutical experiments, and they had secretly mucked up the data by doing things like eating doughnuts on the sly or getting high on glue. But after their blood was tested or their sleep observed, the results were sent out as science.

"I don't really believe in interracial relationships," said Bonnie, looking in a kind of dead-faced way at Sarah.

"The whole *tragic mulatto* thing?" said Sarah with a light, fluffy sarcasm that had flown in from some other conversation entirely. "The whole *what about the children* thing?"

"What?" Bonnie contorted her face as if in pain. She wanted to be respected for the gift she was giving the world and in this room she wanted to be in charge, but now it seemed clear she probably wasn't.

Roberta glared at Sarah. "Sorry," said Sarah. Something gentler returned to her voice. "Sometimes other people's cell phone conversations come in on my fillings." She grinned.

"Really?" asked Bonnie, confused.

"Actually, that happens to me sometimes," I chimed in. "I swear to God. It's very weird."

Sarah tried to make her way back to Bonnie, whom she'd lost. "But, Bonnie, I just wanted to ask you: Isn't the baby half African-American?" Sarah recrossed her legs. She had winced a little at Roberta's "little Irish Rose." I could see she was torn between not wanting to seem confrontational and wanting to know just what kind of racism was here in this room.

"More like a quarter, I think. I don't know. He—my daughter's father—once asked me what I would think of having a child who had one black grandparent."

This did not sound like date-rape chat, or like fling chat. Or chat, really, of any sort at all. But perhaps I was learning a thing or two about chat. Where was Suzanne with the coffee?

"Maybe he was Italian," said Bonnie.

No one laughed, which was excellent. No one laughed out loud.

Suzanne at last came in with coffeepot and cups, and just as she was pouring and passing around the coffee the outside door cracked open. "Is this—" said a man's voice. "Oh, yes, I see it is," and the door opened wide. In stepped a distinguished-looking man: he had a balding head with pewter-hued hair grown long and wavy in the back; it was like he was wearing a head cape. His salt-and-pepper mustache was clipped neatly.

"Edward!" Sarah jumped up.

"Sorry I'm late," he said. His gaze, which had been on her, turned to his own paper cup of coffee, which he sipped from, as if it were not just delicious but urgent, and I could see he was showing us himself, his aquiline profile, his handsome objectness, so that for a minute he did not have to trouble himself to admire us but to soak up our appreciation of him. He had snapped in two the connecting gaze he'd quickly made, then unmade, with Sarah, but one could see it was his habit to almost imperceptibly dominate and insult.

Instead of being angry, Sarah looked happier than I had ever seen her in my brief acquaintance with her. Something in her face softened and relaxed, and a youthful light went on behind every part of it. Despite everything, she was in love with him. I had not seen love very much, and it was hard for my midwestern girl's mind to imagine being in love with a guy this flamboyantly self-involved and, well, old. He could have been fifty or even fifty-four. But Sarah went over to him, clasped his face in her hands, and smooched him on the lips. He patted her on the back as if to calm her down. His deep eyes, his charming smile—I could not then and there see any of it. This was love, I supposed, and eventually I would come to know it. Someday it would choose me and I would come to understand its spell, for long stretches and short, two times, maybe three, and then quite probably it would choose me never again.

"The cab headed out of the airport and got halfway to Pulaski," Edward was saying, "before the driver realized he was headed in the wrong direction."

"Here we say 'Plasky,' " Roberta said quickly.

"Came back through something called Allouez—how do you say that?"

Many of the original French traders seemed to have had such an adversarial relationship to nature, especially water, that everything they named took on their gloom: Death's Door, Waves' Grave, or Devil's Lake, all lovely vacation spots translated from the French. Even in Delton County "the lake of God," *du Dieu,* was known by the locals as Lake Doo-doo. By comparison, "Allouez" seemed welcoming, though perhaps sarcastic.

"Alwez," she said, as if it weren't French at all.

"Edward Thornwood," he said, thrusting out his hand at her.

"Edward. Edward. Yes. Edward. I'm Roberta," she said, clearly trying to emphasize that this was a first-name-only situation. Could the revelation of his last name be a deal-breaker? Would the birth mother in a change of heart later remember it, track him down, take her baby back? I tried to live cautiously—or eventually learned to try to live—in a spirit of regret prevention, and I could not see how Bonnie could accomplish such a thing in this situation. Regret—operatic, oceanic, fathomless—seemed to stretch before her in every direction. No matter which path she took, regret would stain her feet and scratch her arms and rain down on her, lightlessly and lifelong. It had already begun.

Sarah introduced Edward to everyone again, once more as just "Edward," perhaps to help erase the memory of his uttered last name, and he focused his bright gaze and kind words—*so wonderful to meet you, I know this is a complicated time*—on me. This caused visible consternation in Bonnie, who began to look even sadder and more distant, for it was clear Edward thought I was the birth mother and that I was the one who needed to be charmed. Bonnie desired and required the focus of this meeting, if not this entire day, to be on her. Could she not be the star even for that long, just once, given everything, giving everything away as she was doing?

"Edward, Bonnie here is the birth mother," said Sarah.

"Oh, I'm sorry," he said, nodding toward her but failing to summon the same energy he had had for me. I wondered if being mistaken twice now for a possible mother portended something not so sparkling for my future.

"Care for some more coffee?" asked Suzanne. She lifted the pot and toasted his cup with it.

"No, thanks," he said. And then we all chatted some more. Edward was a researcher—no longer associated with a university. He did research on eye cancer.

"How did you get interested in eyes?" asked Roberta brightly.

"Well," said Edward, seated on the loveseat with Sarah. He gave a look of innocent, empirical glee. "At first I was interested in breasts."

"How very unusual," said Roberta.

I let out a small amused hoot—a mistake.

Bonnie simply stared at him.

"But there is a kind of eye cancer in mice that benefits greatly from a chemical that's in grapes and red wine, actually—it's called resveratrol—and I got interested in that. Of course no big pharmaceutical company is interested because it's a natural product and not patentable, and the big companies control the research grants—"

"But you have some outside interest," said Roberta to the rescue. These birth mothers wanted rich, rich, rich. They wanted to know their babies would have all the things they hadn't. And the babies would. They were cute; they would be fine. The person who most needed adopting, it seemed to me, was Bonnie.

"Oh, yes. There's some interest," he added quickly. He could take a lawyer's cues as quickly as Sarah. "But it's not like I've invented a killer robot or anything as glamorous as that." There was silence, so he continued. "Unfortunately, artificial intelligence is very artificial. In my opinion."

Sarah piped up awkwardly. "Here we are with my professional kitchen and his lab and despite all that chemistry our bodies could never get anything cooked up between us." There it was again: adopted kid as default kid. In nervous ingratiation Sarah had crossed some line—of privacy and sensitivity, perhaps even of honesty—though I didn't know it then. Edward gave her a sharp look. Nonetheless, Sarah continued. "Not a green thumb in the house," she said. "Even invasive species won't grow in my garden. I have the shyest vinca in the world."

What did it mean to have the shyest vinca in the world? It

seemed sad but perhaps necessary, like the retirement of an aged ballerina.

Bonnie began to shift in her seat and even her expressionlessness began to recede into the distance so that yet greater expressionlessness could take its place.

"Bonnie, do you have any questions?".

Then the sudden attention to her, which she had earlier seemed to want, startled her. Her face went red with heat. Perhaps there was in fact a chemical found in nature that could prevent eye cancer, cancer of the tear ducts, though I doubted it. I could see her eyes start to redden as well, and soon bright water was shining across them like sunlight with no sun. Her hands moved slowly to her hair. The full force of what she was doing was slowly coming to her once again.

"I am only a hospital aide right now." She did not say the word *bedpan,* but she didn't have to. "I would like to go back to school."

"We can help you with that," said Sarah.

"Uh, actually, that's not allowed in this state," said Roberta. "But certain smaller gifts might be."

"I mean, we could help—in other ways. Advice and things." Sarah was both pathetic and game. You had to hand it to her.

"I just want the best for my little girl," Bonnie said firmly. "Will you raise her Catholic?"

"Of course," lied Sarah, who leaned in generously to pat Bonnie's hand. Because I was closer, I threw my arms around Bonnie. I don't know what came over me. But it seemed we all were a team. A team of rescuers and destroyers both, and I was in on it and had to do my part. Bonnie briefly went to bury her face in my shoulder, then pulled herself together and sat back up. Sarah gave us an astonished look.

"Well, Bonnie," said Roberta, "shall you and I go back into my office and discuss things?"

"Yes," said Bonnie. They got up and closed the inner door

behind them, leaving the three of us standing with Suzanne, who added, "I've seen a lot of heavy stuff in this room," and then busied herself with file folders.

"If this wallpaper could speak," said Edward. He studied it quizzically. "Or maybe it already can."

"This wallpaper wouldn't speak," Suzanne said, glancing up at it. "It would bite."

We sat back down and flipped through magazines. *Adoption Choice, The Adopted Child,* and *Sports Illustrated.* One for the dads. I looked at an article in *Time* about baby boomers and their lonely work habits and aging pets.

In ten minutes Roberta and Bonnie reemerged. "I have some wonderful news!" said Roberta. "Bonnie has decided she would like you to be the parents of her baby."

This ceremony of approval was a charade—everything had been decided before we got here—and as with all charades it was wanly ebullient, necessary, and thin.

"Oh, that's wonderful," said Sarah, and she rushed forward and put her arms around Bonnie. This threw Bonnie off balance a little, and she grabbed the back of the sofa to steady herself. Edward as well stepped forward and gave Bonnie a hug, to which she responded stiffly. But then Bonnie turned to me, and by this time she may have warmed to the idea of hugging, or to the idea of me, because she stepped forward and threw herself upon me again, her silent tears dampening my shoulder. Her back heaved slightly—just once—and then she stood straight.

"Well, we'll be in touch, I suppose," said Bonnie hopefully, while her face wore a look of devastation and dashed vanity. Her moment in the spotlight was coming to a close—the spotlight itself was dimming and she was slowly stepping backwards.

"The annual Christmas card," said Sarah. "I'll send you one every Christmas with all the news."

"And pictures," said Bonnie in a low, stern voice she hadn't spoken in before. "I want pictures of her."

Sarah said, "Of course. I'll send photos." She gave Bonnie a final hug and murmured loudly enough for us to hear, "Be happy."

"Yes," said Bonnie tonelessly. She turned toward me one last time and I then, too, gave her a final hug. Bonnie whispered in my ear, "*You* be happy."

And then she seemed to be disappearing like an apparition. Through the darkening afternoon window one could hear the scrape of a plow outside in the street, but inside was where it was snowing. It was snowing in here in this room and it was all piled up around Bonnie, falling on her head, piled up on her shoulders. Of course it was only a bluff, the large, imposing dirigible of her, and now she had just spluttered to nothing. She was something flat and far and stuck to the wall. I wanted to take her with me, to go to her and lead her out with us. Where would she go? What home could she possibly have? Suddenly we were all going our separate ways. We were to meet Roberta tomorrow at the foster home and there meet the child. I waved to Bonnie, a kind of queen's wave I hoped she'd construe as friendship, but no movement came from her at all.

A kind of stunned trio, Sarah, Edward, and I stepped outside into this town of . . . what? A tundra of closing mills, pro ball, anxious Catholicism. The late-afternoon air of our exhalations hung in brief clouds before us. The thought balloon of my own breath said, *How have I found myself here?* It was not a theological question. It was one of transportation and neurology.

"Let's go seek a fish fry," said Sarah, and happily took Edward's arm.

"Let's do," said Edward, sounding to my ear like a southern gent in a corny old film.

We piled into the Ford Escort, no longer by the black car and with only one small silver scratch, and drove around a little haphazardly, passing the stadium, whereupon Sarah said, "So here's where all the Catholics gather and pray for the Packers to win."

We wound up at a supper club called Lombardino's, which over the bar had a sign that read BETTER TO OUTLIVE AN ELF THAN OUTDRINK A DWARF. There were drawings of Vince Lombardi on the napkins and placemats and even the teacups; to my surprise, I had to tell Sarah and Edward what a supper club even was.

"We're from the East," said Edward. "They don't have them out there."

"They don't?" This seemed unimaginable to me.

"I mean, there are steak houses, but they're not the same. We love supper clubs but without really knowing what constitutes one. We kind of get it, but we always like to hear the exact definition from someone who grew up out here," said Sarah.

Always. Out here. So this was a thing they did, a tourist's game. "Well, a supper club is just, well, it's got these carrots and radishes in a glass of ice like this," I began lamely, with no words coming, just a sense of the obvious. It was like describing my arms. "And there's always steak, and fish on Fridays, and fried potatoes of some sort. There's whiskey sours and Bloody Marys and Chubby Marys, and supper, but there's no real club. I mean, there aren't members or anything."

"What's a Chubby Mary?" This was Edward and Sarah practically simultaneously.

"It's a Bloody Mary with a chub sticking out of it."

"A chub?"

"A fish. It's dead. It's small. At first you see its head just poking up through the ice cubes, but believe me, the whole thing is there."

Edward and Sarah were sitting across the table from me, grinning as if I were the most adorable child. My face heated up in response to what I felt was mockery. For a second I wanted to stab myself.

"They're probably in the back, giving everything a quick parboil then tanning it with a torch," said Sarah.

"Sarah thinks nothing is really cooked anymore, just toned with a butane lighter."

"Sometimes that's true." Sarah shrugged.

"We often blowtorched the weeds at home by hand," I said. "But that's organic weed control—not cooking."

"No, it's not. Cooking." Sarah smiled briefly again as if I were still just the cutest thing but no longer what she was looking for in this job.

Edward took his wineglass and toasted Sarah. "Happy birthday," he said.

"Thank you."

"It's your birthday?" I asked.

"Yes, well, in all the rush of events, who can even care!"

I was tempted to ask how old she was, but then I remembered I already knew. Instead I said, "So, you're a Capricorn!"

"Yeah," she said tiredly.

"Like Jesus!" I said. Having a Jewish mother, I was still inclined to think of Jesus not as the messiah but as, like, a celebrity.

"And like Richard Nixon," she sighed, but then smiled. "Capricorns are a little boring. But they're steady. And they work very hard, aiming for the highest thing." She drank from her birthday wine. "They toil purposefully and loyally and then people just turn on them and destroy them."

"And tomorrow's our anniversary," said Edward.

"That's right. But we never celebrate it."

"Well, it's a little on the heels of your birthday, but we celebrate it."

"We do?"

"Sure," said Edward, smiling. "Don't you remember? Every year on that day you put on a black armband and then I go looking for you and find you on top of some bell tower with a bag of chips and some Diet Coke and a rifle."

Sarah turned to me. They were in performance. They were performing their marriage at me. "There's a lot of pressure having a birthday and an anniversary so close together. It's a stressor." She raised her glass in a toast. "What does that elf and dwarf sign mean?" she asked. I was now the official translator.

"I have no idea." Perhaps they would suddenly, brutally, fire me.

When the bill came, Edward reached for his wallet but couldn't find it. "I must have left my wallet in the car," he said.

Sarah was already pulling out a credit card. "You should get one of those waist-belt change purses," she said to him.

"Too much like a colostomy bag," said Edward. They both looked amused, and for a freak minute I believed they were perfect for each other, a feeling I would never have again.

"Should I pay for mine?" I asked awkwardly.

"Absolutely not," said Sarah, signing for the bill, not looking up.

The next morning I awoke in my own suite—the Presidential Suite, it was named—to Sarah's phone call.

"We're off to see the baby," she said. "Would you like to *go with*, as you real midwesterners say?"

Was this perfunctory politeness—or perfunctory rudeness? Was I supposed to decline and let them have their appropriately private meeting? Or would declining get me fired, as it might suggest that the baby was of no real interest to me? I had come this far with them—it seemed I had to say yes. It was a decision made in the dry terror of cluelessness. Why was I never quick to understand? At the end of a transaction, for instance, when a store clerk handed me my purchase and said, "Have a good one," I always caught myself wondering, *A good WHAT?*

"Yes," I said now. The thick drapes at the windows were outlined in sun. I pulled them open with the plastic rod and the morning burned in—clear and ablaze above a snowy parking lot. The ceiling I could see now bore a maize maze of water stains, and the walls of the room had bullet holes in them. The Presidential Suite! Well, I supposed, even presidents got shot. The wall-paper peeled in triangles at the seams, like the shoulder of a dress dropped to show a whore's plaster skin. There was a fake thermo-stat, one of those thermostats to nowhere.

"Can you meet us in the lobby in thirty minutes?" Sarah asked doubtfully.

"Of course." I looked over at the in-room coffeemaker and wondered how it worked.

As soon as I saw them in the lobby, I realized my mistake. They were looking at their watches, holding hands, then looking at their watches again. Their glance up at me was quick, perfunc-tory, and when I got into the car and sat in the back like their sullen teenage daughter I could see that this was not an outing I should be on. Edward started to light up a cigarette, and Sarah swatted it away.

"Afraid of secondhand smoke? There's conflicting science on that," he said.

Sarah gave him a look but said nothing. From my awkward place in the backseat I remembered a headline from the student paper. "You know what they say about secondhand smoke," I said. I was a girl still finding her jokey party voice and borrowing from others'.

"What?" said Sarah.

"Leads to secondhand coolness."

Edward turned in his seat to look at me. I had pleased him with this stupidity, and he was getting a better look at me to see who I was today.

"Did you have a good breakfast?" he asked.

"I did," I lied.

"Sometimes that's all it takes," he said, turning back around, and I studied his hair-cape some more, its weird, warm flip.

The foster home we pulled up to was in a working-class subdivision. The foster family's name was McKowen, and on their garage was a big letter *M* in bright green plastic.

"Are you ready to scootch?" Edward asked Sarah.

"I so am," she said.

Edward twisted back toward me. "That's Sarah's idea of the quintessential mom word: *scootch*. Scootch over. Scootch in. Everybody's gotta scootch and the moms are the scootch directors."

"That's right," said Sarah.

"I can kind of see that," I said, sounding doubtful rather than agreeable as I'd intended. Sarah turned the car off, checked her reflection quickly in the rearview mirror, scrutinizing her teeth in case they were dotted like dice with the scorched remnants of breakfast, then opened her door. The driveway was shoveled, and we all scootched out. The slam of our doors all in a row made me think of a squad car pulling up and the cops hopping out and going cautiously for their guns. Sarah was first to the porch, eager and businessy, and rang the bell. Edward and I were still trailing behind her like the rookies. She was already standing with the storm door propped open against her shoulder. She was loosening her scarf. When the white wooden door of the McKowens' opened, she removed her hat, which had pom-poms on its ties. She quickly, unnecessarily poofed up her hair. "Hi, I'm Sarah Brink," she said, and thrust out her hand. "We're here to see the baby?"

The woman who answered the door was large and blond and seemed to have a bit of a limp as if one hip were stiff, though all she was doing to suggest this was shifting her weight in the doorway. "Nobody told us anyone was coming," she said tersely.

"Roberta Marshall said she made the appointment," said Sarah as we pulled up behind her.

"Who's that?"

"She's with Adoption Option?"

"No, we're a foster family for Catholic Social Services, and no one has called us about this at all."

"Oh, dear." Sarah turned and looked at Edward, her eyes welling a little. I was getting this strange kidnapper feeling and wanted either to run for it, clear to Canada, or to bust in there and grab somebody. I hadn't eaten breakfast, and I had to calm my mind.

Everyone stood there breathing and no one knew what to do at all. The woman in the doorway was studying us closely. I wondered what we looked like to her. Overeducated, well-preserved liberal types from Troy with their college-age daughter. Or some kinky ménage à trois. Also from Troy. To the rest of the state, Troy was the city from which all kink and pretentious evil sprang. I often thought of it that way myself.

The woman at the door, Mrs. McKowen, sighed, as if defeated. "I don't know why they call them organizations. They are all just a mess." She widened the aperture between door and doorjamb. "Well, you're here, so you might as well come on in and see Mary."

"Mary?" Sarah hadn't bothered asking about a name—she clearly had her own name picked out and Mary wasn't it.

"The little girl. You do want to see her, don't you?"

"Oh, of course. This is my husband, Edward," Sarah said hurriedly, "and our friend Tassie." I nodded at Mrs. McKowen and she squinted at me a little, clearly wondering who the hell I could be.

We walked into a living room with yellow walls, a green rug, and a brown plaid couch. The television was blaring morning TV. Brightly colored plastic blocks and inexpensive cloth animals, fuzzy and fresh—a caterpillar and a bumblebee—were scattered on the floor. There was a teenage girl hovering in the back doorway to the unlit kitchen, and she just watched us without saying anything. The baby Mary was dressed in a pale mint green onepiecer, the feet of which had been cut off so she could fit into it. She was too big for such clothing. She was not really a baby at all but looked almost two, yet she was still in a wheeled plastic walker, which was placed in front of the television, which she was watching. Just some crap talk show, it looked like to me—"So you left him because he wouldn't take his Zoloft?" a well-coiffed woman was asking another on the TV screen—not even a program for children. Mrs. McKowen came in and flicked it off. "Mary, look, you've got some visitors!" The little girl turned in her conveyance and gave us a full-lipped smile. Her teeth were tiny white shells. She had silky dark hair, skin that was a mix of biscuit and taupe, and eyes that were black and bright: she looked like a savvy Indian rug merchant. She flung her arms in the air to be lifted. The walker she treated sort of like a little office. And now she wanted out.

"Hey, baby," said Sarah, picking Mary up, but the child's feet were caught in the walker's canvas leg holes and the whole contraption lifted as well, a little disastrously, and Sarah could not untangle Mary's feet, and Mary began to cry.

"Oh, dear, that thing is caught on her," said Sarah. I stepped forward to help, and to his credit Edward did, too, and we pulled the walker off the child, but by this point Mary was crying for Mrs. McKowen and wriggling in Sarah's arms, trying to get away.

"Oh, Mary, come here, child," said Mrs. McKowen, and she took Mary from Sarah and comforted her. Mrs. McKowen looked back at Sarah drily. "Do you have experience with children?"

"She's a little old for that thing," Sarah said, trying not to sound flummoxed.

"Why don't you all have a seat?" said Mrs. McKowen, and we quickly did. The teenage girl in the shadows remained there. Sarah was next to Mrs. McKowen, who sat the now calm Mary in her lap. Edward sat in a chair near the TV. I noticed that he miscalculated social distances, and it was an impediment to his charm. He was either too close or too far away. Eighteen inches, I read once, was exactly the right distance, but he seemed never there, even metaphorically. Now he was mostly far and still.

"Do you want to say hi to your visitors?" said Mrs. McKowen to the toddler. "You want to go to your new mama?"

"Mama?" said the little girl, and she twisted around toward the teenager still hanging back in the shadows. This sudden attention caused the teenager to disappear entirely. And that's when it became clear that the teenage girl was the one raising this child. Mrs. McKowen was taking in the support money, and the teenager, who perhaps had no life beyond this faux motherhood, was about to have her heart broken in a new and different way for teenagers. "Mama?" cried Mary again, looking in the direction of the dark kitchen. I guessed that the girl had secretly, quietly encouraged Mary to call her "Mama."

"Hey, baby?" began Sarah, ingratiatingly, and the little girl looked at Sarah.

Thus began their tentative approaches toward each other. Each was playful and affectionate. Sarah scooched closer and made her fingers crawl like a spider up the little girl's arm. The little girl smiled and hunched her shoulders up by her ears and said, "Neck," indicating that she both did and didn't want to be tickled there, so Sarah both did and didn't, getting the mix just right. And soon Mary was on Sarah's lap and playing with her watch and touching her opal earrings and Sarah was making the goofy sounds and talking in the high-pitched agitated and ingratiating voice that adults around babies did naturally if ridiculously because look, see, it worked.

The hovering teenage girl in the doorway seemed to step backwards, into an actual engulfing shadow or perhaps a china closet. This seemed to loosen the tongue of Mrs. McKowen, who began to exhibit that midwesternism of tone that was the opposite of what was typically aimed for even in a city like Troy, where friendly things—*Hello, Can I help you?*—were said with acerbity and anger in the cadence. Here, as in the country where I grew up, very provocative things were said with an innocuous lilt. Tone was all. Gift wrap was all. Perfect the wrap, and you could put whatever you wanted in the box. You could put firecrackers. You could put dog shit.

"So," said Mrs. McKowen, "have you met the birth mother?"

"Yes," said Sarah.

"And you're sure you want that woman's child?"

Edward began to cough. "Excuse me—is there a bathroom I might use?"

"Why do you say that about the birth mom?" asked Sarah.

"Oh, I don't know," said Mrs. McKowen. "I guess, well, the lady's not the sharpest tool in the shed.

"Washroom's around the corner," she said to Edward.

Edward got up, turned the corner, and abandoned us.

"She wants to go back to school," said Sarah.

"Sikhool," repeated Mary.

"Yes, school," cooed Sarah.

"Yes, school," said Mrs. McKowen, sighing. "She's always talking about that."

"You see her often?"

"Well, it's a requirement of Catholic Social Services that she come here to visit the child once a month. Creates an opportunity for bonding, which they don't want to be accused of having deprived her of. Also an opportunity for change of heart. Which I don't see coming about in any complete way." She paused. "You believe her story about the rape?"

"What rape?"

"Lynette?" called Mrs. McKowen, and her loud voice caused the toddler to burst into tears. "Could you come feed Mary? It's getting to be on towards lunch."

The teenage girl stepped out from the shadows and toward the baby, who burst into a watery smile at the sight of her.

"Lynette, this is Sarah and . . . her people," she said with a vague wave toward me and toward Edward, who had just returned from his quick pee.

"Hi," said Lynette, and she picked the baby up and away from Sarah, settling her easily on her blue-jeaned hip, then took her out of the room. That was that.

"She didn't tell you she was raped?" said Mrs. McKowen. Now that the baby was gone there was a certain force in the question.

"No," said Sarah.

"Hmm," said Mrs. McKowen.

"Maybe she wasn't."

"Maybe not."

"Maybe she just wanted an excuse for what she was doing."

"Maybe. Don't see how that works, though," said Mrs. McKowen, who then said no more, and soon she stood, walked to the door, and opened it.

We left, looking for lunch.

"Let's see, where shall we go? It's early, so we should miss the crowds." Sarah turned on the car radio. The radio was on some sort of soul station and was playing a rap song with extreme female moaning in the background. "You gotta do it, roll it, run it, up it, down it. Gotta do it, roll it, run it, rock it . . ."—a conjugation of every sort. Edward flicked the radio off disdainfully. But Sarah turned it back on. "Sex is the only good thing the world has given them. At least listen to it."

I could see she was getting ready to enter a new understanding of society. It would be artificial and touristic. It would be motherhood in a safari suit. But how not? It was better than some. Probably it was better than most.

We found a metal-edged diner, went in, and sat at the counter side by side, letting our coats fall off our shoulders and dangle from the stools, anchored by our sitting butts. The counter had been freshly wiped with some piney disinfectant and right where we sat there was an old red Coca-Cola dispenser that resembled the outboard motor of a boat. I sat between Sarah and Edward, like a child. This they seemed to like, but it made it hard for me to have any appetite at all. I could not eat, as if eating were the most inappropriate and irrelevant and perhaps even revolting thing we could be doing right then. At one point I turned too quickly and the wrist edge of my sweater sleeve knocked some french fries to the floor. When I was younger I could get away with not eating something I didn't like by claiming to my parents either that it was too rich or that it had fallen on the floor. (Later I would use this with people: "She was too rich" or "He fell on the floor—what is there to say?") And here I was now suddenly verklempt by my indifference to food. I was floating away from myself. My breath would go musty and sour if I did not eat, so I tried. I ordered a vanilla milk shake and sucked it down. Edward and Sarah would occasionally reach across me to touch each other—a hand on a thigh, or upper arm, or shoulder—and then retreat into their separate and separating spaces. Everyone was quiet, though I wasn't sure why.

We returned to the hotel, headed to our respective rooms. I noticed that when older people got tired they looked a lot older, whereas when young people got tired they just looked tired. Sarah and Edward looked a little aged; our early lunch had not refreshed them and some worry had knotted their mouths and generally dragged their features downward. They were waiting for a phone call, they said, and they would call me after they got it.

"OK," I said, and crawled back into my room and into my bed with my clothes on. I'd brought only one book, the Zen poems, and was finding their obliqueness fatiguing and ripe for parody. I decided instead to investigate the official Judeo-Christian comedy, and pulled the Gideon Bible from the nightstand drawer. I started at the beginning, day one, when God created the heavens and the earth and gave them form. There'd been no form before. Just amorphous blobbery. God then said let there be light, in order to get a little dynamic going between night and day, though the moon and stars and sun were not the generators of this light but merely a kind of middle management, supervisors, glorified custodians, since they were not created until later—day four—as can happen with bureaucracy, even of the cosmic sort. Still, I thought of all the songs that had been written about these belated moon and stars and sun, compared to songs about form. Not one good song about form! Sometimes a week just got more inspiring as it went along. Still, it was truly strange that there was morning and night on day one though the sun wasn't created until day four. Perhaps God didn't have a proofreader until, like, day forty-seven, but by that time all sorts of weird things were happening. Perhaps he was really, completely on his own until then, making stuff up and then immediately forgetting what he'd made up already. People were dying and coming back and having babies and then not able to, so their handmaidens would instead. Then I slid into the nap I knew the lunchtime milk shake would bring on if I just let it.

I awoke to a faint knocking on the door.

"Tassie? It's Sarah. We're going to go to the hospital for the baby's checkup. Do you want to come?"

"Yes, I'm coming," I said, then hurried to the door to open it, but it slammed into the brass slide lock through which I peered, dazed, as if through bars, at a slim slice of Sarah.

My nap had not effectively rebooted me. Sarah was wearing

her winter coat, but I could still see she was shrugging beneath it. "The agency is switching foster families and they have an appointment this afternoon at the hospital for our little girl." She was also wearing that hand-knitted hat with the ear flaps and pom-pom ties. Were these back in style? Had they ever been in style?

I had to close the door on her completely in order to undo the lock and open it again, this time wide. "Let me get my shoes on," I said.

"This was supposed to be the Presidential Suite," she said, gazing into the room at the holes in the wall.

"Well, even presidents get shot," I said.

"I was just going to say that myself," she said, smiling. "But I didn't want to scare you."

I didn't know whether this was interesting—that we were both thinking the same gruesome thing—or even whether it was actually the case. Perhaps it was just rhetorical ESP: Kreskin's Guide to Etiquette. But even if it was true, that we were about to say the same thing, did this connect us in some deep, private way? Or was it just a random obviousness shared between strangers? The deeper life between two people I had yet to read with confidence. It seemed a kind of vaporous text that kept revising its very alphabet. *An exfoliating narrative*, my professors would probably say. *The paratext of the possible.*

"Sorry this is so beat up," she added.

"It's OK."

"Our bedspread is even more lurid than yours," she confided. "Maybe hunters come here in hunting season. We're in the Packer Suite, which is green and gold with footballs on the wallpaper. I kept thinking they were walnuts. The balls, I mean. Edward had to clarify."

"Ha! Well, at least the water pressure's good!"

"Yes, well, we'll wait for you in the car out front," said Sarah, turning to go. Was she trying to keep some irritation out of her voice? Of course! Once again I realized I wasn't really supposed to go with them to this, but I had forgotten and in my sleepiness had said yes.

In the car they made small talk about the carseat they had just purchased at Sears. It was next to me in the back, still with some plastic around it. "It looks safe," I said blithely.

"They make them better now," said Sarah. "The kids are more securely locked in. Kids used to be able to leap out in no time."

In the hospital lobby, a new transitional foster care person was carrying baby Mary, who was now sporting a hat and had been bundled into a pale blue snowsuit that was perhaps institutionally owned and intended for boys. "Hi, I'm Julie," said the woman. "I'm a foster parent for Adoption Option. I just fetched Mary here from the CSS foster home—there was a little bit of a scene at the door." She loosened her hand just slightly from Mary and flapped it toward Sarah like a seal flipper.

"Oh, really," said Sarah, shaking her hand. "I'm Sarah."

"Yes, I know. And you must be Edward and you must be Tassie." She gave us each a nod, still hanging on to Mary.

"A scene?" asked Edward, not letting this go.

"Well, the birth mother had made her decision—she was switching agencies—but this foster family was a little upset. They were reluctant to let the child go, and the changeover, I'm afraid, was a bit dramatic."

"Really?" Sarah looked worried. "What happened?"

"Oh, I'll spare you." Julie sighed and touched the little girl's nose, making her smile. She turned back to Sarah, hesitating. "You met their teenage daughter, Lynette?"

"Yes."

"Enough said," said Julie. "Wanna hold your child?"

"Let me see if she'll come to me," said Sarah. She reached toward the little girl and said, "Come here, baby." The little girl went with her calmly, and Sarah settled her happily on her canted hip.

An elderly African-American woman came walking by and she looked at all of us, but especially at Sarah holding Mary. "Is that your child?" she asked Sarah doubtfully.

"Yes, she is," said Sarah, smiling in a dazed way as if she had just been smacked gleefully in the head.

The older woman stopped and looked at Mary, then Sarah. "Well, that's the most beautiful child I've ever seen," she said, and then moved·on.

Edward turned to Julie, and said, "That woman was hired by Adoption Option."

Julie laughed. "I doubt it."

"You don't think the agency might be worried because there's a dearth of white babies and they need some added promo?"

"Edward," chided Sarah, but she was beaming, and now so was Mary.

Dearth.

Mary *was* spectacularly pretty. I was only just now noticing it. Perhaps the blast of outdoor air had freshened her face, or the light blue of her snowsuit flattered her coloring—who could say. She was a beautiful thing. Her smile was impish but sweet, and her deep dark eyes had presence and considerable intelligence peering out beneath her flannel hat. She was a watchful child, and despite all the upheaval she had the aura of a deeply loved one. Still, there was something in that light blue alone that showed her off to advantage. The color looked like a different color on her— one that all the little girls of the world would want and snatch away from the boys if they could see it this way, this aqua of the angels. One of the few times I'd ordered clothing from a catalog— with my mother's MasterCard—I'd ordered all the items the black models were wearing. The color of the fabrics—oranges, greens, turquoise, and ivory—looked so good against the models' skin, but when they arrived and I put them on *me,* they looked like crap. My own skin, with its splotches of pale red and blue, made me a queer shade of lavender. I looked like a dead thing placed inside a living. So whenever I heard the word *dearth,* a word that sounded like a cross between death and birth, a miscarriage perhaps, or the sleeping car in a train wreck, this made-up color—the lilac of lifelessness—was the thing that leaped to mind.

"Baby Mary?" said a receptionist carrying a large file, and Julie pointed to Sarah. "That's us," she said.

The receptionist smiled at Mary and chucked her cheek. "Looks like she's been eating a lot of squash and carrots!" she said merrily.

It was the beginning of a long stretch of thinking I was hearing things.

"She's biracial African-American," said Julie.

"Oh! Well. I've got the birth mother's file here, too, which you are allowed to look at. The last name, of course, has been whited out for her privacy."

"Yes—Edward? You want to stay out here and look at the file? You're the scientist. Julie and I will go in with the baby."

"Sure," he said.

That left me in the lobby with Edward. At last I had stayed behind—but with Edward and the thick medical history of the birth mother. I sat next to him on an orange leatherette sofa as he patted the file and looked at me. "Shall we see what it has to tell us?" He was looking through me; some other thought had erased me, and he soon pulled his gaze back entirely.

"I guess," I said. He turned his attention to the file. He had assumed the brusque amiability of someone used to having assistants.

It seemed an utter invasion of privacy looking at all these descriptions of personal and bodily matters, but on all the pages of the medical records Bonnie's name was whited out. Sometimes the entirety of it, sometimes just the last name. The afflictions that ran in the family were heart disease, bipolar disorder (the suicide of an uncle), acne, and curvature of the spine. For the patient herself there were many pages of influenzas, psoriasis, depression, anxiety disorder, shingles, herpes, high blood pressure, and at the end pregnancy resolved with a caesarean. There had been some drinking at the beginning of the pregnancy, a six-pack or two here and there. Edward stared at that page, reading. "Catholics will confess," he said to me without looking up, and then turned the page. I was trying to match up all this medical history with the large, stiff, overplucked Bonnie that I had met. On one of the pages—a sonogram page that a radiologist had attached to another report—someone had not noticed the patient's name and so had neglected to white it out: *Bonnie Jankling Crowe.*

"Oops," said Edward, noticing as well but not pointing to it, though he didn't have to. Now we would both know forever. "Let's not tell Sarah," said Edward. "She's got a slightly obsessive side."

"Oh, OK," I said. And so I entered a small conspiracy with him. I no longer knew anymore what I was consenting to when I said whatever I found myself saying. Yet it didn't seem to matter.

Edward now decided to close up the file. "Nobody's perfect. Everyone has a relative or two that's come down with some crud or stuck a fork in someone's eye or dynamited a perfectly good shed."

This astounded me. "Absolutely," I said.

He stood and tucked it under his arm as if he were already regretting having shared it with me, and then he walked across the lobby and got a drink of water. I watched his figure stooped over the bubbler—his longish hair fell forward into his face. He was still wearing his coat, but it was open and dangled like collapsed cloth wings. Turning, and sweeping his hair back with one hand, he came back to sit on the orange sofa but sat farther away from me, turned to smile quickly and perfunctorily, then resumed a kind of staring out into the space of the room, one elbow propped broodingly on the sofa arm, his hand positioned across his own mouth, as we waited for Sarah to return. At one point he turned to me and said, "One shouldn't buy babies, of course. As a society we all agree. And mothers shouldn't sell them. But that is what we keep telling ourselves as these middlemen get richer and richer and the birth mother continues to empty bedpans while wearing her new wristwatch." He paused. "They're only allowed to receive tokens, like a watch. Nothing real, like a car. The nothing-but-a-watch law is considered progressive, since babies must not be sold, or exchanged for cars. And so they are exchanged for watches."

"It's all morally confusing, isn't it," I ventured.

"It sure is," he said.

Sarah came out smiling, holding baby Mary, who was now clutching her and snuffling back tears. Julie trailed behind them. "They had to take blood from her foot for an AIDS test. She's really too old for that not to hurt."

"And she's too young to have AIDS—unless the mother has it. Why don't they test the mother?" Edward was suddenly into the various offenses involved in all these procedures.

Julie shrugged. "You can't do it that way. State law."

There were a lot of laws. We were not allowed to bring the medical records out of the hospital, so Edward returned the file to the receptionist's desk. We could not just leave with the baby. We had to leave with Julie, too, and go back first to Adoption Option and sign papers. In the parking lot Julie said, "Wait a minute, let me get something from my car," and while she trotted to her car Sarah said quietly to Edward, "Anything in the medical records we should worry about?"

"Not really," he replied.

"Not really?"

"No," he repeated with emphasis. "It's no different really from anyone else's history."

"No different really?"

"Don't pounce on my adverbs," said Edward. "No. Honestly."

"You just stepped on my toe."

"What?

"You just rammed into me a little and stepped on my toe."

"Sorry. I'm sure our car rental agreement covers it."

"Yeah," said Sarah, sighing. "Darling, remember when we murdered someone and American Express took care of everything?"

That same joke! But Edward wasn't smiling. A shadow passed between them. A sepia tinge came over Sarah's eyes. A horse-drawn sled jingled its harness bells off in the distance: this town would turn winter into a holiday if it killed them. "The family that sleighs together stays together," Sarah murmured to me. Or, that is what I thought I heard, though there was no levity in her voice. She took one hand briefly away from Mary to squeeze mine in reassurance. Or in promise. Or in regret. Or in happy hope. Or else in some secret pact that involved a little bit of everything.

Julie came back bearing a white plastic trash bag, which she jammed into the backseat with me, Sarah, and baby Mary. She got in the front, with Edward, and came with us, as she technically, as of the moment, was the custodial parent.

Edward was fussing with the heater. "A car that controlled the outside weather as well—now, that would be climate control," he was saying.

"Hey, baby," Sarah kept murmuring. "Hey, baby, baby." She turned to me and in a stage whisper said, "You know at my age, your estrogen starts dwindling and you cannot speak to anyone in a civil voice. But then a baby comes along and look how one speaks."

"The legal fee is billed into the total, but you'll receive a separate receipt for that in the mail." Roberta, too, looked with surprise at the separate checkbooks. "The payment for foster care is also included."

Sarah was directing Edward: "Nine thousand one hundred twenty-seven and fifty cents," she said quietly, but it might as well have been shouted from the rooftop.

"Does Bonnie get nothing?" asked Edward.

"You can get her a watch," said Roberta. "No money. That's illegal in this state."

Sarah put her hand on Edward's arm. "We'll get her a really nice watch," she said.

I peered inside the plastic trash bag. It was amazing to me that you could still be the tiniest thing and *have stuff*. On the other hand, it also amazed me that there was so little of it, and so it seemed sad that a human being was going through the world accumulating all this needless crap and yet also pathetic that this was all she had. She herself neither knew nor cared, I was sure. Inside the bag there was a stuffed yellow caterpillar, a green blanket, some plastic blocks with letters on them, a cardboard animal alphabet puzzle, a stuffed monkey in a little denim leisure suit.

"Congratulations," said Roberta. "You have yourself a beautiful baby."

"And no *drugs*," added Suzanne in a kind of happy hiss. "That's excellent."

In the rental car on the way home back to Troy, Sarah sat vigilantly in the back next to Mary-Emma, who was soundly asleep in the carseat Edward and Sarah had purchased at Sears, along with clothes, during my nap. "Well, we've done it," said Edward. "The future's going to be a little different now. We've now got a horse in the race."

There was a long pause, our tires hitting the gray slosh of the road. For driving, a January thaw was always preferable to actual ice, but when it was over things froze more treacherously than before. And in its melting and condensing the roadside snow turned to clumps reminiscent of black-spotted cauliflower. Better never to have thawed. "I once went to the track," mused Sarah. "I was eleven and I went with my uncle, who came with all these statistics on the horses—a stack of papers the size of a phone book. He was poring over them, figuring out which horse to bet on, and I said, 'Uncle Joe, look, there's a horse named Laredo and I have a dog named Laredo.' And my uncle just looked at me and put his papers away and said, 'OK, let's bet on that one.' And so we did."

"Did it win?" I asked from the front seat. Edward seemed already to know this story. He continued along the bleak winter road. What was it—was it Doppler radar?—that involved the difference in pitch between the leading end and the trailing end of the reverberation? I had taken a physics course last year with a short unit on sonar.

"Did it win?" I squeaked out again into the sharp silence of the car—but no one said anything. Edward was a scientist and so was used to heading straight into the unanswering darkness with his climate-controlled car. Snow began to fall. Large snowflakes in a lazy swirl, the flutter of ballerinas down a spiral staircase—a classic snowfall, one for the movies, one to bag and sell. For driving, however, it was a scary fairyland. Still, it was hypnotic to watch, and soon a great fatigue came over me, and after some time I thought I heard Edward say something and then Sarah's voice say very quietly, "Well, all sex is a form of rape. One could argue." And then she added, "Please, in this weather, don't drive with one hand." I looked out the window and saw a white convertible sailing past us with the bumper sticker GUILT SUCKS: HAVE SOME FUN! The driver was a little white-haired lady hunched scowlingly over the wheel. "Did you hear me?" asked Sarah, and

Edward's middle-aged face turned slightly, tensed with an adolescent's wordless hate. He appeared to continue to steer with his right hand lightly holding the bottom of the steering wheel, his other hand shoved defiantly and absurdly in his pocket. At Sarah's request I turned on the radio, which filled the car with a soft murmur. "How many teams with a dome for their home field have won the Super Bowl?" it was saying. "And now here is Luigi Boccherini's 'Festival in C'!" We passed through the marshland village of Luck, whose municipal welcome sign read YOU'RE IN LUCK. And though on leaving I spied no sign saying NOW OUT OF LUCK, every aspect of it soon was implied. Edward had taken a wrong turn, and we had to turn around and go back through the town. YOU'RE IN LUCK another sign again said, and I imagined a horror movie wherein we never found our way out of this town, and kept driving back into it again, its greeting a maddening taunt.

Eventually, I must have fallen asleep, and when I awoke there was an achy pinch in my neck. The car engine was off and we were in front of Edward and Sarah's house. "It's good to come in the front door with a new baby," Sarah was saying to Edward. "There's a superstition about bringing a baby in the back. Plus, it's politically incorrect."

"There's not a soul around," said Edward. I looked at my watch: midnight. I was feeling like a sleepwalker, needed at this point only for whatever I could help carry into the house from the car, and so I found myself lugging Mary-Emma's plastic trash bag of cheap plush toys as well as a grocery bag of miscellaneous snacks for the car, which had neglected to announce themselves—Ritz crackers, Nutri-Grain bars, a plastic six-pack of flavored water—and so were entirely unopened. The carseat Mary-Emma was in was a newfangled double one, with an interior upright seat set within another, and so the insert could be lifted out with Mary-Emma still in it. Edward managed the awkward weight of this with just a little tug, and Mary-Emma stirred only slightly while Sarah clawed in her bag for the house keys. We pushed in past the gate, Edward fussing with the broken hinge, and stepped carefully down the steps then back up the porch stairs to the front door. Everything in this January night possessed a lunar stillness and a lunar thrill. You could see the earth from here!

Inside the house Sarah headed for the dining room, turning on two small lamps as she went. Edward placed the sleeping Mary-Emma on the table, still in her seat, her snowsuited legs and arms dangling off, her chin sunk into her collar. She'd had a big day, whether she knew it or not.

"Well," said Sarah, looking at her.

"Yes, well," said Edward.

Sarah was still wearing her yarn cap with the earflaps and the dangling pom-pom ties, and she took the right pom-pom and tossed it around her head like a tether ball. It made a muffled cable-knit thwack against her head. "Now what?" she said.

We all might have burst into hysterical laughter, and we probably would have if a sleeping child weren't propped in the middle of the dining room table, next to two candlesticks, a Stengel sugar bowl, and some salt and pepper shakers. Adoption, I could see, was a lot like childbirth: *Here she is!* everyone exclaimed. And you looked and saw a pickled piglet and felt nothing, not realizing it would be the only time you would ever feel nothing again. A baby destroyed a life and thereby became the very best thing in it. Though to sit gloriously and triumphantly in ruins may not be such a big trick.

"Well, I should take Tassie home, is what," said Edward.

"And leave me here all alone?" Sarah said in mock terror, still in her goofy hat. "You must be joking." She clutched his sleeve.

"*You* must be joking," said Edward.

"I am. I'm joking," said Sarah.

Sort of, I thought. And then she said it herself.

"Sort of." She smiled. There was a flash of mutual disgust between them.

Then Edward drove me back to my apartment. "Thank you for helping us on this very complex mission."

"You're very welcome," I said. What else was there to say?

"We'll see you in a couple of days. I'm sure Sarah will phone very soon."

"Sounds good," I sang out into the dark of the car. *Sounds good,* that same midwestern girl's slightly frightened reply. It appeared to clinch a deal, and was meant to sound the same as the more soldierly *Good to go,* except it was promiseless—mere affirmative description. It got you away, out the door. Once again.

IV

Classes did not start until the following week. But nonetheless I could feel the semester winding itself up as if with the hand crank of a Gatling gun, readying itself for unleashing. The spring semester! It was both aptly and inaptly named. Since it had not yet officially begun, I slept until noon, then woke and made a sad little breakfast of poor man's baklava: a large biscuit of shredded wheat with honey poured over and chopped peanuts sprinkled on top. The kitchen was still in its state of neglect. More strawberries in the refrigerator, which it seemed I had only just bought, had once again withered, turned this time the turquoise-gray of a copper roof. The bread, too, had a powdery blue mold that would have made a lovely eyeshadow for a showgirl—perhaps one who also needed the penicillin. The heel end of another loaf, weeks old, was sitting on the counter in a plastic bag with what looked like a snake inside: a coil of mold with orange and black markings. It was the Frugal Girls' Museum of Modern Art.

The landlord had returned to not stinting too badly on the heat. Happiness. In the mail a check came from Sarah for three hundred dollars—it seemed both too much and too little, but I did not actually bother to calculate the hours and what the pay should have come to. I went to the bank and deposited the check and took back a hundred of it in twenties to spend on new books and food. I sat in my apartment with the most inane sorts of magazines, all left there by Murph, which I read with an avidity and dementia typically brought on by hair salons and winter.

"Four Things Men Find Hot." I could never find all four—they were seldom listed numerically or in a conspicuous place. Once you had the magazine open, you had to dig around among the ads (which was their ploy), trying to find them scattered there, and even when you did they were always in slight disguise. Clearly no one at any of these magazines knew for sure what men found hot, though they were hoping you would believe they did. Or maybe everyone at these New York City magazines knew only gay men, and so the things they knew that men found hot they were afraid to actually tell their readers.

Surprise seemed a theme.

As did things with food.

As for the clothing depicted in these pages, I was at a bored loss. It seemed uncool to spend that much money to look like an experimental cake. What would be cool was something different: more murderous, and not depictable. From what I could see, the best look would involve not just something new, but something with insouciant jewelry and ominous leather goods denouncing something old that lay deep within yourself and others. Probably I would never accomplish this. Without explicit instruction I had no feel or instinct, at least not for the new part. I felt, however, that if called upon, I could do the other part—denunciation— but privately. Privately part cool, since I partook of denouncing (silently, violently) all the time.

For several days I let drift take over me. I turned on my computer and aimlessly roamed the Internet. I would click this and then that and pretty soon I was looking at stock car racing or Demi Moore's bare pre-op breasts. A billion ads for herbal remedies and computer security systems flew onto the screen. I took on-screen Oscar quizzes. I googled old friends from elementary school. Nothing. I googled Lynette McKowen. Nothing. I googled Bonnie Jankling Crowe, whose full name I now knew— illegally. Nothing again. I went back to Demi Moore's bare pre-op breasts and wondered about the half-life of regret.

When I went to bed at night I suffered my first bout of insomnia. This is what death would be like, I feared: not sleep but insomnia. To sleep no more, as I had learned in Pre-1700 British Drama. I had never feared insomnia before—like prison, wouldn't it just give you more time to read? I'd always been able to sleep. But now I lay there, fretful as a Bartók quartet. My mind wandered through the night hours uneasily, and it was indeed like prison: when the sky began to lighten, I was in disbelief and filled with terrible, buzzing tiredness.

Once I woke with the feeling that I had actually died in the night. I awoke with a sense that during ostensible sleep I had encountered not just life's brevity but its *speed!* and its noise and its irrelevance and its close. How we glamorized our lives! our bodies! which were nothing more than—potatoes! with a potato's flat eyes and pale pink snappable roots. I lay there in bed in a peaceful form of depression. In another town, one less antagonistic toward religion, this mood—pre-prayer, pre-God, pre-conversion—might have been assigned some spiritual significance. But for people in Troy, God was mind-clutter: a cross between a billboard, a charlatan, a hamburger, and a fairy king. I had always thought God was part of a sensible if credulous denial of death, one that made life doable. How could that be wicked? Why bother criticizing that? Why disparage the crutches of the lame? Why vainly imagine one's own gait unhobbled? Besides, religion gave us swearing. Before Christianity, what was there? "By Jove"? But life in Troy was to be taken without any lucky charms of any sort. It was neo-reformation. The walls of my winter room seemed a silvery, quilted satin, like the interior of a coffin. I began to feel there was no such thing as wisdom. Only lack of wisdom.

Finally, Sarah phoned. "Tassie, how are you—it's been days!"

"Days and nights," I said stupidly.

"I'll say," she said. "Poor Emmie sobbed for two nights. She'd wake up at three in the morning and just cry and cry, poor thing.

She would look out into the dark of her new room and just not know where she was. I would just take her and rock her back to sleep. But now I think she does understand and she seems to have settled right in. I am wondering whether you are free this afternoon? It's time for me to check back in on my maniac restaurant and see how it's doing."

"Is Emmie her name now?" This seemed strange.

Sarah paused. "Well, we found ourselves using her initials right away—M.E.—and before we knew it, well, there we were with Emmie. It suits her, I think."

"Does she still respond to Mary?" I asked, having no common sense.

"Well, I don't really know," said Sarah.

I did not mind the walk to their house. I walked briskly for the first time in days. The stadium in its arc was like a frozen tidal wave outside my apartment. The cold knocked the sleepiness from my head as well as my days-long, tortured hallucination of deep existential vision. The sky was partly clear, with ballooning clouds floating absurdly above, as if for a party that had yet to begin. Low on the horizon there were different clouds, like old plowed snow at the end of a street. I was like every kid who had grown up in the country, allowing the weather—good or bad—to describe life for me: its mocking, its magic, its contradictions, its moody grip. Why not? One was helpless before everything.

In the front of the house the gate at the stairs was still broken. I slipped through and on up to the porch. When I rang the doorbell no one came, and so I knocked with my knuckles on the glass pane of the thick wood door. Sarah opened it dressed in the Madame Curie look I soon learned she favored: a white lab-style coat and black tights. Her matte red lipstick lent a kind of movie version air of Madame: hard crimson elegance in the riverbed cracks of her lips. She didn't want to look like the other chefs in town, with their country-hippie garb, scarves, and flowery print shirts. A restaurant was a science, she would tell me, not a square dance. Perhaps that was where she got it wrong.

"Here, come try this," she said, leading me into the kitchen. The appliances there were of the mammoth stainless steel variety that one did not yet see in Dellacrosse except in the back rooms of feed stores and supermarkets. The cold gray metal of the stove and refrigerator I knew was supposed to be chic, but I preferred the old avocado green of home (not yet a song). On the gleaming stove was a skillet of a paler metal, like white gold. In it were some silvered leaves. She picked one out with her fingers and presented it. I placed it in my mouth, where it seemed to melt slightly and then not, hanging on with a woody toughness. The flavors were a mix of candy store and forest.

"What is it?" I asked, still chewing.

"Carmelized sage." She looked at me hopefully.

"Awesome," I said, and meant the word in its every meaning.

Sarah beamed. "There's a direct path between earth and heaven, and that is caramel," she said. "Add a few grains of hand-raked Norman sea salt—and voilà!"

So this is what Americans were busying themselves with in Normandy now that it had been liberated from the Nazis: hand-raking the sea salt. Soldiers' tears shipped thousands of miles and sprinkled on a fried leaf. Look D-Day in the eye and tell it that!

"Delicious. Am I the first customer?"

"You are," she said. "I hope you don't mind."

"Mind?—"

"Oops—and I forgot about these." She opened the oven and with a terry-cloth potholder took out a couple of picture books. "These are from the library. I baked them to get rid of the germs. I always do that with library books. I'm told you can microwave the germs out, but I don't completely trust that."

tions on the counter. And you'll need to be watchful with that baby gate upstairs. I don't want her tumbling down. Or *you* tumbling up!" Then she paused. *We stand there blank as walls.* "Baby-gate! Now there's a scandal. You're so young, I'll bet you don't even know how the word *gate* came to mean *disgrace*."

"Watergate," I said, though I wasn't positive.

"Well, that's right! Though that was well before you were born."

"A lot of interesting things were."

"Yes. Well. Oh! Besides the plating we did have one good thing last night: a winter minestrone made with heirloom beans and your father's fingerlings. A big hit."

I smiled agreeably, but I couldn't imagine those potatoes sitting in soup. As if she could read my mind, Sarah said, "We sliced them. Right at their bumpy little knuckles."

It was a brutal thing, food.

"Everyone loved it. Oh, before I forget," she added. "There's ipecac in the cupboard next to the sink. I'm not even sure how you use it—it's for situations where poison is swallowed. A woman down the street said, 'You're adopting?' And I said, 'Yeah, what do I need?' And she said, 'Ipecac.' And I said, 'That's it?' and she said, 'That's all I know.' So now that's all *I* know." Here Sarah looked at me mischievously, her look a complicated room one might wander through, exploring for quite some time if there were any time. "If anything goes wrong, whatever the hell you do, don't phone *me*. I've left a number for emergencies. It's 911." She smiled.

"I'll dial the paramedics directly," I said, smiling in return.

"Thatta girl. Sorry I have to rush. They are burning the herbal holiday centerpieces as I speak and smoking fish over them." She hurried out the back door.

I could hear her car start up and drive away. But then suddenly she was back—the car, the clamber up the stairs, the bursting return through the back door. "I forgot something," she said, and stepped over to the counter, opened a drawer, and grabbed a kitchen knife, which she stuck gleefully in her leather bag. "A concealed weapon, or a chef's tool? Who can say? Already, driving around in winter with a shovel in my car makes me feel like a serial killer." Then she flew off again.

The instructions, typed and printed out from a computer, were slid into a book entitled *Your Baby and Child.* I took them both into the living room, where I sat on one of the pillow-ticking sofas, flipping through the pages of the book first. I looked at the chapter "Older Babies" and noted boldfaced headings such as "Beware of lightweight carriages" and "Don't try to keep your baby clean." I would have gotten both these things wrong. *Treat him like a manual laborer. Skin is the most washable material of any in your house.* The advice seemed counterintuitive and random, as if it had said, *Whack him along the the neck with scarlet mittens from Belgium.* Sarah's pages seemed sane by comparison. *Tassie, When Emmie gets up you will know: she whimpers then goes into a full cry. Reintroduce yourself to her. The changing table is right there in her room (where the crying will be coming from). All the changing supplies are on the shelf. There are sippy cups for milk and juice in the kitchen and she can have whatever she wants to eat—that is, whatever you can find.* Sane except for this part: *I have arranged for some risotto to be FedExed to her but I will also bring her something home from the kitchen tonight.*

FedExed risotto? I looked in the cupboard, and in addition to a jar of matzo balls that looked like something from high school biology, I saw little jars of organic peas, carrots, and bananas for toddlers. I knew babysitters had a bad reputation for eating baby food, and although I was hungry—a starving college student!— I would try to avoid opening one up right away. Perhaps later. The bananas, I knew, were puddingy and delicious. I had heard of a woman who once, in a pinch, served banana baby food as a dessert, in parfait dishes, at a dinner party in Dellacrosse.

I stared at those bananas. Since Mary-Emma was going to get FedExed risotto, maybe . . . I could not resist. Besides, she was old for this food and could eat regular bananas, a bunch of which sat on the counter. I twisted open the top and wolfed it down with a spoon, then rinsed the jar and tossed it into the recycling, which was a clear plastic bag torn to hang on the knob of the back door. Though most things about the house announced themselves with clarity, others I had to figure out.

From upstairs came a whimper, then a full cry. Sarah hadn't shown me around the house, so I had to find the staircase myself. There were actually two staircases, side by side, meeting at a win-dowed landing midway, and then they merged and became one, going the rest of the short way up, where a plastic gate, suction-cupped to the wall, blocked one's path. I stepped over it with a kind of scissors kick and then made my way toward the cry. I passed a bathroom with walls painted the pale brown of a paper bag; on the sink was an assortment of prescription pills in their vials, as if someone were collecting beads, getting ready to make a necklace. I passed a bedroom with a mission bed that had perhaps failed at its mission, and a cherry dresser that perhaps had not. Atop it was a jewelry box with the phyllo thin drawers of a bee-keeper's hive.

The baby's room as promised appeared to be on a higher floor yet, the door to which at first I could not find. The crying was at the west end of the house, but when I opened doors to find a staircase I found only closets. There was a short pause and then full-scale wailing began.

It was maddening trying to figure out how to get to it. I wan-dered in and out of the rooms in a low-level panic that prevented me from taking full notice of them, though they seemed both ele-gantly pastel and cluttered to my darting, searching eye. At the east end of the hall, on the left, I saw an open doorway. I lunged toward it, found yet another stairwell gate locked in place. But the actual wooden door was swung wide open, so I stepped over that gate, too, onto steps thickly carpeted in dull earwax gold. Through a tiny window at another landing, framed in the cross pieces, I could see spiny winter treetops and telephone wire. The staircase wound around, and then there it was, the nursery spread out beneath the eaves. The angled ceilings and walls were painted a pale wheat yellow, like a chablis, and at the windows at either end of the space hung curtains of sheer white over heavy, room-darkening shades. A double nightlight in lurid orange plugged up the electrical socket just to the left of a changing table and dresser. Emmie's white crib, with its Winnie-the-Pooh bumpers and bedding, was in the far corner, and she was standing, clinging to its rail. In the short time that I'd not seen her, her silky black hair had fallen out and in its stead tight, blondish-brown curls were growing in, the start of an afro, really. It looked almost like a wig. When she saw it was me, her crying momentarily stopped in wonder.

"Hey, Mary-Emma," I said, returning her, at least halfway, to her former name. She looked at me, then resumed wailing. But when I went to lift her out of the crib, she was eager, and clung to me and quieted down. She was warm and soft and smelled of powder and pee. I took her to the changing table, where she lay passively. I pulled off her balloon-print trousers and disposable diaper, which was made of a soft, strangely layered paper I'd never seen before and which peeled away from her pink-brown bottom like the paper from poultry giblets. The room was dark from the still-drawn shades, and the air was moist from a humidifier. I fumbled around on the shelf over the changing table for a plastic box of wipes and accidentally knocked it to the floor.

"Uh-oh!" said Emmie. She already knew both the sound and the language of things going wrong.

"It's OK," I said. The wipes were in a heater, and so the falling was loud. Luckily none of the wipes came out and the heater light stayed on, so I assumed nothing was broken. Heated wipes! I know my own mother would be appalled by such things. As a baby, I would have gotten the chilly wipes of winter, or frozen dabs with unheated cotton balls, or a quick tepid washcloth, if I was lucky. My mother probably soothed my diaper rash with ice cubes from her soda glass. Still, I did not feel sorry for myself. I felt sorry for Mary-Emma and all she was going through, every day waking up to something new. Though maybe that was what childhood was. But I couldn't quite recall that being the case for me. And perhaps she would grow up with a sense that incompetence was all around her, and it was entirely possible I would be instrumental in that. She would grow up with love, but no sense that the people who loved her knew what they were doing—the opposite of my childhood—and so she would become suspicious of people, suspicious of love and the worth of it. Which in the end, well, would be a lot like me. So perhaps it didn't matter what happened to you as a girl: you ended up the same.

Once Mary-Emma was changed and sprinkled piney and dry with some silky herbal rice starch, I carried her downstairs, stepping awkwardly over the plastic baby gates. I found myself saying "Wheeeee!" and "Upsy-oopsy." Mary-Emma just looked at me with neutral interest. It was a look I'd forgotten and never saw anymore in grown people. But it was the best. It was fantastically engaged: scholarly, unjudging, and angelic. We stood on the landing, deciding which staircase to descend. "Which one?" I asked her. "This one?" Ah, once more: the uncertainty of the adult world. And she thrust out her arm and pointed toward the one that led to the kitchen. She knew her way around already, or was at least acting like it for purposes of displaying authority. I seemed to have little authority whatsoever but to be instead her happy maidservant. The tinier the child, the more you were the servant, I knew. Older children were more subservient, less queenly and demanding.

In the kitchen I sat Mary-Emma on the counter, then stupidly turned away for a second to open a cupboard door. Sitting there, she started to twist, and I lunged and caught her just as she was sliding off the shiny granite toward the floor. Her face seemed to smile and sob at the same time, a look that said *That may be fun for some people but not for me,* and I placed her securely on my hip, feeling the biceps in my arm already beginning to strengthen and my jutted hip on its way to socket stress and limpage.

"Let's get you a snack. How does that sound?" I scanned the cupboard shelves. Had I eaten the best and sweetest of the baby food already myself?

"Oag cool," she said, pointing at the freezer.

"Yes, it's cool in there," I said, still scanning the shelves. I looked in the refrigerator, where there were several bottles of water from Fiji. This was the first time I'd seen water from Fiji but not the last. I didn't believe it was real. Selling water from Fiji seemed like a trick for the gullible, like bottled Alpine air at a carnival.

Mary-Emma's legs began to kick, and her heel in my thigh was a soft spur. Would I not please giddyap? "Oag cool!" she repeated, still pointing.

I opened the freezer door and saw, amid the ice cube trays, chilling vodka, a plastic file folder, and a pound of ground coffee, what she wanted: frozen yogurt pops.

"Ah, OK," I said, and pulled them out. I set her on the floor and then sat there myself and we both ate blackberry frozen yogurt pops and were happy. "Hmm, delicious," I said.

"Dishes," she repeated, creamy lavender all around her mouth, giving her the appearance of a struggling drag queen.

What a miracle food was. In case I had given her too much, I buried the wrappers in the trash.

———

When Sarah returned, Mary-Emma rushed to her and grabbed her around the leg. Sarah massaged her head. I provided a report, much of which I'd actually written out on notebook paper, with the times of Mary-Emma's waking up and eating and playing. "She loves that frozen yogurt," I said. "Hope it's OK: I gave her, uh, a couple."

"Oh, yes, that's fine. I just hope they continue to make them! When I was little Dannon made this delicious prune yogurt that came in a waxy brown eight-ounce container. Well, now they don't make any of those things. Completely gone. Although I was in Paris last year and found some there."

I nodded, trying to imagine the very particular sadness of a vanished childhood yogurt now found only in France. It was a very special sort of sadness, individual, and in its inability to induce sympathy, in its tuneless spark, it bypassed poetry and entered science. I tried not to think of my one excursion to Whole Foods, over a year ago, where I found myself paralyzed by all the special food for special people, whose special murmurings seemed to be saying, "Out of my way! I want a Tofurkey!"

I could feel my tiredness most when I at last lay down. But first I walked home through the dark afternoon. Although the season had already rounded the corner and was on its move toward longer days, the sun still did not make it very high, but just kind of scooted along the side of the sky, pale and sheepish, like something ill, and darkness came over the town early and caused everyone just to give up on their days by four o'clock. The low snowbanks were whiskery with specks of black.

In my apartment the radiators hissed and the windows were frosted deep into the mullions from the steam that hit them and froze. In my room I kicked off my boots and my socks came with them, my toes sore and as knobbed as Chinese ginger. Who knew life with a baby would be so draining? On the night table sat some mint tea that had been steeping there since morning, stone cold and medicinally brown. I sipped a little, its soggy bag falling against my mouth; then I gargled and drank the rest. I got out my translucent Plexi bass, like an answer to ice itself, and put on my headphones and plucked a little Metallica, a little Modest Mouse, plus a nothing bass part for "Angel from Montgomery," and a bit of "Rock-a-Bye Baby." I lay on the floor again and tried to sing like Ndegeocello. I made up a meandering tune that sounded like a bullfrog gulping his pain. In my mind an organist struck electric chords at expected intervals. Expected by me, at least. I felt I knew how to sing along, which most bass players, busy trying to find the midway place between melody and rhythm—was this searching not the very journey of life?—wouldn't have bothered trying. Nonetheless, I was told I looked funny doing it—a bass face to beat the band, someone once said—so I rarely did it in front of anyone. What girl was not reluctant to be ugly? Still, I had started to experience the silence of this apartment as a sorrow, and singing helped, though only so much. I fell asleep with my clothes on, randomly sprawled on the bed as if a tornado had hit and lifted me up, then dropped me down and moved on, bored.

The next day at the Thornwood-Brinks' I took Mary-Emma ice-skating. I put her in her snowsuit, stuffed her into the stroller, and wheeled her down over the bumpy ice to the little neighborhood park, where there was a small flooded lagoon off the lake that the city had cleared for skating. There had not been a lot of very cold days, and a truck that had driven out onto the lake proper had fallen through, so the lake itself was closed except for a small racing pen. But people were allowed to skate on the flooded lagoon and were doing so.

In the warm-up house I rented us both some skates—Sarah had left a twenty on the counter for this—and then we stepped out onto the nicked and bumpily formed ice. I propped Mary-Emma up, bracing her with my legs, and scooted her around. It was all new to her and she laughed like it was a joke. Her skates were double-bladed, and when I let her go she could glide a little on her own but then made off with a choppy step just running artlessly across the lagoon until she would hit a yellowish carbuncle in the ice and fall forward, her snowsuit cushioning her landing. She would then lie there staring into the cracks of the ice; beneath it were wavy weeds and lily pads frozen cloudily in place as if in a botanical glass paperweight. "Fish!" she cried to me, and I went over and she was poking with her mitten at the ice, believing the flora to be fauna. "Well, kinda," I said. She was happy, the sun was shining, and she got up again and took off in her choppy gait. She had great spirit for this sport—it seemed to come naturally to her—and then I remembered her birth mother, who had spent her Saturdays skating with the nuns, and I thought, *Well, of course.* She had inherited Bonnie's ability to skate. And now this is what Bonnie would miss: someone to skate with who wasn't doing it out of charity. Someone she could teach to skate. It seemed, momentarily, a loss like several limbs. I watched Mary-Emma tear across the rink then fall forward again. She just lay there, staring into the ice, mesmerized.

"Well, the sous-chef totally botched the *mignardises,*" said Sarah when I got home, "but that I should have expected. Hey, baby," she said to Mary-Emma, and lifted her quickly up. Sarah was still wearing her white chef's coat, which was now smudged with brown grease. There was a cut on her hand and two burns on her arms. "In everything I do there seems to be some part missing. I'm discovering that it is almost impossible to be a mother and also do anything of value outside the house. But that *almost* is key, and I'm living in the oxygenated heart of that word." Her face brightened. "These bumper stickers that say EVERY MOTHER IS A WORKING MOTHER are bullshit. Propaganda of the affluent. And an insult to actual working moms with jobs. I've taken to tearing them off when I see them!"

"Tossa," said Mary-Emma, pointing happily at me.

"Did you get a snack?" Sarah asked us both in a high chirpy voice.

"We got some cider with whipped cream in the warm-up hut," I said.

"Cider with whipped cream?" Sarah looked aghast.

"Oh, was that a bad idea?"

"I've just never heard of cider and whipped cream," said Sarah. "I mean, really, I'm a food person but—cider and whipped cream? My God—what a thing to do to cider!"

"It's pretty common around here." I shrugged. I had grown up squirting whipped cream on hot cider; was it a perversion of some sort? Frankly, that wouldn't have surprised me.

"Dairy with everything, I guess. I'm going to put all my dessert cheeses in the front window at Le Petit Moulin. Lure them in with dairy, then give them . . . sauteed ground cherry!" This was the light, flighty side of Sarah. "Or perhaps a little sherry," she added.

Almost always, on good days at least, I was a joiner.

"That should make them merry," I said, accidentally uttering the name that seemed never uttered in this house except by me.

"Or cause some hari-kari!"

Sarah smiled and bounced Mary-Emma while she spoke: "Very, very, very." Which again rhymed with the name she clearly hoped to bury. Mary.

"Tossa!" cried Mary-Emma again, leaning toward me.

Sarah looked vaguely troubled. "What perfume are you wearing?" she asked me. "You smell so good." She set Mary-Emma down, and Mary-Emma came running at me and then at Sarah, in a kind of game, back and forth.

"Perfume?" I was overheated from skating and had not yet taken off my coat; I wasn't sure she was correctly identifying the odor—if there even was one. Bodily attention of any sort from others I wasn't used to, and it made me want to run and hide.

"You smell so nice—what is it?" She looked at me hopefully, her eyebrows arced with inquiry. She pushed her hand through her hair. Its brightness seemed to have disappeared, and it seemed now a flat, tannic hue. When she raked her hand through it, I could see that it was thinning; beneath the cat's-cradle crisscross of her part, she had a kind of comb-over thing going on, elaborate zigzagging layers at the top to hide the scalp bursting through. Age was burning the edge of her hairline, and when her hand flicked through the strands, before they fell back in decoration, her forehead protruded shiny and round as an apple.

"I'm not sure," I said. "Garlic?" I knew people always lied about their perfumes and claimed it was soap, as if it were vanity to attempt more. Actually, I sometimes after showers dabbed on a kind of aromatic oil that Murph had given me for my birthday, a slim bottle called Arabian Princess. In the current world situation it seemed unwise to advertise this, in case I was mistaken for the mascot of Osama bin Laden, though I was pretty sure Murph had simply got it at the food co-op.

"Well, if you find out, let me know."

"I think it's from the co-op," I said.

"Really? Well, I'll sniff around there then." Sarah picked Mary-Emma up and nuzzled her. "How was skating?"

"Good," I said.

"Good!" repeated Mary-Emma.

"See how she's really chattering and opening up!" said Sarah, giving her a kiss on the head. "She is, after all, two."

"Good!" cried Mary-Emma again, and then she leaned out of Sarah's arms to come back to me.

"Oh, you want to go to Tassie, do you?" said Sarah, and she let her go, passing Mary-Emma to me, some maternal hurt scurrying to hide behind her thin-as-a-piano-string smile. "You'll really have to tell me the name of that perfume you've got on, if you remember it," she said, sighing. "Otherwise, I could be arrested at the co-op for loitering." Something was wrong—perhaps it was Sarah's tight mouth: a choking wire that had somehow garroted me. I could not speak. A whole minute of silence passed between us. "Well," she said finally, "I should let you go." And she took back Mary-Emma, who began to squirm and fuss.

Classes began in a deep cold spell, a high of one-below for the week. This was more like the winter weather of memory. Cold burst into the room from a mere open kitchen drawer, forks and knives piled like icicles. Our landlord's generous heat was nothing in the face of this. The stem of the doorknobs on the front door conducted the cold from outside so that even the inside knob froze the hand. Cold air seeped through the slits of the electrical sockets. Clothing pulled from the closet was chilly, and in the basement laundry room of our apartment house clothes that did not dry completely in the dryer emerged white with frost. A glass of water put on the nightstand at night might be ice by morning. One looked out through the window, when one could, through pointed icicles that were like the incisors of a shark; it was as if one were living in the cold, dead mouth of a very mean snow-man. Kay, the woman upstairs who had no life, decided as an experiment to throw boiling water off the upstairs back porch. She let us know by paper notice slid under our doors that this would happen at eleven a.m. on Monday, and so the rest of us gathered and watched it hit the air in silence and come down as slow, quiet steam and slush. We'd been told it would turn instantly to pellets midair, but perhaps something in the water—chlorine, or the salts of the water softener—kept it from doing that. On the street, the wind was so bitter, it seemed to bypass cold and become heat. Breathing burned the nostrils. Cars on every block wheezed and gagged and would not start. The combination of the cold weather and dry indoor heating had caused the longer nails on my picking hand to weaken, crack, and break beneath the quick, stabbing the pink hammy skin below, so that my fingers bled and I had to bandage them before I went out.

And then it warmed just enough for a blizzard, followed by another, as if the prairie were in a hiccup. Winds howled in the chimneys and under eaves, knocking ice blocks from the roof. And then when the air was finally still, a stupor descended, induced by accumulated snowdrifts, which were banked against the sides of houses like a comforter thrown over to calm an agitated dog. There was in the air a cold resignation good for reading.

My Intro to Sufism was taught by a self-described "Ottomanist," which made me think of someone lying back with his feet up on a padded footstool, with a remote, in autumn. He looked charmingly rattled and had his arm in a sling. He was Irish, and he spoke in the airy *r*'s and staccato of County Brokencanencork, as Murph liked to refer to the entire country of her forebears. "For those of you who are in any way concerned about my teaching the class," said the professor, "believe me: I know more about this topic than anyone in this department. And for those of you concerned about my teaching while on painkillers for my arm, believe me: I also know more about teaching while high than anyone else in this department."

I sat next to a tall, handsome brown-skinned boy, who smiled at me and then sent me a note, as if we were in high school. *What am I doing in this class?* he wrote. *I am Brazilian. What are you?*

I didn't know what I was in this particular context. I wrote back on his sheet of paper, *I am a quasi Jew. What am I doing here?*

I don't know, he wrote back.

In capital letters I wrote, *WHAT IS THE BEST WAY TO KILL MYSELF? WOULD A PEN TO THE NECK BE QUICK?* Then passed it back.

He read it and beamed, smothering a laugh that brought forth a slight snort. The professor, who was speaking, looked glancingly in our direction and then away. The boy next to me wrote in all capital letters: *YOU DEFINITELY SHOULD NOT BE IN THIS CLASS.*

I'm not sure what Sufism is, I wrote back. I slid him the paper.

I'M NOT SURE WHAT WINTER IS, he wrote once more in all caps.

Welcome, I scrawled. *Usually it's not this warm*—a reversal of the old local joke. *Usually it's not this cold,* we used to say to visitors during a midwinter thaw.

WHAT???!!!!! he wrote with great energy.

I feel that mysticism isn't really happening here in this course, I wrote.

IT ISN'T.

Are you quasi mystic? I wrote.

I'M PESSI-MYSTIC, he wrote back, *AND OPTI-MYSTIC. BOTH.*

After class, I went home and with my earphones on picked around on my electric bass, pressing my fingers into the steel strings, toughening my calluses. I loved "Twinkle, Twinkle, Little Star," which I referred to as "Mozart." I played and sang aloud over and over again the line "How I wonder what you are," which without any audible accompaniment, to Kay-with-no-life upstairs, I knew sounded like the mad howling of a simultaneously sexed-up and brutally injured alley cat. She had already told me this. Honoring the classics, I apparently nonetheless sounded undone in agony. When I felt finished, when I felt expressed and spent, I found an old pack of Murph's Marlboros and smoked one in front of the bathroom mirror, blowing the smoke up and out, and turning my head slowly this way and that as I did. In the dim lights I did not look so bad.

Sarah and I made one trip to the courthouse, to pick up copies of the provisional adoption papers from the judge's office. After six months they would be signed and Mary-Emma would officially be Sarah's. And Edward's. Until then she was in their foster care. On our way in we passed a bench in the corridor on which sat a row of young boys awaiting hearings of various sorts. Some of the boys were as young as nine. They were all black. We carried Mary-Emma past them and they all looked at her and she at them, everyone entranced and baffled. In the judge's office the clerk and envelope were waiting for us. Sarah took the envelope with a smile. "Is this your other daughter?" the clerk said of me.

"Twenty's a cute age," Sarah said to me later in the car home.

Once she and Edward asked me to stay overnight, like a bona fide nanny, and I said OK. They were going to have a date night together and would be out late, so my just staying over would be the most civilized thing. This worry about civilization seemed tardy for just about everyone. "Sure," I said.

When I arrived for their Saturday-night date, Sarah said to me, "Don't be afraid to rock Emma against your bare skin. Breast to cheek, belly to belly. I do it all the time. It soothes adopted children who haven't been genuinely nursed."

"OK," I said.

"It's a good thing you're not actually nursing," Edward said to Sarah. "You'd probably try to make a cheese."

Sarah rolled her eyes. "He keeps thinking I'd make some boutique cheese!"

After they left, Mary-Emma and I spent the evening watching so many different toddler videos—baby songs and train stories— that she beamed with happiness every time the FBI warning came on at the start of a new cassette. I made cookies. I did my animal imitations. I gave her a bath and in the bathroom tried some of Sarah's wrinkle tonic on my own chapped cheeks and then rubbed the extra into Mary-Emma's knees, which were dusky and dry. There were also jars of cream made from Andean snails and lotions from Japanese sake; we stuck our fingers in and smoothed the little dollops into our arms.

And though she was too old, when her bedtime arrived, I lifted my shirt and bralessly rocked her to sleep in the uphol- stered glider in her room, both of us falling asleep there. When I snapped awake, there was a figure in the doorway: Edward. I pulled my shirt down groggily.

"We're back," he said quietly.

"Should I go home?" I asked.

"Not at all," he said. "Make yourself at home in the guest room downstairs. Good night."

And I placed Mary-Emma in her crib and crawled off down- stairs to the second floor to sleep in my underwear. Edward again appeared in the doorway there. "All went well?" he asked, smiling.

"Yes," I said, from under the covers.

"Well, good." There was a long silence with a slowly fading smile in it—his. "Well, good night, then," he said. *Handsome is as handsome does,* my mother used to say. *Dashing dashes.*

"Good night." And when he left I got up and pressed the door tightly shut.

In the morning Mary-Emma dashed to all our rooms, newly, wordily singing, "Time-for-to-get-up my daddy. Time-for-to-get-up my mama. Time-for-to-get-up my Tassa." Sarah made pancakes and we poured syrup on everything, even into our coffee. For stray minutes we seemed like a family, laughing and chewing. I felt included. We were all in this together.

But family life sometimes had a vortex, like weather. It could be like a tornado in a quiet zigzag: get close enough and you might see within it a spinning eighteen-wheeler and a woman.

"Thank you for our date night," Sarah said to me when I left. Her face looked tired and drawn. With every new word or phrase Mary-Emma learned, one seemed subtracted from Sarah.

On the weekday mornings that I walked to the Thornwood-Brinks' the sharp air turned my cheeks to meat—on one of Sarah's menus lying on the counter I had once seen the phrase "beef cheeks"; maybe this was how they were made! My nose dripped profusely when I stopped at curbs and crosswalks. But when I kept moving—the snow so cold it squeaked like Styrofoam beneath my boots—single clear drops, like baubles, collected just inside my nostrils and dangled pendulously until I dabbed at them with a gray carnation of Kleenex that had died long ago in my pocket, never to wake again. Moreover, the dabbing caused the tissue to disintegrate further, and soon it was little more than crumpled, powdery ice against my nose. My too-thin socks, also, left my feet cold even in good boots. Why was it that here in Troy country girls had the thin cotton socks (from Home Dollar) and the suburban girls had the thick ones (J. Crew or L.L.Bean)? Was it that we just had bigger feet and no room in our shoes? Or did we not think of the weather as something separate from us, although we should have? Perhaps we accepted the weather as being us, weren't terrified of it, carried around all its severity and storminess inside us, as a kind of defeatedness. Our outer veneer was thin and meek and weak—

futility!—and part of our defeat. Our inner giving up, self-designed to simplify life, matched the outer, and left us merely dazed. Thus, the socks. And thus other things.

Edward was sitting alone at the kitchen table when I came in. His hands were pushed inside the green sweater sleeves of each opposite arm, like those of a girl trying to stay warm, but his hair—its mix of old road snow and smoke—gave him the steely look of the wise elder. The contradiction—the hair, the girlish hands-up-the-sleeves—was unusual to my eye, and if you studied it, perhaps some conclusions could be reached about the nature of his character, but I didn't then appraise it with any purpose, and the look of him just seemed to produce a slightly odd and comic swirl of hybridity. On the sides his hair was receding and thinning, something you noticed more after a haircut, which I could see he'd recently had. The balding of men! I had once seen a documentary that traced the lives of ten boys from the age of seven on, and with every installment more and more scalp emerged on the subjects; the film, intended to examine the struggles of masculinity and social class, was one long glacial retreat of hair.

"Well, hello," he said. "You come bearing a lovely warm perfume!"

The heat of the house quickly thawed every part of me but my toes.

"You're not at the lab today?" I asked, listening not for his answer but upward, for any sound of Mary-Emma. I thought I heard a repeated bleating sound that could simply have been a plastic smoke alarm with a low battery.

"I was waiting for you," he said.

"For me?"

"Waiting for you to get here so I could leave." His hands came out of his sleeves.

"Am I late?"

"Not really," he said. His expression was mysterious: a stern, amused indifference. The look of maverick science, perhaps! I knew the Mayo Clinic was showing some interest in his work. "Sarah's working down at the Mill, as we say. She'll be back at six. She thought even though it's cold that you might bundle Emmie up and take her for a walk in the wagon. You'll see there's a red wagon on the front porch, which may work better than that stroller on the ice."

"Yes, I saw the wagon coming in."

"Good," he said, fixing me with his gaze.

For a moment I was forced to study him back. His nose, bony and beakish in profile, was wider and tuberous when looked at straight on. His eyes were trying to do something with mine, but I wasn't sure what. He seemed too old for our eyes to be doing anything. Not only had the years eaten their way into his hairdo, two prints of scalp astride a central silvery lock, but it seemed he had darkened the roots, perhaps with the shoe polish I'd seen at the bathroom sink upstairs. His shoes were always brown. Like Sarah's, his hair was a production, of nature and art: it was as if his face had washed up on his head, like a tide, and left its mark, and then some artistic boy had come along to the same beach with a little paint.

"Sarah believes that babies should be aired," he said finally. "She also believes in forcing hats on babies even when they're screaming against it. She believes in doing this because they look so cute that way and we want a lot of cute pictures. Apparently." He sighed. "And so we just shove the hats on."

"Beauty is painful, as the supermodels say."

"Right!"

The alarmlike bleating was intensifying. "Is that Emmie?" I asked.

"Yes, that is. I'll leave her to you."

I went up to find her and behind me heard the back door shut, the car start and rumble out of the driveway and away.

Obviously I didn't know how long she'd been crying. But her face was puffy and swollen, her cheeks fever-bright. The hot stink of diaper was in the air; she would need to be changed. "Hey, baby!" I chirped, and she swung her arms up to be lifted out of the huge crib.

"Tassa," she said, as if reminding herself. She was needy and sweet. Her new life story, beginning here, would perhaps be a triumphant one. And when I picked her up and held her, she seemed something so very lovely and uncorrupted—no matter what terrible tale she had actually been plucked from.

Pulled steadily, the wagon bumped along the icy walk to Mary-Emma's great glee. "Whoops-a-daisy," I would say—the wagon would tilt and then fall back, or get stuck in a rut and need a sudden tug that would knock her back hilariously. She would giggle and exaggerate her own falling, leaning every which way in her new puffy pink snowsuit, a small drip of clear mucus appearing at her nose, which she would fetch with her tongue. If we stayed out too long her face would be chapped and as red as a radish. Even with her darkening skin. These kinds of details I was learning. When it seemed too cold I would look for inside venues. Up on the main street of the neighborhood I would take her to a supermarket that had handicapped access and let her race up the ramps, play with the electric doors, attempt hide-and-seek in the aisles. Or I would stop at the mattress store, wheel her in, and look over the place, the real idea being to let her run around and jump from bed to bed while I discussed springs and firmness with the salesman. He would sometimes look worried, seeing her leaping around. "Do you mind if she does that?" I asked hopefully.

"Oh, no," he would say, but with a slightly sickened look on his face as out of the corner of our eyes we watched her bouncing and flopping and squealing.

Because the upcoming March Democratic primary *was*, in

effect, the general election—since no Republican had been elected to city government, perhaps ever—the city plows spent much time in the weeks before the primary clearing the streets. In Dellacrosse we might have gotten some summer road repair in time for the fall showdown—PHIL POTT FOR CORONER (Dickens lives!)—since there the Republicans had a prayer. But here in progressive Troy, apparently, mass seduction by the incumbent had to happen early, and so the mayor resorted to assiduous snowplowing. The plows seemed to come from everywhere, with their front shovels angled like petrified fish lips. The scraping of metal on ice and then on the street surface itself set a steady metallic treble line to the low rumble of the trucks. In consideration of the spring soil and grass, Troy had also bought a truck that instead of salting the roads sweetened them with beet-sugar brine, and its drip along the streets looked like the trail of a sad thing with bad kidneys.

I took Mary-Emma up toward Wendell Street, which was the only street nearby with actual restaurants and stores and other businesses, probably nine establishments in total. It would have passed for the downtown of a tiny village, and I knew the sidewalks were more cleanly shoveled there. On Wendell we headed through the salted-to-slush ice toward the neighborhood branch of the public library. I would show her the children's books, and despite Sarah's preference for baked books, we would sit at a table near the radiator and read. Few people were on the street, but the ones we passed smiled at me, then looked at Mary-Emma and then back at me, their expressions not exactly changed but not exactly the same: upon seeing us together, our story unknown but presumed, an observation and then a thought entered their faces and froze their features in place.

But then a car on the opposite side of the street, full of teenagers, it seemed—I could not tell how old they were—slowed down and looked at us from across the lane. I kept going, headed for the library, but glancing back I noticed that the car had pulled into a side street and was now turning around, coming back down Wendell in the lane closest to me. It pulled up to the curb. A guy with a bright orange mohawk, a big silver ring in his brow, silver studs like cake decorations up the cartiliginous rim of his ear, and a thick black leather jacket that made him look as if he were wearing an expensive chair, leaned out the window. Two other boys were in the backseat—if taciturnity could kill!—and a very ordinary-looking brown-haired girl was at the wheel. I thought the mohawk guy was going to leer at me. Or maybe he would ask to see my breasts or shout that he wanted to put them in his mouth or maybe he would offer to do things with his studded tongue, lick me up, lick me down, suck me head to toe, or maybe he wanted my juicy lips on him or to tell me I had a fat ass but he liked fat asses or that I had a skinny ass but he liked skinny asses and wouldn't I like to get my skinny ass or my fat one into this fine car with him and his friends so he could do all these fine things? Instead, he glared right at little Mary-Emma and shouted, *"Nigger!"*

Never before in my life had I understood so deeply what it meant not to believe one's ears.

"My-kull!!" exclaimed the girl inside driving. The boys in the back snickered a little, and she swung the car away from the curb. The rear tire spun and flung snow into the wagon, which made Mary-Emma laugh at first and then, when the rock-frozen snow hit her face, made her cry. I hadn't known any of this was possible in this town. Dellacrosse, perhaps—although I'd never actually heard it there— but here? Here was so proud of itself. Here was so progressive and exemplary. Here was so lockstep lefty. Here was so—white. The only color they knew here was the local one they took on for camouflage and convenience. If this were Salt Lake City, I knew, half the people here would have happily been Mormons. Instead, righteous and complacent and indistinguishable from one another, they were all members of the ACLU and the Freedom from Religion Foundation.

"Fuckers," I found myself saying. I picked Mary-Emma up just to hold her, letting the wagon roll slightly away and bang into a parking meter. She was so swaddled in her giant slippery snowsuit that I could hardly hang on to her. But I carried her into the coffee shop we happened to be near and sat her on the couch by the gas fireplace and unzipped her snowsuit to warm her there. The log was fake and the fire rolled around it blue and cold as water—an ornamental fountain more than a hearth. Mary-Emma's hair was damp and pressed to her head. Well, I would get her some hot chocolate. "Foggers," she said to me, and then we both laughed. "Don't say that, though," I added, in warning.

"Oh, my God!" cried Sarah. "Oh, my God, oh, my God. That's it, that's it." She began pacing around the kitchen after I told her what had happened. I did not repeat the actual word that My-kull had said but just used the phrase "the *n*-word." I was holding Mary-Emma, who was playing with my hair, lifting it up and then letting it fall in my face, laughing when I would blow on it and make it move.

Sarah continued. "My God! Who knew this was possible in this city? At the little folk music festivals in the county parks in summer you see all kinds of mixed-race families. I thought this was the perfect town . . . OK, not perfect, but I thought this was the best possible situation for Emmie. I thought we would not be letting her down by bringing her here, and now I see my own naïveté." The finger-raking of her hair, which had become familiar to me, began now with two hands.

"Perhaps if you are black, there is nowhere, really," I said, thinking of the boy in Sufism, and Sarah just stared at me.

"I'm forming a support group. Don't laugh."

But I wasn't laughing.

"I'm going to use the very mechanisms of this town against it——this goddamn self-satisfied town that . . ."

"That drinks its own bathwater!" I said, borrowing a Dellacrosse expression for Troy. It was a metaphor and not a metaphor and is what the outlying areas of the state all felt: that Troy was a piece of smug, liberal, recycling, civic-minded monkey masturbation. That it was gestural, trying to make itself feel good—which in Dellacrosse meant "better than everyone else." That it wasn't real. *That* was the true crime. Its lack of reality. Whatever that meant. Also, once a year some rural girl came to Troy for the weekend, drank too much, and ended up raped and beaten to death in some apartment or park.

Sarah looked at me with sudden searching concentration. It was a look I was coming to know and it was one I felt inside of me often, a feeling of aghast but childlike scrutiny: it said, *Why are there more space aliens on this planet than there used to be? Or are we the space aliens and are the human beings, uh-oh, coming back?*

"Yes," she said slowly, then picked up speed as if snapping herself out of a daze. "Well, I guess all towns sort of drink their own bathwater. But they don't all have cruelty-free tofu! I'm going to get a support group going, and I'm going to bring families of color into this home, and we are going to discuss things and pool our strengths and share our stories and plot our collective actions and all that shit. Would you supervise the children?"

"What children?" I knew that the owner of the Moroccan restaurant on Wendell had children. Would they come? Last October someone had shot up the restaurant sign with actual bullets, then ripped it off and rebolted it upside down.

"The hypothetical children. The ostensible children. The imagined children. That kind." She smiled.

"Sure," I said.

"Tassa hair up 'n' down," said Mary-Emma, still playing with it as if it were silky string.

And so the weekly meetings got their start. Every Wednesday evening I would be upstairs with the children: Mary-Emma, two four-year-olds named Isaiah and Eli, a five-year-old named Althea, and a girl named Tika, who was eight and who sometimes helped me with the little ones and other times just sat in a corner and read *Harry Potter.* Often other families would make an appearance: an Ethiopian doctor and her sons, a seventh-grade boy named Clarence and a fourth-grader named Kaz. There was an Adilia, a Kwame, and more. They were mostly "of color," as was said by all the adults downstairs, a range of shades from light to dark, though most of the parents downstairs, I noted, were white. Most were the transracial, biracial, multiracial families Sarah and Edward knew thus far in Troy, and probably more would be recruited. Upstairs I built Lego forts with the kids, or thought up little hiding games or wrestled or sang. Their voices were boisterous and fun and, being kids, they had their own words: "Nanana-booboo, you can't catch me," they would tease one another. The way in which the play-taunts of children resembled the calls and cries of animals was interesting to me. Only once did Sarah summon me downstairs to help her make a quick emergency dessert for the group: we microwaved the peach baby food and spooned it as hot puree over ice cream. "We used to eat this in Dellacrosse all the time," I said, changing the facts slightly.

"Really!" said Sarah.

"Yes. Sort of. It was better than some old raisin cream pie— pudding and pits we called that pie."

"Pits?"

"My mom always bought cheap raisins with the stems still on and poking out." I continued dripping the hot peach liquid on the little scoops of ice cream, which had been dug out of the carton with a melon baller. Naked, they looked ready for ping-pong.

Everyone, except the children, exclaimed over the dessert's deliciousness.

"You can just eat the ice cream," I told the kids upstairs.

And amid the shared stories of public school biases and gang statistics and the strange comments of acquaintances, remarks would waft up through two floors, out of interest and earshot for the kids, but if I strained I could hear.

". . . and I walked into the school for the conference and there was the teacher shaking Kaz and banging his head against the wall . . ."

". . . institutionalized bigotry can subtly convince you of its rightness. With its absurdity removed, its evil can compel . . ."

"And even the adults pat her hair as if it's the funniest thing they'd ever seen on a mammal . . . and of course available for public patting, like a goat in a zoo . . ."

"There's a great woman on the south side who does hair . . ."

"Of course homework is just a measure of the home! And so the kids of color will always fall behind . . ."

"The African-American peer group is the strongest and the Asian-American is the weakest—that is, Asian-American parents have power that African-American parents do not."

"School is white. And school is female. So it's the boys of color who have the hardest time, and if they're not into sports the gangs will lure them in . . ."

"I guess we sort of knew that already, but still."

"It's all so unfair."

"Where are the reparations for slavery, or for the Indians, who got some of the money back, just not a lot of the land."

"I don't think the casinos count."

"Oh, baby, they count."

"You know, there are people in our department sitting on piles of inherited money who object to a black person making five thousand dollars more than they do. 'It's the principle,' they say, and you just don't know where to begin with that one."

"You know, the Jews got reparations from the Nazis, but who got the actual money? Well-to-do Jewish grandchildren who hardly need it at all. In Ohio and Brazil there are grandchildren of Nazis who are truly destitute . . ."

"All right, where are we now? How did we get onto this?"

"What?"

"Would anyone like more wine?"

"At this point we could use a little gin . . ."

"Well, even the Indians got a few casinos—"

"We discussed that already—"

"But no one in Africa or here ever received reparations from anyone . . ."

"Is that true?"

"Sonya Weidner's working on that—aren't you, Sonya?"

"Well, the Jews are working on that."

"Really?"

"How the hell should I know?"

The nonverbal sounds were like wind—coming in rushes and then falling back. There were bursts of sinus explosions, which were what laughter was in winter, followed by low rumbles of sighing and dismay. There was the pouring of wine and the eating of hors d'oeuvres while trying to speak.

"Racial blindness is a white idea." This would be Sarah.

"How dare we think of ourselves as a social experiment?"

"How dare we not?"

"How dare we use our children to try to feel good about ourselves!"

"How dare we not?"

"I'm in despair."

"Despair is mistaking a small world for a large one and a large one for a small."

"I'm sure that's what I'm doing."

There was a cawing sound that could have been a pack of dogs or geese returning or simply the radiators starting up.

"Let's face it: we're all living in a bubble of some sort—of every sort."

"Look at the way banks are making loans these days. No matter how many times people watch *It's a Wonderful Life,* they still don't get it!"

The opinions downstairs were put forth with such emphasis and confidence, it all sounded like an orchestra made up entirely of percussion: timpani and cymbals and the bass notes of a piano. Even a snare drum would sound stuttery, feathery, and hesitant by comparison.

"You and your academic diversity! Diversity is a distraction."

"Not in the Amazon, it ain't. It's glue. It's the interlock of the interlocking pieces."

"The Amazon! Is that where we are? Look, the whole agenda, like feminism, or affirmative action, is decorative. Without a restructuring of the class system, the whole diversity thing is a folly."

"Oh, I see! A communist! A revolutionary who wants to challenge simple college admissions diversity as being unrealistic as a mechanism of social change. I love this. Let me come to your dacha next week and I'll explain everything . . ."

"Another false dichotomy. Don't you agree, Edward? Mo's just setting up a false dichotomy? It doesn't have to be diversity or socialism, affirmative action or class equality. One is easier to do, granted, and doesn't cost anything."

"It costs! In terms of diversion and resources, it all costs!"

"That's a load of crap!"

I had once seen a load of crap. It was carried to our house in Don Edenhaus's truck and dumped right at our barn for composting into fertilizer.

"You are one of those right-wingers who puts on the Halloween costume of a socialist so you can infiltrate the left and get them to listen to your criticism—but I'm not listening . . ."

I turned toward my charges and said as if in mimicry: "Ladies and gentlemen, we are pleased to present 'It's Time to Shut UP!' starring me!"

"And starring me!" laughed the little girl named Tika.

"And me!" copied Mary-Emma, and we all staggered around the room with our hands over our mouths.

In our sequestered nursery behind and above the baby gate at the stairs, there was scarcely an argument. Sometimes there were squabbles involving Legos, which Mary-Emma was too young for and would stick in her mouth. One of the parents, well intentioned, always brought them. Once, Mary-Emma, initially delighted and gracious about other children in her room, fell into a heap of sorrow and rage over a stuffed talking Elmo. And once someone called someone else a "dingbat," but it was a word so unfamiliar to everyone, including the speaker, that no one's feelings got hurt. Mostly they all played nicely, even if they brought more energy into the room than either Mary-Emma or I was used to. Sometimes they asked me questions.

"Do you go to college?" asked Clarence.

"Yes, I do."

"Do you like it?"

"I do."

"You do?" exclaimed Tika.

"Well, not every day is perfect."

"I want to go somewhere where every day is perfect."

"Me, too."

"Me, too!"

"Me, too!" and then we screamed the laughter of absurd desire. It was like some strange mocking echo of the conversation downstairs.

I sang "There Was an Old Woman Who Swallowed a Fly." "I don't know why she swallowed a fly, perhaps she'll die." Not one of them had heard it before—perhaps it was considered too gruesome for children now, with its heartless "She's dead, of course" at the end, but they all were mesmerized, including Mary-Emma, who began trying to learn it. I had to keep pulling Legos out of her mouth, and because she was becoming toilet trained I hurried her twice to the new potty in the bathroom—such was her excitement at company. From downstairs there came talk I hoped the kids didn't hear.

"This whole town is racially inexperienced and so there is racism on the ground floor of everything."

"Including this house. No offense, but you can't exclude *anything*."

"I understand."

"I heard years ago of a white family with an adopted African-American boy, and once he turned thirteen they had a security system put in so he would feel safe when they went out to parties. The system involved the summoning of the police at the slightest thing, even a motion at the windows, and so of course what happens? Once, while the parents were at a Christmas party, the police burst in, and seeing a teenage black male just standing there, they blasted him in the chest."

"Did he die?"

"Not right away."

Sometimes there was a simultaneous quiet upstairs and down, like a blanket of snow, as if at that moment no one anywhere in the galaxy knew what to say.

"Did you teach the children a song about eating live animals?" began a message on my machine from Sarah, which started out as if it were a reprimand and then headed another way. "Well, whatever it was, they loved it and loved you. Thank you. Next Wednesday it would be great if you could come early. Say at four or five if that works for you. Let me know. Thanks!"

Geology, Sufism, Wine Tasting, British Lit., Soundtracks to War Movies. There was a rumor that several of us were about to be thrown out of Wine Tasting, as we were underage and some computer or other—not the original one—had just noticed. Just as well, perhaps. A grasp of oakiness had continued to elude me. I got citrus and buttery and chocolate, but violet, too, proved difficult. Was it all just baloney? The grind of the semester seemed to be taking place off to one side of me. Still, I did try. I would do my work at night, dive into the blue of my computer screen, which would wash on like a California pool. Then, after swimming in it for a while, I'd come tiredly to the surface with bits of this or that—in my hair, if not my head. My computer desktop indicated I was at least working on things. I was starting, then starting over fresh without deleting the first thing: my screen looked like an aquarium where a hundred tiny square-finned fish had died, randomly frozen in place. Except for the Sufism, taught by the Donegal don, classes marched along forgettably. In the Neutral Pelvis I was also learning about the cantilevered torso, the inner space, and the choral *om*. But in Sufism we learned that Rumi was a man in love, and the absence of the beloved entered all his cravings, which it really didn't do with Doris Lessing. In Geology we were learning the effects of warmth and cold, which at bottom I began to see was what all my courses were about. In Soundtracks to War Movies we were given a list—every war from the ancient to now, *Gladiator* to *Black Hawk Down*—and we were to see as many depictions as we could and note their melodies.

———

With Murph gone, I moved my desk away from the window, where the leaking draft would chill and hunch me. I made the computer screen itself into my sole window. From here only I would look out into the world. I googled my father to see what others were saying about his produce and to check out his website and what it indicated about the coming spring crops. I googled Sarah and Le Petit Moulin and learned that she had once cooked dinner at the White House for President Clinton. Perhaps it had gone badly and this is why she'd failed to mention it. Wine before swine? Pearls before martians? Perhaps she had served actual swine. Apparently she had indeed served them pork, local and organic and deposited in what I now thought of as a diaperlike tortilla. Tortillas seemed to me a mistake. She had also served them a walnut and buttermilk sorbet. Perhaps there was also a salad—mesclun with lemon-shallot dressing (I was making up names of dishes in my head: Kiwi carpaccio! Funnel of fennel! Couscous with frou-frou!)—and surely other things. But only the pork and sorbet were mentioned. I googled myself, my laptop screen becoming not only a window but a mirror. I wanted to see how I was doing out there in the world, or rather not I but the other Tassie Keltjin I'd discovered who was a grandmother and an emergency 911 volunteer outside of Pestico. *Mirror, mirror, on the wall.* Weekly I would google her and see how she was doing. One week she celebrated her fortieth wedding anniversary with her husband, Gus. Another week she tied for second in a pie-baking contest. And then one day I googled her and her obituary flashed up on the screen, and that is when I stopped googling her for a while.

When next I went to the Thornwood-Brinks' it was Edward who again greeted me at the kitchen table. Did he not have the speed-dating of fruit flies to chaperone?

He smiled at me in a warm and charming way that made me look behind me to see if someone else was there. No one was.

"I wanted to let you know that the cleaning gay is coming today."

"I beg your pardon?"

"I'm sorry. He's gay. He cleans. I call him the cleaning gay. Sarah yells at me for that. The cleaning *guy.* His name is Noel. Though he sometimes likes to be called Noelle. His vacuum cleaner used to frighten Emmie, but now she's obsessed with it. He sometimes lets her push it around. That's all OK."

"Sounds good," I said. "Is she napping now?"

"She is," he said. And gave me one of those smiles again, full of craggy warmth and intelligent twinkle. I turned around to see once more if someone was behind me. And then he left.

When Noel came, noisily bursting through the back door with buckets of cleansers and sponges, I introduced myself.

"Just call me No*elle,*" he said of himself. "When I was little they used to call me Noel, Noel, the toilet bowl. Although now I have thought of painting that on the side of my van. It might be good for business? I don't know."

"How long have you been working here?" I asked.

"Too long," he sighed. "Though I love Sarah. She's fabulous."

"How about Monsieur?"

He sighed and leaned on his mop. "Gay men don't like straight men."

"Really?" I somehow doubted that.

"Why should they?"

I shrugged. "No reason."

"Little Emmie's a doll, isn't she? I'm so thrilled for Sarah. I hope they'll get a swing set out back for her."

"That would be good," I said.

"Today's my birthday," he added.

"Happy birthday. How old are you?" He looked somewhere in his thirties.

"Sixty," he said. "It's a biggie."

"Well, you sure don't look that!" Although even as I was saying it, beneath his dyed black hair I could see the leathery skin and rheumy eyes of age, or the fumes of harsh cleaning fluids, whichever it was.

"Actually, it's not my birthday."

"Oh," I said.

I had read *some* Lewis Carroll—but clearly not enough.

"I'm just trying that out—it *is* coming up, so I'm trying it out on people." A test. Perhaps it was a test of me as well. Still, I thought we could be friends. There was a nice kind of upstairs-downstairs vibe I was getting from him—we two could be the downstairs. Or was it upstairs? We would be the back stairs.

"Well, as I said, you don't look sixty."

He flung his hands at me. "Oh, don't say that! It makes me feel worse, like you're lying. Look! Emmie!" I turned and there she was, having awoken, rashy-cheeked and tumbleheaded. She'd made her way over the crib rails, down the stairs, past all the gates.

"Tassa!" she said, and ran and hugged my legs.

In Sufism I continued to sit next to the Brazilian. *WHAT THE HELL IS THIS PROF SAYING?* he wrote to me.

"He's actually very smart," I murmured back. "He's talking about the four stages of the *tariqa* and their rituals. There's a lot of piety, renunciation, and yearning for Paradise."

Then he leaned toward me and whispered, "I can see you don't join that easily in complaining. That's a good quality. But so is joining easily."

Walking out of the lecture hall he said to me, "Did you know it's blackbird days—*i giorni della merla*?"

"What is that? I've never heard of that."

He studied me for a moment. "It's a celebration of the white blackbird who has taken refuge in the chimney, which blackens him with soot. It celebrates the soot."

"Interesting," I said, thinking of Mary-Emma and other possible myths of the white blackbird.

"It's Brazilian," he said.

I nodded. My head filled with the renunciation of renunciation. And a yearning for yearning.

I began to dress for him, relying mostly on a new gray-brown sweater dress I had bought in a boutique downtown with my new wages, a store where the clerks were chicly eager to help and where each item of apparel was in a color called Peat or Pumice or some such word. There were subtleties of neutral hue I'd never encountered before: Pebble, Pecan, Portabella, Peanut, Platinum, Porcelain, Pigeon, Parmesan, Pavement, Parchment, Pearl, and, ah, Potato. There were the brighter colors, too. One could recite them all like a jump-rope rhyme. Paprika. Pinot, Persimmon! Pimento! Pomegranate, Pine! Poplar, Pistachio, Peacock, Petal Pink, Polar Peach, Pumpkin, Pepper, Plum, Pineapple. Periwinkle, Peridot, Primrose, Palm, Pea, Poppy, Puce. My new dress was in a shade called Oyster, which was a lot like Fig Gray, I noticed, and which I called Stick, since it was the color of a stick. Growing up far from the sea, what did I know of oysters? It was the same hue as a muddy russet potato before the potato was hosed off. I felt it made my eyes dark and my hair shine, but maybe the color appealed because unlike so much else I owned it was not a yellowish shade of green that threw itself in with the natural tinge of my teeth. On days I wore the dress, along with my water bra, the Brazilian was friendlier. Soon, and after an unfortunate but not totally annihilating laundering, I was calling the dress "shtick." Did he not know these were not my real breasts, or not really? Did guys even bother to want to know? Girls were walking around wearing these soft protrusions and guys were just going "Do-dee-do" like Homer Simpson. Perhaps when God said, "Let there be light," in the original and correct Bible, still undiscovered, he also said, "Let there be do-dee-do." Thank you, God.

After class the Brazilian and I would walk out together. He was tall and long-limbed beside me, and my walking close to him, in matched stride with him, made me feel in possession of a prize. One time we made it all the way to a coffee shop, where I asked him whether he'd like to have coffee with me, and he said no.

"Coals to Newcastle and all that," I said, flustered. "Why would a Brazilian drink coffee in America—don't know what I was thinking." I turned to go.

"I'd like a Coke," he said.

"OK," I said. "They have Pepsi in there. Is that all right?"

"OK," he said. He had a smile that made you realize that some skulls contained an entire power plant set up in miniature inside, and the heat and electricity they generated spilled their voltage out through the teeth and eyes.

"Teach me some Portuguese," I said over coffee and cola at a back table near a table of zines and flyers.

And what he taught me, phrases from little songs—*Ahora voy a dormire, bambino, / Porque llevo el pijama: si! no! si! no!*—I repeated and rehearsed at home and even taught Mary-Emma. They could have been Etruscan for all I knew. *Negro, blanco, / Me gusta naranja!* I learned much later it was actually Spanish with some Italian thrown in. Except for the words to "Happy Birthday," none of it was Portuguese at all.

Thus began my protracted misunderstanding of Romance languages (in high school I had taken German with Frau Zinkraub; on the tops of all my quizzes I drew pictures of Panzer tanks with Hitler on top in a salute; I had tried Latin, but *in situ* there had been no one to speak it with—and so what was the point? I would do things like imagine *ergonomic* meant "thereforeish"). Romance languages eluded me both generally and specifically; nothing was as cryptic and ripe for misunderstanding as the physical language of a boy's love. What was an involuntary grimace I took to be rapture. What was a simple natural masculine compulsion to be in, to tunnel and thrust, I saw as a tender desire to be sweetly engulfed and at least momentarily overpowered by another's devoted attentions. What was an urgent, automatic back-and-forth of the body I thought of as the eternal romantic return of the lover. Kissing was not animal appetite but the heart flying up to the lips and speaking its unique attraction and deep eternal fondnesses in the only way it could. The juddering of climax, as involuntary as a death rattle, I took to be a statement of hopeless attachment. Why, I don't know. I didn't think of myself as sentimental. I thought of myself as spiritually alert.

Uh-oh, as Mary-Emma would say.

"Are you a virgin?" he had asked.

"Yes," I said. That he couldn't tell already, that it wasn't spelled out all over my face and demeanor, thrilled me. To be funny, I rolled my head with a harlot's abandon and purred, "I am." I fell back, the way a cooked onion slid apart, in all its layers, when bit.

Later I would come to believe that erotic ties were all a spell, a temporary psychosis, even a kind of violence, or at least they coexisted with these states. I noted that criminals as well as the insane tended to give off a palpable, vibrating allure, a kind of animal magnetism that kept them loved by someone. How else could they survive at all? Someone had to hide them from the authorities! Hence the necessity and prevalence of sex appeal for people who were wild and on the edge.

If only I could have dated someone who was both insane and criminal. If only I could have dated the criminally insane! I could have doubled my fun and entered the purest, highest exhilarating erotic and narcotic trance! and if I'd lived to tell the tale, perhaps come to my senses sooner. I was in a fused condition of ecstasy and retrospective rue almost always, and from the beginning. "I love you," I would say, and he said nothing at all. But no shame rose in me to rescue or silence me. "I love you," I said again. And then I added, "Is there an echo in here?"

"There is," he would say, smiling. His teeth were the color of cream. His gums the pale lox pink of a winter tomato. He wore wrapped around his neck a black-and-white scarf—a print I thought of as Middle Eastern, though it could have been a Navajo tablecloth, for all I knew.

"Yeah, I thought so." I would tenderly smooth the strands of hair off my own face, myself.

I had told Murph that I had a crush on a South American and while I was out she called from her boyfriend's one night and sang into the phone machine: "Pedro Pedro bo bedro, banana fanna fo fedro, fee fie mo medro . . ."

His name was Reynaldo, and as the snow melted, I began to bring Mary-Emma—in her Radio Flyer wagon or in her stroller—on walks to his apartment. To bring him a present—a doughnut or Danish or a hot mocha—I would stop in the market on the way there, in a section of town where there were actual black people shopping (unlike the Wednesday-night rumors of such). Some would look at me, then at Mary-Emma, and then at me again and smile. They seemed to be welcoming me into the community. Some would say hi to Mary-Emma. There were only a few bits of unpleasantness from women. Two black women and one white one scowled at me: I was a tramp. For some black women I clearly had encroached upon their men and produced this baby; besides, what did I know about bringing up an African-American child in this world? (Nothing.) To the white woman I was a whoring girl messing around with anyone. This was all said in looks, so the truth could not be uttered, but I saw again and again what it was simply to walk into a store for a doughnut and have a wordless racial experience.

But mostly black people were smiling and warm to us. Everyone loved a beautiful baby, no matter what.

"Hey, sweetie!" they said. And Mary-Emma would smile or hide her face in her own shoulder.

Once, I thought I saw Sarah's car following us, but when I turned saw nothing.

When I brought Mary-Emma, Reynaldo and I did not kiss or touch at all in front of her, but often I returned to his place with her after having left his bed for work just that morning, wanting badly to see him again soon and right away. It was neither near nor far—one could get there in twenty-five minutes without much trouble, and when we arrived he was very kind to us both. He loved the doughnuts. He loved that particular mocha coffee. He was taking a photography class and took pictures of us with a new digital camera he had just bought—we said "cheese" in three languages, and then "keys" and then "please," and when we were not paying attention he would suddenly sneak up and snap our picture from the side. Or freeze us in the frame, I should say. Digital cameras were still new, and seemed magical, as right in the moment he could have you look through the frames and say which picture you wanted. He made me some strong Brazilian morning tea, to last the whole day, and poured juice for Mary-Emma. She poked around and got into things, but he had a real xylophone, which he let her play, with both the soft cotton-dampened mallets and the harder wood ones with their zingier sound, and it all delighted her. She struck hard and with every note turned to look at me with amazement. "Here, let me show you," Reynaldo would say, and he would take two sticks per hand and bounce them around on what I thought of as a double-decker keyboard. She seemed to love Reynaldo because he was attentive and appreciative, and perhaps because he was brown (the colorblindness of small children was a myth; she noticed difference and sameness, with almost equal interest; there was no "Dilemma of Difference" as my alliteration-loving professors occasionally put it; there was no "Sin of the Same"), but she also loved him because of that xylophone. He played the only American song he knew, a folk one with verse upon verse of wide water and longing and woe, one that ended ". . . like the summer dew." And then he was very quiet, saying, "Shouldn't it be 'like the summer *does*'?"

"Where have you been?" asked Sarah.

"What do you mean?" There was something in her voice I'd not really heard before. I wondered if this was her restaurant voice. Not as sharp as the coulis-and-quenelles voice. But perhaps a beef-cheek-and-parsnip-gnocchi voice.

"I was driving home and I saw you on Maple Avenue coming from what seemed quite far away. And Edward told me he's seen you headed the other way, fast as can be, Emmie in the stroller and you just zipping along God knows where to."

"I'm sorry. Should I not take her for walks?"

I'd never felt accused before. Perhaps I had never *been* accused before. I had, however, never been responsible for very much before, not really, and had little practice in having my actions observed and found lacking. Well, once, in ninth grade, I had tried out for cheerleading. But could that even count? When I went to fly into the air with one knee up, one leg back, one hand on my hip—a stag jump, it was called—I'd come down in a heap and the observing was quickly over.

Sarah's voice softened. "Oh, of course you should." And then she seemed to let go of the topic entirely—just let it drop and skitter—and so I didn't say any more on the matter right then.

———

With my new money—Sarah had already given me a raise—I bought a used Suzuki 125 motor scooter, which I kept on the front porch and rode to classes or to Reynaldo's, and a bedside reading lamp I ordered from a catalog. The catalog showed a man sleeping peacefully while his model-wife read a book in soft but focused light. In real life, however, the light was so intense that that same man would have had to wear sunglasses. He would have had to set up a little pup tent on his side of the bed. The lamplight was as bright as the noon sun, and as I studied next to him, Reynaldo could not sleep. Yet another pretty picture of love I'd not questioned, just bought. I turned off the light and fell behind in my reading.

It seemed now that the town had started to throw off the monochromatic winter to reveal its bright lunatic pajamas beneath. Though the robins had not yet reappeared, cardinals were whistling their mating songs. The remaining snowbanks were made dingy with rain. Only once did a late light snowfall blanket the town with a deathly quiet—a quick reminder before the winter left for good—an *amuse-bouche,* a *mignardise,* a *déjà vu,* a *je reviens:* I had dropped French long ago. *Au printemps!* The evaporating snow left the sky a lurid yellow at night. The streetlights shone off the remaining drifts, and for a few days all remained milky and low.

But soon again the journey from crocus to daffodil to peony resumed. Flowers that intended to impress only bugs had accidentally enchanted not just me. Gardens began to emerge. Every third day there was a hot lemony sun, with the lawns starting to green from rain and melted snow. The fraternity boys started to wear shorts and the siberian violets blued the yards. Still, you could sometimes see, in a shady north corner, a small black-flecked pile of snow so solid and condensed it could not melt. It was as if it had changed, biochemically, into a new substance, like the silica on Mars that was the tag end of some water or other.

Wavy thickened tulip leaves had burst the beds and flopped down, still forming their tight bullety pods, but at an angle (only the largest tulips stayed straight, I said to Reynaldo, when kissing him; beneath him at night I was being taken to places so high and starry, I feared I was taking years off my life, the way astronauts are said not to live especially long). The early tulips were caught in leafy show, the petals still prayers sealed in a leprechaun's clutch. St. Patrick's Day came and went without even a single green beer to drink. My days were too busy and full, and without Murph—who seemed to have completely vanished except for the waxy smell of her unclean hairbrush still sitting there in the bathroom, along with her black dental floss and soap and an assortment of other items—what was the point of green beer?

My strolls with Mary-Emma kept me alert to gardens and the softness of the air. The hyacinths, with their gravity-defying construction—fat botanical bumblebees with their look-Mom-I'm-flying paraphysics, which in the presence of actual gravity showed the botch of this ambition—soon bloomed and tipped. Clumps of daffodils huddled near trees, and spring phlox pinkened the hills of the park. What in June would be weeds and brush were now forsythia and the starry purple spikes of bachelor buttons (surely never worn by any bachelor ever). If I went up alleyways to better view other people's backyards, and if I didn't pay too much attention to the motley assemblages of trash cans, the alleys seemed like Irish lanes, or at least pictures I'd seen of country roads in Kerry. I'd contemplate the surreal dangle of the bleeding hearts or the columbine with their tiny eccentric lanterns in the most hardscrabble places—close to warm concrete—sprouting skyward and groundward simultaneously. If no one was looking I'd pick one for Mary-Emma. As with a snapdragon blossom you could turn one into a little talking puppet. There was a delicate hinge like a jaw, which you could squeeze open and shut. You could do little mocking imitations of your mother in the truck at the farmer's market. You didn't even need to be sitting in an actual truck to do it.

"Look, Mary-Emma!" And she would. It was a beautiful thing, having a little girl in tow. Why hadn't my own mother known? Perhaps there was too much winter permanently in our veins.

Mary-Emma would point toward the street sewers, seeing a raccoon scuttle in. "Cartoons down there!" she exclaimed.

Dwarf irises, bearded irises, and the first mosquitoes emerged simultaneously, each with their subtly striped gray-violet plumage. Where were the bearded dwarves to add semantic meat to the flowerbeds? Well, some yards did have ceramic gnomes in their yards à la Germany.

The strengthening light sparkled in the trees' new leaves, and the thick bosomy smell of lilacs floated in waves across our various paths. The humid spice of honeysuckle hung over the garbage cans. I even met the threesome next door, who finally emerged after winter, looking very beautiful. The woman—I remembered her name was Catherine—smiled at Mary-Emma. And Mary-Emma did not smile back but hid behind my leg.

"She never says hi to me," said the woman, Catherine. The two men had continued on ahead. "I hope it's not because I'm white!"

I stared at this crazy, Satie-playing woman. "A lot of people she knows are white," I did not say, "including her parents," and so I said nothing but just watched as she trotted up ahead to be with her men.

In the Thornwood-Brink flowerbeds were the strangest blooms of all: tall leafless stalks crowned by purple floreted globes. They looked like probes, or sentries, or gaslights, or wands, the handsome goons of the garden. Alium, they were called, and in actuality were giant mutant chives. Their bulbs were like onions, and squirrel-proof, and they were supposed to be a kind of accent flower, but Sarah had planted them thickly all around the house in a kind of fierce, orchardlike fence, as if to enhance TV reception.

"Look at this!" exclaimed Sarah at the front door, pulling a printed sheet of paper from her mailbox. "The plant nazis are back! Apparently I have buckthorn and nipplewort in my yard and they would like me to get rid of them pronto! You know, the thing with plant nazis is that they *start* with the plants . . ."

The dogs next door were wild with their games. In the sky the returning geese were winging over, their honking alto bark like the complaining squawk of a cart.

"Last year they were after me about the nap of the lawn! They said I was mowing in the wrong direction and it disrupted the look of the neighborhood to have the blades of grass bent in a slightly different direction in one of the yards! I was mowing this way"—and here she tipped her whole body—"when I should be mowing thattaway." She tipped her body back the other direction. Indignation gave her a dancer's energy. And the warming weather caused her nervous thinness to emerge from beneath her usual thick sweaters.

One of the pictures Reynaldo took of Mary-Emma that I liked best showed her looking upward at the camera in hope and joy, and I took it to Kinko's and had it blown up and then I went to Walgreens with Mary-Emma herself in tow and bought a shiny red made-in-China frame. The African-American cashier looked quickly at me and then at Mary-Emma and said, "You should braid her hair. No black girl's worn an afro since 1972." Then she handed me my receipt without looking at me. I took the purchase back to Sarah's, put the photo, which was in my backpack, into the frame, and then propped the whole thing on the dining room table as a gift. I could hear Sarah on the phone in the kitchen, working out the wording details on this week's menu. " 'Sheathed in bacon'? I don't think so. It sounds—well, I don't need to tell you what it sounds like. And look at that chicken again: there are too many adjectives in front of it. It's like we're trying to hide something."

"Whossat?" I whispered to Mary-Emma, pointing at the dining room wall, toward the sound of Sarah's voice.

"Mama," she said, smiling.

"And whossat?" I pointed at the picture of her on the table.

"Emmie!" she said, excited.

"That's right," I said, and I danced her around the living room. The windows were open and we could hear the dogs yapping and chasing each other next door. When I spun and stopped I then saw Sarah just standing there in the dining room. Oddly, I could smell her: she was wearing my perfume.

"Who took this?" she said, indicating the photograph on the table.

I was taken aback, as if struck by a mechanical hand belonging to no one. "A friend. I thought you might like it." Sharp heat plucked and pinched at my eyes. I had only wanted to please and surprise her, but now I felt suddenly very tired. I glanced at the photo again, to try to see it from her point of view, and noticed that in it Mary-Emma was sitting on Reynaldo's prayer rug. I hoped it looked like a yoga mat.

"What friend?" she said, looking stern and troubled.

"A friend of mine," I said stupidly, as I was now afraid and unsure. At this point Sarah seemed to lose concentration. Out front a car was idling high but driving by slow, the bass of its stereo deep in a rap song, vibrating and loud. It was a local hit, one recorded here, and it went "Out of Troy! Black Boy! You show your indignation, you end up on probation!"

"Whoever that is, they keep driving past: this is the fourth time this week and the second time today. That's not your friend, is it?"

"No," I said. "My friend is Brazilian." As if this explained everything, the innocent photography, the innocence generally. *A maiden knows her love like the sky the distant grass.* That is, knows her love sort of, and from aloft sees not a blade. My head was full of middling poetry, only some of it my own.

"There it is again!" she exclaimed, and then she turned quickly to get to the front window to see, I assume, if she could actually make out the driver, the car, the spinning rims, the license plate.

She turned back toward me. "Have you noticed this car going by anytime before?"

"I don't know what car it is."

"Well, any car going by with a thundering bass and slowing down on this block?"

Actually, I had noticed it. The rap music and the car. You could hear its approach, the car turning the corner, the music booming like a furnace firing in a basement below you. I was attuned to the bass notes. But what I had noticed more, and what concerned me more, was the phone ringing and then when I answered it, as Sarah had instructed me to do, "Thornwood-Brink residence," there was a long silence, then a hang-up. My thoughts had wandered to Bonnie, that she was home alone, not getting her life together at all, not nearly as she had hoped, not even close, and was instead lying fetally on a sofa in a position of seller's remorse, tears of devastation streaming down her cheeks. How not.

But I could see now that Sarah's concerns were not with Bonnie but with the mysterious, gone-missing birth father. I could see she imagined that it might be he who was driving past, having somehow found out Mary-Emma's new address. He had not officially signed off on any papers. And though the agency had done all the things it was supposed to do, advertise in the local papers and seek him out in the halfhearted legalistic manner that fulfilled their obligation, it was easy to imagine a young guy in a bar or at work or walking with a cousin on a nice day back from church or home from school and suddenly hearing he had a child given up for adoption, and somehow wanting the child back. Had she not imagined the birth father as one of the Green Bay

Packers, as I had? A minor celebrity, handsome, carefree, with no time for a relationship, let alone a child? At the very least she should have imagined him as perhaps the wayward son of one of the aging running backs.

"I'm not sure that I've paid that much attention," I said.

"OK!" Her face reddened. "Have you paid attention to *this*?" She pointed wrathfully at the photo. "The photographer? Have you paid attention to him? Who is this person taking pictures of Emmie?"

I did not say anything, because I could no longer speak.

The car with the booming rap song trawled by once more. "There it is again!" Sarah cried, and raced to the window. I could see her lips moving silently, memorizing, and then she went quickly into the kitchen and wrote down the license plate number on a Post-it.

"I've put the license plate number by the phone. If you see that particular car again, let me know."

"OK."

"It's just . . ." And here she moved both hands through her hair in anguish, her words a kind of muttering to herself. "My whole life feels like a horror show of slowly moving cars . . ." I didn't know what she meant by that—a funeral? "Look, I'm sorry. I've upset you," she said. She touched my shoulder in what might have been tenderness, but I was too frozen to discern exactly. "Thank you for the picture. I understand. It's a lovely picture. She looks darling. But no more. Do you understand?"

"Yes," I said automatically.

"It's not that I don't trust your friend. It's just, I might not trust his Rolodex."

"I don't think he has a Rolodex," I said daftly.

Sarah's eyes bore down on mine. "Now I'm going to tell you something I didn't tell you before. I never phoned the references you listed on your résumé. I hired you because you seemed angelic to me. You gave off an aura. I didn't phone one person on your list. Or, well, I phoned one person, but they weren't home. I didn't care what any of them said. I was a snob about you. I trusted my own instincts completely."

I didn't know what to tell her. Like everyone, I felt I was a good person. How could I tell her she should have phoned the references? How could I tell her, *Why would you place your child in the hands of someone whose references you never checked out?*

"I can see that you love Emmie, and I know she loves you. She says your name when she wakes up from naps. You are, sometimes, the first person she asks for. I don't mean to sound suspicious of your friend, but I don't want him taking pictures of Emmie. When you go for walks with her, go someplace else, not to his place, not with him." She put her hand on my shoulder and smiled. "Love is a fever," she said. "And when you come out of it you'll discover whether you've been lucky or—not."

I was silent and so was she.

"I am concerned for you just as I would be for anyone," she added strangely.

I went into what my mother called okey-dokey mode. I grabbed for the midwestern girl's shielding send-off. "Sounds good," I said.

I began to find back routes to Reynaldo's. One did not have to go down the most obvious streets. If I took the alleys, past the flowering bushes and the refuse and recycling bins, I could travel unseen, with Mary-Emma and her kick-ass American stroller bumping along the pebbles and potholes all the way to Reynaldo's. There we would nuzzle and chat and he would make pepper water or early-morning curry, which I then believed to be Brazilian cuisine, and we would eat. Mary-Emma would play, and the pictures Reynaldo took—for his photography class—he no longer gave me, just showed me, and they were mostly taken from behind her as she studied something in her hands, an ashtray or a clock. She could have been anyone's child in the world. He would play soccer with her and teach her phrases and songs. He always said *"Ciao"* when we left, and Mary-Emma had begun to repeat it, and wave. "*Ciao,* Airnaldo!"

When I brought her back home she was often dozing from the stroller ride and I would take her directly upstairs to the attic nursery, where she promptly woke up. I could hear Sarah on the phone: ". . . roasted figs, braised wild boar with dried Death's Door cherries, uh-huh, veal sweetbreads with chestnuts—this is very Sheriff of Nottingham! I mean, it's springtime. Where is the spring? Where are the new potatoes, asparagus, ramps and fiddleheads, vinaigrettes and roux? How about that lemon sorbet with the chopped basil on top?"

Dementedly, and because Mary-Emma would not take a nap now, I made a clapping song out of "ramps and fiddleheads / vinaigrettes and roux," and after Sarah got off the phone Mary-Emma and I went downstairs and performed it for her, risking that Sarah might feel mocked, but she didn't—I hoped.

"Like our song, Mama?" asked Mary-Emma. Sarah seemed both amused and embarrassed, and her laughter contained the slightly hysterical, undulating edge of each.

"Oh, thank you for this, I guess," she said, and Mary-Emma ran to her and threw her arms around one of her legs, pressed her cheek against her thigh. Sarah petted her head. "I feel like this restaurant is driving me mad!" she said absently. "Someone just accused me of raping the forest floor. Because of the fiddlehead ferns. And because of the veal, one of the waiters is going around the kitchen bleating 'Mommy, Mommy!' "

"Mommy!" Mary-Emma repeated happily, and Sarah smiled.

"It's sort of funny," I said, shrugging. "Though sad, too."

"It's only once a week that we change the menu—why should it be so hard? And then the absenteeism! of the sous-chef alone—not to mention the waitstaff. I'm going to keep all the messages from my voice mail and make a CD of excuses I get from employees: *Can't come in; I'm coughing blood . . .* and I'm going to play it full volume at the end-of-the-year holiday party."

"Mama," said Mary-Emma, cooing—wanting, perhaps, Sarah's leg to go slack.

Sarah continued to pet Mary-Emma's head, but at the same time she rolled her own neck around. "When I roll my neck around like this," she said, sort of smiling and sort of not, "I hear the scariest sorts of crunching sounds."

"That happens to me," I said.

"Ach," said Sarah, with her eyes closed. "Every year we do too much with venison and ground cherries. It's like stuff you'd scrape off your car."

Once I brought Mary-Emma back from a walk and found Edward there at home, alone, laughing with someone on the phone. When he hung up, he was still in a good mood. "Papa," Mary-Emma said mirthlessly, but she lifted her arms and he swooped her up into his.

"How'd your day go?" he said to me rather than to her.

"Fine," I said.

"Fine," she said. She began unzipping her own jacket. I walked over to help her take it off since Edward was holding her. This caused us to have to maneuver together.

"Things well with you?" Edward said to me warmly.

"Oh, I think so."

"Lot on your mind?" I didn't know where this interest in me was coming from. Did I seem gloomy and preoccupied? Out of reach of his charms?

"Oh, I don't know. There's classes, of course." And lest he think I was complaining that work and school were too difficult in combination, I hastened to add, "Plus, my brother's thinking of joining the military."

"Oh."

"I'm hoping he doesn't"—this was true—"and it's been on my mind, I guess." This last was not strictly so, but it should have been. Why wasn't it?

"It'll toughen him up, show him one or two things about the world," said Edward. "What does not kill him will make him stronger," he added prosaically, needlepoint Nietzsche.

"Yes, but what if it *does* kill him?"

And here between us passed a look of pale apprehension, some past, some future, the details of which I couldn't yet know, but each blasting into the room and meeting there, draining the blood from our faces. Only the voice of Mary-Emma—"Papa! Oag cool!"—returned us to the warm crumbs of the present.

"Nietzschean philosophy doesn't get its hands dirty with *that*," he said, making his way to the freezer. He was suddenly a scientist again. "And neither should you. Philosophers are good at parties but not for cleaning up after. But really: Let me tell you something. Don't be your brother's keeper. Don't worry about brothers. Take it from someone who has a sister. Worry about yourself. The brothers? They're not really worried about you."

Schoolwork was alternately tedious and mesmerizing. I took the notes my professors wanted me to. In the library, in the margins of my books, I wrote "nature equals disorder." I wrote "fate versus free will." I wrote "modernism as argument against the modern." I listened endlessly to the music from *Schindler's List*. Then *The Bridge on the River Kwai*. Mostly, however, I was alone in my room with Rumi. Murph continued to stay away, although once she sent me an e-mail that described a long fight she had had with her boyfriend and then the kissing and other acts of contrition that had pasted them back together. Another e-mail I got was from my brother. *Dear Sis,* it began. *Only you could perhaps talk me out of this, if you wanted to, but only if you wanted to, because*

I'm not sensing anyone having any strong desire with regards to my future except myself and it is this: to do something real. I don't care what part of the world I end up in as long as it isn't Delton County.

Then he sent another e-mail that began simply, *Please read this new one and ignore previous e-mail,* and so I ignored the first but failed to read the new one, seeing nothing dangerously swaggering in anything he'd sent so far.

Spring warmed the air. Light fell from the sky like sugar from a bowl. At night, if I slept at home, without Reynaldo, he would phone. "Are you asleep?" he would always ask.

"No."

"You sound as if you are. Quick. How many fingers am I holding up?"

He would make me laugh.

Noel, Noel, the toilet bowl. Noelle turned off the vacuum cleaner when he saw me. "It's finally my birthday," he said. "Really. I put a patchouli sachet in the vacuum bag for the occasion."

"Well, happy birthday," I said, and together with Mary-Emma in my arms sang him "Happy Birthday" in Portuguese. As we finished the last lines— *"muitas felicidades, muitos anos de vida!"*—we sang them with great articulated gusto, as at the concluding ring it reminded me of "Ina Gadda Da Vida." Clapping began behind us, and I turned.

There were Sarah and Edward. Only Edward was smiling. "Very nice," said Sarah, looking at me. She was wearing a gold sweater knit in tight roseknots so that her slim arms looked like ears of corn. On her head was her thick cotton chef's toque. "What language is that?"

"Portuguese," I said. "I think."

"Portuguese," Sarah repeated, nodding her head.

"It's my birthday," said Noel, to help me out.

"Yes, well, happy birthday, my dear Noelle!" She kissed him on his cheek and then threw one arm around him and kept it there. I could see he'd been working for her for years.

He pointed at her but looked at me to tell me this: "I love her!"

"Yes, but, darling, you left your Diet Coke in the freezer and it exploded again." Sarah would not smile. Or rather, she would not smile big.

I turned with Edward and Mary-Emma as we headed back to the kitchen. Edward was shaking his head. "He's always doing that with the Diet Cokes," he said.

I went to warm a muffin in the microwave for Mary-Emma, and Edward suddenly stopped my arm. "Look," he said. "There's a moth in there." Without putting the muffin in, he pressed On to see what the moth would do. This penchant for torture, in the guise of curiosity, was the same sick experimentation of certain doctors, of bored boys, of lunatics, and it was in Edward, too. The moth was not singed. Neither did it flutter and combust, as a heartless data-seeker might have predicted. As I myself had predicted. Had I missed my own latent calling as Mad Inept Scientist? The moth did nothing at all, just stuck whole to the plastic wall of the oven. Probably the poor creature had already been dead for some time. I cleaned it out with a paper towel, then warmed Mary-Emma's snack.

"Well, I wanted to see," said Edward.

Thoughts of Bonnie preoccupied me. I dreamed of her at night. She was always approaching to say something but then said nothing. She floated. She zoomed. She burst forth from adjacent rooms. There were no doors and then suddenly one would appear and swallow her. She would emerge through a wall. She was always empty-handed. She was gaining weight. Her clothes were the pale gray of plastic copy machines and desktop printers. She would not speak. I couldn't get her ever to say a word.

At the Thornwood-Brinks' the phone rang a lot, and when I answered it there was a long pause before the hang-up. Then for a while the phone calls seemed to cease.

Worried that Bonnie had taken her own life, I googled Bonnie Jankling Crowe again, expecting to find, as ever, nothing. I instead found a notice from a Georgia newspaper about someone named Bonnie J. Crowe who had been found murdered in an apartment in Atlanta. No known suspect. No evidence of robbery. Investigation pending. My heart leaped up. Of course! I thought. This would be exactly the sort thing that would happen to poor doomed Bonnie. Here I was worried she was suicidal when in fact getting herself murdered would be more her style.

But how would she have had the money to get to Atlanta? Might she have sold her new gold watch for which she had traded a child and been ushered into a retirement from if not all happiness at least all things Mary? I went on eBay and discovered a gold watch for sale there by someone who went by bonniegreenbay. And how many Bonnie Crowes were there in this world? How many bonniegreenbays? I had to stop. I had discovered too much. I had learned things there was not a test on: I had to get back to my studies. The soundtracks to *The Longest Day* and *Saving Private Ryan* played incessantly in my apartment.

On Saturday nights I visited Reynaldo on my own. I no longer wore the water bra—that jig was up, or that jug-jig, as Murph called it. He did not seem to mind my lack of dairiness, as we said of cows. In fact, he seemed enthralled or at least very attentive, and once said he preferred small-breasted girls. ("And you *believed* him?" a later boyfriend would say to me cruelly.) If the gray dress was not available, I would be forced to make an outfit from all the different black things I owned, which were all a slightly different black: there was the bluish black and the olive black and most oddly the reddish black—all faded or shiny or worn to a hue unique unto itself and impossible to wear with anything else that was black. I would add a silvery swampy sweater, with dangling balls or quartz for earrings, like a third and fourth eye in the dark against my hair. I wore lipstick that made my mouth look bloody. I wore mascara that by morning had collected like soot in the corners of my eyes. I wore an army green jacket that looked unexpected with a fuzzy ivory scarf looped around the collar like the scruff of a chow.

As if adorned for a costume party's idea of a terrorist, I wore my Egyptian scarab necklace and my Arabian Goddess perfume and a clumsy blue ring made in the backstreets of Karachi. I was politically incorrect. The idea was a surprise attack. Which seemed to work. Often we didn't talk at all. His arms were soft and strong. His penis was as small and satiny as a trumpet mushroom in Easter basket grass. His mouth slurped carefully as if every part of me were an oyster, his, which made me feel I loved him. He would pull away and look at me happily from above. "You have the long, pettable nose of a horse," he said, "and a horse's dark, sweet eyes." And I thought of all the horses I had seen and how they always seemed to be trying to get their eyes to focus and work together. Their eyes were beautiful but shy and lost, and since they were on opposite sides of their heads like a fish's, one of them would sometimes rear up in skepticism and fear and just take a hard look at you. I felt nothing like a horse, whose instincts I knew were to run and run. I had mostly in life tried to stand still like a glob of coral so as not to be spotted by sharks. But now I had crawled out onto land and was somehow already a horse.

There was a tender but energetic adhoccery to our sex, the way there is when young people are not embarrassed by their bodies—what they look like and what they want. Kissing was urgent yet careful, luminous and drinklessly drunk. He hovered—quivering, tense, and flight-bound—I bucked, humped, and arced, a dancer in a sea lion suit. Afterward, he would sometimes say,

"That was one for the scrapbook!" When I slept in his bed, I slept deeply and long. When I went to the Thornwood-Brinks' directly from there, I would sometimes walk, sometimes take my Suzuki scooter. Sarah would flee the house with arbitrary explanations: "I don't want the Mill to become one of those precious little restaurants with everyone so serious in their white jackets like they're technicians in some sort of lab. Though look at me." She pointed to her own Marie Curie getup. "I look like a dental hygienist." This was the sort of snobbery I noticed even among the most compassionate Democrats. I could hardly say I was immune. What was education for, if not to acquire contradictions? At least it looked like that to me. "I mean, Edward works in a lab and he doesn't even wear a white jacket. Though maybe he should . . . And yet honestly, *some* discipline is required in every kitchen. I left a note for you on Emmie. She's got a tiny bit of a cold and the Tylenol drops and instructions are right there on the counter. Bye!"

She had bought a new attachment for the bicycle, which I would put Mary-Emma in instead of the wagon, and we rode around the park that way, while Mary-Emma sang and hummed herself to sleep, her voice wobbly on the bumps. I would pass the town's few black and Latino kids fishing in the pond for dinner, and I would think of the absurd disparities of everyone, how Mary-Emma was now a little African-American princess while these poor kids at the pond were the casualties of a new pull-away-and-don't-look society. Here is where churchlessness had gotten us. Not that far. And so I often admired Reynaldo's piety. Still, the kids were having fun fishing. But I could see they hadn't yet caught a thing. Nonetheless, it was spring, and they were young, and even hedge fund managers couldn't take that away from them.

On Wednesday days when I was with Mary-Emma, the noon whistle would blare and the dogs next door would go barking mad in choral reply, as if saluting some larger king dog. On Wednesday nights, as if echoing this, the house once more filled up with visitors and their remarks. Contentious shards of discussion floated upward like dust shaken from a rug.

"Postracial is a white idea." This again. It had all begun to sound to me like a spiritually gated community of liberal chat.

"A lot of ideas are white ideas."

"It's like postfeminist or postmodern. The word *post* is put forward by people who have grown bored of the conversation."

"And the conversation remains unresolved because it's not resolvable. It's not that kind of conversation. It's merely living talk. Whereas you put *post* in front of it—what is that? It's saying 'Shut the hell up. We're tired and we're going to sleep now.' "

"If you reject religion, you reject blackness."

"Black culture here is just southern culture moved north, that's all."

"Well, that's not all."

"Blacks have preserved the South up here—the cooking, the expressions, the accents—better than the southern whites who've moved here have."

"Why is that?"

"Uh—isn't that obvious?"

"Southern whites who've moved north live among the northern whites? And blacks live collected together in segregated neighborhoods?"

"I'm here representing the Pottawatomie, the Oneida, the Chippewa, the Winnebago, and the Ho-Chunk. I am here to tell you we weren't successfully integrated because we weren't given real jobs, let alone intimate jobs in your homes and on your property. Only on high bridges and tall office buildings. Your relationship to us from the beginning wasn't even exploitive. It was homicidal."

"Dave, sit down. You're mostly white."

"Is this the pot calling the kettle black?"

"I think when the pot calls the kettle black the pot is merely expressing its desire for community. It's also expressing the pot's habit of calling bullshit on the kettle."

"We can't solve history. We have to work with what's now."

"What's now is my son's white grandparents only just now got around to putting him in the will with the other grandchildren. They want to be congratulated left and right. Good God—he's ten years old. It took them ten years!"

"What's now is these self-admiring people who say, 'I don't care whether a person's black or green or purple.' As if black were a nonsense color like green or purple."

"What's now is I walk in behind Kwame when we go out to eat and I can see that the hostess is afraid of him—a thirteen-year-old black guy coming into a restaurant. I'm white so they don't know I'm his mother and am right behind him. They don't know I'm seeing them. But what I'm seeing is what Kwame experiences all the time. She sees that hooded sweatshirt, she grabs the pager, and then says stiffly, 'Can I help you?' Not 'Here for dinner?' or 'Good evening.' "

"I've got a time machine in the trunk of my car."

"Oh, I know. And the relatives all love them when they're little but then when they're older and don't look cute to them anymore, look out: they see they have a young black man as a grandson, or an African-American girl full of vim and sass. The sexualized black teenager just so doesn't work for them."

"Let me tell you: even the white ones are a shock."

Laughter.

"Is it racism or racial inexperience?"

"Oh, we're back to that."

"Girls have it bad, too."

"I said girls."

"Of all colors."

"And don't get me started on Islam!"

"And why are we so hateful about black Muslims, for decades these Chicago neighborhoods have been tense about every god-damn mosque and yet we went way out of our way for those honky Bosnian Muslims?"

"Honky Bosnian Muslims?"

"Honey, be quiet and just drink."

"A suffering sweepstakes—now there's a fool's game. Who invented the term *suffering sweepstakes* anyway?"

"People who aren't suffering. People who find it a spectator sport. Can't one say 'Ouch' without being told to shut up? What 'suffering sweepstakes'? A sweepstakes involves a prize! Besides, everyone who really is suffering knows someone who is suffering worse. Suffering *is* relative. Or at least it is with my relatives!"

"Who invented the term *suffering succotash*?"

"Here's a suffering sweepstakes: War was devised to offset the number of women who died in childbirth. The young men killed actually equaled the young women who died. But now it's all out of whack . . . so it looks like the old men are plotting to kill the young in order to get all the hot chicks."

"So that's why war was invented. To get rid of the competition. Mother Nature had put too much competition in play."

"And who is doing all this engineering again?"

"Father Nature."

"Ah."

"Nate—as he's known to his friends."

"Nate."

"Yup."

"Here's a suffering sweepstakes: Both Black Hawk and Otis Redding died in this county. But Black Hawk gets a bar and a golf course."

"He was pursued like a rat. He should get a statue."

"Is there a statue?"

"Is there a statue for Otis?"

"I think there's a granite bench."

"A granite bench? He would have preferred a golf course and a bar."

"A fool's game."

"And this pertains to our discussion how?"

"Since when did pertaining pertain?"

"Oh, yes, military recruitment of minorities."

"The schools are off to begin with. Busing and integration are never done right, and so it's a fool's game."

The fool's-game person again. Or the fool's-game person's brother.

"Look at the schools in this town. The only one that's not failing black kids is the magnet one where whites are only twenty percent of the school. Now, that's empowering! Put them in a white school, they are all relegated to the tech courses. They get put in the basement with the vocational teachers. Then they have dropped out by junior year, while the white parents continue to hoard the resources for their gifted and privileged. They want money for stringed instruments! They demand it! They get violins, we get viol*ence*. Man, you'd better get some money for some black teachers, I say."

"Plus, the school boards are hiding the real numbers. The figures they offer show only dropout rates from senior year. If you drop out before you're not in the tally, because you're going to make them look bad. You're MIA."

"So the numbers are a fairy tale."

"They're a bad fairy tale."

"Told by a bad fairy."

"Oh, I think I know who you mean."

"Stop!"

"The weird thing is that as fudged numbers go, they are still socially and racially unacceptable."

There were murmurings and bursts of laughter and indecipherable ebbs and crashes of seeming silence that would suddenly bring forth from a great distance, like the approaching music of Ravel's *Bolero,* some new monotonous melody.

"So what are you saying? That nothing short of a revolution will do?"

"Well, maybe."

"Well, that's hogwash."

I had once seen a hog washed. In whey. The hog was Helen, and she really liked it, the slop of the whey, then later a cool hose.

"It is the most unhelpful stance."

"Darling, maybe it looks unhelpful, but it seems to help others. I mean, someone has to be an idealist."

"That kind of idealism is cynicism of the most extravagant and ostentatious sort."

"Everything has to be doable here and now?"

"Everything has to be less stupid."

One of the biracial girls—Althea—stepped forward toward me with a joke. Her face was lit bright with it. "Why do black people get so tall?"

"Why?"

"Because their knee grows!" she squealed with delight.

"Who told you that?" I asked, and she pointed to one of the white girls in the corner. My having been told this joke was a source of such hilarity that both she and Althea covered their faces with their hands and laughed so hard that I laughed, too.

Reynaldo and I went to movies on campus, ones I deemed romantic date movies, and he would shift his legs around restlessly and joke about the drama's predictability. "Oh, I knew that they would do that. Of course."

"How did you know?" I whispered in the theater's musty dark.

"A call came in on my cell phone."

And I would squelch a laugh, then minutes later he might say in his intermittent accent, "My cell phone says she turns and walks away right now but then looks quickly over her shoulder." And of course he would be right. And I would laugh. We would go back to his house and drink tea.

"The first time I used a cell phone I felt so ashamed walking along talking. Talking to no one. Like a mad person. But God when he made this great world put everything in it. He knew what to put in it so we could someday have cell phones."

"Kiss me," I would say.

Sometimes we would go to a Palestinian rally, then come home, light little tea lights, and go to bed, candlelight vibrating the room like a handheld camera. He kissed like he'd been kissing for decades. I tried to learn what he knew.

At night he wrapped himself around me, legs and arms, and we slept spooned like that until in sleep one of us had to move a little. Still, we never let our skin pull entirely away from the other. "Do you believe in spiritual mistakes?" he whispered into the dark one night.

"Yes," I said.

"Do you believe an entire country could embark on a spiritual mistake?"

"Yes."

"Do you believe an entire country could *be* a spiritual mistake?"

"Yes."

And though he continued never to express a single word of love for me, not in any of his several languages, I could not take a hint. Let the hint be written across the heavens in skywriting done by several planes—I was dense. Even skywriting, well, it wasn't always certain: it might not cover the whole sky, or some breeze might smudge it, so who could really say for sure what it said? EVEN SKYWRITING WOULDN'T HAVE WORKED!

Several years later, I would wonder why I had thought my feelings for this man were anything but a raw, thrilling, vigilant infatuation. But I still had called them love. I was in love. I had learned the Portuguese and the Arabic for *love,* but all for naught. At night in his apartment bedroom, with only the little red eyes of his stereo and phone and laser printer to light up the dark, he told me in a sighing way how I was his only friend, how he had just moved here in January after his business in New York fell apart— a delivery business that took things to and from New Jersey and Queens in a white van painted NO PACKAGE TOO SMALL. After 9/11, his van could no longer make it through the tunnels and bridges in a timely fashion. As a brown man, he was constantly pulled aside and fleeced for drugs. One by one, he lost clients. Packages did not arrive quickly enough. And by December he had sold the panel truck to a white man and with the money was registering online for classes out here. "I thought I would go back to school a little."

I liked the way he said "a little." "Why out here?" I asked him.

"Good question!" he said. Some friends in New York had recommended it. "Besides, there are no tunnels for everyone to be terrified of."

"No, no terrorism. What you have to worry about here is— *corn mold*!"

"You are a farmer's daughter," he said.

"Did you have any green card issues, running that business?"

"Green card?"

Neither one of us really knew how that worked.

"Immigration status and all that."

"Oh, no. No problem there. How do you think Mohamed Atta got in? It's easy. Hasta la vista, baby."

"I wonder if Mohamed Atta ever said 'Hasta la vista,' " I said now.

"Oh, I'm sure he did," Reynaldo said quite seriously.

And then he would turn me over and begin to massage me, his fingers made of some kind of steel, and like the cracker and digger used to splay open a lobster his hands dug in. The muscles of my back and neck and legs slid apart, and even my feet seemed to spread like the bones of a fan. When I would reciprocate he would say, "Take your long guitar nails and scratch my back," and so I would.

"Where does it itch?" I would ask.

"Uh, yes, over there."

"Don't do that there-over-there thing. You've gotta say up, down, left, or right."

"Copy," he said, and then, "Yeah, right there, right in there, a little back and over . . ."

"See, no, don't do that back-and-over stuff."

"I said 'right.' "

"But not the directional right. I'm not a psychic. The itch travels. But the—"

"—witch does not?"

"Yeah, the witch does not . . ."

"Ah, but she is lovely."

Most everything was beyond words, in a plateau of pleasure and pain that lifted out the tongue and stomped it on the floor.

On the other hand, for him I seemed just a diversion. After lovemaking he would turn on his back and stretch and proclaim his relaxation.

"Relaxed? You just feel relaxed —that's it?"

"Oh, no," he said, turning to look at me. "I also see fireworks and Jesus flying by in a cape and all that."

"Good!" I would let him mock me. I would find any time, any moment, any excuse to get on my Suzuki and zoom over to him. I would go bareheaded, letting my hair whip stick-straight in the wind. I had stopped wearing my helmet in all things, though I would sometimes don a muslin headscarf to keep my hair out of my teeth, and would walk into his apartment wearing it. He thought I'd called it "Muslim" rather than "muslin." He would place his hands on my head as if he were blessing me. "You could have my child," he would whisper, and I would hum and nod and say "OK." But it was Mary-Emma, whom I already loved, whom I would imagine us having, we would have her, and love her, her giggle, her smile, her caramel skin. And sometimes it was true: the three of us would go out together, and we were like a family. If he had loved me, or even if he'd just have said so, I would have died of happiness. But it didn't happen. So I didn't die of happiness. Words for a tombstone: SHE DIDN'T DIE OF HAPPINESS.

Wednesday nights Sarah's group still congregated and the remarks once again quickly wafted upward toward the attic nursery. The laundry chute conducted them even more than the staircase: maybe the words just climbed the stairs themselves, not even halting on the landings. The voices were alternately operatic, vaudevillean, sybillant, and tedious. Sometimes what sounded like singing was mockery. Sometimes what sounded like mockery was a request for food. Sometimes comments sounded seasick, or shopworn, or shot down, or like a station on the radio.

"The healthcare system and the school system and social security have to have means testing. It has to be the reverse of the way it's been: poor people in, rich people out."

"This whole racial blindness thing. These people who insist they don't notice what color other people are. These parents who come to pick up their kids at daycare and pretend they've never noticed Jared's skin. I wanna say, 'Honey, if you're racially blind like you say, that's something of a handicap. Let me give you a cane! You'll notice, by the way, that it's white. Or maybe, since you're colorblind, you won't.' "

"The phrase *race card,* as in 'playing the race card,' where did that come from?"

"O.J."

"Before that, I think."

"*Race card*—what the hell does that even mean? Another white idea."

"Hey, as I said, we white people had a lot of bright ideas."

"A black person can't accuse a white person of playing the race card, as the white race card is played every day."

"In fact, it's not really even a card. It's more like a deck."

"It's more like the whole game."

"Do you know Alta?"

"She's an awful fake poet. Oops—did I say that?"

"I do feel I know a whole lot about her body just by reading her work."

"Oh, her work is so fake, that's not even her body."

"A poet with a body double."

"I would like a body double—just for grocery shopping."

"Do you get those looks in the aisles when you're with your kid? That look that says *I see you've been messing around with colored people—we hope you're paying cash.*"

"I think I know what you mean."

"The suspiciousness."

"And the suspiciousness of religion, too. I find that antiblack."

"Don't get me started on Islam." It was the don't-get-me-started-on-Islam person.

"What is the purpose of busing? They bus in the poor black kids and then segregate them anyway, sticking them in the basement, in the shop classes."

"Were you here last week? Or was it longer ago that we were already talking about that?"

"When I first brought Kaz in to have him tested, to see whether he should be entering school as a first-grader or a kindergartner? And I sat outside the room listening while this lady gave him some crazy-ass test that went '*Foot* is to *shoe* as *blank* is to *muff.*' He was five years old! How's he supposed to know what a muff is?"

"Someday he will!"

"Stop! I mean, that is just the most antique and ridiculous analogy! I think he said something completely random like 'rabbit.' And afterward she came out to me with this worried look and said he was learning disabled and we would have to put him in special ed. He was five years old!"

"They track them early, for funding purposes. They need the numbers to be high enough for hiring. So the black kids take it in the teeth."

"The internal segregation of even integrated schools is famous."

"They have no concrete agenda other than that?"

"It's pretty much a crock."

I had seen quite a few crocks in my life—some of them moldering in barns, some cracked, some of them beautiful. All of them empty. I couldn't remember a one that had had anything in it.

"It sure does give you a sense of what it is to be African-American in this world."

"Well, yes and no."

"Thank you."

"Sorry to bring up hair again: Someone mentioned someone before, a woman who can do black hair? I need an address. I'm getting grief for Emmie's afro."

"Yeah, she should have some braids!"

"Elva down on South Elm can—she is cool and loves the kids. On Christmas she goes down to the homeless shelters and gives everyone free haircuts, black or white."

"Is this Sarah Vaughan on the stereo?"

"Sure is."

"Man, listen to her scat."

"And you say you don't believe in such a thing as black culture."

"I don't."

"Ever heard Julie Andrews scat?"

"I don't believe in gay culture or white culture or female culture or any of that. It's just so . . ."

"Dream world, baby."

"Ever heard Julie Andrews at all?"

"Hey, you don't need blue eyes if you got blue earrings."

I didn't know what they were talking about most of the time. But sometimes, in recalling certain remarks, the context would clarify them. Certain phrases, like a dusting of sand, would float across my mind and heat to a sort of glass. I'd seen scat! And now here it was as an admirable thing.

"Vaughan takes 'Autumn Leaves' and turns it into *Finnegans Wake*."

"Is that your argument?"

"Yeah. Kind of an Irish one: over beer. I am drinking beer."

"When we were in France, the French customs officials looked at us in a bewildered way. 'But look,' they said, as if they were pointing out something we had failed to notice. 'You are white and your son is black—how can this be?' As if it defied science or as if we had never regarded our own skin color before. And I had to say in English, and in anger, 'This is what an American family looks like!' "

"The rest of the world doesn't understand the ungovernable diversity of this country."

"Diversity made even more extreme by capitalism."

"And by Karl Rove. I was once in a restaurant and saw Karl Rove sitting across the room. For five minutes I thought: *I could take this steak knife and walk over there and change history. Right now.*"

"And?"

"Well, as you can see I chose to stay a free woman. Would anyone care for a timbale?"

"Is there meat in them?"

"Oh, stop already with the meat. She's become an actual member of PETA."

"Not yet."

"No. That's good. Though I give them ten years and you watch: they'll win the Nobel Peace Prize. Last year I gave them fifteen years, but I think the climate is changing very quickly in their favor. The rationale will be that humane treatment of animals can only mean more humane treatment of people."

"I have a problem with these animal rights people."

"Yeah, me, too. They instantly start comparing animals to black people. They say, 'We did the same thing to black people.' And you say, 'But they were people.' And they say, 'Yes, we know that now, but that's not what they were saying then.' And you say, 'Well, many people were saying it then. And no one now, that I know of, is saying a cow is a person.' "

"A species-ist!"

"There are Austrians saying that chimpanzees are people."

"And don't get me started with the primate research. There is such eagerness to lump black people with apes. Beasts of any kind."

"That's done even to the Jews."

"Well, Austrians . . ."

"What do you mean, 'even'?"

"I mean nothing. I meant even chickens. I've heard the PETA people compare what goes on with chickens to what went on with the Jews."

"Well, how else are you going to make them sit still in their nests and do your taxes if you don't cut their legs off?"

"Your sense of humor is too dark."

"Don't say 'dark.' It's racist."

"Have you noticed that when people say 'I'm not racist' you instantly know they are?"

"It's like those completely unself-aware men who say, 'I am not sexist,' and you want to say, 'Darling! Of course you are!' "

"I wish people would get it straight and say 'birth parent' and not 'biological parent.' Everybody's biological."

"That's in part what's too bad about everybody."

"And I don't like the use of the word *adoption* for animals. The humane societies use it all the time, but it's confusing to chldren who are adopted."

"I once heard I. B. Singer speak of the holocaust of chickens."

"And now there's that other one, Peter Singer."

"Are you sure you don't mean Pete Seeger?"

"The ethicist who says kill the deformed babies but don't eat meat."

"Oh, he's a horse's patoot."

I had seen a horse's patoot. I had seen plenty of them, and the large swatch of tail that like a creature unto itself swept the flies away.

"Too many Singers."

"Now we're back to Sarah Vaughan. Yes. I'll have a timbale."

I'd seen a crock. I'd seen a horse's patoot. It was a timbale that I'd never seen.

"Too many Sarahs."

"No such thing!"

"Too many timbales. Please! Have another one."

"There's the argument that people are so cruel to one another that until we take care of that we'll never get square with animals."

"And then, as I was saying, there's the argument that humanitarian practices with animals will cause us to improve our relationship with people. We'll say, 'Wait a minute: We don't even do this to animals. Why are we doing it to people?' "

"Sometimes it doesn't matter where you begin."

"Is that really what the moral ethicists are saying now?"

"I don't know about them all. My field is actually dairy science."

"Their argument is that unless an animal is expressing all his native animalness, he is being cruelly used and his life is unworthy. You would think that would then cause them to see death as a mercy. But the death is not the issue. It's the life."

"I would think the actual killing is the issue—how is it to be done?"

And here I thought I heard Sarah's voice. "How to kill chickens: Enough to feed the planet? I mean, have we learned nothing from the Holocaust? Can't we just round them up and gas them?"

More laughter all around. "That would express the Jewishness of the chickens—or do I mean the chickenness of the Jews?"

"That's why we got Israel, baby. We're not chicken anymore."

"This is such bullshit. Even humans don't get to express the fullness of their native humanness. You think the homeless person sleeping in his windowless car is expressing his humanness? And yet everyone breezes by and carries on. It makes bullshit of our finest intentions."

I had seen bullshit. I had seen chickens run after it and eat it warm.

"All I know is, gee whiz, you water your plant! A plant you would water! A deformed child no?"

"Would anyone like some water? Is your wine OK?"

"No, it's not OK! I need another one!"

"I thought we were supposed to be talking about interracial families."

"Sonya won't stay on subject."

I had once seen a comedy sketch in which a host chloroformed a dinner guest to keep him from saying one more word.

"Everything's genetic! It seems there's a gene for everything! Sad but true, or maybe not so sad."

"Or maybe not so true."

"All I know is that our son has the jock gene. And he is adopted—obviously. Not one person in our extended family has this gene. We go to all his games and he's like a Greek god out there, and we are in the stands looking like the peanut vendors."

I could hear Edward's voice. Proximity to science and scientists and academics had caused him to speak in a kind of mimicry of professors. He would use the phrase *if you will*. A lot. "Let's call it recombinant rehydration, if you will." And Sarah's voice would pounce. "Edward. Let me give you a pointer: Lose the *if you wills*."

There was a long pause. "I would rather throw sand in my eyes."

Some merriness. Most of the voices I never really recognized.

"Just kidding."

"What melting pot? It doesn't really melt all the stuff you put in the pot. There is DWB, driving while black, and there's DWJ, driving while Jewish. Guess which gets you pulled over and searched?"

"I'm not that well read on the subject."

"Perhaps you are not that well read."

"Anyone who's read all of Proust plus *The Man Without Qualities* is bound to be missing a few other titles."

"I'm sure."

"You know those automobile window shades to prevent baby sunburn? Did we need one? Of course! But he argued no— Edward, you did! You argued with me!"

"Because she's not white?"

"Here is my security system: me. A black man in the house. It scares away everyone."

The soft weight of feet on the carpeted steps. I looked up from my place on the floor with Mary-Emma. A woman appeared in the doorway, brown, tall, slender, her hair in neatly braided dreads, her head looked like a pot of vines, her figure stylishly offset with dark and bright. No one said "Mama" and ran to her. Not one child claimed her. Only two even looked up. Edward appeared behind her and touched her arm and she turned. Then they both receded, stepped back, disappeared.

At the end of the night, when the parents came up to fetch the kids, several asked their children how the evening had gone and the kids said "awesome" or "sucky"—there was no middle ground, nothing that wasn't a thrill or a debacle. I loved the way the black women grabbed their boys and pulled them close. I loved the white dads carrying their black daughters up high. Only Mary-Emma with her little smile said nothing at all as one by one the children left her room. Downstairs, I heard Sarah's voice alone with Edward in the kitchen.

"You emptied the top rack of the dishwasher but not the bottom, so the clean dishes have gotten all mixed up with the dirty ones—and now you want to have sex?"

Was I hearing things? Was this the grassroots whimpering of an important social movement, or was it a small, deep madness? If two things fell in the forest and made the same sound, which was the tree?

I picked up Mary-Emma. With a clean wipe I dabbed at some chocolate near her mouth. "Go hug your mama," I said, putting her back down and sending her dashing into the kitchen to interrupt them.

I called "Good night" and slipped out the door. Out of politeness I left quickly to go live my life. I had not ridden my Suzuki but still put my hair in a scarf, as if I had. I was a *sharmoota,* with a *hijab* tied not properly, under the chin, but—a concession, the middle ground—behind, at the nape of my neck, like Grace Kelly in *The Country Girl.* Or was it *Rear Window?* I walked and walked and then, as in my recurrent dreams where I was flying but only a few inches off the ground, unambitiously but still airborne, I began slightly to run. On my way, I broke off a blossoming stem from a neighbor's crab-apple tree and through the moist April night I made a brisk, hot beeline toward Reynaldo's. I would put the stem in water when I got to his place.

But when I got there something was wrong. There was no light coming from his windows. I climbed the stairs and tapped on his door. Uneasiness coursed through me, and finding the door unlocked, I slowly turned the knob and went in. I found him sitting in what had become an emptied darkened apartment, in the middle of the floor, with his laptop blazing its light up at him. It reminded me of the aluminum foil we would put on my mother's old album covers in order to catch the sun in summer and burn the pallor from our faces. All the other furnishings were gone. Everything—the bed, the xylophone, the table. On the wall was a single poster, white letters on black: *A vast silence reigned over the land. The land itself was a desolation, lifeless, without movement, so lone and cold that the spirit of it was not even that of sadness. There was a hint in it of laughter, but a laughter more terrible than any sadness . . .* I knew it was from the opening page of *White Fang,* a book I had read in seventh grade. I had never seen this hanging in his room before, though maybe now it simply stood out, being the only thing there besides Reynaldo himself and his laptop. He slammed the laptop cover down and looked up at me, or at least toward me. He was sitting on his prayer rug, which was facing east. I remember when I had thought it was a yoga mat, like my brother's. I kicked off my shoes at the door, as he sometimes liked me to do, but I was not relaxed: my jackhammering heart was rising to my throat. The thought occurred to me that so much vibration might loosen my fillings.

"Hello," he said, unsmilingly and as if from a great bleak distance. He flashed the light from a key chain my way, then lay it on the floor where it was our only illumination. He glanced at my face and then away. There was a cup of tea on the floor beside him, and he picked it up and drank from it while looking at the wall. I had seen this exact same expression and movement before—where? (Edward. I'd seen it in him the very first day I met him.) In the future I would come to know that look as the beginning of the end of love—the death of a man's trying. It read as Haughty Fatigue. Like the name of a stripper. There was the sacredness, immersion, intrusion, and violence to the ordinary that preceded romantic love, and then there was Haughty Fatigue, the stripper, who stole it away.

"What's going on?" I asked. There was nothing to put the crab-apple branch in or on, and so I just stood there holding it. In its droop I could see it already beginning to fail, an aspect of flowers I had studied in paintings of them.

"I'm moving to London," he said. "I've had the xylophone sent to your apartment. It should show up there in a few days. Mary-Emma can play it there. And you, too, of course."

Was the Jack London poster a clue? A code? Everything had grown strange. Things between us were dissolving like an ice cube in a glass: the smaller it got, the faster it disappeared. Thus would the whole world end, I'd been told.

"I'm not part of a cell," he said.

"That never crossed my mind." Though now it did. He had accepted some assignment. That must have been it. There was some manipulative mullah in his life—rumors abounded of quiet recruitment everywhere, though these were whispered and sometimes whispered as jokes. "Why London?"

"The English are simultaneously critical and stiffly uncomplaining—a stage Americans bypassed altogether, having gone from a dullard's stoicism to a neurotic's whining in less than half a century."

"That is such a bullshit answer."

"I'm part of an Islamic charity for Afghan children. That is all. They think I'm part of a cell. I'm not. If anyone asks you, if they question you when I'm gone, please tell them that I'm not."

There was no room in this conversation for "What about us?" The conversational space had suddenly filled with other creatures. Perhaps we had at last reached that stage of intimacy that destroys intimacy.

"You are Brazilian. What kind of cell would you be part of? A bikini wax cell?" I had once found a copy of a lingerie catalog in his pile of newspapers. When I picked it up and looked closely, the address label bore my own name. On one of the few occasions I'd had him over he had apparently taken it from my apartment, unbeknownst to me, perhaps to look at the bosomy models. Now that he was apparently leaving for London, all kinds of things I had refused to think about for very long came blowing back as if by dusty gusts aimed to tear up the eyes.

"I'm not Brazilian."

"You're not?" Of course he wasn't. Why hadn't I figured that out? Where were the bossa novas? Why did he not know a single phrase of "The Girl from Ipanema"?

"About that I lied."

"Why? Where are you from?" Perhaps he would turn out to know the words to "Kashmiri Love Song," my favorite song by Rudolph Valentino. My hands were truly pale! Even if he did not love them by the Shalimar. My heart tapped against my chest like fingers on a tabletop.

"Hoboken, New Jersey."

"Hoboken? Like Frank Sinatra?"

He snickered a little, a look of hard pedantry in his eyes. "Even the very first revolution in America was conducted from New Jersey."

"Gambling and disease. Right from the start. Are we doing American history?" I looked at his familiar and beautiful face. He was leaving me as mysteriously as he had first appeared. An agony. The exit like the entrance—but reversed. A palindrome: *gut-tug.*

"You are an innocent girl—though you are not pure. But still, I believe you are innocent. Especially for a Jew. That is good."

"A Jew?"

"Yes." This pronouncing voice did not sound like him, and he could see that I could hear that and seemed to give me a small, quick breaking-character smile meant to slip out and be received by me beneath this script of departure.

"That means you aren't going to tell me anything more, are you." I began to twist the bottom hem of my T-shirt into a coil. In life, as in movies, one sometimes could mistake a robot for a living being. "What's happened to your voice? You're speaking without contractions. How can you be from New Jersey?"

"When you find out who you are, you will no longer be innocent. That will be sad for others to see. All that knowledge will show on your face and change it. But sad only for others, not for yourself. You will feel you have a kind of wisdom, very mistaken, but a mistake of some power to you and so you will sadly treasure it and grow it."

"How about if I first just find out who you are." I had been the minibar—and not the minbar—in this temporary room of lodging. It was BYOB and I had brought the beer. "You are a haddi: some sort of jihadist."

"It is not the jihad that is the wrong thing. It is the wrong things that are the wrong things."

"Thank you, holy warrior, for the Islamofascist lecture."

"As Muhammad said, we do not know God as we should."

"And whose fault is that? That's not yours or mine! Maybe God has not stepped forward enough. Maybe God has not done a sufficient job of meet-and-greet."

I suddenly felt like an old Indian chief, one who sees that the world has changed irrevocably, and that the younger generation would never know the old one, even the strongest, slumped on their horses at the end of some trail. But if Reynaldo could feel the uncertainty of his own path, perhaps we could feel our despair together. Despite everything, I had not thought of him as irretrievably religious. He would not eat a bratwurst, but who could blame him? The hot ones snapped with fat when you bit in. The cold ones were death itself . . .

"I didn't know you had all this blasphemy in you," he said. Was that a smile?

"Yeah, well, sometimes the creation exceeds the creator. You know? A computer can beat a chess champion, a son can out-smart a father." I would not get into Frankenstein. "Maybe the Bible, with its vain, wailing God, is telling us that the creation, too, is more divine than the Creator. Look at that! I've said that and not been smote!"

"Sometimes these things take time," he said.

"The smoting?"

"Sure. Everything."

"Great." And then I added, "How about a kinder, gentler jihad?"

"One must listen to God."

"Well, God should speak up. He mumbles."

"He has made us his messengers."

"How nice for him that he has his own staff and some out-of-town offices."

"We are his sheep —"

"I didn't mean that kind of staff."

"—as well as his wolves."

"That sounds really, really complicated."

"Mankind is the source of all suffering."

"And the source of all God." I had crossed a line. "But as I said, the creation is often greater than what created it." Hubris or intelligent design?

He was silent, with a smile that wasn't a smile. I found myself falling toward him, as if the rush of feeling tearing through me could magically be made into useful affection: perhaps if I tried to kiss him—but he pulled away. And then slowly I got up, stepped back, one careful step at a time as he spoke. My crab-apple branch had fallen near him.

"There are a billion Muslims in the world," he said.

"So, what? I should be able to find another one?"

He fixed me with a powerful stare. He had that ability to summon up great concentration in his face and eyes. "There is that possibility." For a moment pity for us both glistened his eyes. "You can't get blood from a stone," he said sadly. Referring, I supposed, to love. It was an expression he liked and had used before with me.

"Yes, you can," I said. I was always trying.

"You can?"

"One can. You can."

"How is that done?"

"You go to a quarry."

"A quarry?"

"Yeah, if you go to a quarry there is always some body that's been dumped there."

He laughed.

"The Koran doesn't prohibit you from laughing at gruesome humor?" I would mock him a little—why not?

"No," he said.

"In every book there's a lot of white spaces—"

"Silences . . ."

"So who knows what's going on, really, between the lines? All those meaningful silences!"

But then, feeling he was being mocked, he let his face go bloodlessly stony, and suddenly he looked finally and completely packed up and gone. Locating the living him would be like finding a miner in a collapsed mine: I could drill and dig and shine lights into various passageways, but the likelihood of my seeing him again, at least as he once was, well, the chances were not that good.

"You avoid a lot of difficult things in conversation," I said.

"I hope so!"

"You lied to me," I said finally.

"A lie to the faithless is merely a conversation in their language."

This sounded like one of the many fortune cookie fortunes marking time in the pages of my books. "I was never faithless to you."

"Not in your definitions, no."

"Is this where you go on about desiccated America? Don't you understand? I agree with you!"

He said nothing.

"You're not taking flying lessons, I hope!"

He shook his head. "No."

A roll of toilet paper and two white pills shone from the windowsill near me as I backed away. "What are those?" I said, pointing at the pills. In my chest my heart had gone from the rapid flicking of a playing card on bike spokes to the loud erratic knock of a sneaker in a dryer.

"They are for emergencies. And for cleanliness, obviously. The pills? They're from Brazilian potatoes—two interests of yours."

"Really."

"Potatoes and Brazil."

"I understood what you meant." Fear and sorrow flared up simultaneously like fires that put each other out. Feelings of any constructive sort deserted me. "As much as you want this world to end, it can't. The seeds to everything are being stored, as we speak, in boxes in the permafrost of Norway."

"Who will find them?"

"People will."

"Yes, I'm sure you're right."

"You are?" On the other windowsill was a small package of tampons. "Why do you have those?"

"In case of emergencies. Worst-case scenarios: they stanch wounds."

"Really."

"When they ask you to name my friends, you will have to say you don't know, because you don't know."

"I don't know." Why didn't I know? "This kind of political and spiritual despair," I said desperately, recalling something once heard on a Wednesday. "It's mistaking a small world for a large one and a large one for a small."

He smiled but he kindly didn't laugh. "You have no idea what you're talking about," he said.

"Maybe. But maybe not." These were the words of a child. But it didn't mean they were untrue. "Perhaps you are being recruited by a plant. What if you are a victim of a scheme?"

"What if I *am* the plant," he said, feigning playfulness. "What if I *am* the scheme?"

"Listen! The jihadist leaders—they don't respect outsiders. They think these fervent recruits are all crazy, coming from another country as they do, and they use them and laugh at them."

"Who told you that?"

"The Donegal don. On a day when you were absent."

"What?"

"He knows Arabic and collects chatter. That's what someone told me."

"He 'collects chatter'! Listen to you!"

I just stared at him, feeling this was it: that I would never see him again.

"It is not the jihad that is the wrong thing," he repeated. "It is not a war that is the wrong thing. It is the wrong things that are the wrong things."

It was like Gertrude Stein speaking from inside a burka. I continued to step backwards, and my bare toe hit something sharp, perhaps a tiny carpenter's nail poking up from the floorboards. In a kind of yoga stance I lifted up my foot, which was bleeding. I squeezed and I could see blood drop darkly to the floor, though nothing was stuck inside. Lifting my foot, however, just seemed to cause it to drip more. There was that roll of toilet paper on the windowsill, and I hobbled over and ripped some off, winding it around my toe.

"Are you OK?" he asked, sounding almost like the sweet boy I knew him to be, deep down, although that part no longer mattered.

"Yeah. It doesn't hurt," I said.

"They think I'm part of a cell, but I'm not, I swear. I hope you will always believe that."

"In the name of Allah—oh, yes, I believe."

I put my shoes back on.

It was like the classic scene in the movies where one lover is on the train and one is on the platform and the train starts to pull away, and the lover on the platform begins to trot along and then jog and then sprint and then gives up altogether as the train speeds irrevocably off. Except in this case I was all the parts: I was the lover on the platform, I was the lover on the train. And I was also the train.

"In the name of Allah."

In the name of la-la-la-la-la-la-la-la-la-la-la. I took off, out into the street, crying. I ran and ran and never turned around and no one came running after me. I ran past the Muslim Students' League, a small house not far from Reynaldo's, painted turquoise and white; a makeshift mosque of some sort, I knew, had been constructed in the back. Reynaldo himself had been part of a team that had helped paint it. At this time of night no one was in or near it at all; at times during the day I had seen it ominously busy. Nothing, I thought, should be busy. All should be slow and sparse. I ran past a block I usually took but that was being ripped up for sewage pipe replacement, and in the middle of the street was a municipal barricade with a sign that said ROAD CLOSED. Beneath it but still on the sign a graffiti artist had sprayed, in black, *I love you.* In the sky were starry poisons, like the hundred spiders that, throughout a human life span, are said to drop into one's mouth, while sleeping with a dropped jaw. I ran north and north and north and could perhaps have run all the way to Canada, where, paralyzed with sadness and exhaustion, my arms and fingers would stiffen upward and I would, in one of grief's mythic transformations, become a maple tree, my sappy tears cooked down to syrup for someone's flapjacks.

The interesting thing about a wound in the foot was that the pressure of just standing on it, not babying it, stanched the bleeding and healed the thing: Was that a robustly New Age truth or what? ROAD CLOSED *I love you.* When I got home I stripped naked and climbed into a filling tub, sat waist-deep in water and let loose with deeper weeping. The toilet paper I had wrapped around my toe was shredded and came off in milky wisps and fronds, floating all around in the water, and when I went under completely—to disappear, to clean, to alter my conscious state, whatever that was—the shreds swam toward my head and clung to my hair. When I could hold my breath no longer, I burst back up and saw that the warmth of the bath had caused my toe to start bleeding again, so that bright crimson swirled riotously through the water like life sprung free—though it was really a hello from death. I got out of the bath, wrapped myself in a towel, and then spun and spun, the towel falling away, my wet hair whipping droplets through the room, and I kept whirling until I felt neither death nor life but a kind of dizzying transport, which I was pretty sure wasn't Sufism, or the radiant depths of my soul lifting from bottomland to lovely storm: it was more like low blood pressure combined with PE—something I'd experienced a lot as a child—a slight separation from the body, to serve as a reminder of what you were.

V

The clocks were wound forward an hour, and light flew down early and persisted into evening. My sleep was shallow, and the nights were long and full of chiding conversation from people who seemed actually to be in the room. But when I awoke there was no one. The apartment was muggy. The prairie, increasingly, I had noticed, could not hang on to spring. It was as if there were not enough branches to grip it, hills to hold it—it could get little traction, really, and the humid heat of summer slid right in. Soon the chiding conversation of hovering people was replaced with a feeling that I was being bitten by bugs I couldn't see. Everything I ate seemed to collect in a clayey ball in my bowel, and my pulse would stop in my sleep then start up again in a hurry, discombobulated, waking me from dreams of blind alleys, naked running, and wrath. I would get out of bed with the scary meat-step of a foot that had gone to sleep and toenails that had loosened oddly, lost a firm grip on the actual toe— all this from a broken heart.

I had not mopped or swept the floors in months. I had used paper towels when there was a spill and hoped that eventually the entire apartment floor would get wiped up this way. This method of cleaning the floor, in patches, I imagined was like writing a poem every day until you eventually said everything about the human condition there was to be said. But it didn't really work that way, even in poetry: grimy corners remained while certain floorboards got burnished to a slippery hellish gleam. Sometimes, when out of paper towels, I would use one of the wipes I often packed in my backpack for Mary-Emma, and I would start with the counters and work down: it seemed I could clean almost an entire room with just one—that was the sort of delusional housekeeping I was becoming a devotee of.

Not one person asked me about Reynaldo, which made me realize just how private and isolated our affair had been. Temporary and vanished. Like *Brigadoon* with headscarves. My own emotions felt a disgrace. There was apparently no indication left of me in his apartment—except the blood—and no one came knocking on my door. I felt as blue as the lips of a fish, which was really just a line from a song I had going through my head. "The grass don't care / the wind is free / the prairie—once a sea—don't sing no song for me." Bad grammar was totemic for bass player grief.

What I really felt was this: chopped down like a tree, a new feeling, and I was realizing that all new feelings from here on in would probably be bad ones. Surprises would no longer be good. And feelings might take on actual physical form, like those sad fish lips, a mouth speared into a gasping silence, or worse. I swung my hair and slapped the face of my bass like Jaco Pastorius, squinting the neck into a fretless blur; perhaps one day I would dig those frets out with a file and fill them with epoxy, too.

Sometimes I would awake too early in my bed and would feel my foot flap beneath the sheets, and I wouldn't know at first that it was mine. I felt only the movement of the cool sheet, and it felt like someone else was there, in the bed with me, but I would quickly turn to see there was no one; it was always just me. At night before I fell asleep I was not above staring at the phone. *Are you there? Yes. Are you falling asleep? Not really. How many fingers am I holding up?*

In reality, no one asked me any questions whatsoever. No one said a word, except Sarah.

"Did you see in the papers the story about this student who

disappeared? They found blood in his apartment but they don't know whose."

"Really," I said.

"This wasn't the guy who was taking pictures of Emmie, was it? Or a friend of his?"

"Not that I know of."

"You see, that's the problem: *Not that I know of.* There's room for possibility."

Her look at me was a darting thing. I just stared at her without seeing all that much, and I must have looked crazy with unhappiness, because she then came up to me and smoothed my sweater sleeve and petted my arm. "I'm sorry," she said. "I don't know why I'm going on like this."

"It's OK," I said. It was quasi OK.

She returned to her theme menus. Invasive Species Night: the mustard-vine gnocchi; the steamed zebra mussels; the soup of wild carrot and wild parsnip; the salad of chicory, mustard garlic, fig buttercup, watercress, and burdock. Napkins of human hair! Well, that I just invented, piping up to amuse her, but she said, "Hmm. Yum." And then there was Endangered Species Night: wild rice and free-range bison; American eel gratin and Chanticleer chicken with short and thick parsnips. Eating endangered species made some ecological sense, she claimed—if it was tasty and grew popular, people would save it?—but I wasn't paying complete attention. The general idea was that food always survived. I wondered.

"I'm off to the Mill!" Sarah would shout up the stairs. I could see the edge of her white jacket.

"Ciao, Mama!" Mary-Emma would shout down. She was saying so many words these days. "I feepy," she said when she wanted to go to bed. She loved to watch old Esther Williams movies, which I brought her from the university library, but they either revved her up or wore her out.

"OK. Let's go."

"I die," she said.

"Well, someday. But not for a very long time."

"I die into the pool!" And she took a flying leap onto her new futon, which Sarah had just bought to transition her out of the crib.

Twice, back in my apartment, the phone rang, and when I went to answer it there was just all this terrible noise: muffled speech, electronic moaning, whooshing sounds of water. "Hello?" I cried repeatedly into the mouthpiece. But I heard only eerie underwater groans. The caller ID on our Radio Shack phone said "cellular call," nothing more. Dialing star-69 gave me nothing. Later, comically and perhaps correctly, I imagined it was Reynaldo's cell phone, that he still had me on speed dial and accidentally bumped the keypad and was taking me into the bathroom with him. Some bathroom somewhere. Probably it was flushing noises I was hearing. Or maybe he was on the other side of the world in a hot zone and his phone was trying to blow up something—it wasn't called a cell phone for nothing—and the secret blow-up code had instead misdialed and reached romantic interference: me.

I began to miss Murph. All I needed was her company, a sense of her presence again. Every day I felt that if she would somehow come back into my life, things would be brighter.

And then astonishingly, she did. As if I'd wished it on a lucky penny: at this perfect time for me, Murph returned, which if it had been earlier would have been a slight bummer as I had recently been using her stuff, bullshit things like her "hair ionizer," which I had imagined had made my hair shine and took the static out, and her mister—a "handsome mister," I used to call it—which lightly sprayed mineral water on your face. But as brokenhearted as I felt now, I was using nothing, just letting static electricity streak my hair across my teeth! I had let my face crumble to sand. And then I just walked in one afternoon and there she was, sitting on the couch. She'd arrived the same day as the xylophone and had herself just wheeled it in off the porch.

"This is cool," she said, pointing at it.

"Hi!" I exclaimed. I dropped my books and hugged her. I was so happy to see her.

"Yes." She smiled.

"Are you? High?"

"Yup."

"As a kite?"

"As the Hubble!" She looked tired. "I feel like a veteran."

"Of highness?"

"No."

"Of what, then? Hineyness?" Ritual ribaldry was part of the Muwallahin Sufic way, if I remembered correctly.

"A veteran of the gender wars."

"Yeah, well, me, too. But I'm afraid those were never declared."

"Fucking do-nothing Congress! And we never got a parade or anything!"

"We've got marching bands," I said, pointing in the direction of the stadium.

"That's not a parade," she said.

"It's a quasi parade."

She and her boyfriend had also broken up. "He put me in the freezer," she cried, "and didn't even have the decency to chop me up first!" And so together we stayed in our apartment, smoking cigarettes and making up tunes for our grief. "He played me like a yard sale lute! If he calls here, give him the tone, man."

But he never did.

"Do you realize," I said, "that when women have orgasms

scans show large parts of their brains go completely absent on the screen?"

"Yes, well, that corresponds with my anecdotal research in the field."

"Mine, too."

I would get out my bass, though the strap was always slipping—"Wait, let me put this strap on," I invariably said, and Murph would cry, "Hoo-hee!" There wasn't an innuendo anywhere she couldn't be the first to locate and illumine with her hoots.

We played all the things I'd recently made up. Though in real life a boy's love was a meager thing, we liked what a boy's love could do in a poem or a song. "Driftless Dan, he had no plan / Prairie Pete, he got cold feet / Great Lake Jake was hard to take . . ." And so we would give back our own grieving songs of sorrow at love's mystifying impersonations. We even had a song called "Mystifying Impersonation." Also a sad, slow one titled "Why Don't the Train Stop Here?" which Murph thought was too country; even when I changed the *don't* to *won't,* she found it unfocused, with its verse about a church turned into condos, though I liked that part best. "It's like 'They paved paradise and put up a parking lot,' " I protested.

"It's not," she said. "Believe me. It's not." She knew how to speak without gentleness or malice, either one, and preferred my song "Everyone Is You—in Your Dreams," based on something someone told me once about dreams, but also a defiant anthem to rally us against the narcissism of the betraying lover! Oh, yeah: impotent vengeance, baby, sing your song! What could be better than words that worked every which way? Who cared if the train stopped here or not? I would lay in the rhythm with my electric bass and she would throw herself into that xylophone with ecstasy and pain, a nearby cigarette perched on a saucer, sending out its smoke like the tiny campfire of two tiny prisoner squaws. Who knew she could play?

"It's really just a toy," she said. "Anyone can."

"That's not really true," I said, unconvinced and impressed. Murph's hands and arms moved up and down the keyboard with the undulating movements of a squirrel—sine and cosine interlocking. She would then suddenly stop and point at me with her right mallet, indicating that it was time for my solo, and I would let it rip—or try. Murph liked our collaborations better than such lone efforts by me as "Dog-Doo Done Up as Chocolates for My Brother," and we seemed best on the rocking ones, like "Summer Evening Lunch Meat," a song we had written, combining the most beautiful phrase in English with the ugliest, and therefore summing up our thoughts on love. "Summer evening" was what God had provided. "Lunch meat" was the hideous human body itself. When I lay the rhythm in with my bass, when I did it right, Murph could take over with the xylophone and it sounded great. Well, maybe not great. A little stupid, but sweet. "Let your bass-face shine!" she shouted. Probably my features were contorted in concentration and transport. In between the more rollicking stuff, in useful weariness, we found ourselves sailing even on our waltzy ballads:

Did you take off for Heaven
and leave me behind?
Darlin', I'd join you
if you didn't mind.
I'd climb up that staircase
past lions and bears,
but it's locked
at the foot of the stairs.

Are you in paradise
with someone who cares?
Oh, throw down the key to the stairs.

One can see shining steps
and think love is enough,
Then sit at the bottom and wait.
The climb up to sweetness needs more than my love:
darlin', please just open the gate . . .

Can someone just open the gate?

"I want to write something, too," said Murph one evening, and because it was night, and because we'd had two beers apiece, she grabbed my bass and picked awkwardly away at a new song, written right there from scratch, from a four-stringed see-through, each of us making up a line and the other one supplying the next line, and so on.

Why did I let you make off with my head?
Now when I go out I pretend that you're dead.
But if I glimpse you,
don't know what I'll do,
'cause I've never been as crazy
'bout someone as crazy as you.

Madness is sadness—
I loved you the most.
Now my future's the house
for your lunatic ghost.
Why are the leaves still bright green
and the sky so damn blue?
Can't they see I'm just crazy
'bout someone as crazy as you?

She wanted to rhyme "don't abhor us, that would bore us, just adore us" with—"Which is it?" she asked. "Is it *clitor*is or clitor*is*?"

I didn't know. Why didn't I know? "It may depend on which you have," I said.

To say all this made us laugh our heads off does not begin to express its consolations. Soon every night I'd get out my electric and we'd do every tune we knew how in easy keys of G-minor and E-minor, with riffs that were like climbing the same three stairs over and over. We started making up songs that had no choruses, just one cursed, merciless verse after verse, complaint like a flipping knife wandering around, debating, resting no place at all. In line after line, we tried to compose meaningful phrases with twinned endings: *sinister* to rhyme with *minister, cubic* with *pubic, flatbread* with *flatbed, bearable reason* with *terrible treason, lucky* with *Kentucky*—well, the songs angrily made no sense. We took turns, each of our verses sounding like the rhymes of stalkers bleakly drunk with love, a little hope like dust beneath our nails, from where we clawed, though all was flawed, still, now, our lives were shorn of plot, cuz baby you were all I got, waiting out here in the parking lot, beneath the stars, outside of bars, there I am, baby, there, there, idling in the fescue, waiting for your rescue, but you're nowhere, why don't you care that love is rare—*my love is rare!*—I'm going to drive to see . . . what you think about me.

We reached a point at which it was a good thing there was no chorus.

One night we got dressed in bag-lady clothes, got a shopping cart filled with beer, and went down by the railroad tracks just to howl like wolves. This was late-stage Sufism, mid to late.

"When we make our CD?" said Murph as we trudged back home, "we'll put a razor blade right inside each and every one."

"And those little bottles of gin," I added. "And a pistol."

"You're great," said Murph, putting her arm around me.

"Yeah, well, I feel like I'm headed for a future where I'm just every guy's sister," I bleated. "I think the fact that I read *The Rules* in Mandarin didn't help any."

Murph smiled, but what she said next was unsettling. She put her hands tenderly to my face and said, "Look at you! You're nobody's sister."

Outside in the flowerbeds the yellow irises had unfurled in the sun with their lolling nectarine-pit tongues. There was a kind of ticking, humming all around, as if every living thing were contemplating bursting.

"I'm wondering why Emmie has been singing this particular song," said Sarah, pointedly, in the kitchen. She had her chef's hat on, the one that wasn't a conventional toque but a brimless canvas cap.

"A song?"

" 'Prairie Pete, he got cold feet'?"

"Oh, yeah," I said. "I made that up."

"That's OK," she said, as if I needed forgiving, which I could see I might.

"I've also been singing regular standards with her," I added hopefully.

"Yes," she said. " 'I Been Working on the Railroad.' I've heard her sing that. There's just two things I'm worried about with that: the grammar and the use of slave labor."

I wasn't sure I was hearing things correctly. Her sense of humor was still not always explicit or transparent or of a finely honed rhythm, and it sometimes left me not in the same room with it but standing in the hall. The words "You're serious?" flew out of my mouth.

"Kind of." She looked right through me. "I'm not sure." And then she went upstairs, as if to go figure it out. When she came back down she added, "Correct subject-verb agreement is best when children are learning language, so be careful what you sing. It's an issue when raising kids of color. A simple grammatical matter can hold them back in life. Down the road."

"Yes," I said mechanically.

"We are pioneers," she said to me. "We are doing something important, unprecedented, and unbearably hard." And then she left again, and I turned away to hide my own teariness behind a door, because I was tired and wasn't exactly clear what Sarah was talking about.

"Tassa?" came Mary-Emma's worried voice.

I hauled out all the Scottish airs and mournful Irish drinking songs I knew, full of *yonder*s, *e'er*s, and *loch*s, but there were also a lot of *bonnie*s, and when I came to those I feared something terrified entered my face, because Emmie just stared at me, sensing something was up, a rock in the road. I couldn't tell whether that word resonated with her or not. Still she was always wanting to learn the songs herself. "Bonnie-oh, oh bonnie-hey, nonny-bonnie pretty day." The phone would ring and I would stop, dead in my tracks. If Sarah were there, she would answer it, and mostly I was relieved to hear her voice. "Quesadilla soup? No, we don't serve that, that's our competition . . . Yes, of course it's their secret recipe. They have to keep it a secret, since if you knew what was in it you'd never order it again." But sometimes I would hear her say, "Who is this?" then slam the phone down.

Because Mary-Emma had not only moved from a high chair to a booster seat but had for a month been sleeping in her "big girl bed," the futon on the floor, I often lay next to her at nap times, reading and singing and sometimes dozing off myself. Sometimes we were awakened by Noel and his vacuum cleaner as he made his way through the house, an iPod lit up in his apron pocket, his headphones blocking all noise. It was the first iPod I'd ever seen, and when the vacuum cleaner wasn't on I could hear the tinny sound coming out of the earbuds and Noel singing along in a broken and transported way, not hearing his own voice, and so sounding as if he were deaf. Still, I could make out one of the songs he played over and over, a Bonnie Raitt one, "I Can't Make

You Love Me," the words to which I recognized but didn't really know. If there were a song called "I *Can* Make You Love Me," I would have memorized it long ago.

Noel saw me and smiled and turned his vacuum cleaner off. He pulled the earbuds out. I could see his eyes were wet with tears.

"It's hard to listen to this song," he said.

"It's sad," I agreed.

"My old boyfriend auctioned himself off to it at an AIDS benefit 'Love Slave' auction."

"God, I wish mine had done that! And that was the last you saw of him?" I no longer could understand the world, and so I would only pretend to try.

"Sort of."

"You broke up?"

"Well, he caught HIV that very night. And died—just last summer."

"Jesus. I'm sorry."

"Thanks," he said.

"I think Bonnie Raitt owes you a new song."

"Somebody does," he said.

Easter Monday and no classes, as if it were Canada. I buzzed up on my scooter. The lawns were greening brightly, though the sky remained a furry shade of pearl. Dogs barked next door. As a belated Easter present I had brought Mary-Emma two goldfish, in deli containers. I would find a clear glass bowl to put them in—Sarah seemed to have a hundred.

Inside the Thornwood-Brink house there was holiday detritus: a three-foot chocolate bunny, a Brio train set. There were actual eggs that Sarah had boiled in different colored teas to make an elaborate marbling. They were all piled together in a single flax basket.

"I see you put all your eggs in one basket," I said, I thought wittily, but she didn't hear me.

"Emmie's asleep," said Sarah. "Even that Suzuki of yours didn't wake her."

"Oops," I said. "Sorry." Possibly I was getting used to her oblique and random reprimands. I put the fish on the table.

"Those are cute," Sarah said. "I promise not to entertain any thoughts about seasoning them." She was at the kitchen counter, mashing the bulbs from the Christmas paperwhites into a bowl, forming a paste. "I thought I should tell you about something." She stopped for a second from her work. "Something that is happening." Even in her stillness she looked busy and tense. "But you know? Let's have a glass of SB." SB was sauvignon blanc. I knew that now. A month ago I would have thought she was referring to the Super Bowl, or an SB vintage Gibson guitar, or her very own initials. "I've got a bottle in the fridge. It's been a good long time and so it's chilled to the center of its little bones. Yum."

She stopped the flower bulb mashing. "Let's go sit in the living room." She brought the wine, a Screwpull, and two wineglasses, and we sat on the pillow-ticking sofas, the same as we had when I'd first interviewed with her.

"We mustn't tell Edward we drank white and not red," she said. "Are you underage?" she asked.

"Under what?" I said, smiling and sipping, and Sarah just waved her hand through the air. "Well, if you drink more than one, don't get back on that scooter."

"One's good. I'm good with one."

She sipped from her glass and rolled the SB around on her front teeth. "I like a wine that's oaky."

"Oaky and . . . just a little dokey," I said. I was learning nothing very serious about wines but after a single sip of one was clearly willing to say anything.

Too preoccupied to smile, she seemed on the brink of something. Not for nothing were people named what they were named.

"There are things that are happening and I feel you should know," she said. Her face bore a look I'd seen before: it was one of bravado laced with doom, like fat in meat.

An *uh-oh* feeling overtook me. I gulped at my SB.

"But first you should know that there's an unfortunate backstory. Which I'll have to tell you. But you must understand: it was years ago and we were different people then." She fell back in a sunken way against the cushions, while I leaned forward from mine.

"You and Edward?" I asked, swallowing more wine, which was grassy and cool. I never knew anymore whom people meant when they said "we." College had done that to me. In Dellacrosse, I had always known whom people were referring to. I also didn't really know what people meant when they said of themselves that they were "different people then." It seemed a piece of emotional sci-fi that a small town would not have allowed. *Whaddya mean, you were a different person? Don't give me that hoodoo! I've known you since you were knee-high to a coot!*

"Edward and I," she said. "We were living out east, in Massachusetts. We were named Susan and John and we had a son."

Was I shocked? I couldn't even tell anymore. No one, it seemed, was who they said they were.

"Are you startled?" She raised her eyebrows, waiting for me to say something.

"Are you serious?" is what I chose. It seemed one could just say *Are you serious?* for the rest of existence and it would never be unjustified and would always have to be answered and so would keep the conversation going.

"Susan and John." She shook her head.

"Were those your middle names?"

She paused. "In a way."

She was about to go on when we heard Noel at the back door, with his stabbing, fidgeting key in the lock and his clanking pails and mops.

"We may have to continue this some other time," said Sarah, leaning forward and putting her wine down.

"OK," I said, still sipping. Noel came into the living room, with his tie-dyed sneakers, bearing a bouquet of daffodils for Sarah. I knew they'd been cut from the previous client's yard.

"Why, thank you!" she said. "Would you like some wine?"

"OK!" he said, smiling. "It'll go with my Diet Coke," he said, laughing nervously.

He seldom picked flowers from Sarah's garden (for the client after her), though once he had snipped some hydrangea from her shrub and she had warned him to cut from the bottom next time; he'd cut a big blank hole in the bush. She felt poorer people were entitled to do things that rich people weren't. It was in lieu of a revolution. And less bloody all around. I had heard her say this on one of her Wednesdays.

"We'll talk later," she said to me. And I brought my wineglass to the kitchen sink and just dumped it, then went upstairs to check on Mary-Emma.

She was lying there wide awake when I peeked in.

"How are you?"

"You got brown eyes," she said. "I of brown eyes."

"That's right."

"I want blue eyes like Daddy."

"No, you don't. Your eyes are perfect. They need to be brown like mine!"

"OK," she said. She was at an age where she would awake from a nap and suddenly be an inch taller, or be speaking in whole sentences, or in the grip of bleak and disturbing ideas.

"Wanna go to the park?" I asked.

"YEAH!" she cried out happily.

"First I have to show you: I brought you two Easter fish." We went downstairs and looked at them. They were still in their take-out containers, so I took a clear glass mixing bowl from the cupboard and poured them in. They swished around and bumped noses. "What should we name them?"

"Juicy!" Mary-Emma exclaimed.

"Juicy?"

"This one's Juicy. And this one's, this one's . . . Steve!"

"Steve?"

"Yeah. They're brothers." She stared at them until she looked a little cross-eyed and bored.

At the park I pushed her on the swing, higher and higher, and when she got off she dashed over to the slide and I gulped anxiously, fearing its dangers, but let her go. It was a fast slide, and from our previous visits I knew that children typically shot out from the flattened scoop of its slippery, sun-heated metal and landed on their faces, their thighs burned. Mary-Emma was no exception, but none of it fazed her. She and another girl had started a little game together, and they giddily took turns on the slide and then tried to make each other laugh at the bottom by assuming outlandish poses. Sometimes one would pretend to be unconscious or dead while the other one forced her back to living, which was indicated by giggles and brought about by tickling or pouring sand onto bare bellies or into hair. Sometimes it seemed to me that children believed death occurred in different forms than adults did, in varying degrees, and that it intersected with life in all kinds of ways that were unofficial. It was adults who felt death exerted a lurid sameness over everyone. Why couldn't it be as varied as life was? Or at least have its lurid sameness similarly gussied up and disguised?

Afterward, the girl's mother came over to me. "My Maddie just loves your little girl," she said to me, shouldering her bag and getting ready to go.

"They do seem to like each other," I said. I would let her think I was the too-young mother.

"What is her name?"

"Mary-Emma."

The woman grew awkward but purposeful, in my experience, a bad combo. "Do you think they could get together for a playdate someday?" the woman asked. "Maddie doesn't have any African-American friends, and I think it would be good for her to have one." She smiled.

I was stunned into silence but only for a moment. Suddenly all the Wednesday nights I'd ever overheard distilled themselves into a single ventriloquized sentence: "I'm sorry," I said to the woman, "but Mary-Emma already has a lot of white friends."

I didn't wait to examine the woman's expression or to mitigate it with softened thoughts. I stood and picked up Mary-Emma, canting my hip and nestling her there. I took her home, wheeling the empty stroller in front of me. She did not swing and kick herself away in order to be put down and run ahead. She was tired.

The idea that Mary-Emma would be used like that—to amuse and educate white children, give them an experience, as if she were a hired clown—enraged me, but walking fiercely and pushing the stroller hard over the sidewalk cracks helped work it off. Back at home in the kitchen we fed the fish little pieces of bread, which they nibbled at, and which might not have been the ideal food, especially for Juicy, who died within days, though Steve was tough and hung on, unkillable.

In general in the early afternoons I would feed Mary-Emma lunch, put a clean Pull-Up on her, and tuck her in for a nap. I sang her "Swing Low, Sweet Chariot," even though it was about joining people in death and planning the afterlife as a jolly place for friends and loved ones. Would this lead to a preoccupation? Was the grammar off? She stared at me wide-eyed while I sang. "Sing it again," she said after I had sung all the verses I knew.

"Now you take a nap," I said, "and have a really sweet dream." I thought I might bring her dirty clothes downstairs to the laundry room in the basement. Usually I tossed them down the laundry chute, but this time, with little else of immediate concern, I decided perhaps to be helpful and do a load of Mary-Emma's clothes. Sarah had gone out.

But when I got downstairs to the basement (which was carpeted and where Mary-Emma and I sometimes played on rainy days), I noticed there was a light on in the laundry room. I walked in anyway, and there stood a young woman I'd never seen before. She was pretty in the pale, speckled, toadstool way of redheads: enchanting, possibly poisonous, simultaneously prosaic and exotic. She was busying herself with an iron, touching the hot surface with a licked finger, though it did not yet let out a sizzle.

"Oh, hi!" I said. "I didn't mean to startle you! I'm Tassie."

"Yes," she said. "I'm Liza." I could see that her immediate task was to seal by ironing the new tea bags filled with Sarah's own tea.

"I look after Mary-Emma."

"I help out with the laundry and stuff," she said. She saw that I was holding some clothes. "Here, let me take these—I do all Emmie's stuff together with Dreft."

"Oh, OK," I said. "You'll see there's some signs of—" And then just behind her I saw, at the bottom of a foreshortened door that led to some kind of wine closet or pantry a man's good brown shoes, and pant cuffs, hiding in the shadows. Research into wine had taken a new form. It was like seeing the shoes of the person Dorothy's house had landed on in Oz. Witch's feet under the short door, although these shoes took you anywhere but home. "You'll see some signs of the park. Grass and dirt."

"No problem," she replied.

"Sounds good," I said, and then I turned and left.

———

"I met Liza," I said to Sarah upstairs when she came in the back door later that afternoon. "The laundry lady."

"Oh, good," said Sarah brightly, setting a bag of groceries down on the counter. "Now you've met just about everyone—except the guy who shovels and mows."

"Noelle doesn't do that?"

"Noel? No."

"And not Edward."

"Uh, nhew, not Edward." She did not look up but just kept pulling grocery items from her bag. Broccolinis and fresh eggs.

"Mary-Emma's napping upstairs, so I thought I'd go now."

"Oh, yes, that's fine. Can you come on Friday, by any chance?"

I flew home on my Suzuki. There was a final exam in Soundtracks to War Movies, and though I'd listened to *Platoon's* Adagio for Strings night and day, I still hadn't watched *The Best Years of Our Lives,* which was required, and which I finally did, under a blanket on the couch. I loved the guy with the hook hands. They didn't give men hooks anymore. Everything was plastic and digital and disguised. A proper pirate was no longer possible. Hook hands would be useful for playing bass, or for high shelves at home, or for toenail cleaning, and if he, your man, your hook-hand husband, scratched his head with one, no thought he came up with could possibly be dismissable or dumb. Love should be helpful. Love should contribute something.

On Friday Sarah tried again to tell me her secret. The secret of Susan. Susan's secret. Once again she sat me down with more sauvignon blanc while Mary-Emma was napping.

She began by talking about hair, which lessened my foreboding. "I'm still getting criticized for Emmie's hair."

"People don't like her afro," I said knowingly.

"Ha! You've been informed. Yes. They feel it should be grown long and then braided, even on a child. I guess they feel that she is

Rapunzel and will need that hair to escape me, the witch who has adopted her and wants to cut it off."

"No one could think that."

"We've been confronted with a difficult situation of our own doing," she said. She poured more SB. "This is very briary," she said, "this wine."

"Briary. Yes." I would have to remember that for the final.

And then she began her story. Or began it again.

They were driving in a car along the turnpike, John, Susan, this new mysterious child, their son, Gabriel, with the name of an angel but obstreperous and four years old, in the backseat. He wanted ice cream now and wailed for it. "Quiet, kiddo," said John in the front, a little heatedly. But Gabriel began to lean forward in his carseat and plunked John on the head with his fist and grabbed his flipped and capey hair. John shouted in pain.

"Stop that, Gabriel," said Susan, whoever Susan was. "You'll cause an accident." She was caught between these two male energies, one grown and one growing and unformed like a fire. Still, the grown one looked ablaze himself, with the quick sparky burn of an electrical accident. One must let the males of the species have their go at each other, she had once been told. Who had that been? Who had said that?

"No!" shouted Gabriel, and John turned while driving and swatted the child on his knee.

"John," said Susan in a low warning. Gabriel himself did nothing. He did not cry. Instead he removed one of his own shoes and from the backseat leaned in and hit John over the head with it.

"Hey, stop that! I'm driving! Susan, get him to stop!" Why could she not get him to stop? Trucks roared by in the slush.

"Stop that, Gabriel," said Susan, twisting back to calm her boy and trying to confiscate the shoe, but the child was focused on

Dad. He leaned forward and whacked John on the head again. He was a difficult child. He could be sweet. But then there was this wild part. A loose wire aggravated by close quarters.

"Ow, God. That's it!" said John. He cranked the wheel and swerved the car onto the shoulder of the highway, putting on his blinkers, crunching along the gravel shoulder, heading toward a scenic view rest area up ahead. Cars honked angrily behind him. He shifted into park and then swung around and undid Gabriel's carseat restraints. "If you cannot behave in this car, then you cannot be in it. Get out right now!"

"John, we're on a turnpike!"

"There's a picnic table up there—he can wait there. We've put up with this long enough! Our parents wouldn't have put up with this!" The refrain of a generation, uttered in bewilderment.

"Our parents wouldn't have done a lot of things."

"Well, maybe they were right. Get out!" he shouted at Gabriel, who looked only a little stunned. Suddenly the little boy was compliant. He clicked the handle and quickly got out, pushing the door shut as hard as he could. He began walking toward the picnic area, with his one shoe. No one was there and the tables were covered with the same sooty spring snow that had become slush on the road.

"Oh, God, now look what's happened," said Susan. "I'm getting out with him." She turned to gather her bag from the backseat. The car began rolling slightly.

"I can't believe he did what he was told for once!"

"John, he has one shoe on. Turn into this rest area right now." She felt around in the back for her bag and perhaps the other shoe. Where was it?

"I can't stop here, apparently. I've either got to get completely off the shoulder or . . ."

Trucks blared their angry elephant sound behind him.

"You must. Stop. Here."

"I'm trying," he said, but when he pulled the car ahead he overshot the rest stop turn and there was only a steep ditch to drive into unless one got back on the road. Someone blared a horn behind them, and now the pressure of the honking traffic caused him instead to feel he had to merge, and when he drove the car forward to avoid the ditch, he studied the vehicles in his rearview mirror, then pulled quickly into traffic.

"What are you doing?!" Susan's voice was a gaspy shriek.

"I couldn't get back in the lane and make that turn both."

"Slow down and pull over! I'm getting out."

"How can I do that here? I can't without causing an accident. Just wait," he said. "Bear with me here." He sped up instead. He seemed to think that speeding up would be better, to get the whole thing over with faster. "We're going to have to be a little inventive! Though I've heard of someone who did something like this."

"*Like what?!* Let me out!" She undid her own seat belt and turned around again in her seat. A whimpering sound was forming at the back of her throat.

"Don't worry. It will be a kind of time-out for Gabriel," he said, now appearing a little panicked and checking his rearview mirror again. What was a time-out? Was time literally stopped while everything else continued without it? People were pulled out of time? But not by Einstein. This was done by people who were the opposite of Einstein. "He needs to understand one or two things about the world, and perhaps this will help. We'll get off at the next exit and circle back and pick him up." The circle tour of manhood. John's face was starting to tighten with anguish, the grip of regret. "Bear with me. We're going to improvise a bit." Susan saw Gabriel in her side-view mirror, receding to something tiny until the road's turn took him out of her vision entirely.

———

At this juncture something exploded like a gunshot in the kitchen—Noel's forgotten can of Coke—and we both jumped. Liza came up from the basement with a basket of clothes. Even though I had met her only once before, now she seemed to be everywhere.

"I'll bet it's that damn Coke can of Noel's," Sarah said, opening the freezer and seeing brown frozen droplets sprayed all over it.

Sarah sighed. "Liza, would you like a little wine?"

"Oh, yeah," she said, and she listed out loud what was still in the washer and what was still in the dryer and what was hanging and what was folded, what was still wrinkled and what was pressed. I was full of apprehension. "Tassie," added Sarah, starting to write Liza a check, "we'll talk later."

"Sounds good," I said, and left quickly. As I did, a FedEx deliveryman had stepped up to the porch with an overnight package—probably risotto!

I rode home on my Suzuki, climbed into bed, and tried to read for my literature class: *"Dog in the manger!" I said; for I knew she secretly wanted him . . . Deep into some of Madame's secrets I had entered—I know not how . . . I know not whence . . .* I pulled the sheet over my head. "You OK?" shouted Murph from where she sat at her computer.

"No," I replied, but in our apartment this did not make the least impression.

There was actually only one more Wednesday. The usual sparkiness of the notes had a fizzled edge, like the jagged dissolution of a warming orchestra that had suddenly decided not to play. The chorus was dominated by a new woman's voice, someone whose diction was as clipped and quick as an auctioneer's.

"The only black people you know went to Yale."

"Yeah, all the white people she knows went to Yale as well."

"Whitest person in the world is Dick Gephardt—have you ever noticed that? He has no eyebrows! He's translucent!"

"He wasn't graphic enough to become president!"

"See or be seen."

"Did you say, 'From sea to shining sea'?"

"Now we're doing deafness?"

"What?"

"Deafness jokes. I love them."

"And don't get me started about Islam!"

Once again, the don't-get-me-started-about-Islam guy. Was he fishing? Was he a spy? It was hard to listen from two flights up and follow when the kids I was supervising were after me to sing "Knick-knack-paddy-whack-give-your-dog-a-bone"—the alternative words to the Barney love song, which they found exotic and hilarious.

"We should all work in soup kitchens."

"Why I *do* work in a soup kitchen. I am raising an African-American child in the twenty-first century."

"Here's what else we should do: little windmills in our yards, solar panels on our roofs . . ."

"And wooden shoes!"

"I have faith in this new generation."

"Not I! They are all sleepwalking!"

"Have you noticed that the biracial kids all find each other? They are emerging as their own group."

"They call themselves 'mixed,' not biracial."

"For the kids, having a black mother is more prestigious. So many of these mixed kids have white mothers, and so even they've formed *their* own group. That's what Jazmyn tells me."

"We're so busy telling young people about the world, we forget there are ways they know more than we do."

"Yeah, no, I agree. These students are the best of both worlds. They are serious grown-ups, principled and worldly and gentle in ways we weren't. And adorable, in a way they won't be in ten years."

"I know what you mean! You want to eat them right up. Get your lips on their chests. There's nothing wrong either with using a knife and fork."

"The hazards of a college town."

"Would anyone care for a beer, or are you all drinking wine?"

"I'm worried about all the precious culture that comes now from nowhere: that is, it comes from trust-funded children's book authors. 'The Adventures of Asparagus Alley' and such things. Adults are living increasingly as children: completely in their imaginations. Reading *Harry Potter* while every newspaper in the country goes out of business. They know so little that is real."

"Yes, you've mentioned this before."

"Sorry. I guess I need more people to talk to."

"When a tree falls in the woods and no one is there to hear it, did it really fall? I realize that's not how the expression goes . . ."

"If a tree falls in the woods and there's no one there, that's lucky. That's how the saying *should* go."

"What?"

"We're doing deafness jokes *again*?"

"What?"

Deafness, somebody's, was no doubt the reason I had ever been able to hear these people at all. From two flights up, I had often not known exactly what I was hearing, but still the sounds rose, in various key signatures and tempos. The acoustics of the house had always been odd. Remarks were suddenly loud, bursting up through the air vents and the stairwells and laundry chute, or suddenly quiet. Was this just the human mouth, or was it the mind as well? Back to the woods: If two things fall in the forest and make the same sound, which is the tree?

"What's most galling is the way school integration is used to educate whites, not blacks, to give whites an experience of race rather than blacks an experience of algebra."

"The one black principal we have in this town has banned hats."

"Soon the mooning, herniating jeans. In a way? I hope so."

"When you are white and you adopt a black child, don't you feel yourself pulled down a notch socially?"

"In terms of how you are treated and the new concerns you face?"

"All the things we've been talking about from the beginning. Everyone has stories."

At eight the parents arrived upstairs to fetch their kids, their teeth dingy with zinfandel, their lips etched and scabby with it. Most kids ran to their parents with great energy, though some, engaged with a puzzle in the corner, refused even to look up. Once again, I loved the way the black mothers would come upstairs and grab their kids, just pull their oldest son's head to their breasts and say "Hey, baby!" There had only ever been a few black fathers on Wednesdays, but again they, too, were physical, pulling their boys close with an embrace. Some of the parents tried to give me extra money, as a tip, and though I didn't feel comfortable taking it, I couldn't make my lips form the words to refuse them. On her way out one girl, Adilia, said to her sister, "You just don't think you're living unless you're tormenting somebody, do you?" Her father turned to me and said, "Sometimes these people we believe are children are actually midgets."

I waved, like the widowed aunt seeing everyone off at the train station. I leaned over and pressed Mary-Emma's head to my chest. I said good night.

I went home and googled the *n*-word, opening up a sewer that went on forever.

———

For the final installment of her dread tale Sarah should have switched to red wine. Not just for the color but for the fortifying warmth. Instead she had a greenish SB she said was not just briary but also loamy. "It is painful, appalling, really, to have to tell you all of this, though you'll see, there are reasons," she said. "It's not that we are not what we seem. Though I suppose our names once being something else might make you think otherwise."

"Yes." How could it not? "But hey, what's in a name?" I said. One could always find suitable moments for Shakespeare.

She put her wineglass down, placed her hands on her brow, and then let her fingers spread upward through her hair. "I can't remember where I was."

Where would she plunge in? Sometimes one is swimming in a lake and aims for a slant of light, only to discover it is brightly colored scum.

"You were in the car," I said. And then I wanted to clap my hands over my ears but failed to do so.

"Yes. It was of course a nightmare," Sarah said. She shook her left wrist a little, staring at her watch, as if she were reading a magazine. "I just pulled this watch so quickly out of the jewelry box, an earring got stuck on it." And she showed me some gobbledy-gook metal tangle on her watchband. The surrealism in this house was like a poltergeist.

"We were in the car," she agreed, and suddenly stood up and paced around the room while she spoke.

Susan grabbed his arm. "John! He's only four! What are you doing?" While John was speeding up, time was beginning to slow down.

John shook his arm away. "Let me drive! You're going to get us into an accident!" He had already exited and was negotiating the cloverleaf that got him back on the highway going the other way. "Look, he's still there: I can see him," he said.

She had grown up in a family where men were always cruel to other men—in what seemed a conventional way. She had never known what a woman's role should be in these masculine rites, which were all a kind of refinement of malice. They were polish through pain. *One must let the males of the species have their go at each other.* Whereas girls just went directly toward polish. Polish via polish—in this way one didn't have to be internally reworked.

Still, why had she reached around to get her bag? It had cost her a minute. What did it, or even the shoe, really matter?

"He's not up by the picnic table. He's just on the shoulder, standing there crying! The traffic is so scary and loud!"

"I'll wave to him so he knows we're coming."

Speed was John's solution. He pressed on the gas. As they sped by on the opposite side he honked his horn. At this, Gabriel, seeing his parents speed by, took a tentative darting step out onto the freeway but then withdrew. Was he headed toward the median strip to signal to them? That's what it seemed, though this happened so slowly, time unwound so hesitantly, nothing was clear. The slowing of time, the careful opening up of each moment, was a gift to use if you could figure out how. This gift of time, this opportunity, was an opportunity for rescue. If rescuing behavior could be summoned. The ability to summon it was a survival mechanism, and those who survived would pass this time-slowing capacity on to their progeny. But behind glass, where Susan was, it was difficult to use, difficult to find the appropriate action even toward her child—should she throw herself from the car?—and so she subjected each moment not to an action but instead to interpretations.

Was Gabriel just trying to greet them? Or was he trying to get to them? Was he wanting to be with them after everything and all? The forgiveness of children was one of God's sunny gifts.

Susan, now once again completely twisted in her seat, the shot-gun seat without the convenience of an actual shotgun, began to shout. *"Turn! Turn! Turn!"* To every thing there was a season.

"I can't!"

"Cross the median strip! Get back to him! Drive over there! John, you've got to get back there before he tries to run out!"

"We'll be there soon!" This obedience to the rules and flow of traffic was perhaps the way of science. Certainly it was the way of experiments.

"U-turn now!" She grabbed the wheel. The car swung bumpily across the median strip and a police siren went off in the distance behind them. As if in duet, there was a high-pitched singing in Susan's ear that could be heard by no one but her—a wheezy screaming without body or noise—a hollowing wind in the head. And as things slowed for them, enough to think and take an action, she could see, looking ahead for their running boy, that though one car had slowed down to let him make a dash for it, another car, not seeing, had already greedily sped up to pass on the left, and before everyone's eyes Gabriel became the flying golden angel after which he was named.

"I'm not sure what just happened," said Susan, who kept repeating these words, and opened the door as the car was still moving. As they reapproached the rest stop, which was on the right, vacant and devoid of picnic or rest, and where the scenic view would remain a mystery, Gabriel was lying far away on the left, across the highway from it, on the muddy median. Several cars had stopped and Susan stumbled from theirs while it was slowing. She fell, then got back up. Traffic was beginning to rub-berneck. She ran across the lanes, between the cars until she got to him: his eyes were open and there was a spasm at the mouth; she threw her coat over and beneath and around him like a bunting. Time was still in slow motion but no longer in a way that could even in theory be made use of.

There was a trial date and there was a hearing and there was a prison sentence not long enough to suit either of them. They pleaded guilty to every charge, large and larger. The judge tilted his head and massaged his face with his hands: he had seen much worse. His job was a curse and he'd grown used to worse. And so, astonishingly, he suspended their sentences. Their loss was considered, by the court, sufficient.

They changed their names and drove a thousand miles west.

"Our lawyer was too good," said Susan.

Throughout the telling of this, thank God, Mary-Emma was upstairs, dreaming her dreams. Her parents had gone from a couple who would be different, who would be better than anyone, who were determined to be better than most, to a couple who would be different because they were worse.

"That woman who would sit there and somehow let a man make that kind of mistake is gone," said Sarah.

"She died," I said.

"Gabriel died." My ears were scorched. A bass line from a Peter Gabriel tune thumped absurdly in my brain.

"But Susan, too," I said.

"Susan," Sarah repeated, as if in a trance. "There is not enough dying that can happen to Susan." Sun came out momentarily from behind a cloud and briefly washed her with a cleansing light, then moved on as if it had changed its mind, leaving her in the dark once more.

I wanted to go home and watch movies for the rest of my life. I wanted to see larger and more ravenous and less pathetic monsters than these.

"We did not have the nerve, in our convicted but legally unpunished condition, to look anyone in the eye anymore. Not where we lived. We did not even hold a decent memorial.

How we stayed together I cannot fathom." She was pacing again. "And yet, how could we not? We were each other's only consolation. The sort of redemption that was required of us only *we* understood."

"Of course," I murmured. Although how together they had remained seemed possibly a matter of debate.

"Strangely, it's easier to get on with life, to forget one's losses and misdeeds, if one is not formally punished. People often think the opposite, but it's not true. Proper official punishment creates a double punishment and gives wholeness and enduring shape to an experience that otherwise is allowed with time to fade and blur and be denied."

Fade. Could events return, retrace their heavy-footed passage, to the place from where they had accidentally come? Could even a child grow vaguer and . . . *fade*?

"Much has been made of the doom of not remembering. But remembering has its limitations. Believe me, it is good to forget."

"Yes," I said. Though everything that I ever forgot I always remembered again later, so perhaps it didn't count.

"Sometimes when I reconsider this event, as a route to forgiveness, I recast it and make it Susan who is actually driving. Yet it still comes out the same. Sometimes."

I didn't know whether it mattered. I didn't know what to say. I felt as if I were watching the lion lady being eaten by the lion.

"It was an accident," I said.

"Negligence is the legal word. One of them, at any rate."

In my mind I did a quick survey: pride, weakness, uneasy deferral to power. Paralyzing strangleholds of the unconscious, amnesia of convenience, dark twists of character, and secrets in the past? Babbling during grief? Jokes while dying? Hadn't I had a midterm on these?

I was now at the bottom of my wineglass, where there was no further loam or briar to assist.

a lot of stairs. And steps. Stairs and steps both. There are always obstacles."

"Yesterday at the bank I accidentally made off with the suction canister at the drive-in teller. Maybe what Emmie really shouldn't have is a mother who is too busy."

This again seemed to negate *me*. I was the one who was hired to neutralize or at least mitigate the busyness. But I hadn't succeeded and could feel myself being neutralized and mitigated instead.

Here Sarah leaned forward and put her hand on my cheek, which reminded me of Murph. Why were people doing this all of a sudden? "Of course, Emmie has you. That's been nice." The hand came down and her gaze turned away. She seemed to be speaking to no one in particular. "So I didn't name her Maya or Kadira or Tywalla: I named her Emmie. Was that so wrong?" I could see she felt under some critical eye, as she had from the beginning. "You know what my neighbor across the street said to me? 'I always see the babysitter with the baby, but I don't see you.' Day and night, I'm down working at the Mill."

Where were effective, urgent words when the world most required them? I felt I needed to persist. But it was like all bad dreams: the dreamer, even while dreaming, thinks, *What is going on here? What am I supposed to do?* In pleasant dreams, equally strangely, one always seemed to know.

She continued. "Women chew up their lives trying to heal themselves from the bad arrangements they've made with men; all this healing is not attractive. It's boring." And then she added, "Anything that does not throw a young black person into despair is all for the good. Unfortunately, I don't qualify as that. I officially don't qualify."

"Nothing's ideal. You are her real mother now," I said boldly.

"You're not getting it!" she said sharply, her face flushed with exasperation. "We have been caught in our own home cooking."

"Home cooking?"

She sighed. "That's restaurantese for throwing something back in the pot when it has fallen on the floor. Deceit. It means deceit. Even if by some miracle we challenge the agency and win, we will have a public story. Emmie will be shunned!"

"No, no, that's not possible."

"Yes!" she said as if I were an infuriating dimwit. "We all will be spoken of! And when Emmie is old enough, she will hate us."

Perhaps I'd become like the teenage McKowen daughter we'd all glimpsed at Mary-Emma's first foster home. Perhaps I was clinging to something that wasn't mine to love. Perhaps I was treasuring love that wasn't mine to treasure. My hands were twisting at each other in a way that my mother used to yell at me for. When I was young she would just lean over and swat them.

Sarah grabbed the glasses and I followed her back into the kitchen.

The people in this house, I felt, and I included myself, were like characters each from a different grim and gruesome fairy tale. None of us was in the same story. We were all grotesques, and self-riveted, but in separate narratives, and so our interactions seemed weird and richly meaningless, like the characters in a Tennessee Williams play, with their bursting, unimportant, but spellbindingly mad speeches. Only Mary-Emma seemed immune, undeviant, not part of that, though she was, and had her own soliloquies to be sure, and would have them up ahead in life—how not?

Sarah opened the refrigerator, which lit her up again. "The whole thing fills me with terrible thoughts. I suppose I should manage a better philosophical stance. Certainly the French would! They would have the proper comedic perspective." And here she paused. "Of course, they also have jokes that end 'And then the baby fell down the stairs.' " She had sealed her rooty puree into a

Rubbermaid bowl, the puree I'd seen her chopping many days ago already. She was no longer thinking it should be stashed here.

"Please," she said, handing it to me. "Don't eat this. Just keep it in the back of your refrigerator at home. I'll ask for it again, but I don't want it lingering around here right now. Not with the kids coming Wednesdays."

"What is it?" I asked. There would be no more Wednesdays. I already felt that.

"It's, um, a kind of poisonous paste that, well, gets stains out. Just don't get it confused with parsnip tapenade."

"What's it made of?"

"It's . . . nothing. But don't mix it up with food."

Then I realized it was that paperwhite puree I had just seen her mincing, mashing the bulbs with a cheese slicer and a pestle.

"Does it work? In the laundry?" I asked. Meekness returned to cover me and blur my sight like a veil.

"Supposedly," she said, with mystery and evasion. "Perhaps someday I'll have Liza try it on some stains. If you keep it cool and moist and scrub it in with a brush it's supposed to work. Take it home with you, please, just for now. I'll ask for it back later. But here, take it." And she thrust the sealed plastic container at me. I took it. Put it in my backpack. It reminded me of tales I'd read of people carrying yeasts in damp handkerchiefs from Europe— a break with one world and a beginning in another, where one would culture and grow things from the old. Or perhaps one could kill someone instantly with this. Or cure a wart. I didn't know its uses, really, but obligingly took it anyway, back to my house, where perhaps I would grow a whole new life with it, or clean a rug, or do nothing.

Tragedies, I was coming to realize through my daily studies in the humanities both in and out of the classroom, were a luxury. They were constructions of an affluent society, full of sorrow and truth but without moral function. Stories of the vanquishing of the spirit expressed and underscored a certain societal spirit to spare. The weakening of the soul, the story of downfall and failed over-coming—trains missed, letters not received, pride flaring, the demolition of one's own offspring, who were then served up in stews—this was awe-inspiring, wounding entertainment told uselessly and in comfort at tables full of love and money. Where life was meagerer, where the tables were only half full, the comic triumph of the poor was the useful demi-lie. Jokes were needed. *And then the baby fell down the stairs.* This could be funny! Especially in a place and time where worse things happened. It wasn't that suffering was a sweepstakes, but it certainly was relative. For understanding and for perspective, suffering required a butcher's weighing. And to ease the suffering of the listener, things had better be funny. Though they weren't always. And this is how, some-times, stories failed us: Not that funny. Or worse, not funny in the least.

I forgot about the container in the fridge. As with the wasabi at Christmas, I was careless with takeout. Things mounted in the refrigerator and the sink as Murph and I let a life of spring rains, warming air, romantic dissolution, and pointless essay writing make further mincemeat of domesticity. I got panicked and tried to combine the work of several classes: "Sufic Perspectives of Brontë's Exfoliating Narrative" or "Meeting at Shiraz: Sufic Per-spectives on Pinot Noir." I was having a lot of ostensibly Sufic perspectives. "The Sufic Hymn of *The Dirty Dozen.*" "The Sufic Quiet of the Western Front." "Sufic Mrs. Miniver." I had memo-rized the whistling theme from *The Bridge on the River Kwai,* but this did me no good, as I was never asked to whistle it. Crusty dishes accumulated in the sink, as did a low level of dingy water that would not drain. Half-finished cups of coffee sat on book-case shelves, with flies floating on top. When my papers were returned, question marks appeared in all my margins.

When not working, Murph was going on the Internet, slowly becoming obsessed with astrology. Wanting to see herself outlined in twinkling stars or hoping to bring the heavens at last into fruitful play here on earth, or so it sounded to me, she would say that sun signs were people alone on a mountaintop. They were warm and attracted money and should surround themselves in the colors of wood. The planets whooshed in and out of her conversation. The stars were fire or water or earth or air and contained advice and secrets that would put a box of fortune cookies to shame. When I said, "But how could the positions of the stars and planets have anything to do with our lives down here?" she would just look at me, wounded but portentous. "How could they not?" she would say.

Murph and I both had a lot of schoolwork, and our music sessions dwindled as I took to racing off to the library on my Suzuki. I got a phone message from my advisor and I was forced to drop Wine Tasting, as they had at long last discovered I was underage. The computer had made this mistake with twenty students. My parents would get a partial tuition refund. Across the street in the stadium, football teams were holding spring scrimmages and fans in green and yellow crowded in to cheer them on, even if the games didn't count. Life was spent in all sorts of ways. I watched *The Thin Red Line.* I watched *Apocalypse Now.*

The real problems, as far as I could see, which was not that far, remained back at the Thornwood-Brinks', and the temporary removal from their home of the pulverized narcissus bulb tapenade had not solved them.

"I dropped a course, so now I have some extra hours," I told

Sarah as I was leaving one afternoon, thinking she might like more help. When I looked at her, I no longer really knew what I saw.

I felt she could see this, as she said, "Well, we'll see what happens. I realize I'm not being fair to you, in terms of your schedule and budget. But I'll try to make it up to you." A bonus. I had heard of these. They were always fraught. I recalled that promising hand squeeze she had given me those long months ago in January, waiting in the hospital parking lot. And then, recalling more, something she'd said became clear to me: it wasn't *sleighs* together; it was *slays* together.

A remark like that served what purpose? If only I'd been able to use it in my *Macbeth* paper last term!

Mordancy: there was something that could not really be taught. But it could be borrowed. It could be rubbed up against. It could scrape you like bark.

Once, when I was there alone with Mary-Emma, the phone rang, and when I answered it there was just silence. "Bonnie!" I said sternly. "Is this you?" There were things I would tell her. Things she should know! Things she should know and know now! *"Bonnie?"* And then a familiar voice began to speak. I knew somehow it was the voice of the woman with the beautiful dreads. It was the voice of the woman who did all the deafness jokes. She said, "I'm sorry. I think I dialed the wrong number."

Then one Monday, when both Sarah and I were there, the phone rang again. I picked it up upstairs and heard someone say, "This is Suzanne, Roberta's assistant at Adoption Option . . ." But Sarah had answered it downstairs, so I hung up and went back to Mary-Emma. Steve was still swimming in his bowl, which we had moved to a high shelf in Mary-Emma's room. She and I were doing our song and dance to Diana Ross's "Ain't No Mountain High Enough." There were *ooh*s and *ahh*s and Ross's own breathy *sing-sprecht* at the beginning, which I mimicked, teaching Mary-Emma. When I was very little, it was the only song I knew by a black woman, or the only one my mother knew, for she was the one who had taught it to me. I pointed my thin arms out and up. " 'If you need me, call me.' " I made the fingers to the face sign of talking on the phone. " 'No matter where you are.' " Arms out again, my head smiling and shaking. Mary-Emma did the same. Downstairs the phone rang again and again. " 'No matter how far.' " I could hear Sarah's voice below: "No. Yes. That's true."

I continued with the oblivious and radiant Mary-Emma. " 'No matter where you are, just call my name, I'll be there in a hurry.' "

There was a loud moan from below, which somewhat matched the music. " 'On that you can depend and never worry.' " I ratcheted up the volume. " 'No wind,' " I sang, practically shouting, and then Mary-Emma shouted back, " 'NO WIND!' " " 'No rain,' " I sang. " 'NO RAIN!' " she repeated. And I then lifted her up as I always did and bumped her on my hip in front of the mirror, where we watched ourselves. " 'Or winter's cold can stop me, baby, if you're my goal.' "

And then for a brief minute there was anguished wailing from below that had nothing to do with our song, though I kept on with the music, which had a corresponding whooping cry to it, turning up the volume even louder so that we would hear nothing more from downstairs. I kept Mary-Emma busy for almost half an hour with this. She came in on all the sliding moans and dreamy cries, and also on command repeated whatever phrase I'd just sung. " 'Life holds for you one guarantee, You'll always have me.' " We were practically shouting.

" 'YOU'LL ALWAYS HAVE ME!' "

" 'And if you should miss my love, One of these old days . . .' "

" 'THESE OLD DAYS!' "

" 'If you should ever miss the arms, that used to hold you so close . . . , just remember—' "

" 'JUST REMEMBER!' "

" '—what I told you that day I set you free!' "

" 'SET YOU FREE!' "

And then, during a pause in the song, the front doorbell rang. Just before the chorus. Sarah came dashing up into the nursery. I turned down the music. Sarah was wearing my perfume, the same scent, and her rush upstairs warmed the air with it. Arabian Goddess.

"Mama!" Emmie sang out.

Sarah grabbed her to her chest and began rubbing her back frantically while Emmie played with Sarah's hair, pulling it straight up and seeing if it would stay or fall.

"Quick, Tassie," Sarah said in a sibilant whisper full of panic. "Would you answer the door for me, please?"

"Sure." Then I added, "Uh, what should be my MO?"

"Stall," she said.

I trudged downstairs. I affected a proprietary saunter.

At the door was a woman who either reminded me of someone I knew or *was* someone I knew, or both.

Both it was: it took a while for it all to come into focus, but quickly it did. She smiled tightly and said, "Hello, Tassie—you probably don't remember me. Roberta Marshall."

From the adoption agency. I remembered her well. At least it wasn't Bonnie herself. That might have been too much for me.

"Yes, I do. Hi." I shook her hand. I felt a saucy manner come over me, as if I were not Bonnie or the shy McKowen girl but Amber Bowers in the Kronenkee Perkins Family Restaurant. Whatever Roberta's presence meant here, it could not be good, it seemed to me. She was like the police, but the police dressed up in taupe and beige. A state trooper with earrings. Strangely, I felt protective of the house. I had worked here for what felt like a long time, I guess, and was attached to its very doors and walls more than I realized.

Roberta had never met Amber, so it didn't matter if I pretended for a spell to be her. My teeth were better—thank you, Bess and Guess!—but if I remained tight-lipped she might never see them. I might be hiding all manner of fangs and fossils and other spittable bits. This secret would give me skank power.

"How's little Mary? Is she doing well?" Roberta stared straight into my eyes. If only I'd been wearing a hat with a brim I could angle down over them! If only I'd been accessorized more insouciantly—or accessorized at all—I might have felt myself a real match for her.

Everyone, I only noticed now for some reason, called Mary-Emma by a slightly different name, like she was no one at all. "She's fine," I said, as if I were talking to a spy. Still standing in the doorway, I sank into one hip and leaned one arm up against the doorjamb. I stared at Roberta without inviting her in. I did not know how to smirk—at least, not that I knew of. Not deliberately. Neither did I have any gum to chew. But I could move my mouth around a little as if there were food in my teeth, and so I did, and then I pursed my lips in a manner that hovered on the edge of incivility. This was new for me and not without its fun.

Function and intention gave Roberta a sturdy demeanor. "Is Sarah here?" she inquired, hoping to clear away me, the riffraff.

"Let me think," I said. I actually did need to think in order to figure out what further to say. I wasn't sure what Sarah might want me to do. Roberta was starting to be irked with me. Irritation entered her eyes in a low, cold flame. "Let me go see," I added.

Upstairs Sarah was already standing in the hall, a little paralyzed, but with Mary-Emma dressed in a pink corduroy jacket and a pink velvet headband around her afro. Mary-Emma's head was sunk down on Sarah's shoulder, as if it tired her to be so dressed up; it was getting close to nap time.

"Roberta Marshall's downstairs," I said.

"Jesus, I can't believe she came so soon. I can't even believe she came today." Sarah looked paralyzed. But then breathed deeply and brushed past me, with Mary-Emma, to go greet Roberta at the door.

Sarah, too, did not invite her in, so I could see from the landing, where I watched, near an open black trash bag of stuffed animals, a Brio train, and folded baby blankets, that my instincts had been correct. She did not even open the outer door but just stood, slightly braced against the open inner one.

"Hi there, Sarah. And hello there, Mistress Mary," chirped Roberta from the doorstep through the screen.

Mary-Emma looked at her wordlessly, then buried her face in Sarah's sleeve again.

"Not quite contrary," said Roberta, shrugging off the quip.

"You did not make it clear you were coming today," said Sarah.

"I'm sorry. I thought you understood. Legally, your time is up as foster parents, and if the adoption papers can't be finalized, we move on to the next couple in line. Which means—"

"Which means what?"

"I was getting to that. It means Mary has to be moved into the regular foster care that we use. Just for the time being, of course."

"Why can't we be the foster care?" Sorrow flooded Sarah's face.

"Because you're not. Our agency has specific ones we use. There was that problem with your withheld information, which we've discussed already. I don't want to get into that now."

"Well, we were her foster parents for all these months. I mean, we are still this second, I should think."

"Your being foster parents has been a technicality, as I explained, until the adoption was finalized. Since you're not going ahead, we must make other arrangements."

"You'd move her right now this minute based on a technicality?"

"I'm afraid it's sort of the law."

"I need to discuss things further with my husband, I think."

"You've had all this time."

"Well, yes, but we still need more time. To transition. At the very least. Just to transition. To sit with this decision and make the transition."

"The law doesn't offer that kind of comfort zone. I'm sorry. I wish for your sake it did." And here she slowly opened the outer screen door, insinuating her body over the threshold.

"Hey, Mary! Want to go for a ride?" Roberta stooped to look Mary-Emma in the eyes and made a big, false happy face.

"What are you doing?" Sarah began to lean back into the house.

Roberta began to hold her arms out for Mary-Emma. There was going to be a scene. Sarah swung Mary-Emma away.

"Don't touch her!" Sarah cried, and Mary-Emma began to whimper.

"You can make it easier for the child," said Roberta, "or you can make it difficult." She edged in further, filling the doorway, shoving the screen door now completely behind her hip. She reached out again, worming her fingers around Mary-Emma.

Sarah pulled her brusquely away.

"Sarah," Roberta said scoldingly. "Don't make this a tug-of-war."

Sarah's face became a mask. "Do you have a carseat?" she asked quietly. Defeat was coming over her. Probably there was a kind of shiny bird or spiny fish that did this, gave away its babies, flailed out at its own family, and did it all disguised as a rock to avoid being eaten.

"Yes, of course," said Roberta. The most personal matters were supervised by bureaucracies so that humaneness would not interfere and obstruct. Everyone could shrug and plead the little laws of life.

"OK. Well, I'll walk her to the car. I won't have you just snatching her in the doorway."

Sarah walked her to Roberta's car and put her in the back.

"Wait a minute. I have her stuff," she said, and ran ashen-faced back into the house, grabbing the trash bag from the landing. The original white plastic trash bag had now been replaced with a newer, larger black trash bag, and filled with Mary-Emma's original dowry, plus some other items—clothes, a Gund Pooh bear, the Brio train, a silver cup, and the Diana Ross CD, which I'd placed in there just before tying up the whole thing with its yellow plastic tie. I had also added Steve the fish, tied him tight in a Baggie with water and plopped him on top in a plastic take-out container. It didn't seem like much, traveling the world with just these trash bags. I might have hoped to save Mary-Emma from this particular country-western song—"these plastic bags hold my life, darlin' dear"—or at least this particular verse, but I wasn't strong enough to wave away anything as strong as music, let alone harsh facts. I had tried to be Amber, recalcitrant, oppositional, but had also, like Sarah, ended up as passive, translucent, and demolished as Bonnie, just watching the baby go.

"Here," said Sarah, thrusting the bag in Roberta's direction. In her other hand she had a sippy cup, and she handed it to Mary-Emma through the open car window.

"Mama?" Mary-Emma looked frightened.

"I can't go with you," said Sarah, and simply blew the child a kiss. "But it'll be OK. I promise."

"Ciao, Mama!" Mary-Emma began to cry and thrust her arms from the backseat. Sarah stood curbside, saying nothing. "Ciao, Mama! Ciao, Mama!" Her farewell was not even the language of the mother or the babysitter, but the babysitter's ex. Mary-Emma's cries came floating back through the open window as the car zipped down the street and took a right at the first corner.

I could not believe what Sarah had done.

Of course King Solomon was right. The woman brought before him with the disputed baby, the one who consented to the infant's being cut in half, was not the real mother.

But she was the real wife.

Sarah turned and ran quickly inside. I followed. I have never heard a houseful of such weeping. Inside, Noelle had entered through the back door with his vacuum cleaner and pails. "What's going on?" he asked, placing a Diet Coke once again in the freezer.

"I'm not the one who can tell you," I said. Then I left as quickly as I could.

For a week I busied myself in a robotic way with tasks, half waiting for the phone to ring—to have it be Sarah or Reynaldo or even more hilariously Mary-Emma, as I missed her. I wanted to hear that all these little nightmares were gone—mistakes had been made!—that a lot had been patched up and swung open and glued back, and can you get over here right this minute, you are needed! But one spring day tumbled after another, identical and dull, and the semester seemed to be closing up shop, indifferent to me. I went on two geology field trips, both times as a quasi zombie. I did my final Dating Rocks research paper: "The Plausible Sufic Geology of Stonehenge." I was reduced. I was barely there. When misfortune accumulated, I could feel now, it strafed you to the thinness of a nightgown, sheared you to the sheerness of a slip. Light seemed to shine right through your very hands, your blood no longer red: your skin in the breeze billowing, like a jellyfish. Your float through the day had the reality of a trance, triggering distant memories though not actually very many. The passing of time was the lightest of brushes. Life was ungraspable because it would not stay still. It skittered and blew. It was a mound of random trash, even as you moved through the hours like a ghost invited to enjoy a sparkling day at the beach.

Murph was lying on the couch when I came home one night from the library. I spoke to her but there was no answer. I shook her. She was not rousable. She was clammy and bluish in the lips. When I shook her again there was some moaning. Next to her on the coffee table was the now, on my part, long-forgotten plastic bowl of paperwhite tapenade and a box of crackers that had been knocked to the floor beside them.

"Oh, my God!" I shouted to no one, then I phoned 911. While I waited I pushed my fingers into her mouth to see if I could fetch any extraneous mash still in her mouth. There was a gob of it inside her cheek just sitting there and I rinsed my hand of it, then took wet paper towels to the rest of her mouth. Just once I thought I heard her moan. Where was the ipecac?

An ambulance and a fire engine pulled up in no time at all, and Kay came down from upstairs and stood on the porch, gathering her reports. "Are we going to need some crime scene tape?" she asked. "I've got a big yellow roll upstairs!" The paramedics were three cute boys whose cuteness I didn't notice until I conjured them later in memory. They carried tackle boxes of swabs, needles, tubes, and blood pressure cuffs. They took her vital signs and then maneuvered her onto a stretcher.

Her breathing was shallow but not alarmingly so. Still, they took the silver stud out of her nose and stuck an oxygen mask on her. I rode with her in the back of the ambulance, holding her hands, first one and then the other. "Flower bulbs?" asked one of the paramedics. "Well, there's a first for everything."

"There *is,* isn't there?" I said in a suddenly brightened way, for it came to me that she would live and all would be well.

And she did. There was no killing her—she was like an ox combined with a horse combined with a bear combined with a truck; she was like Steve the fish!—and afterward she seemed her same self, but in my statements to the police, and in my new under-standing of Sarah's self-thwarted potential to kill someone—who else but Edward and herself, unless she wanted Liza and the others thrown in—the parsing of these things was like a blade through light, defying all weapons. I had become vague and unknowable to myself in guilt and inaction. Or rather, perhaps, newly known.

The local lakes were already verdant with scum. I failed my Neutral Pelvis final. I simply forgot to go. When I approached my instructor to say, "But my roommate was throwing up blood!" she said, "That line is as old as the hills." I turned in all my papers and exams. There was not an informed word in them. I had no idea what I was talking about, though here and there I would burst forth with an embarrassing intensity of assertion. I was given Bs.

"Who was that witch you worked for?" asked Murph before she went home to Dubuque for the summer, her stomach pumped, her pulse returned, her courses done.

"She wasn't a witch." I sighed. "At least, I don't think so." I thought about this some more. "At least, not a very good witch."

"A good witch at all?"

"Yeah, maybe."

"Still, I'd like to smack her," said Murph.

I laughed drily. "God, so would I."

She touched my arm. "Don't make your own life your project in your own life: total waste of time. I don't mean that personally. I mean that for everyone. It was revealed to me as I fell back from the great white light of death."

I felt nothing but admiration for her. I felt she was a healer. I felt she could read minds. "Do you ever feel certain people are psychic?" I asked. "Like you know someone and secretly feel they are psychic and that they don't understand this themselves?"

"Yes," she said.

"You do? You've felt this about someone?"

"I feel that about you."

This seemed so much like a joke that I laughed.

"Really." She smiled and embraced me. "Have a great summer." We had given up our lease and neither of us knew what we would do come fall, but it wouldn't be with each other. We had put almost all of our possessions in storage, which was a metaphor for being twenty, as were so many things.

My father phoned to ask me if I'd like to help him with the farm. He had recently started a three-season-spring-greens angle to his business and needed help with it: I would run out in front of his newfangled thresher-shaver and scare the mice away. My brother was packing up for boot camp at Fort Bliss and would be gone all summer and all harvest. Did I have another job? Was I interested?

I said I thought that would be good exercise and I appreciated the offer. As a coincidence, I told him, my other job was suddenly over. I'd come home on the bus on Monday and we could talk about it more. I had to clean the apartment to get our deposit back.

"You will miss Robert's graduation if you don't come sooner. It's on Sunday."

"Well, I'll take the early Sunday bus," I said.

What had I learned thus far in college? You can exclude the excluded middle, but when you ride through, on your way to a lonely and more certain place, out the window you'll see everyone you've ever known living there.

I had also learned that in literature—perhaps as in life—one had to speak not of what the author intended but of what a story intended for itself. The creator was inconvenient—God was dead. But the creation itself had a personality and hopes and its own desires and plans and little winks and dance steps and collaged intent. In this way Jacques Derrida overlapped with Walt Disney. The story itself had feet and a mouth, could walk and talk and speak of its own yearnings!

I learned that there had been many ice ages. That they came and went. I learned there were no mammals original to New Zealand. I learned that space was not just adrift with cold, flammable rocks. Here and there a creature was riding one, despite the Sufic spinning of the rock. The spores of lightless life were everywhere. I think I learned that.

VI

My brother and my father picked me up at the bus station, figuring I'd have a lot of stuff. Robert was wearing his graduation gown but carrying his cap.

"Well, you don't have that much," said my father, puzzled.

"I put a lot in storage," I said. I tugged at Robert's gown. "Hey, congratulations."

"It's more of an accomplishment than you may realize," he said, abashed.

"What time is the ceremony?"

"Not until two."

"And you put on that gown already?"

"You bet."

"We have already taken a thousand pictures," mused my dad.

"You didn't answer my e-mail," said my brother.

"What e-mail?" I asked.

"The last one I sent you!"

"You told me to ignore it."

"No, not that one. The one after that!"

I was slowly remembering that I had archived it for later.

"Is your address still bassface-at-isp-dot-com?" he continued.

I always believed my e-mail address was clever and hip until I heard it said aloud. "It is. Jeez, I'm sorry. I don't know what happened." I would change the subject. "How are you?"

"Great!"

"Really? Nobody's great!"

"Well, it's not great with a capital *G*. It's actually *g-r-a-t-e*. That may not be so good."

"No, it may not be. How did that happen?"

"I got grated on a curb."

"Ha! Did he ever," said my dad.

"Did you just make that up?" I asked my brother.

"No," he said, smiling and climbing into the truck. "I've been working on it for weeks."

"Weeks?"

"Well, not weeks. Months, actually." He was working hard to sound *upbeat* and had landed on *bizarrely merry.*

"Did you leave that Suzuki of yours back in Troy?" inserted my father as we were driving off.

"Yes. I did."

"Too bad!" said my brother. The topic of the lost e-mail had too much regret and belatedness attached to it and was no fun. Unlike the motorbike. "I wanted to see you buzz around the ceremony this afternoon. It would cause a sensation!"

"That's just what I want to do." I stared out the window of the truck. Irrigation sprinklers like the skeletons of brontosauruses were sprawled across the farm fields.

At home I had to help my mother dress, in the room she called "the store." Here she would stack up boxes of apparel that she had mail-ordered but not tried on to see whether she would keep them or send them back. When she was ready she would go through and open them one by one, but until then they stayed in the store—which was in essence a kind of mail room.

"Gail?" my dad called up for my mom.

"We're in the store!" she called back, and I helped her try on something I thought would be fine, and then yanked the tags off for her. "Send the rest back," I said. "But wait—what is this?" There was a beautiful black hat with a feather sticking straight up and a sash dangling down the side.

"That's not for a graduation."

"No, it's not. Unless you're the one graduating: then you could flip the sash as you walked across the stage and blow a whistle with the feather between your thumbs."

"It's for something, though," she said, holding it with more affection than was seemly. "I don't know what yet."

"A party from fifty years ago, maybe."

"Hey, around here? There are a lot of those. And you still can't wear a hat like this."

"Where did you get it?"

"Oh, online somewhere. What does the box say?"

I tried it on myself.

"Very nice," said my mother. "Perhaps I should give it to you."

"Yes, perhaps you should!" I laughed. "I could wear it to all my classes!" I placed it back in the hatbox, which smelled of cedar and insecticide.

The graduation was inside the gymnasium due to a forecast of rain, and in the middle the tornado siren went off and we all just stayed put. Personally, I felt this sound effect was suited to the occasion. The girls all wore high heels beneath their black graduation gowns and wobbled across the stage with great uncertainty, except one who strode quickly, then slipped and almost fell. I didn't know any of them. Pinned to their chests they wore large white peonies that looked like the heads of angora cats. The boys pumped their fists in the air at the slightest inside joke. When Robert walked across the stage to grasp his diploma, the principal, good-naturedly, pretended to hold it back, but Robert smiled, and so did the principal, who patted him on the back, gave him the thing, and sent him on his way. He was liked, I could see that. People really liked Robert. In the crowd his posse called out "Gunny!" and "Gunny, got your gun?" and that's when the full implications of his going off to the army really hit me. Why hadn't I given it sufficient thought before now? Well, that was an easy one to answer, but still. It was not an excuse.

When the tornado siren stopped, we stepped outside and there was sunshine everywhere. It was the season of white flowers; to go with the girls' peonies the school grounds were edged with bridal wreath and daisies. Only one dark rain cloud was left in the sky, like an evil genie, and it was making a hasty retreat in the breeze.

My brother left for the ironically named Fort Bliss the very next day. We took him to the bus station and said good-bye. We gave him little presents. A rabbit's foot key chain. A tortoiseshell toothbrush. I gave him a copy of poems by Rumi and a three-by-five card that said *Here's a reply to your forgotten e-mail: don't forget to write!*, which, in case it sounded like sisterly snottiness, caused me to throw my arms around him and hug him hard. "You put the *soul* in *soldier*," I whispered to him. "Just don't get one of those flag tattoos."

He pulled away from my embrace. "Why not?" he asked, and I could see he was desperate for the knowledge and reasoning behind anything. I could see he felt shorthanded, underequipped, factually and otherwise. Just the night before he had said, "Afghanistan has provinces? Like Canada?"

"Oh, I don't know," I said now, shrugging. He beamed anyway. He was no longer a boy; he had become a young man. How had that happened? Nothing I said or knew had I known for very long, and so its roots were spindly and unsteady and the whole thing unsharable. "Don't be nervous 'bout the service," I said. It was a line I'd heard in a song somewhere. "You'll be fine. Oh, and this," I said more quickly, confidentially, discreetly stuffing a tampon in the side pocket of his duffel.

"Good God, what's that for?"

"Just—for an emergency. Worse-case scenario: it stanches wounds."

"Where do you learn this stuff?" asked my brother.

"From movies," I said. "I've told you that before."

We had brought Blot with us, and Robert knelt down and grabbed the dog's head. "Good-bye, Blot, you bum," he said, pulling the dog close and giving him a rub.

My father thrust a wad of bills into Robert's front jacket pocket. My mother was the most misty-eyed, and my brother, as if to calm and please her, stayed peppy to such an artificial and generous degree that you could see he had no idea what he was doing. Even hoisting his duffel bags, he looked uncertain. My mother leaned in to kiss him and swept her hand through his wavy hair. "Oh, they're going to shave it all off."

"Let's not get maudlin about hair," warned my dad.

"Sell it to a wig maker!" I said, chucking him on the arm. "Get cash!" I couldn't help at that moment but recall the time Robert had put Crisco in his front cowlick to tame it. It had frozen on the way to school, before we even got to the corner bus stop. But by midmorning the grease was melting and dripping down his forehead. I tried not to think of other times when he was younger and would absentmindedly pick scabby barleys from his nose. Now was not the time to think of him as a hapless child.

When the bus hissed and rumbled away, my brother's face still pressed at the tinted window, my mother dabbed at her eyes and could only say, "I'm going to throttle that recruiter."

"Now, Gail," said my dad. Then he added, "If you throttle him, how will I get to hear him yelp and groan when I kick him?" This cheered my mother up.

I began working in my father's baby greens field that very week. My job was to run in front of the shaver, a special attachment on the thresher, which he had contrived himself and which he was amused by and drove proudly like a car, though our field was so small that it was hard for him to make the turn-arounds.

I ran ahead of it with fake feather and plastic hawk-wing extensions on my arms, whacking at the greens to scare the mice so they would not get into the mix. (If we had to take the greens to the triple-wash facility, it ate into the profit.) My father had actually designed my outfit for this, partially from a kite we had once brought to the Dellacrosse Kites on Ice festival. The costume had an aquiline-beaked mask and long wings I slipped my arms through, dipping them as I ran, brushing near the ground, beating the leaves, to resemble an actual predator and to encourage rodents to run from the shaver: nobody wanted sliced mice in their salads. At least not this decade.

I trotted, swooped, and shooed. I was the winged creation of my dad, like Icarus. I could feel myself almost flying, the way I flew in dreams: not very high, just running along and then sometimes lifting off just a little so that my stomach moved up into my heart. For a second. Not unlike my Suzuki on a speed bump.

I would also clear the field of rocks; it was at times rocky as a beach, stones rising to the surface from a quarrylike underworld. I collected them in a loader either to repatch the fish hatchery or to sell at the seed shop. The ones they sold at the seed shop were from China. All the way from China! Everything from China, even the rocks! It was not an expression yet, *like coals to Newcastle—like rocks to Dellacrosse*—but it would be soon, said my father, as it was the confounding truth.

In this manner, most often masked and winged, I spent the summer days. Running twenty feet ahead of my dad as he rode the reconfigured thresher, I would run and dip and swoosh and in theory scare off rabbits as well. Mice darted, snakes did their undulating gumshoe. With my dad in the mornings I had worked up a song: "Squirrels and mice and moles better scurry / when I am a hawk in a hurry / when I am a hawk in a hurry with some fringe on top." Even Miles Davis had liked this tune.

My father worried that I might be getting too good at this task and scaring off all the real predators that would help keep the rodent population down.

"Hey, that's life in the the-ay-ter!" I said. The whole soundtrack to *Oklahoma* played in my head. The sun burned. There was a bright golden haze on all meadows. The sky shone as blue as forget-me-nots, and often the smudged thumbprint of a morning moon hung suspended above. The air before noon was soft, with the coppery smell of dirt. We would mostly work early, and then evenings, when things (me, the lettuce) were cooler. Midday I spent resting and reading, drinking cold lemonade and Coke out of Ball jars that had lost their tops. Sometimes in the afternoon there were thunderstorms so sky-crackingly violent it was like life on another planet entirely. The storms seemed different from the ones of my childhood. These were sky-wide and tree toppling, moving across the state with the fury of marauders— pelting rain and wind that could switch the current of a creek— and then afterward, total calm in the air, sparkle and breeze, as if nothing had happened at all.

Although I avoided most community picnics—I had never liked sitting on the ground with a paper plate while flies bit your legs, or sitting squeezed in at an old picnic table on a bench that gave you splinters—on the Fourth of July I went with my parents to the county baseball field to watch the fireworks. As this was the first fireworks display since 9/11, the county had rented a metal detector and we all had to walk through, the daylilies, in Packer green and gold, in bloom to either side of us.

"As if Al Qaeda has ever even heard of Dellacrosse," said my father once we were seated. "I guess absolutely everyone wants to be on the map. No matter what map it is."

"It's a form of terrorism *not* to bomb this town," I said. My father gave me a look.

"Keep your voices down, you two," said my mother. She had

brought snacks of lemon frosting sandwiched between graham crackers, a favorite of my childhood, and when we were seated she passed the little Tupperware box back and forth to my father and me.

Once the sun set completely, its murky rose stretched taffylike across the horizon, the air grew cooler, and the show began. Like the operation of a rocket ship, the fireworks were staged to burst at designated points across the sky. Peonies and chrysanthemums bloomed forth from spasms and explosions. Were we having fun? Dripping sparkle sizzled and dissipated, then resumed; the deathly silence before each burst began to fill me with dread. Screeches, whistles, booms: the barium green and copper blue held too many intimations of war. We were a glum trio, my parents and I, our necks nonetheless arced and our heads dropped back onto the flattened hoods of our sweatshirts, watching all this lit-up drizzle. Our snack was gone. We had eaten the whole container's worth.

Would it have been so bad to have remained a colony of England? I wondered fiercely with every bang. Would it have been so terrible if every dessert was called a pudding even if it was a cake, to grow up saying "in hospital," to lose a few articles, to spell *gray* with an *e,* to resprinkle the *r*'s, to have an idle king, an idle queen, and put all the car steering wheels on the right? Well, perhaps the steering wheels would be worth fighting for. Perhaps our Founding Fathers had had an intimation of that one.

"There was a lot of smallpox in the eighteenth century," I said on the way home, squeezed between my parents in the front of the truck.

"There sure was," said my dad. "But they started the inoculations around the time of the war, I think."

"Well, we can celebrate that, at least," said my mother. "Sometimes I think it might not have been so awful to be English."

"Oh, my God—I was just thinking the same thing!"

"Tories in the lorry!" exclaimed my dad.

"Well, how awful could it be? England looks great in pictures. You went there on your honeymoon!"

"We would have been colonists," said my dad.

"So? Would we have had to wear big scarlet *C*s around our necks? "

My father leaned past me to say to my mother, "You send a kid to college, and look what you get."

"Corinne Carlten wears a big gold *C* around *willingly*," I said.

"How is Corinne these days?" asked my mother.

"I really wouldn't know," I said, and then fell silent. Every exchange with my parents ended up in some boring place I didn't want to be.

"And how about Krystal Bunberry, since her dad got sick and all."

"Dunno," I said. "She was nice to send that toilet paper, though!"

"If we were still English," said my father, "we'd be drinking more and driving on the wrong side of the road—pretty much what people do on the Fourth of July anyway."

"I don't like all the words in our national anthem," my mother said. She had given up on me and my friends as a topic of conversation. " 'Bombs bursting in air.' What kind of song is that to sing? When sung in large crowds, everyone takes a deep breath and it sounds like 'bombs bursting in *hair*.' "

"Hush," said my father.

Then we all looked out at the road. The high crucifixes of phone and electric poles, in line on either side, multiplied and shrinking in the distance almost to a vanishing point, made me think of the final scene of *Spartacus*.

"Think the corn's knee high?" asked my mom, and soon our truck lights swung and shone onto our own driveway and we were home.

———

I watched movies that I rented from Farm & Fleet. They weren't very good; Farm & Fleet was new to it, and the selection was small, though we never actually used the phrase *slim pickins* at our house; it would have been bad luck. Like placing your pocketbook on the floor or your hat on the bed. But I was watching a lot of Jennifer Aniston movies and documentaries about Brazil and Argentina. I would return them the very next day. Sometimes I would drive around, taking the long way back. It was lovely summer weather, and the shoulders of the county trunks were bruised blue with chicory, then snowy with Queen Anne's lace, for a while mixing, making a kind of weed gingham along the roadsides. Prairie grass flowers had been replanted in places and in others had never left: meadow rose, Turk's cap, lady slipper, laurel.

My mother had taken slightly to her bed. Mrs. Miniver she wasn't. The plants in her mirrored flowerbeds had crept out into the lawn itself, which was soon waist high in weeds, fuzzy and humid, which for ten days in mid-July revealed themselves to be not just sneezeweed but nightshade and phlox. A field of purple. A riot of violet—balloon flowers, foxglove, and sage. It was a weird and beautiful joke that her flower garden had never looked this good before. The hollyhocks stood bright and straight and as high as the windows, with only the slightest of lists. Ghettos of echinacea appeared, and fuchsia-hued tobacco and yarrow, as if it had all made a deliberate decision to do so. Only the unpruned hydrangeas missed her and had begun early their self-cannibalizing tinge to green; lit to the gills with chlorophyll, barren and virginal both, their branches drooped into the dirt with robust pustules of cream and lime. Only in their bowed and defeated eating of the soil did my mother's absence show. Ordinarily she would never have allowed this.

Sometimes in the afternoon, upstairs in my room and still with my hawk outfit on, I would get out Ole Upright Bob, the double bass, dust him off, his bow quiver clipped at the tail beneath the bridge, like a scrotum, and we would rustle up a tune. There was a kind of buoyancy in making these four low strings sing something that was not a dirge. It was a demanding instrument, the stand-up bass—by comparison, my guitar, with its buttery, mushy fingerings, was a toy—and sometimes I just played it with open strings, Miles's "Nardis," which was basic, and which spelled *starry* backwards in Latin, or something, and which I loved, and which didn't take a lot out of me. I had once, in the state music tryouts, played a solo from a double bass concerto by Sergei Koussevitzky, who in 1930 had been on the cover of *Time* magazine. That's about all I knew about him. But either I wasn't that good or the sight of a girl standing beside this huge wooden creature, grabbing its neck and stroking its gut, pulling the music out of the strings by force, made them ill at ease, and I was not selected. The faces of the panel listening were the very embodiment of skepticism made flesh, as if they were all saying *Get a load of this!*, and I had never experienced the weaponry of such expressions before. Subsequently, I drifted away from classical entirely, needing to leave behind the memory of that event. It was an aspect of childhood adults forgot to think about when they encouraged their children to try new things.

My mother came to the doorway once, seeing me winged and wrapped around my bass, one hand moving squidlike down the neck of him, the other bouncing the bow in a kind of staccato, and she said, "No wonder I couldn't sleep. Look at you. What a sight." There I was, I supposed, a bass-faced bird, embracing the sloped shoulders of another bird whose long-necked wooden crested head, like a knight in chess, hovered over my head as if it were a fellow creature advising me what to do. Still, she smiled. I was playing "Bye Bye Blackbird." She thought that it was my own arrangement, but it was one I had copied, or tried to copy—if only I'd had beefier hands and more of them—from Christian McBride.

"Your grandmother used to sing that song!" she exclaimed, and then went back to her room to rest.

I sometimes took to smacking the back of the bass for rhythm. My playing was full of wanderings that would return to fetch back the melody, or maybe only a handful of its notes, before venturing off again. I played a Bach cello prelude I had learned only the year before. It was sometimes fun to do this, make the bass play cello, like making an old man sing a young man's song. Ole Bob would complain and bellow but get through it in a slower, hobbling way, his occasional geezer spritelinesses a farewell embrace of lost youth. It moved me. I had never known my grandfathers, but if they had lived longer, I imagined them looking and sounding a lot like Bob. It was the family name, after all.

I began to miss my Suzuki, and so with my parents' permission I took a bus back into Troy to get it out of storage. My little rented storage bin—years ago a decomposing body had been found two units down, said the manager—was right next to the bus station. And yet after that bus ride I needed to walk somewhere, to stretch my legs. In the storage bin, in addition to my bike there was a box, and I looked in it to find my books from this past year and also the pearls my mother had given me for Christmas, which I quickly removed and shoved in my purse. Once I had locked up again and parked my bike in a public parking stall, I ventured out, making my stride long and purposeful. As I walked, I dug into my bag for my pearls and put them on.

I headed downtown. Troy seemed quiet and empty without the usual bustle of students. It seemed sleepy, out of step. It seemed to be from the dopey, lovely past.

Without realizing it, I was headed in the direction of Le Petit

Moulin. It was Saturday at five, cocktail hour, and the summer sun glossed everything in sight, the tree leaves and the storefront glass; even the Baraboo granite in the sidewalk squares sent out a sparkle. At this hour shadows were cast, in a translucent, notional shale. Halftones shimmied when the breeze jostled the trees.

I would go into the restaurant and see if Sarah was there. I felt the need not just to see her but in some strange way to see if I might work for her again, somehow, in the restaurant, in the fall when I came back to school, and so I went there to find her and to apply for a job. They would probably not be seating until six, so it would just be employees there now.

I walked up past the front window, where cheeses were displayed in old-fashioned glass cheese preservers, which were like cake cases with vinegar at the bottom. I climbed the cement stoop that was the restaurant's entrance. So much for handicapped access. I had never been in this place, ever, and so I couldn't be sure exactly what my breathlessness was from. Near the top of the stairs there was a potted lantana tree, though I didn't know what it was called then or that it cost nine hundred dollars. All I knew was that it looked like a tree from the pages of a fairy tale, its pink blossoms and yellow blossoms . . . How could it produce two different colors —both orderly and ethereal and alive? It had to have been done by grafting or hybridization. It was a preposterously pretty thing.

"May I help you?" asked a young man coming out from behind the maître d's lectern. There were no customers yet in the place, though a cook in a white jacket was seated at the bar, and behind it a bartender was rubbing glasses clean with a towel. Above them hung old mill wheels, collected from the countryside and bolted decoratively onto crosspieces in the ceiling.

"I would like to apply for a job."

"We are not taking any applications," said the young man at the maître d's station.

"May I just fill one out anyway? I'm looking for any kind of work. I'll wash dishes—I'll chase mice out of the salad! Anything!" My own remark amused me, and I chuckled a little to myself, but the young man looked troubled.

"This is our last night."

"What do you mean?" I asked.

"The restaurant is closing tomorrow."

"Oh, my God."

"I know."

"Is Sarah Brink here?"

"Sarah?" This caught him by surprise, and he studied my face for something—either what I knew, or how I knew her. "No," he said slowly. "Sarah's not here."

I looked around. The tables were elegantly done up with woven mats and white napkins. There were peruvian lilies in glass vases on each table and an angle of sun coming in showed only a tiny astral float of dust. Soon, with everyone bustling around, it would be gone. "Well—do you have a free table?"

"Pardon me?"

"I'd like a table. For dinner. Dinner for one. Just myself."

"We don't serve until five-thirty, but I'm happy to seat you, if you'd like."

"I would. I would like that," I said.

"Thank you," I said. He led me to a far table and handed me the record album cover with the printed sheet that served as a menu. Sarah had recycled all her old album covers and placed adhesive photo corners inside so that new menus could be photocopied and slipped in and out. I was given Neil Young's *Harvest*—perhaps there was an agricultural theme to her record selection—and though the wine list and the menu were placed inside I tried to see who was playing bass on this album—was it Tim Drummond? Stanley Clarke? Mingus himself? I had to peek behind the wine list to see for sure. Drummond.

I went back to studying the menu—was it not a kind of poetry? I sipped wine for a half hour, studying each word for its imagery and rightness of sound. There were ramps and fiddle-heads, vinaigrettes and roux—summer had not yet taken these away. Though only now did I realize that roux was not spelled *rue,* as surely it should be and would be soon, at least by Sarah. There were astonishing things: crab mousseline with a shellfish cappuccino. There were fennel-cured salmon noisettes with a champagne foam. Not a Chubby Mary in the house. There was bison carpaccio with wilted spring leaves—might these be my dad's? There were salads of lambs quarters and mint and sorrel with beets and pea shoots and tomatoes that were heirloom, like brooches, and cheeses that had won prizes in shows, like dogs. Both soups and salads wore corsages of squash blossoms and pea flowers. And at last, as I looked down through some of the most amazing writing I have ever read, everything shaved, braised, truf-fled, and "finished with"—cipollini confit! beauty heart radish! horseradish aioli!—there were my father's potatoes: roasted Bo Keltjin Farm butterballs and fingerlings. And there, with a roasted saddle of lamb, were the embezzled gourmet "Keltjin duck eggs"—egg-shaped and egg-sized, as perfect as new potatoes in a can, but with the flavor of sweet butter and apples and briary wine. But not loamy. The flavor was loamless, without loam.

Considering all that had come before on the menu, I tried not to feel that the family potatoes seemed rather minimally described—set forth without the words *spring* or *buttery* or *meaty* or *milky* or *golden* or *crisp,* not even *smuggled,* not even *grown in rich stiff mud to help condense the taste.* Still, there they were, apparently just speaking for themselves. That was something. My father's name had been on this menu all this time, perhaps for years, without my knowing. And since it was just a printed sheet I asked: "May I keep the menu?"

"Of course," said the waiter, who not only refilled my wineglass with Prairie Fumé but offered me a black napkin. "I notice you are wearing black," he said.

I didn't understand. "So I can match?" My jeans were black, but my shirt was actually navy.

"Well, you might not want to get the white napkin lint on your outfit." He backed away a little. "It's up to you."

"Oh, of course," I said. Eating was serious business here, I knew. "It's a good thing I brought my black dental floss!" Maybe I was crazy; he certainly looked at me as if I were.

"Dental floss comes in black? Or it just gets black?" Perhaps he hated me.

"I'm not sure," I said. I stared back at the menu. "How are the potatoes?" I asked without looking up.

"Very good." He smiled. "And there are two things not on the menu that I can tell you about if you want. The first is an almond-encrusted lake trout for thirty-four dollars." Thirty-four dollars for a fish probably caught in the pond across the road from Dellacrosse High seemed, well, high. (And here, silly us, we'd called it *high* school because everyone seemed so stoned!) Oh, the wine: the wine was plummy like juice. Now, here was some real red wine research!

"Thank you." I nodded and put my black napkin in my lap, setting the white one on the side of my seat, in case I had to blow my nose. "And what is the second?"

"Oh. Sorry. It's a skirt steak served with shiitake mushrooms and its own jew."

"Its own jew?"

The boy looked startled. "Yes," he said. "I think so." He looked quickly at the jottings on his notepad he had jammed in his pocket.

"Yes," he said.

"Thank you." I tried to smile. The sound of Delton County was never terribly far away. "I thought for a second there you were going to say, 'a skirt steak with its own skirt.' "

"No," he said, turning and rushing away.

The angle of the sun slowly lowered and heated the room, then lowered some more so that the room began to fall into shadow.

The waiter brought me a baby cup of parsnip puree with watercress and crème fraîche. "What is this?" I asked, and he explained. An *amuse-bouche.*

Would it poison me as the tapenade did Murph? Who cared?

"Right," I said, and lifted the tiny handled cup to my mouth and slurped. I was like a giant raiding a dollhouse. A huge Goldilocks among teeny tiny bears. I felt monstrous to myself. The stem of watercress went up my nose.

I was then brought another tiny thing for a doll: a fig with caramelized phyllo and pine nuts. A candy bar for the gods.

I had never eaten such intricately prepared food before, and doing so in this kind of mournful, prayerful solitude, in a public place, where by this time no one but I was seated without a companion, made each bite sing and roar in my mouth. Still, it was an odd experience for me to have the palate so cared for and the spirit so untouched. It was a condition of prayerless worship. Endless communion. Gospel-less church.

As if a compote were a chauffeur, every dish seemed richly to have one. I ordered the homemade asparagus ravioli—ravioluses!—with thyme and asparagus and chopped herbs, a vegetable tag-teaming itself. Gradually, I felt I had started to ascend into some kind of low-level paradise. It was astonishing to eat food that tasted like this. Was there ever a time on the planet before now when people had eaten this well? Surely people were eating in a way that evolution had no preparation or reason for. It was a miracle, gratuitous, dizzying and lovely. A "celeriac puree" could no doubt mend all cracks, remove all stains, but what was a "torchon"? A "ganache"? A "soffrito"? A "rillette"? Even the *tenderly braised escarole* offered up a phrase in a seemingly new tongue, familiar words reshaped in the high-scoring points and busy luck of Scrabble or Dutch.

I ordered a side of the Keltjin Farm potatoes.

"With *the ravioli*?" asked the waiter coldly.

"I'm related," I said.

"To the ravioli?"

"To the potatoes." I would spare him the conversations I'd sometimes had with Sarah—about the terroir, the key element being sand that would move and let them push out but not too far.

"Oho!" he said, as if this were even funnier.

I ordered a kind of fish called kona kampachi. Was that not the name of an exotic starlet from the 1940s? Did she not wear a one-piece skirted bathing suit, her breasts like pointed party hats? She came served with a lemon half wrapped in a beribboned little net. I squeezed and sprayed and dripped and did not have to pick out the seeds. I'd never before seen a lemon in a beribboned net. A lemon dressed like a fairy princess. *Bring* this *to the homeless shelter,* I heard one of the Wednesday-night voices exclaim. The potatoes arrived perfectly parboiled and could have been strung as a necklace for Barbara Bush.

I found myself eating slowly, ordering more, and staying late. The waitstaff had begun cleaning as I sat there in an almost deserted dining room. "Don't worry. Though we're shutting down early, as it's our last night, there's no need to hurry." I ordered some sherry and dessert cheeses, with their lingering taste of rot, ammonia, and adhesive bandages. There were truffle cheese with specks, twelve-year-old cheddar with crystals of salty sugar, slivers of goat cheese with the consistency of dried toothpaste. Cow cheese, sheep cheese, goat cheese—all the animals of childhood were here. Except for a pig. Where was the pig cheese? I refrained from asking, despite the wine.

I ate a bowl of fresh strawberries drizzled with a balsamic vine-

gar so rich it had the viscosity of honey. The berries were gar-
nished with the same carmelized sage I'd once tasted in Sarah's
kitchen. Every serving I'd had so far, however, seemed tiny and
delicate, so that it seemed less like dinner than a metaphor for
dinner. I began to order more. I ordered a second dessert of homemade sorbets herbally accessorized with chocolate mint, and
lavender and raspberries, their little sacs burst and smeared across
the dish like bloody bugs. I'd heard Sarah speak of these sorbets:
last February she'd said that she would make them in various flavors and colors and put them out on the fire escape to keep them
cold and there they would sit in their little dishes, sparkling all
evening outside beneath the winter moon. When I mentioned
this to the waiter, that I'd heard these sorbets were homemade
and chilled out on the fire escape in cold weather, under the
moon, his face pinched inward, as if there were a small stink in
the room. "Who told you *that*?" he asked.

My scooter was not really intended for a sixty-mile journey at
night, but it would have to do. I gunned it past a slow city bus
that was wheezing its way along, spewing exhaust. Once I was
outside of Troy the smell of manure rose up on either side of me
in the thickening dusk. The sky, which had begun looking the
deep color of a plum, had now opened up in places to a plum's
eerie gold-green flesh. The winds were switching in a way that
made me edgy. Rain moved in like a pattering animal. Riding
home like this—was this stupid of me to do?
   Was the pope Catholic?
   Was water wet?
   Leaves flicked up their silvery undersides. The sky had the
gilded look of storm. Some of the clouds had caught the light of
the receding city, and I could see there was rotation in them. I
went as fast as I could. I sometimes felt my tires skid and would

then have to slow in order to straighten them in time. During one long stretch between two endless cornfields it seemed as if I were just standing still, going nowhere, the landscape was so tiresomely the same. And then the road began to roll and there were trees but the air remained motionless yet with sudden loud gusts. In the dark, one had to swerve to avoid the roadkill—the possums were smashed to slipperiness and the raccoons were large and often stiff with rigor mortis; even in death they could topple you. An unfortunate porcupine on the center line looked like a decorative but treacherous cactus.

I distracted myself with language: *Right as rain*—what did that ever, ever mean? I was a farmer's daughter and couldn't tell you. *Was the rain wet?*—that I understood: sarcastic tropes of obviousness were always the provincial way, and were made even more obvious by individual personal recklessness. Was the pope Catholic? Does a bear live in the woods? Was he a liver in the woods, and would the pope if hungry (and if caught in the woods along with the bear, heaving their respective masses around, snapping the branches and flattening the grass) eat it? And would the pope die if he did?

The rain began pelting me as if it were hail—and perhaps it was hail: cold and stinging. Icy wetness stung my nose and cheeks. Things seemed to be metallically hitting the fender plates of my bike. I had no helmet. My lone headlight seemed to shine its light only a few feet ahead as I kept racing toward it, like a greyhound toward a moving teasing hare. Wind whirled around my ears as if in a vortex, a true gale, my mother's own name: I would be the daughter of storm. Additionally, I had eaten Sarah's food and no doubt would be maddened and end up a gorgon! My hair was being blown and tangled into stiff sticks of straw. The key was not to lose heart. In all things probably. Even for gorgons. And so I was determined not to.

———

"It's not safe for you to be riding that little bike for hours in the dark." Both my parents were waiting up for me. I entered like a drowned thing, my hair whipped to mop strings.

"You're wearing your pearls," said my mother.

I had forgotten. And checked again to feel them. I was drenched.

"They can get wet," she said, trying to hide her surprise and approval. "That's OK. It's actually good for them." And then she added, "We got a postcard from Robert today."

"Really?" She handed it to me.

"No more," said my father, unyieldingly, trying to get my attention. "You're to ride that scooter only in the day."

I looked at my brother's postcard. *Hey you all,* it read, instead of "Dear Family." Who said "Dear Family," anyway? Nobody. *Greetings from deep in the love handles of Texas. Food here is like a cross between* Alien 5 *and* Predator 3. *We are shipping out tomorrow. Love, R.* It was nothing. Said nothing. On the front was a picture of El Paso, with its relentless blue sky like lobelia that had died then gone to heaven and become an invasive. I'd never known a blue sky could look so mean.

"Did you hear me about the scooter?" my father asked tensely.

"Yes," I said. "OK." And then I pulled out a copy of the menu and gave it to him. "I found your potatoes," I said.

"Is that so," he replied.

I did what I was told. I rode the scooter only in the daylight, into town to get soda pop and movie rentals. I sometimes rode it after working with my dad in the lettuce fields, my bird outfit still on, weaving along the county roads with their lettered names—F, M, PD—that stood for nothing that I knew of. The emptiness of them, and the revving on the curves and hills, was another kind of flight. Sometimes the thought again occurred to me that I was the extraterrestrial trying to get back home to outer space. Or somehow, as with my half-Jewishness, perhaps I was only *part* extraterrestrial, a mixed breed, a sci-fi tragic mulatto; as anyone could see, I didn't really know how to get back to outer space at all. I was clearly making a botch of it. The breeze cooled me, even as a bird of prey, though if a storm was brewing, insects began to sense it in panic; slow-flying horseflies the size of bumblebees, as well as gnats and dragonflies, were blown onto my face, catching in my wings and sometimes even in my teeth and throat, if I'd been singing to myself. I would have to turn around and ride back to the house.

Some days, work done, I would just roam the property. Sandy soil was good not only for potatoes but for cottonwoods and basswoods as well, which on our land were giant and shade-giving. I would roam through our tiny ghost orchard, the cherry trees of which had been left unpruned three seasons running now and were spiky, gnarled, and largely fruitless, awaiting, perhaps, a buzz saw, a table maker—or a Russian play! Sometimes I would find an actual clutch of darkening cherries, and as with the apples in the adjacent three-tree cider orchard, I liked to find the fruit that had been slightly roughened. I had a habit from long ago, which my mother had failed to discourage: biting into the bruised spots of apples and cherries, the places under the skin where they had made their own wine, sweet and brown.

Past the old springhouse now used as a shed, past the root cellar built strongly into a small hill near the woodlot, I often headed down toward the fish hatchery with Blot just to look around. Blot himself was mostly interested in locating his old feces from last summer, stools that had turned dry and white as space snacks. "Blot! Get over here!" I would have to call him loudly, lest he tear off on some odiferous, self-seeking pilgrimage, never to be heard from again. Lucy, our nanny goat, was newly tethered for the summer, as she had wandered over to the adjacent construction too often and gnawed on the plywood gazebos.

Beneath my feet the ground sometimes gave way soggily: mole tunnels. Along the path the roots of old oaks had sometimes curled back around on themselves to encircle a clutch of wild-flowers. Others stretched across the path not only like a stair's edge but like the backbone of an ancient animal in an eroding grave. It was amazing to me the charisma of some of these trees, even as the lights were going out in them, the finger-leafed oaks, which were the ragged remnants of old savannah, and the star-leafed maples: my brother and I had climbed them and read in their strong branches. Some had hollowed trunks that allowed you to get right inside, in a sort of hiding cure of some sort, dis-appearing until you felt better; or you could just climb in and pop out for the hellbent surprise of it. The creaturely fire of them never seemed to extinguish itself entirely. Through the years, and at my dad's distracted encouragement (perhaps to get us out of the trees), we had also spent time reinforcing the fish hatchery banks with stones plucked and gathered from the fields. The pond always seemed to need buttressing. We made piles from the round, fist-sized field rocks, before we planted them into the embankment. Sometimes they looked as friendly as our very own potatoes. Other times they looked like piles of tailless rodents, and in certain lights they could startle.

I had an idea that the fieldstones I didn't take to the feed shop for sale to gardeners I would save for the hatchery. Its walls had held largely because we had been children and had been enthusi-astic in our repairs, laying the stones tight as Legos. We'd also used a mortar of assorted grit: sesame seeds, toothpaste, bubble gum, and glue. And although the mortar had long ago washed away, the stones had settled nicely due to our original design and diligence in placing them. Plus, the stream was gentle. Fish still found their way in there and stayed. Certain weeks in summer our breakfast consisted of walleye and toast.

The tennis meadow, as we called it, was on my mind, too, as

something to salvage—but for what? Sedge and porcupine grass had cracked open the blacktop; vetch and vetchling, pennycress and loosestrife moved in along the edges; all manner of night-shade, turkeyfoot, and gumweed had grabbed its opportunity. The court had disintegrated to dry dirt in some spots and was edged in rusty, crumbly mold in others. Remnants of the service lines were now indistinguishable from lichen that had etched the broken edges of the concrete piece by piece. Sedimented mac-adam. "Macadamia nuts!" my father used to joke. He had no use for tennis: it reminded him of his own childhood, which he had left behind, a childhood where, as in England, the countryside meant tennis. What else might it mean? He had been determined to discover what else.

I decided to make a little project out of the meadow. First I took my father's clippers and cut the daisies and pink clusters of milkweed: I thought I would put them in some vases around the house but quickly saw they were crawling with ants. Then I took the mower and rake and took the thistle and pigweed and every other blooming thing down. With my father's blowtorch I com-pletely burned and cleared the space between the two wood posts, where the net would be. The net posts were now cracked and swollen from years of weather. Creeping Charlie wound round them like Christmas ribbon on a gift bottle of wine. I raked out the crumbled court in between, making about a two-foot cleared, charred path. Then I placed along it a twenty-foot runner of indoor-outdoor carpeting I'd found in the barn. I strung a thick old rope between the poles, and I took my collection of Rumi poems and carefully flattened and unstrung it so I could hang folded pages along the crease, tacking them into the rope with pushpins, and I lay underneath and read. It had always been my desire to have a device that might hang from the ceiling with a lit book—why had no one invented this yet?—and this was the clos-est I'd come to experiencing it.

I found time every day to go there, and it was a sanctuary from the bobcats and graders that were still at work in gazebo-land. If it was buggy I would bring some repellent and spray the air, then step through the cloud of it as if it were a spritz of cologne. I lay down and stared up: the shade of these words made a magical tent. Because of the field's sheltering from the breezes, the pages didn't flap around much in the air, and if I wanted to rearrange or reposition them in any way I could do so. While I read, butter-flies occasionally landed, as if to check out these new cousins, and then took off again. I would read Rumi and ponder love and its ecstasies as well as the extinction of the self in divine essence until I found myself fumbling in the pockets of my shorts for a stick of gum. Which I would unwrap, blowing off any pocket dirt, and chew, while still reading. When I grew weary of Rumi, I put up Plath, whose brisk, elegant screams I never grew tired of, until I did, and then desiring something different yet again I began to hang recipes of things, carefully dismantled from old cookbooks my mother no longer wanted. I would study their notation, their confident sorcery, their useful busyness. They were the opposite of poetry, except if, like me, you seldom cooked, and then they were the same. I would take the pages in when done, in case of rain.

I did go swimming—once, at the Dellacrosse Village municipal pool. In normal attire I rode my Suzuki there on the hottest day of August, and then, stripping down to one of my mother's old one-piece bathing suits, the padded foam bodice of which helped keep me afloat, I swam lengths up and down in the turquoise water until I was exhausted.

I didn't see anyone there I knew, except a girl I'd gone to high school with, Valerie Bochman, who already had a roly pink baby who was dashing, diapered, through the sprinklers of the adjacent wading pool while Valerie watched from a towel. Oddly, the baby was not that cute. He looked pale and fat and empty-eyed. I knew Valerie had gotten married but I'd forgotten to whom and didn't know what her last name was now. She'd buried her old name and acquired a new one, like a witness in a federal protection program. How would we girls find each other again when we got to be middle-aged and came back and tried to look one another up in the phone book? We would all be missing. *There* was a protection program for you. Before I headed back to the pine-slatted changing room to shower off the chlorine and stare bleakly at the lime-scaled showerhead, which with its raisiny rubber nozzles had the look of a blueberry Stilton, I gave a weak wave across the pool at Valerie. But she didn't wave back. She just looked at me vaguely, smiling in a noncommittal way that showed no recognition whatsoever. So I left. Perhaps she would suddenly remember me on her way home.

Every night I lay in my bed, staying up past ten, reading. The light from my lamp attracted insects through the holes in one of the screens, and by eleven I would look up at the ceiling and it would be crawling with bugs, small, medium, and large, light and dark, all collecting up there in ominous flocks as if awaiting Tippi Hedren. Once, a leggy winged albino thing landed on my book, and its oddness fascinated me, though I soon slammed it between the pages. Once I awoke in the middle of the night and could see that through the crack between my door and the badly settled frame there was a long sliver of light from the hallway, and fireflies could enter the room; they sparkled in and out like fairies, as if the door were nothing at all, as if there were no separating this room from any other space. They were like visions, really, but ones I'd not had as a child, when I'd slept through the night with a depth and stillness that was no longer possible.

Whenever I put my bird costume on I felt once again like Icarus—·
take that, Professor Keyser-Lowe of Classics 251!—though I realized this wasn't, mythically speaking, either lucky or apt. But it
was becoming the most fun I'd had all year. Sometimes in the
evening, the summer moon a tangerine shard—an orange peel
stuck up there like the lunch garbage of God!—I'd get all set to go
out and my father would say, "Oh, I'm sorry, not tonight, we're
not harvesting tonight," and I would say, "Oh, OK," but then I'd
just go out anyway. Perhaps I was becoming addicted to being a
hawk or a falcon or whatever it was I was. Perhaps I just needed
the evening run. Often Blot would come with me, trotting along
behind. Lucy would look longingly from her rope. The thrushes
whistled their flutey country song: *Run to your home hear me /
why don't you come to me?* They sounded insincere and happy.

Waning light rouged and bronzed the clouds so they looked
like a mountain range. As the dusk washed over, I galloped up
and down the rows of three-season spring mix, and my dreams of
flying would return. As ever, in my flying dreams, I never got very
far off the ground, and now here if I took a leap I felt my wings
supporting me, kitelike, just a split second above the field. I
would hover, buoyed, my wings finding a little air, and so when I
landed I would instantly leap up again, the ball of one foot pushing off—that split-second feeling of almost being able to set sail
was enough of a thrill. Actual sustained flight would have been
beside the point, and too scary to boot. This was my modest
dream come true: unambitious flight. The kind that never even
got high enough for a view.

Alone at dusk I was quiet; I sang nothing. At the field's edges
and near the barn and the root cellar, light still held in the yellow
razzmatazz of the goldenrod. With the first full drop of the sun
the swallows swooped out from their mud nests to feed. Then the

barn bats followed—the small ones darting, then the larger ones, like cougars with wings, crawling their way through the air, ignoring the mosquitoes, heading for the fireflies. I sometimes studied their flight, which would never be mine, and neither did I really want it to be, but nonetheless, the balletic motions, both searching and swift, were things to be admired.

I was perfecting my soar and leap every evening as the sky deepened into night. All the daytime machinery of the nearby construction lay still, and the sawing scherzo legs of crickets began their summer repetitions—like the feisty strings in a piece by Philip Glass. The cicadas throbbed and shook with the rattle of tambourines, the peepers trilled—they all came together in a choral way. Sometimes there was the braying of a lone and distant goose. I would head toward the far woodlot, toward a spot where there was bluegrass with an overlay of rye, something that would have made a perfect soccer field. I would run toward that grass and back, feeling the slight takeoff of my wings, a sudden if momentary weightlessness. The reddening sumacs on the other side of the woodlot were fruiting early this year, and I would sometimes run in their direction as well. If Blot barked too excitedly or nipped at my heels or jumped at my wings, I ran him back to the house and would then return to the fields on my own, keeping to the narrow dirt rows between the baby greens and the kale. I ran and banked the turns and ran again, feeling myself float just lightly above the earth.

And then one evening, the air velvety and vibrating with tree frogs, the occasional bass of a courting bull in the pond thickening the song, the sturdy sky an infinitude of summer stars—what wishing! if one wanted to wish; what guiding of ships! if one were steering one!—there they both were: Reynaldo and Robert. I stopped, my skin hot from running. They were standing side by side at the end of the field, Robert with his yoga mat, Reynaldo with his prayer mat. Each had a cell phone and a volume of poems by Rumi. Their stillness, the fact that as apparitions they seemed to recede and keep the same distance from me always no matter how I tried to close it, and that they didn't say a word before they turned and walked away, melting into the dark, though the sky remained mapped and spangled with constellations, was an omen. Plus they came again the next night in the exact same way, neither vaporous nor cadaverous, but wordless and turning and walking away, this time with a little bruised-up boy who I realized instantly in the way of visions was Gabriel Thornwood-Brink: this made me understand that they were unfindably dead, all of them, and that now the really useful things of life, like stars, would become incomprehensible decoration.

I was not there when the two military officers drove up in their military van to my parents' door to announce my brother's death, though years later I met someone who had done that kind of work for a living. "It's very hard and very weird," he said. "It was the strangest job I ever had. Although completely draped in duty, it was an exercise of total cluelessness, which, for someone who has spent any time in the military, is saying a lot."

It was unclear how and why Robert's death had occurred so suddenly, so soon, so instantaneously—eight weeks of boot camp had been hurried along and they had been shipped quickly overseas, as the all-volunteer army was at the beginning of its being spread too thin. They had only just landed someplace near Helmand Province; they had been there for less than three weeks; there was a BBIED but no QRD, which were all in TK or J-bad along with all the MREs; they were equipped with AKs but even a routine land-mine sweep can go awry. The letter said something different than the person on the phone. In appreciation of our loss a check for twelve thousand dollars came right away, express mail, with *Keltjin* spelled wrong.

The wailing of my mother is not to be recounted. A summer of having taken to her bed had not strengthened her for his death at all but seemed instead to have cut a groove for the mourning of it. One night she came downstairs simply to shout at my father. "We never should have named him after you! Jews understand that. It's bad luck! Why did you want that so much?"

"I thought you meant it was bad luck for me!" my father shouted back. "And I didn't mind that. I didn't care about some old world hocus-pocus."

"Well, look at that old world hocus-pocus now!" she cried, then rushed back upstairs. My father hadn't been there when the officers had come, and he, too, had gone into a state of stunned silence, though he did say heatedly, "I'm going to make some phone calls." Though I'm not sure he ever made enough to satisfy himself. A demining expedition. An ambushed foot patrol. How about a whack on the head with a backhoe? Fractured by a fork-lift? The boys stayed too long in the nighttime mountains even as the monkeys screeched their warnings. According to the PL or the CO. A BBIED. There was apparently a brand-new way to die: by cell phone. And there was supposed to have been a quick-recovery deployment by an OEF convoy. But the DU didn't have the ECDs up and running. No one actually proposed the possibility of Robert's own fright and ineptitude or of "friendly fire," but the jumble of alternative explanations raised suspicions. My father, the NOK, was spoken to incessantly in acronyms and gruesome euphemism. "KIA by Talib RPGs," they said.

"Well, I want a real explanation—ASAP!" my father cried in a voice of heat and ice. "What you mean is that his leg is in a tree somewhere?" Another officer had come to sit in our living room to explain things further.

"Actually," said this uniformed man, "his leg was obliterated. His hand was in a tree. It was very high up. We had to leave it."

———

My father did not lie in bed in the mornings the way my mother did, but busied himself in the fields without me. "You should rest," I said to him.

But he said, "I can't lie there and just think. It's too scary to lie there and just think." Sometimes he spent the days just chopping wood.

My mother covered all the mirrors in the house with pillow-cases and scarves. The mirrors in the flowerbeds she covered with sheets.

Robert's body was flown home to Chicago and from there two men drove it the five hours north to the funeral home in a Hummer, as if here in Dellacrosse even the dead might need the protection of such a vehicle, though the body did require a refrigeration unit and so perhaps this was why. The driver, on greeting my father, gave him my brother's dog tags, which my father took like they were a fistful of change, in one hand, not looking.

The funeral, at a former Lutheran church Robert himself had never been to—one that was now Unitarian, for people who felt that God should be elected democratically and after a long campaign—seemed dominated by his friends. Chuck Buzlocki. Ken Kornblach. Cooper Dunka. They stood up, gearhead after gearhead, and you had to hand it to them: they had one boring story after another about Gunny, which moved them all to both laughter and tears. We his family sat startled and mute as if we did not know any of them, including the person they were talking about. Yet hadn't we just seen all these boys at graduation? Listening to them, I realized why Robert's grades had been so bad.

The minister made only the vaguest mention of God, in terms that made God seem a design and a force but a little indifferent to our fates and therefore unworshippable. Like a railway system. It could get you where you were going, wherever that was. A transit authority! But it wouldn't counter your own devotion with love. Here and there in the church sanctuary there seemed to be a prayer, but each sat in my ears nonsensically.

> Our father who art a heathen
> Hollow be thigh name.
> Thigh king is dumb
> Thigh will is dun
> on earth as it is
> at birth.

I had nothing against prayer. Those who felt it was wishful muttering perhaps had less to wish for. Religion, I could now see, without a single college course helping me out, was designed for those enduring the death of their sweet children. And when children grew stronger and died less, and were in fact less sweet, religion faded away. When children began to sweeten and die again, it returned.

But sitting there, I began to realize that part of me didn't believe Robert was dead. Part of me thought perhaps the whole thing was a prank. Like everyone, Robert would have loved to have attended his own funeral. Of course, one did always attend one's own funeral. But usually one was so deep in the role of the dead person that one didn't get to pay attention to the nice things people were standing up and saying about you.

The minister continued calling for others to come forth, to step up and speak, and a few more did: one teary girl and a geometry teacher. "I loved Gunny," they both said. The girl read a poem called "Gunny Finally Got His Gun," which was unbearable.

At the end my father stood up and shambled to the front. He clutched the lectern and looked out at all the gathered and just stared. It was not an especially uncomfortable silence as the whole occasion was so uncomfortable that his silent staring didn't really add anything additional. Yet he did bear a look that to me seemed to say, *How have your own repellent and ridiculous sons remained alive when mine has not?*

He began with a story. "When Robert was little he liked secretly to swing on the ropes in the haymow. Both my kids seemed always to love the feeling of flying, and so sometimes I looked the other way. Perhaps this was bad of me. Knowing when to look the other way and when to jump in has never been my strong suit. Once when he was about six he fell from the rope, down off the mow, and hit his chin against a rusty old bucket. He came to me holding the metal pail and said, 'Daddy, don't yell: I know I'll need stitches and a shot, but it was awesome.' "

This story had nothing more to it, and my dad just stood there, as if searching for another one that might be more engaging to the crowd, something more revealing and entertaining, as even at funerals people shamelessly hoped just for a moment here and there to be amused. But I could see that this one story summed up everything for him. I stayed seated with my mother, who was not doing well. She was wearing the black hat with the feather sticking straight up. She drew the dangling sash of it across her quivering lips. I was wearing my hair pulled back in a black barrette fashioned in the shape of a crow. "What can a man say about losing his boy?" my father cried out, finally. He had raised his voice as if he were calling. "His only son? Well! I miss him more than any words can remotely convey. He was not just a good son, a good person. He was the very best kind." That was all he said before his face clenched and purpled and he had to turn and come back down. My mother had given him a handkerchief, which he did not use to dab at his eyes but instead pressed completely over his face, like a barber's hot towel. When my father walked back toward us from the pulpit, he took my mother's hand and led her outside, leaving me behind. Organ music started up and everyone began to leave, to go out into that September sunshine to comfort my parents. I simply sat there. Soon the organist, too, got up and left, giving me a smiling nod as she did.

Alone in the church, I did not move for a long time. Then I craned my head around and couldn't see anyone at all, and so I slid out of the pew and went up to the coffin, which was on a gurney draped with a heavy velvet blanket. On top of it was the cognac-colored casket, a large varnished thing, a shiny parlor piano with a flag draped over. I petted the lid of it. A yellow jacket, the kind you see trolling the trash cans at picnic spots, was walking on the edge. I took off my shoe and smacked it. Then in wiping it off with the folded program that had Robert's photo on the front and the list of biblical readings inside and on the back the stunningly absurd numbers 1984–2002—what could they truly mean, especially with a bee's guts now yellowing the second two?—it occurred to me that the coffin might be unlocked. I jabbed my fingers into the corner crack. One could open it—so I did. When I lifted the lid, the flag slid to the floor. It was not one of those fitted flag casket coverings they later made plenty of.

Within, as if placed in a quilted quitar case, lay a smashed guitar: a uniform of green, part pine, part portabella, part parsley, with parts of a man inside. I put my shoe back on and my program in my purse. "Hey there, Robert," I said, but was afraid I might cry. I knew there were superstitions about touching dead people. But one belief had it that if you touched one you would never be lonely again. I climbed atop the gurney, up into the coffin, and fitted myself inside to nestle next to him. I was thin from all my weeks as a hawk in the salad fields, and I curled in against him, even with my purse, panting shallowly, as I hardly dared to breathe, dreading some stench or other. But one had to breathe. His smell at first seemed a chemical one, like the field fertilizer used by the agribiz farms. Field fertilizer! You could not make up stuff like that! Though the interior of the casket was quilted white, like a beautiful suitcase, what I could see of my brother looked like garbage tossed inside. He had no legs, it seemed, so there was room for mine. Beneath his uniform he was wearing a hooded sweatshirt put on backwards so that the hood could be pulled up over his face. I carefully pulled it down to see. Beneath the hood someone had stretched a clear plastic shower cap over his features. Beneath the shower cap, which I didn't dare touch, I could see his nose and jaw were gone but there was still his full lower lip I knew so well, now lavender, and blistered, and the upper one, with its smattering of gingery freckles beneath the whisker stubble that still seemed fresh and black as pepper. His skin, what little I could see, had the jaundiced look of bad weather that had come and not left. His stammerless stillness seemed the loneliest and most dumbfounding thing.

"Robert," I whispered. "It's me." We would be kids again, lying in the woods somewhere, except the smell was starting to seem horrible, and I was curled against him in such a way that I realized he'd been stuffed with things, styrofoam or something, as so many parts of him were missing. One sleeve was filled with stuffed newsprint, a paper sausage, which crunched when I lay my head on it. The hand protruding from the uniform cuff was a mannequin's hand, knuckleless as a fish. I could see that death had settled him, flattened him, the way that a salad—of, say, three-season spring greens—flattened and settled after initially being fresh and buoyant and high in the bowl. How he had once been fresh and buoyant and high in the bowl!

In case I started to cry, I pulled the lid down back over us, a sateen ceiling, and it became very dark inside, although the hinge side of the lid, I could see, was not flush with the rest and there was a line of daylight there I could make disappear by closing my eyes. The space grew hot and cramped.

I could hear Robert's friends come back into the church. Suddenly they became pallbearers again. "Hey, the flag slipped off," said one, and they put it back on. "Bad luck," said another. "Shut the fuck up," said a third, and soon we were being trundled out of the church to the hearse. I listened for my father's voice but didn't hear it. We were lifted up and slid into the vehicle and then I did hear my father's voice. "Where's Tassie?" and then my mother's: "I don't know. I think maybe she went on ahead to the cemetery with some friends."

I would lie in there with my brother forever. I would rescue him from this heap of trash that was oblivion, perhaps our old mending mortar of gum and glue and sesame seeds would help; a good drink of water; a snack of cheese. We could send out for pizza and Coke. The hearse started and we rode off to the edge of town near the Dellacrosse Village Cemetery. A name that seemed to suggest that all who were buried there lived in a kind of village. Well, we would have a kind of brute picnic of things when we got there, perhaps; we'd snap the bones of the drummer's drumsticks and see whose wish came true. I petted Robert and the crumbledness of him and the terrible smell—like moldering shit in a plastic pencil case—made me no longer feel I was close to him. I'd been closer to him in the lettuce field that night. This was not actually, truly, him in this fetid spot.

My nose began to bleed. I had thought I was crying but then I could taste the metal of it. I had little experience with nosebleeds, and my mouth filled with coagulated clots like small chunks of liver. I wiped my nose and could feel the clots amid the mucus and blood. Still I lay next to his remains—there was no more apt word for the cobbled-together form I was curled against—I would lie there and preserve him somehow with memories. I would reassemble him with chat. I would say *Good morning* in the morning. I would say *Good night* at night. Not to do so ever again was just unthinkable. I would lie there and tell him the story of every movie I'd ever seen. I would not be no guy's sister. I would lie in there until—until I began to weigh my options.

When we arrived at the parking lot and the funeral men set up the gurney and the pallbearers again came to carry the body out of the hearse, I decided to make my presence known. It was getting out not exactly when the getting was good but at least before the smallest crowd. As Robert's friends lifted the casket onto the gurney I pushed up on the lid, poked my head out, and made my presence known. I clambered out the rest of the way. The light of the world hurt my eyes.

"What the hey?" one of Robert's friends exclaimed.

"It's Gunny's sister," said another.

"What were you doing in there?"

And then my mother came running over, tears raining down her face, and she just brushed me off and held me and motioned to the boys to close the casket lid.

In the cemetery there were rifles fired in the air in salute. More guns for Gunny. I recall that. There was a concrete park of angelic gargoyles or beastly cherubs—who could tell one from the other? There were white crosses and covered pots of geraniums and perfectly coned yews. There was a drummer, as I had expected, though no one broke his sticks and made a wish. There was "Taps," mournful and familiar:

> *Day is done,*
> *Gone the son.*
> *It will stun,*
> *No more fun,*
> *Have a bun.*

And then the bridge off which the bugler hurled his lungs:

> *Night is nigh.*
> *Say good-bye.*
> *People die.*

There was a large flag folded neatly, amazingly into a triangle, then given to my mother, who neither held it to her heart nor thanked the skilled folder. She hurriedly crammed the thing into her handbag. And then the driving home. There were casseroles people had brought with tinfoil over the top, and the kitchen table was piled high with them. It looked like someone had died. And since someone had, this look at least did not contribute to any lies. I went upstairs to my pink room and basically stayed there for a month.

My parents arranged for a medical leave from school for me and I was told I should rest until I felt better. Our house had become a kind of *krankes Haus*. The local newspapers were brought to my room and I tried to read them. In our county, I learned, all the loons were stuck: I would just be one of them. But in fact it was widely reported that all the county's loons were flightless, had caught a kind of botulism—from the fish they ate that had drunk bad water. Was this tainted water from clinic runoff or the natural occurrence of toxins in a lily pad? Who knew? There were some arguments on each side. But the birds' wings had frozen in place, so the birds not only couldn't fly but drowned right there in the water. Other articles told of ducks, deranged by mercury, who were reputedly wandering off from their nests and then making new ones, forgetting to go back to the first. I lay in bed, sick and not eating, storky beneath the sheets, my thoughts landing arbitrarily on this or that, like light moving past a window. The fulfillingness of my life's every day had not just faltered but completely stopped.

The weather cooled; Japanese ladybugs, brought years before as pest control for the soy, had taken over the farmhouses, ours included. They formed shiny orange coverings on our windows and doors, and if you brushed at one it bit you. At night the ones that had made their way inside spent their time whacking themselves against the lampshades.

Songbirds, drunk on fermented mulberries, and leaving purple fecal puddles on branches and railings, once again got themselves confused and failed to get going south, lingering instead in the bare trees.

On Hoopen Road three cows were electrocuted in a storm.

Life was unendurable, and yet everywhere it was endured. I was reliving my old homework from Mythology for Freshmen. The work of grief, where only unsteady progress could be made, seemed at first Herculean. Then Sisyphean. Then Persean. Then Echovian. Then one was turned finally and prematurely into a flower or a tree, with a flower's curvature and a tree's yearning reach. Paralyzed. But with shoes. And dinner. And chores. I did *improve,* to use a medical verb, without actually feeling better, and as the autumn weeks went by more and more I left my room and began to help my father with the harvest and sometimes even rode with him, taking the small roads, among the drumlins and moraines to Chicago, delivering potatoes and our three-season spring mix to some restaurants, as well as occasionally setting up at the farmers' markets there. My father wore my brother's dog tags wherever we went. Certain moments the whole earth seemed a grave. Other times, more hopefully, a garden.

We would start off bright and early into the rising sun, the ground billowing up its dew in such heavy, magical vapors that when one was in the troughs of the highway one couldn't see a foot ahead and the fields looked as if they were on smoky fire, preparing for the visitation of ascending or descending gods. Which could it be? Perhaps it was true what people used to say about our county: outer space was interested. But then the air would clear and the day would be awash in light. I studied the third-cutting hay rolled into tight coils on the fields and placed at perfect distances from one another, as if by an art department.

One had to get on with life, out of good manners if nothing else. My dad and I would strike up random conversation. "Seahorses give birth," I would begin. "But they're male. Why do we even call them male, if they give birth?"

And my dad would be silent, driving, considering. Then he would speak. "Because they insist on it. They don't want what happened to ladybugs to happen to them. These ladybugs have masculinity issues to beat the band!"

I tried to laugh. I appreciated his trying to acknowledge me, be with me, though it had become difficult for him. Ahead of us ballooning clouds floated there absurdly, as if for a party that had yet to begin. Groups of geese crawled through the sky, their metallic honks declaring their departure south.

We would stop somewhere to eat and do just and only that: stop and eat. We got BLTs and soup and then would continue on our way. The brilliant gold leaves and grasses, the drying roadside timothy and bluestem, all looked on a nice day like a hymn to sunlight, when in fact, if one actually thought seriously about the situation, the mechanism of their dialogue with the sun had been shed entirely. The honey locusts had gone first, raining shimmering trails of seedlings into the gutters of the streets in town. Then the yam- and ham-hued maples. A papery caramel of leaves or a trail of maize or both lined every road we were on. How like the end of love to leave a beautiful corpse. When they weren't gold against blue, like something royal, the oaks bore the flat blackish red of a blood orange, and my father and I would drive along staring out at them through the windshield, each of us thinking our own thoughts. One evening migrating songbirds, oriented toward the moon, mistook a red-lit cell phone tower for their destination and we watched as they all shredded themselves in the tower's steel supports. More disastrous love performed in symbols. As we passed, my father slowed down, then sped up again. Silence was not the worst thing, though it still contained sorrow and making-do. Here and there a rabbit scurried across our path.

"Are rabbits nocturnal?" I asked.

"Yep."

"Well, why do you see them in the day as well?"

My father was quiet for a long time. "They work in shifts," he said finally.

Fattening in the butt, shy, petty, carsick except in a truck, perhaps I was more suited to country life than I'd ever understood. When we got back at night, my father would slam the truck door and look at the vast and watchful sky. "That's a hell of a heaven up there," he would say. Inside he would sit before the nightly news, which had just begun a semimonthly honor roll of American servicemen, fresh-faced privates, killed in the Middle East. Their photographs were shown, a few at a time, in silence, with their names and ranks and hometowns printed beneath. They were the faces of babies, babies in hats, and on the rare occasion that there was someone older, an officer, my father would shout: "Aha! All right! They got a lieutenant colonel!" A light bird. Once a full bird—a colonel—elicited my dad's bitter whoop. Each soldier's face stared out from the glass TV screen like a sweet, accusing child in the good-bye window of a terrible, terrible nursery school. My dad began to smoke my mother's cigarettes, Camel Lights, which had never affected her health very much, but which left him hoarse and hacking, at least at night; the brandy piled up near his chair, first in shot glasses, then whiskey glasses, then coffee mugs. The night we saw my brother's picture in the honor roll we all just happened to be there together, both my parents and I, and we were stunned into motionlessness. Robert's, too, was the face of a baby with a hat jammed on. The hat was absurd, conferring nothing but a dark decoration as if to anchor the composition of the photo. His eyes were caught in the headlights of something—foreign policy? a bored remark of the cameraman? the portentous burst of the flash?—and he was not smiling. "Robert looks tired in that photo," my mother said finally.

"He does," agreed my father, who then turned off the television and left the room.

The clocks were set back and the sun began to set at four. I opened up my laptop and began e-mailing Murph. She was taking the year off, working with schoolchildren in Baton Rouge. I told her about my brother, and she sent back a horrified and sympathetic e-mail along with a song she'd written for me. It was kind and stupid and full of *death* rhyming with *breath, brother* with *another, war* with *core, cry* with *why.*

In my archives I stumbled upon the final e-mail that Robert had sent me what seemed so long ago—just last spring—and I froze when I saw it. How had I not read this? Why had I just shoved it away as if it were nothing? What was wrong with me? I was no guy's sister. My eyes stung and shrank, but I opened it to see, in a blur, finally what it said.

Dear Sis,

I don't know if you realize how I'm always watching you up ahead there in life, and how it has seemed to me you always know what you're doing, and how I admire that. Probably it all seems different to you, and maybe this is just a kid brother speaking, but to me you have always seemed smart and independent and sure of yourself, figuring out everything. Or it looks like that. To me. Maybe it's a girl thing, though let's face it: you are very different from Mom. Perhaps I am more like her, because, I have to admit, I'm a little lost here and that is why I am writing to you. Right now I feel only your words could keep me from doing what I feel I may end up doing—and if it is not a good idea but mere desperation and confusion, then regret is on the way. And yet I think it is the right thing despite what some might say. What most people say bounces off of me. But you saying "DO" or "DON'T" might sink in. Nobody else's remarks seem to register. Should I join the military? Will the army be a good experience? If they ship me right away to Afghanistan, will I regret it? or will I be glad to eventually have the extra tuition assistance to help Dad out in sending me to college, or even DDD! (Just kidding.) Remember what Mr. Holden always said in Science: Only in physics does gravity plus inertia equal orbit. Sometimes I know guys meet other guys in the army and when they get out they set up businesses together. What have you heard? Please get back to me with all your wisdom and advice ASAP! Talk me out of this, if you can!

Love, your dearest and of course favorite brother,
Robert "Gunny" Keltjin

P.S.: Without my little string collection I'd probably go crazy.
P.P.S.: That's a joke.

Once again I was struck by his written voice, which contained none of the haltingness or hesitant construction of his speech. When I looked up from my screen and turned to look out the window, I could see the autumn migration of the turkey vultures, with their uncanny ability to smell death and come clean it up for you, though this year they were a little late. A hundred of them glided in the sky without flapping, their feather-tips like fingers conducting the turns with hardly a motion.

I wanted to go back in time. Just to send an e-mail—was that too much to ask? When Superman went back in time, when he flew backwards around the world at top speed, though he looked very tired, it still seemed as if he might manage a passenger, like those dolphins who give rides to kids. I wanted Superman to take me whooshing with him backwards around the globe. Just to send an e-mail. That was all. Not so much. But what would I say? What grammar, what syntax would hold together sentences in this whizzing flight back? *Both my kids seemed always to love the feeling of flying.* What punctuation as strong as aeronautic stitchery would I know to bring with me? The apostrophe in *don't* held together by our bubble gum and seeds? It would do. For a moment or two.

After letting it float like a dying dentist-office fish on my computer screen, I locked Robert's e-mail back up in the archives and never looked at it again. The laws of metaphysics were sometimes sterner than the laws of physics: You can never go backwards. Though the scientists tell you that you can. No information can escape from a black hole. Though the scientists insist some does.

The scientists and the comic books were in cahoots!

Meanwhile, everyone else knew that things were simple and straight ahead: a life bumped around like a bug in a window, then one day just stopped.

I knew from freshman physics that there was a quantum mechanics theory that allowed for something being dead and alive at the same time: if a particle could also be a wave, if it could morph and part company with itself, then an entire being composed of those particles could also go wavy and be in two places at once, heaven and hell, bar and ballpark, life and death. Parallel universes existed for all options. In theory. And observation of one universe was the only thing that deprived the other of its reality.

Only a few other times did Robert make appearances. The first time I awoke in the middle of the night to find him pacing around my room in the dark. He was speaking. He said, "I keep waiting for it to hurt, but it doesn't hurt yet. Maybe it will hurt later." And then he added, "Apparently it's an insult to the residents of the afterlife to ask where you are, to imply you're not sure which place you ended up in. You're supposed to know! You're supposed to know just by looking! Without inquiring! But damn! It's hard to tell!" Another time I found myself unable to sleep and when I sat up to get some water I saw that he was standing by my dresser, holding a sign that read YES I AM A MAN. Another time I awoke to find him sitting wordlessly at the foot of the bed. He looked the same as when he was alive except he was wearing a shower cap, a different one, perched back on his head, and he was holding the fake mannequin hand, turning it over and over as if it were an interesting stone he'd just found. He held it up to his eye and looked skyward with it as if it were a telescope. "Robert, what do you want?" I asked him, but he said nothing, perhaps because it had always been so—he had never known what he wanted, and now not even in death. I blinked my eyes closed and opened them again and he was still there. "Robert, what are you doing here?" There was more silence. I forced my eyes shut again and when I opened them, I said, "You mustn't feel sorry for yourself!" He was still peering around the room with the mannequin hand. At that I closed my eyes for several minutes solid and when I opened them again, he was starkly, everlastingly gone.

I guessed that only at the last possible minute did the soul in a determined fashion flee the dying flesh. Who could blame it for its reluctance? We loved our lives more than we ever knew, and at the end felt the bounty of them, as one would say in church, felt even the richness of their missed opportunities, or just understood that they were more than we had realized during the living of them and a lot to give up. Sometimes I imagined that just before oblivion, as one lay dying, one got to have a brief fare-well meeting with friends: one last dream drink in a cozy spot of the mind. Even sputtering hardware, before its final burn-ing out, gave back its pleasures as best it could. There was a song! And wasn't this a compelling trade, sensation for spirit and vice versa? This exchange was lifelong and perhaps heightened at death: the thirsty draped about the bubbler for a drop. These were the sorts of notions that had been raised in all my classes, and we had chased them round and round like dogs maddened by their tails.

When I went into Robert's old bedroom with my mother, to help her put his clothes in boxes for Goodwill, I lifted his winter coat off its hanger and a bat flew out the cuff and out of the room to nowhere we could find. That was the last life any of his clothes ever had, at our house at any rate.

The holidays of fall had all merged like a suburban megalopolis. Halloween had bled into Thanksgiving, which had already become pre-Christmas, just as Kenosha had become Racine had become Milwaukee. Pumpkins had wreaths! Hunting season began on Veterans Day, and men who had never once been in the military dressed themselves in the bright color of circus lollipops and prowled the fallow farms for deer. Sex workers, whose high season was the hunting one, temporarily set up shop in a rented store-front on County H called Dance, Drink, and Din-Din, right smack next to Home Dollar. My birthday came, and because I was at last of drinking age, my father bought champagne and he and my mother proposed a toast. "To our sweet and lovely Tassie," said my dad. "Twenty-one! Time flies so fast, I have to lie down just thinking about it."

I'd read once of a French geologist who had confined himself in a dark cave for sixty-one days, though when he emerged, he thought it had been only forty-five. Time flew! No matter what.

"At least we got one of you out of childhood," added my mother.

"Gail," my father warned her.

"Sorry," she said. Her face had become round and bloated. Mourning had widened instead of thinned her. Perhaps it was the calming pharmaceuticals she'd recently been prescribed. She now, behind her large glasses, had the double-triple face of the middle-aged, her most forward face, the one she used to have, framed again in yet another oval of flesh, a cameo of meat. In fact, fat had settled in around the entirety of her. Instead of going on a diet, she said, she would stick a wick in her belly and burn it off for Hanukkah.

I googled the other Tassie Keltjin again, to see if something was being done to honor her increasingly distant memory, and if not, to see if people were even a little bit sorry that she had died. Perhaps they would be. Perhaps they should be. "If the universe is big enough, everything that can happen will happen, so that if we could look out far enough we would eventually discover an exact replica of ourselves." This I had read in the paper. In the *Science Times.* It was like a cosmic version of the infinite number of monkeys who given an infinite amount of time ultimately write *King Lear.* Which in evolutionary terms was a scientific fact. When you thought about it.

The other Tassie Keltjin was still dead and it was no big deal to anyone. No one was doing squat.

After Thanksgiving, I went back to Troy. My father had begun experimenting with winter spinach grown in a propane-heated hoop hut. This kind of spinach—thick, tender, grown slowly— was in demand in Evanston and Chicago, where he hoped to sell it in time for Christmas. He smiled and said he hardly needed me, that I should get back to school before I turned into a damn fool.

There were days I felt hard, bittersweet, strong. People died, but then if you forgot they had died, even for a minute, they could achieve a kind of immortality; that is, they kept on living, even though they were dead. My Suzuki back in storage, I walked everywhere. The gothic spires of campus seemed defiant thrusts at God, or poles for the stripping saints. Haughty Fatigue! The zoology quad, which we cerebrally called "the hippocampus," was now being ripped up for some sort of construction and there were cranes and backhoes and concrete barriers to walk around. At the kiosks near the union I stopped regularly to read the film society posters.

I found an apartment, one with a girl named Amanda Prague, who'd grown up in Pardeeville, Wazeeka, and Mukwanago, and she was, she announced, as if needing to get this out of the way, a quarter African-American, a quarter Oneida, a quarter Czech, a quarter Irish.

"That's a lot of quarters," I said.

"Sure is," she said, nodding and shrugging. She needed a roommate, since the one she'd started with in September had gone home midsemester with mono. "You seem quiet," she said. "If you want it, it's yours." So I signed on, wrote down her phone number for my own, and moved a few items into her empty room, which had a bed, a dresser, and a lamp. I added a quilt, a pen, and a clipboard: What else did I need? I would wait until later to ease her into the idea of my bass guitar. The storage bin a mile away still held not just the Suzuki but also the xylophone. I would stay mum about these as well, for now, though perhaps by March I'd be riding my scooter once more, like other girls I'd seen: helmetless and serene, with the angelic hypnotized look of the already dead, as traffic veered all around.

———

the window the cheeses Sarah used to display beneath their glass covers were still there but were now curling, blueing, browning: the grana and govarti, the cocoa cardona. No one had put them away. The twelve-year-old cheddar, which on a good day was like sugared gold, was now cracked and snowy with mold. The white pasty goat cheeses had yellowed and greened. The restaurant had been closed up in a rush, and no one, not one person all fall, had cleared out the window. I stared at these decaying cheeses as if they were living things, dying unfed in a zoo, which in a way they were. They were misshapen and yet on display, a person's collapse and sorrow concretized behind glass. Negligence in the restaurant world! I thought I saw in one of the goat cheeses the teeth marks of a rat. No doubt in this town someone had already written a letter to the editor about it.

By mid-December I'd registered for my spring semester classes, had found a part-time job as a barista in Starbucks, and was getting ready to go home for Christmas and then move back here more completely in January. It had not been that hard to find work, as reservists had been called up in preparation for war; shops and restaurants and computer stores were suddenly short-staffed. On the bulletin board inside the Starbucks door I saw a handwritten sign that read BASS PLAYER NEEDED FOR BAND, and I tore off one of the phone number flaps that were cut into the bottom like fringe and stuck it in my pocket.

Meanwhile, I liked the whirring of hot milk into cups, the pumping of syrups, the listening to international music I'd never heard before. I learned to make art—peace signs, ferns, space alien heads resembling Munch's *The Scream*—in the cappuccino foam. It was our job to be friendly, and people were friendly back. My hours were not boring. There were random spells of this and that, cast as if by a merciful clown-god. One morning, a woman

Yet again, another December, and I found myself looking for a job. The low matte sky was like a black-and-white photo of a sky. Which made it seem strange rather than familiar; its strangeness was not made friendlier by its resemblance to a photograph. A vast and depthless sky should not resemble a photograph any more than it should resemble a rug. With the exception of occasional thoughts like this? I was hanging on. I had a new résumé printed up, and in addition to the Schultzes and the Pitskys back home I added the Thornwood-Brinks to my list of references. I did not rule out some dubious employment choices: a want ad that read *Tap into Collective Wisdom, Make $ by Predicting Future Events;* another asking for human subjects for a pharmaceutical company drug trial; or a position as the new "Bad Girl," whom a guy could hire to write love letters to him so he could leave them around the house to make his girlfriend jealous. I also applied for a job that involved pretending to have certain physical symptoms, for labs and clinics involving medical students and doctors in training. "Describe some vague abdominal pain," a man in a white lab coat commanded me.

"It's sharp for a few seconds and then it kind of goes splat and hovers for a little while behind my right rib—before it glides slowly, diffusely south."

The man was silent. "Is there nausea?"

I was surprised by his question. Perhaps I was doing well at this. "No. Well, yes. Sometimes."

"Do you have acting experience?"

"I feel like I do now," I said. But I was not called back.

One day, with a propelling pang, I ambled toward downtown. Along the lake, the slick black scalps of the water signaled a coming storm. I walked past Sarah's old restaurant and saw that although it was closed, no one else had yet taken it over. There was a padlock on the door. The sign reading LE PETIT MOULIN was still in place, though the last three letters of *Petit* had been pried off—no doubt to hang on a dorm room wall somewhere. In in line paid for the coffee of the guy behind her, and then he turned around and paid for the customer behind *him*. And then that guy paid for the woman behind him, and it went on for about forty-five minutes until there was a lull and no one was in line at all. A quiet period of no customers broke the chain—but still: it was a piece of magic while it lasted.

Outside the window of the shop, students had begun the protesting of Bush's military buildup, his plot hatched with neo-con intellectuals who, like aging former members of a high school chess club, wanted a tournament they could win. They would sweep up pawns and swoop in with rooks. DON'T BOMB IRAQ read the student placards. "War is not the answer," the protesters chanted, and "Not in our name," whatever that one meant. On my breaks I went out and marched with them, decrying the juiced intelligence, or were we hailing the *juste* intelligence? My hearing may have dimmed from the espresso grinders and the hiss and gurgle of the steamer wands, and I wasn't a hundred percent sure on the chants. Whichever. I was on the side of dissent and despair. On their breaks people came in and ordered holiday lattes. Anxiety, cold, and political disbelief we offset with ginger-bread and common cause. Or so we imagined. I gave people free dirty chais and red-eyes, so-named for their extra shots of espresso. Or black-eyes—coffees with two shots, a drink we privately called a "dickwheeler," not only because we imagined this is what such a drink could do, but because someone named Richard Wheeler had come in once and charged three of them on his credit card.

Where would all of Bush's soldiers come from? We wondered about this aloud. "Deployed means to have all your ploys removed," we said. The former Starbucks manager, herself a National Guard weekend warrior, had already been taken. "I hear they're looking at the middle schools," joked one man bleakly. "Hey—eighth-graders are spry, and they like to win!" Afghanistan was already thought of as the good war, and I was told even by some who were marching for peace, when they learned, that my dead brother was a hero.

"Really?" I asked.

"Well," I was warned, while people threw back their caffeine and put on their gloves, "no hero can bear up under too many *really*s."

One evening the phone rang and Amanda said, "It's for you." Almost tenderly she handed me the receiver.

I pulled the phone with its long cord into my bedroom and closed the door only partway, so as not to seem to have secrets that might disturb. "Hello?"

"Hey, Tassie Keltjin, it's Ed Thornwood!"

"Oh!" I was too startled even to say hi.

"I know this probably comes as a surprise to you. A little blast from the past."

"Yes," I said.

"But the not-too-distant past."

"No, not too." Blasts from the past were like the rooms one entered and re-entered in dreams: they would not stay nailed down. When you returned to them, they had changed—they suddenly had more space or a tilt or a door that had not been there before. New people were milling around, the floors undulated, and the sun shone newly, strangely in the windows, or through the now blasted-open ceiling, or else it shone not at all, as if having fled the sky.

"How are you?" he asked.

I would never really again know the answer to that question. I believed my life would never again be set up to know. "OK, I guess."

"Well, good. I'm OK myself, I guess." I hadn't asked. I hadn't

known to or how to. There was a long pause. "This is not the reason I'm calling, but I do think you should know that Sarah and
I have split up."

A little later in life, when this time seemed distant and
shrunken, and every friendship from it had dwindled, I would
encounter many women with lives sadder than Sarah's. Still,
without much concentration, I could always get her weird story
back—though it was stored dreamlike on my brain's highest
shelf—and I could make it seem the saddest of them all. It was
like *Madama Butterfly*, except Sarah was also Pinkerton and Kate.
The difference between opera and life, I'd noticed, was that in life
one person played all the parts. Still, it wasn't, strictly speaking,
Sarah's story. In the end I felt it belonged as much or more
to Mary-Emma, whom, I realized, I had never stopped uncon-
sciously to seek, riveted by little girls who would be her age in
stores and malls and parks. I would do a double-take every time I
saw some dark, lively girl of three or four or five or six—the years
piled on. I would get close and look close, which is what I realized
Sarah somewhere must surely be doing. And Bonnie. If she was
alive. And even Lynette McKowen. Emmie! A little girl with four
women wondering after her, looking for her, sort of, without her
even knowing. That was love of the most useless kind, unless you
believed in love's power to waft in from a burning sky to the
unseen grass it had designated as its beloved, unless you believed
in the prayers of faraway nuns, unless you believed in miracles
and magic, rapture and dice and Sufic chants and charms behind
curtains and skillful clouds at smoky, unfathomable distances.
Love and virtue—their self-conviction was an astonishing thing:
a pantomime of wishes, a sham dream that made actual, detectable,
dreamable dreams as real as rock. When I imagined all of these
women with their hearts seeking and beaming their futile, worth-
less love through the air toward Mary-Emma, I pictured them all
in a line, part search party, part refugee camp, and in my mind I

set them on a path that went over hill and over dale and even on into meadows and trees. Of course I was with them. And because I was, and because it was all in my head anyway, to the parade I added Helen the pig, just to be picturesque. Plus Lucy, our nanny goat, as there should be some real kind of nanny. And just because I wanted to, I added Robert. To be with him a little, since I missed him and in my mind I could do as I pleased.

"I'm terribly sorry," I said. Sarah had once made me a mixed CD, full of songs she'd listened to when she was young, with lyrics about the wonder of the slowly perfecting world. *A new day is dawning. My friends, we are changing. Ain't it powerful . . . sunrise of a nation.* The words seemed to have come from the medieval period of another planet.

Love is the answer, said the songs, and that's OK. It was OK, I supposed, as an answer. But no more than that. It was not a solution; it wasn't really even an answer, just a reply.

"An inevitable thing, I guess," said Edward. I could not think of him as Ed. "And really probably all for the best. She has gone back east—to New York this time."

Somehow I found this move of hers difficult to believe. I remember Sarah once saying, "To live in New York you have to have won the lottery *and* your parents have to have won the lottery *and* everyone has to have invested wisely." She would also look at me very enigmatically and say, "In New York all the white babies have brown nannies. We've done the reverse. Give me five."

"New York City?" Where did I think she was going to go—Prairie du Chien? (A town only I was obsessed with as a bleak fate, since it meant not even "prairie dog" but "dog prairie.") And then suddenly it seemed to me that New York was where half-Jewish people had to go and where I would go too someday. Even though, as Sarah once said, on every corner they sold pretzels dotted with the kind of salt used here to de-ice driveways.

"Yeah, well, don't get me started," he said.

I knew that divorce was at a rate among everyone that it used to be only among movie stars. In marriage everyone had become a movie star. You wanted reality TV? There it was. What would be so wrong with arranged marriages? There the coldness was put in the parents' hearts right up front rather than grown later, so unpleasantly, in the hearts of the lovers.

"Listen, I got your number from the people at Starbucks who called here asking for a referral. I'll have you know I sang your praises. To the skies. And so I thought I'd give you a call. Since I found myself thinking about you."

Could no kind of sorrow knock such ventures out of him?

"Well, yes, thank you," I said. For me, Edward's voice seemed to come bearing the cries of so many others, unbeknownst to him. And when I tried to conjure his face it was the face of a mouse that as it scurried somehow left the trail of a snake.

"The Starbucks manager who called me wanted to know whether you were clean and reliable! That made me laugh. I said of course that you were all that and a thousand things more." I was silent and so he continued. "I don't know what we would have done without you."

What was there to say? "Look what happened regardless"? We had entered a darkening wood.

He continued, blindly. "There was much I came to understand about my heart last spring when you were in the house with us."

Had his research not helped him with the functioning of the human eye? With understanding the basic mechanisms of sight? Perhaps things were not going well at the lab!

I said nothing merciful. I said nothing at all.

He pushed on. "It's strange how as you get older some of the things you learn come from young people. Young people do come along seeming to know more. You end up thinking, as a scientist, *Good grief, evolution is true!*"

I withheld the encouraging chuckle I supposed he wanted.

"With your help, and with others', I've come to realize that life, while being everything, is also strangely not much. Except when the light shines on it a different way and then you realize it's a lot after all! Still, in the end, I imagine we will always look back and think: *Too little, with too little in it.* Because at the end the light's dimming, of course. There is no such thing as wisdom—that is the only wisdom. But there is lack of wisdom. I try to remember that."

This assertion of paucity and barrenness he'd gleaned from me? This light show? This tra-la-la of no wisdom? What had I learned from him but that he believed, or had once believed, that boys should learn the hard way about the world?

"Yes, well," I said, "the truth shall set you free—and then what?"

"Then what, indeed." He cleared his throat. He had lost the *if you will*s perhaps, but now there were *indeed*s. Which seemed worse. "Well, I was wondering if you'd like to go out to dinner with me sometime," he said.

Sacrifice the children to propitiate some ancient god. There were a lot of gods and they all wanted something.

"Dinner?" I asked. These days I ate little for meals: mostly a single bowl of red barley boiled to a swarm of slick, fat ticks. I would melt butter on the whole mess and eat it in front of the TV.

"Yes. Dinner."

"Dinner?" I said again in disbelief. My grandmother, when asked once at her ninetieth birthday party what words of advice she would offer young people, given her particular perspective at the end of life, had at first simply scrunched up her face and said irritably, deafly, *"What?"* But she was just buying time. And when the question was restated she looked around at her whole family, the kids and grandkids, and said loudly, "Don't get married!" We were stunned. It was if she had said, "Shoot to kill." It was if she had said, "If you just shoot to wound, they get up and come at you again." I used to think that those essentially happy and romantic novels that ended with a wedding were all wrong, that they had left out the most interesting part of the story. But now I'd gone back to thinking, no, the wedding *was* the end. It was the end of the comedy. That's how you knew it was a comedy. The end of comedy was the beginning of all else.

"Yes," Edward said.

The gothic knell of a wedding bell, the hangman's rope grown straight out of the chest then looped like tasseling around the tables. Rat teeth raking the cake. Beauty could not love you back. People were not what they seemed and certainly not what they said. Madness was contagious. Memory served melancholy. The medieval was not so bad. Gravity was a form of nostalgia. There could be virtue in satirizing virtue. Dwight Eisenhower and Werner von Braun had the exact same mouths. No one loved a loser until he completely lost. The capital of Burma was Rangoon.

My fortune cookies, too, had lost their frolic: *Bury your unrealistic dreams or they will bury you.*

But not in bed.

"Dinner?" I said again. Being oneself was no great accomplishment. It was not being oneself that was hard.

Then he paused. "Perhaps this is too sudden of a phone call." His voice had become weary and tart. "Too out of the blue for you, maybe."

Amanda came to the doorway of my room, poked her head in and mouthed, "Wanna split a pizza?"

I nodded my head. *Yes.* She disappeared.

The earth was not perfectly round but pear-shaped. And according to black hole experts, ninety percent of the universe was missing.

Still, there was always a circus somewhere.

"Dinner?" I repeated into the phone. My knuckles looked white as opals. *O whatever-God, unprompt mom of all steps, still no forwarding address?*

Edward remained silent, as did I. What was I alive for? I would not always know or make it my troubled concern. For now I simply became aware of my own noisy breathing. Windy exhalations, I had been told, seemed louder on the phone than they actually were. Inevitably, winds had an unpredictable drama. Prevailing westerlies did not always prevail: sometimes things blew up from the south and created little eddies—*little eddies!*—of stewing weather. I slowly moved the receiver away from my face and it seemed to keep on going, floating toward the cradle, vaguely guided by my hand. Air rushed to cool my cheek. Outside, in the early night, it was already beginning to snow.

Reader, I did not even have coffee with him.

That much I learned in college.